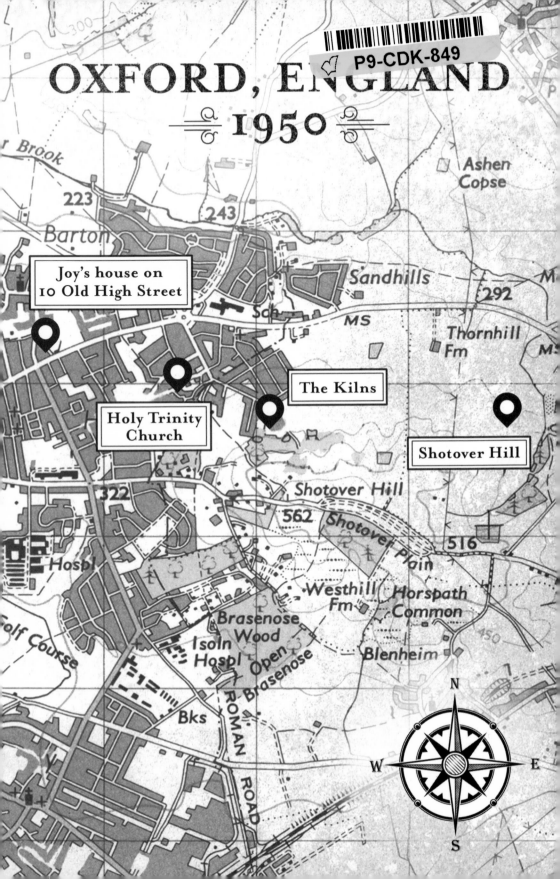

OXFORD, ENGLAND
1950

Joy's house on
10 Old High Street

The Kilns

Holy Trinity
Church

Shotover Hill

Ashen Copse

Barton

Sandhills

Thornhill Fm

Shotover Hill

Shotover Plain

Westhill Fm

Horspath Common

Brasenose Wood

Isoln Hospl

Open Brasenose

Blenheim

Hospl

Golf Course

Bks

ROMAN ROAD

ACCLAIM FOR PATTI CALLAHAN

Becoming Mrs. Lewis

"Patti Callahan seems to have found the story she was born to tell in this tale of unlikely friendship turned true love between Joy Davidman and C. S. Lewis, that tests the bounds of faith and radically alters both of their lives. Their connection comes to life in Callahan's expert hands, revealing a connection so persuasive and affecting, we wonder if there's another like it in history. Luminous and penetrating."

—PAULA MCLAIN, *NEW YORK TIMES* BESTSELLING
AUTHOR OF *THE PARIS WIFE*

"In *Becoming Mrs. Lewis*, Patti Callahan Henry breathes wondrous fresh life into one of the greatest literary love stories of all time: the unlikely romance between English writer C. S. Lewis and the much younger American divorcee, Joy Davidman. Callahan chronicles their complex and unconventional relationship with a sure voice, deep insight into character, and eye for period detail. The result is a deeply moving story about love and loss that is transformative and magical."

—PAM JENOFF, *NEW YORK TIMES* BESTSELLING
AUTHOR OF *THE ORPHAN'S TALE*

"Patti Callahan's prose reads like poetry as she deftly unearths a lost love story that begs to be remembered and retold. I was swept along, filled with hope, and entirely beguiled, not only by the life lived behind the veil of C. S. Lewis's books but also by the woman who won his heart. A literary treasure from first page to last."

—LISA WINGATE, *NEW YORK TIMES* BESTSELLING
AUTHOR OF *BEFORE WE WERE YOURS*

"*Becoming Mrs. Lewis* is at once profoundly evocative, revealing an intimate view of a woman whose love and story had never been fully told . . . until now. Patti Callahan brings to life the elusive Joy Davidman and illuminates the achingly touching romance between Joy and C. S. Lewis. This is the book Patti Callahan was born to write. *Becoming Mrs. Lewis* is a tour de force and the must-read of the season!"

—MARY ALICE MONROE, *NEW YORK TIMES* BESTSELLING
AUTHOR OF *BEACH HOUSE REUNION*

"Patti Callahan has written my favorite book of the year. *Becoming Mrs. Lewis* deftly explores the life and work of Joy Davidman, a bold and brilliant woman who is long overdue her time in the spotlight. Carefully researched. Beautifully written. Deeply romantic. Fiercely intelligent. It is both a meditation on marriage and a whopping grand adventure. Touching, tender, and triumphant, this is a love story for the ages."

—ARIEL LAWHON, AUTHOR OF *I WAS ANASTASIA*

"Patti Callahan took a character on the periphery, one who has historically taken a back seat to her male counterpart, and given her a fierce, passionate voice. For those fans of Lewis curious about the woman who inspired *A Grief Observed* this book offers a convincing, fascinating glimpse into the private lives of two very remarkable individuals."

—NEW YORK JOURNAL OF BOOKS

"*Becoming Mrs. Lewis* illuminates the raw humanity of seeking faith in a distrustful world. We've heard C. S. Lewis's narrative. Here, Callahan keenly demystifies poet Joy Davidman's story and in the telling, shows us the power of a greater love. I was wonderstruck by this novel."

—SARAH MCCOY, *NEW YORK TIMES* AND INTERNATIONAL BESTSELLING AUTHOR OF *MARILLA OF GREEN GABLES* AND *THE BAKER'S DAUGHTER*

"This finely observed accounting of writer Joy Davidman's life deeply moved me. Patti Callahan somehow inhabits Davidman, taking her readers inside the writer's hungry mind and heart. We keenly feel Davidman's struggle to become her own person at a time (the 1950s) when women had few options. When Davidman breaks free of a crushing marriage and makes the upstream swim to claim her fullest life, we cheer. An astonishing work of biographical fiction."

—LYNN CULLEN, BESTSELLING AUTHOR OF *MRS. POE*

"With an artist's touch, Patti has woven flesh and bone onto an unlikely love story and given us a glimpse into a beautiful and storied romance. I read this through an increasing sense of awe and admiration. By the final page, I realized Patti had crafted an intimate and daring literary achievement."

—CHARLES MARTIN, *USA TODAY* BESTSELLING AUTHOR OF *LONG WAY GONE* AND *THE MOUNTAIN BETWEEN US*

"This book is a work of art. Intelligent. Witty and charming. *Becoming Mrs. Lewis* is a stunning foray into the wilds of faith—from doubt and discovery, to the great adventure of living it out. Patti Callahan's invitation into Joy and Jack's love story is as brilliant as the lives they led. I'm left as spellbound as the first time I met Aslan . . . with these characters now just as dear."

—KRISTY CAMBRON, AUTHOR OF *THE RINGMASTER'S*
WIFE AND THE *LOST CASTLE* SERIES

"In *Becoming Mrs. Lewis*, Callahan peels back the curtain and allows a glimpse into Joy Davidman's extraordinary life and her love and marriage with C. S. Lewis. With captivating prose, Callahan carries the reader across the ocean from New York to Oxford and into the private heart of this tender love story."

—KATHERINE REAY, BESTSELLING AUTHOR OF *DEAR MR. KNIGHTLY*

"In this unforgettable story of love and passion, piercing intellect and the power of the written word, Joy Davidman has come to claim her own resurrection, and the results are astonishing. Patti Henry has achieved a bold literary magic: *Becoming Mrs. Lewis* heals the cracks in the firmament of our hearts."

—SIGNE PIKE, AUTHOR OF *THE LOST QUEEN*

The Bookshop at Water's Edge

"With an eloquent and effective narrative, a realistic continuing theme of unbreakable relationship bonds, and a fantastic multilayered story line of secrets, regrets, and a good dose of teenage drama, this is a solid summer read . . . [a] low-country treasure of new beginnings and an old mystery."

—*LIBRARY JOURNAL*

"A look at what family really means, and how the past affects the present in so many ways. The writing is superb."

—*RT BOOK REVIEWS*

"A great summer read about finding yourself and returning home."

—*POPSUGAR*

"Henry creates a world that feels rich and real—readers can practically hear the rushing river, see the ocean waves, and smell the hydrangea bushes . . . [an] atmospheric look at friendship, forgiveness, and second chances."

—*KIRKUS REVIEWS*

"This is a great beach read of the Dorothea Benton Frank and Anne River Siddons variety."

—*BOOKLIST*

"*The Bookshop at Water's End* carries us along the graceful curves and outwardly serene story line of two childhood friends returning to their summer riverside home. But like the river she writes about, Patti's plot roils with strong undercurrents of murky secrets, tragedy, and the pulsing tides of self-discovery. No one writes about the power of family and friends like Patti Callahan Henry. *The Bookshop at Water's End* is a must-read for your summer!"

—MARY ALICE MONROE, *NEW YORK TIMES* BESTSELLING
AUTHOR OF *BEACH HOUSE FOR RENT*

"I adore Patti Callahan Henry's new novel. *The Bookshop at Water's End* is a juicy summer read about family secrets, forgotten friendships, and the power of books to change our lives."

—JANE GREEN, *NEW YORK TIMES* BESTSELLING
AUTHOR OF *THE SUNSHINE SISTERS*

"Patti Callahan Henry's stories are always woven with magic and mystery, and *The Bookshop at Water's End* knots these elements into a deeply satisfying and heartfelt tale of loss and betrayal, friendship and forgiveness. The sun is shining, the tide is turning, summer and Patti Henry's latest masterpiece beckon. Resistance is futile!"

—MARY KAY ANDREWS, *NEW YORK TIMES*
BESTSELLING AUTHOR OF *THE WEEKENDERS*

"From the very first page, Patti Callahan Henry draws you in like the tide, revealing long simmering secrets that will test family and friendships and explores the question: do we tell our stories or do our stories tell us? In lush, lyrical prose, Henry explores the power of forgiveness, especially in ourselves. Every page was a treat."

—LAURA LANE MCNEAL, BESTSELLING AUTHOR OF *DOLLBABY*

"Patti Callahan Henry has written the best novel of her career with *The Bookshop at Water's End*. I absolutely adored it and predict it will be one of the most loved books of the year. In fact, it's so good I wish I'd written it myself!"

—DOROTHEA BENTON FRANK, *NEW YORK TIMES*
BESTSELLING AUTHOR OF *SAME BEACH, NEXT YEAR*

Becoming
Mrs. Lewis

OTHER BOOKS BY PATTI CALLAHAN

BECOMING MRS. LEWIS

A Novel

The improbable love story of
Joy Davidman and C. S. Lewis

PATTI CALLAHAN

THOMAS NELSON

Since 1798

Published in Nashville, Tennessee, by Thomas Nelson. Thomas Nelson is a registered trademark of HarperCollins Christian Publishing, Inc.

Extracts by C. S. Lewis copyright © C.S. Lewis Pte. Ltd. Extracts by Joy Davidman copyright © D & D Gresham. Reprinted by permission.

Thomas Nelson titles may be purchased in bulk for educational, business, fund-raising, or sales promotional use. For information, please e-mail SpecialMarkets@ThomasNelson.com.

ISBN: 978-0-7852-2450-1 (hardcover)
ISBN: 978-0-7852-2843-1 (hardcover signature edition)
ISBN: 978-0-7852-2581-2 (international edition)

Library of Congress Cataloging-in-Publication Data

CIP data available upon request.

Printed in the United States of America

18 19 20 21 22 LSC 5 4 3 2 1

To Joy and Jack
With great love

The consolation of fairy-stories, the joy of the happy ending; or more correctly of the good catastrophe, the sudden joyous "turn" . . . is one of the things which fairy-stories can produce supremely well.

J. R. R. Tolkien, "On Fairy-Stories"

PROLOGUE

"You would not have called to me
unless I had been calling to you."
ASLAN, *THE SILVER CHAIR*, C. S. LEWIS

1926
Bronx, New York

From the very beginning it was the Great Lion who brought us together.
I see that now. The fierce and tender beast drew us to each other, slowly,
inexorably, across time, beyond an ocean, and against the obdurate bul-
warks of our lives. He wouldn't make it easy for us—that's not his way.

It was the summer of 1926. My little brother, Howie, was seven
years old and I was eleven. I knelt next to his bed and gently shook his
shoulder.

"Let's go," I whispered. "They're asleep now."

That day I'd come home with my report card, and among the long
column of As there was the indelible stamp of a single B denting the
cotton paper.

"Father." I'd tapped his shoulder, and he'd glanced away from the
papers he was grading, his red pencil marking students' work. "Here's
my report card."

His eyes scanned the card, the glasses perched on the end of his
nose an echo of the photos of his Ukranian ancestors. He'd arrived
in America as a child, and at Ellis Island his name was changed from
Yosef to Joseph. He stood now to face me and lifted his hand. I could

1

have backed away; I knew what came next in a family where assimilation and achievement were the priorities.

His open palm flew across the space between us—a space brimful with my shimmering expectation of acceptance and praise—and slapped my left cheek with the clap of skin on skin, a sound I knew well. My face jolted to the right. The sting lasted as it always did, long enough to stand for the verbal lashing that came after. "There is no place for slipshod work in this family."

No, there was no place for it *at all.* By the time I was eleven I was a sophomore in high school. I must try harder, be better, abide all disgrace until I found a way to succeed and prove my worth.

But at night Howie and I had our secrets. In the darkness of his bedroom he rose, his little sneakers tangling in the sheet. He smiled at me. "I've already got my shoes on. I'm ready."

I suppressed a laugh and took his hand. We stood stone-still and listened for any breaths but our own. Nothing.

"Let's go," I said, and he laid his small hand in mine: a trust.

We crept from the brownstone and onto the empty Bronx streets, the wet garbage odor of the city as pungent as the inside of the subway. The sidewalks dark rivers, the streetlights small moons, and the looming buildings protection from the outside world. The city was silent and deceptively safe in the midnight hours. Howie and I were on a quest to visit other animals caged and forced to act civil in a world they didn't understand: the residents of the Bronx Zoo.

Within minutes we arrived at the Fordham Road gate and paused, as we always did, to stare silently at the Rockefeller Fountain—three tiers of carved marble children sitting in seashells, mermaids supporting them on raised arms or sturdy heads, the great snake trailing up the center pillar, his mouth open to devour. The water slipped down with a rainfall-din that subdued our footfalls and whispers. We reached the small hole in the far side of the fence and slipped through.

We cherished our secret journeys to the midnight zoo—the parrot house with the multicolored creatures inside; the hippo, Peter the Great;

a flying fox; the reptile house slithering with creatures both unnatural and frightening. Sneaking out was both our reward for enduring family life and our invisible rebellion. The Bronx River flowed right through the zoo's land; the snake of dark water seemed another living animal, brought from the outside to divide the acreage in half and then escape, as the water knew its way out.

And then there was the lions' den, a dark caged and forested area. I was drawn there as if those beasts belonged to me, or I to them.

"Sultan." My voice was resonant in the night. "Boudin Maid."

The pair of Barbary lions ambled forward, placing their great paws on the earth, muscles dangerous and rippling beneath their fur as they approached the bars. A great grace surrounded them, as if they had come to understand their fate and accept it with roaring dignity. Their manes were deep and tangled as a forest. I fell into the endless universe of their large amber eyes as they allowed, even invited, me to reach through the iron and wind my fingers into their fur. They'd been tamed beyond their wild nature, and I felt a kinship with them that caused a trembling in my chest.

They indulged me with a return gaze, their warm weight pressed into my palm, and I knew that capture had damaged their souls.

"I'm sorry," I whispered every time. "We were meant to be free."

PART I

AMERICA

To defeat the darkness out there, you
must defeat the darkness in yourself.

ASLAN, *THE VOYAGE OF THE DAWN TREADER*, C. S. LEWIS

Chapter 1

Begin again, must I begin again
Who have begun so many loves in fire
"Sonnet I," Joy Davidman

1946
Ossining, New York

There are countless ways to fall in love, and I'd begun my ash-destined affairs in myriad manners. This time, it was marriage.

The world, it changes in an instant. I've seen it over and over, the way in which people forge through the days believing they have it all figured out, protected inside a safe life. Yet there is no figuring life out, or not in any way that protects us from the tragedies of the heart. I should have known this by now; I should have been prepared.

"Joy." Bill's voice through the telephone line came so shaky I thought he might have been in a car wreck or worse. "I'm coming undone again and I don't know what to do. I don't know where to go."

"Bill." I hugged the black plastic phone against my ear and shoulder, the thick cord dangling, as I bounced our baby son, Douglas, against my chest. "Take a deep breath. You're fine. It's just the old fear. You're not in the war. You're safe."

"I'm *not* fine, Joy. I can't take it anymore." Panic broke his voice into fragments, but I understood. I could talk him off this ledge as I had other nights. He might get drunk before it was all over, but I could calm him.

"Come home, Poogle. Come on home." I used the nickname we had for each other and our children, like a birdcall.

"I'm not coming home, Joy. I'm not sure I ever will."

"Bill!" I thought he might have hung up, but then I heard his labored breathing, in and out as if someone were squeezing the life out of him. And then the long, shrill, disconnected buzz vibrated like a tuning fork in my ear and down to my heart, where my own fear sat coiled and ready to strike.

"No!" I shouted into the empty line.

I knew Bill's office number by heart and I called him back again and again, but it rang endlessly while I mumbled a mantra: "Answer answer answer." As if I had any control from where I stood in our kitchen, my back pressed against the lime-green linoleum counter. Finally I gave up. There was nothing left for me to do. I couldn't leave our babies and go look for him. He'd taken the car and I didn't have help. I had no idea where he might be other than a bar, and in New York City there were hundreds.

Isolated, I had only myself to blame. I was the one who'd pushed for a move from the city to this banished and awful place far from my literary friends and publishing contacts. I'd begun to believe that I'd never been a poet, or a novelist, a friend or lover, never existed as anything other than wife and mother. Moving here had been my meager attempt to whisk Bill away from an affair with a blonde in Manhattan. Desperation fuels one to believe idiocy is insight.

Was he with another woman and merely feigning a breakdown? This didn't seem too farfetched, and yet even his lunacy had its limits.

Or maybe it didn't.

Our house in the Hudson Valley at the far edge of the suburb of Ossining, New York, was a small wooden abode we called Maple Lodge. It had a sloping roof and creaked with every movement our little family made: Bill; Davy, a toddler who was much like a runaway atom bomb; and Douglas, a baby. It often felt as if the foundation itself were coming undone with our restlessness. I was thirty-one years old, surrounded by books, two cats, and two sons, and I felt as ancient as the house itself.

I missed my friends, the hustle and bustle of the city, the publishing parties and literary gossip. I missed my neighbors. I missed myself.

Night surrounded my sons and me, darkness pressing in on the windowpanes with an ominous weight. Douglas, with his mass of brown curls and apple cheeks, dozed with a warm bottle of milk dangling from his mouth while Davy dragged toy trucks across the hardwood floors, oblivious to the scratches they dug.

Panic coursed through me as I roamed the house, waiting for word from Bill. I cursed. I ranted. I banged my fist into the soft cushions of our tattered couch. Once I'd fed and bathed the boys, I rang my parents and a couple of friends—they hadn't heard from him. How long would he be gone? What if we ran out of food? We were miles from the store.

"Calm down," I told myself over and over. "He's had breakdowns before." This was true, and the specter of another always hung over our home. I hadn't been there for his worst one, after a stint in the Spanish Civil War before we met, when he'd attempted what I was frightened of now—suicide. The leftover traumas of war rattling and snaking through his psyche had become too much to bear.

As if I could cure the panic from a distance, I imagined Bill as I met him—the passionate young man who sauntered into the League of American Writers with his lanky frame and the wide smile hooded by a thick moustache. I'd immediately been drawn to his bravery and idealism, a man who'd volunteered and fought where needed in a faraway and torn country. Later I fell deeper in love with the same charming man I heard playing the guitar at music haunts in Greenwich Village.

Our passion overwhelmed me, stunned me in its immediacy as our bodies and minds found each other. Although he was married when we met, he had reassured me: "It was never anything real. It's nothing like you and me." We married at the MacDowell artists colony three days after his divorce was final—symbolizing our bond and dedication to our craft. Two writers. One marriage. One life. Now it was that very passion and idealism that tore at him, unhinging his mind and driving him back to the bottle.

Near midnight I stood over the crib of our baby, my heart hammering in my chest. There was nothing, not *one* thing I could do to save my husband. My bravado crumbled; my ego crashed.

I took in what was quite possibly the first humble breath of my life and dropped to my knees with such force that the hardwood floor sent a jolt of pain up my legs. I bowed my head, tears running into the corners of my mouth as I prayed for help.

I was praying! To God?

I didn't believe in God. I was an atheist.

But there I was on my knees.

In a crack of my soul, during the untethered fear while calling for help, the sneaky Lion saw his chance, and God came in; he entered the fissures of my heart as if he'd been waiting a long time to find an opening. Warmth fell over me; a river of peace passed through me. For the first time in all my life, I felt fully known and loved. There was a solid sense that he was with me, had always been with me.

The revelation lasted not long, less than a minute, but also forever; time didn't exist as a moment-to-moment metronome, but as eternity. I lost the borders between my body and the air, between my heart and my soul, between fear and peace. Everything in me thrummed with loving presence.

My heart slowed and the tears stopped. I bent forward and rested my wet cheek on the floor. "Why have you waited so long? Why have I?" I rested in the silence and then asked, "Now what?"

He didn't answer. It wasn't like that—there wasn't a voice, but I did find the strength to stand, to gaze at my children with gratitude, to wait for what might come next.

God didn't fix anything in that moment, but that wasn't the point of it all. Still I didn't know where Bill was, and still I was scared for his life, but Someone, my Creator it seemed, was there *with* me in all of it. This Someone was as real as my sons in their beds, as the storm battering the window frames, as my knees on the hardwood floors.

Finally, after wandering the streets and drinking himself into a stupor, Bill stumbled into a cab that brought him back to us just before dawn. When he walked through the front door, I held his face in my hands, smelled the rancid liquor, and told him that I loved him and that I now knew there was a God who loved us both, and I promised him that we would find our way together.

———

As the years passed, our coffee table became littered with history and philosophy books, with religious texts and pamphlets, but still we didn't know how to make sense of an experience I knew had been as real as my heartbeat. If there was a God, and I was straight sure that there was, how did he appear in the world? How was I to approach him, if at all? Or was the experience nothing more than a flicker of understanding that didn't change anything? This wasn't a religious conversion at all; it was merely an understanding that something greater existed. I wanted to know more. And more.

One spring afternoon, after we'd moved to a rambling farmhouse in Staatsburg, New York, a three-year-old 1946 *Atlantic Monthly* magazine was facedown on the kitchen table and being used as a coaster for Bill's coffee mug. I slid the mug to the side and flipped through the magazine as our sons napped. The pages flopped open to an article by a Beloit College professor named Chad Walsh. The piece was titled "Apostle to the Skeptics" and was an in-depth study of an Oxford fellow in England, a man named C. S. Lewis who was a converted atheist. Of course I'd heard of the author, had even read his *Pilgrim's Regress* and *The Great Divorce*—both of them holding a whispered truth I was merely beginning to hear. I began to peruse the article, and it was only Douglas calling my name that startled me from the story of this author and teacher who'd reached American readers with his clear and lucid writing, his logic and intellectualism.

Soon I'd read everything Lewis had written—more than a dozen books, including a thin novel of such searing satire that I found myself drawn again and again to its wisdom hidden in story: *The Screwtape Letters.*

"Bill." I held up Lewis's book I was rereading, *The Great Divorce,* over dinner one night as the boys twirled their spaghetti. "Here is a man who might help us with some of our questions."

"Could be," he mumbled, lighting a cigarette before dinner was over, leaning back in his chair to stare at me through his rimless spectacles. "Although, Poogle, I'm not sure anyone has the answers *we* need."

Bill was cold hard correct—believing in a god hadn't been as simple as all that. Every philosophy and religion had a take on the deity I hadn't been able to grasp. I was set to give up the search, shove the shattering God-experience into my big box of mistakes. That is, until I contacted Professor Walsh, the writer of the article, and said, "Tell me about C. S. Lewis."

Professor Walsh had visited Lewis in Oxford and spent time with him. He was turning his articles into a book with the same title and he replied to me. "Write to Mr. Lewis," he suggested. "He's an avid letter writer and loves debate."

There Bill and I were—three years after my blinding night of humbleness, three years of reading and study, of Alcoholics Anonymous meetings and debate, of joining the Presbyterian church—when an idea was born: we would write a letter to C. S. Lewis, a letter full of our questions, our ponderings, and our doubts about the Christ he apparently believed in.

Chapter 2

Open your door, lest the belated heart
Die in the bitter night; open your door

"Sonnet XLIV," Joy Davidman

1950

Didn't most everything begin with words? *In the beginning was the word*—even the Bible touted that truth. So it was with my friendship with Lewis.

I descended from my second-story office in our farmhouse into the frigid January day to grab the mail. Two separate trains of thought ran along the tracks of my mind: What would I cook the family for dinner? And how would my second novel, *Weeping Bay*, be received into the world in a few months?

Frosted grass crunched under my boots as I strode to the mailbox and opened it. As I flipped through the pile, my heart beat in double time. On top of the pile of bills, correspondence, and a *Presbyterian Life* magazine was a letter from Oxford, England. I held the white envelope with the airmail stamp of a young King George in profile, his crown hovering over his head, in my hand. In slanted, tight cursive handwriting, the return address stated *C. S. Lewis* across the top left corner.

He'd finally written a reply. I ran my gloved finger across his name, and hope rose like an early spring flower in my chest. I needed his advice—my life felt unhinged from the new beliefs I'd thought would save me, and C. S. Lewis knew the Truth. Or I hoped he did.

I slammed shut the metal box, icicles crackling to the ground, and slipped the mail into my coat pocket to navigate the icy walkway. My sons' quarrelling voices made me glance at our white farmhouse and the porch that stretched across the front—an oasis before entering. Green shutters, like eye shadow on a pale woman, opened to reveal the soul of the house, once pure but now clouded with anger and frustration.

The front door was open, and four-year-old Douglas came running out with Davy, age six, chasing close behind.

"It's mine. Give it back." Davy, only an inch taller than his little brother, brown hair tangled from the day's wrestling and playing, yelled and pushed at Douglas until they both caught sight of me and stopped short, as if I'd appeared out of nowhere.

"Mommy." Douglas ran to me, wrapping his arms around my soft hips and burying his face in the folds of my coat. "Davy kicked me in the shin," he wailed. "Then he pushed me on the ground and sat on me. He sat on me too hard."

Oh, how God loved to make a variety of boys.

I leaned down and brushed back Douglas's hair to kiss his round cheek. In moments like this my heart throbbed with love for the boys Bill and I had made. Davy's lithe body and frenetic energy were from Bill, but Douglas's sensitivity to mean-spiritedness was mine. He'd not yet learned to cover it as I had.

"This is all nonsense." I rustled Davy's hair and took Douglas's hand in mine. "Let's go inside and make hot chocolate."

"Yes," Davy said with gusto and ran for the house.

All the while the letter burned in my pocket. *Wait*, I told myself. *Wait*. Expectancy always the thrill before having.

Davy flew through the front door, but not before riling Topsy, who now barked as if to warn us of a monstrous intruder.

"Be quiet, you fluffy mongrel," I called out, "or you'll make me sorry I ever rescued you." I stepped over a pile of toy trucks in the foyer with Topsy fast at my heels. By this time in our lives we'd gathered a menagerie of animals—four cats, two dogs, a bird, and now Davy wanted a snake.

Bill was in his refurbished attic office, typing as fast as his fingers knew how, working on his second novel to pay the bills, which were piling as high as the snow would soon be. The shouting and barking and bedlam must have stirred him from his typewriter, for suddenly there he stood at the bottom of the stairwell.

Douglas cowered, and I reached for his hand. "Don't worry," I said softly. "Daddy won't yell. He's feeling better."

Bill's hands were limp at his side in a posture of defeat. At six foot three inches, my husband often gave me the impression of a reedy tree. His thick, dark hair was swept to the left side like an undulating wave that had collapsed. He was sober now, and his verbal lashings had subsided. AA was doing its job with the Twelve Steps, spiritual sayings, and group accountability.

He pointed at the spilled basket of library books beside the door, then pushed up on his rimless glasses. "You could pick all of that up, you know."

"I know, sweetie. I will."

I darted a glance at him. His blue button-down shirt was wrinkled and misbuttoned by one. His blue jeans were loose on him; he'd lost weight over the past months of stress. I, meanwhile, had gained—so much for life being fair.

"I was trying to write, Joy. To get something done in a house so full of disarray I can scarcely focus."

"Dogs. Kids." I tried to smile at him. "What a combination." I walked into the kitchen. I wanted to defuse any anger—the argument that could ensue would be a repeat of a thousand other quarrels, and I wasn't in the mood. I had a letter, a glimmer of hope in my pocket.

Davy climbed onto a chair and sat at the splintered wooden table and folded his hands to wait. I shook off my coat and draped it on a hook by the door, placing the mail on the kitchen table. Except for the letter. I wanted to read it first. Wanted something to be just mine if only for a small while. I slipped off my gloves and shoved them into the pockets to conceal it. With bare hands I dug into the dirty dishes piled in the sink—another reminder of my inadequacies as a housekeeper—and found the saucepan, crusted with tomato soup from the night before.

This house had once been the fulfillment of a dream. When Bill's *Nightmare Alley* was released and Tyrone Powers starred in the movie, we'd found ourselves flush with cash for the first time in our lives. It was just enough money to buy this patch of farm upstate. We didn't know that dreams coming true weren't always the best thing. That wasn't what the stories told.

I turned to Davy, my voice full of manufactured cheer. "We might get snow today. Wouldn't that be great fun?"

"Yes," he said, swinging his legs back and forth to bang on the underside of the table.

Bill strode into the kitchen and stood by quietly, watching me clean the crusted pot.

"More bills," he said, rifling through the mail. "Fantastic."

I felt his eyes upon me and knew they weren't radiating with love. Love dwindled, but each day I gauged what remained. Companionship? Admiration? Security? At the moment it felt like rage. I lifted the clean pot and wiped it with a green dish towel from the side of the sink, then turned to him with a smile. "Would you like some hot chocolate?"

"Sure." He sank into a chair next to Davy. "Mommy is going to warm us."

I opened the old Coolerator—more white coffin than fridge—and stared at the lonely shelves. Wilted lettuce, an open can of last night's tomato soup, milk, eggs, and a pan of ground beef that had gone the dark, foreboding brown of rancid meat. I needed a trip to the market, which meant another afternoon of writing would be lost. My mood curled over like the spoiled meat, and I hated my selfishness that cared more for the page, the writing, than for my family's meals. I didn't know how to change, but oh, I was trying.

I watched as the milk came to a slow boil in the pot; then I poured the chocolate flakes into the white froth, transfixed. Outside, the first snowflake fluttered into view, then melted as it settled on the windowpane;

it was a natural wonder and it lifted my heart. The bird feeder hung from a low branch, and a cardinal paused there and turned its black eye on me. Every simple thing radiated for a brief moment with extraordinary beauty, a daily grace.

I poured the melted goodness into three mugs just as Douglas came barreling into the kitchen.

"Did you forget about me?" he asked, his hands overhead like he wanted to fly.

"No, my big boy, I did not forget about you."

We gathered around that table, my three boys each holding a mug of hot chocolate and I a cup of tea. I wished for whipped cream to top it off for them. Why did the everyday-ness of my life sometimes feel constricting, when the everyday-ness was *everything?*

I had other family, my parents were still alive, but I had no immediate desire to visit them. My brother worked in the city as a psychotherapist, yet I rarely saw him. Aside from our new Presbyterian church community, *this* was my family.

There on our acreage in upstate New York, I felt isolated from the world, yet I listened to the news: Truman was president, the atomic bomb was still all the talk—what had we unleashed in splitting that atom? Apocalyptic chatter everywhere. In the literary world, Faulkner had just won the Nobel Prize in Literature.

"Thanks, Mommy." Davy's voice brought me back.

I smiled at him, at his chocolate moustache, and then glanced at Bill. He leaned back in his chair and stretched. He made such a handsome picture, the "perfect mythical husband" I'd once called him during our great falling-in-love. I sometimes wondered how I appeared to him now, but my survival instincts didn't leave room for vanity. My brown hair, long and thick, stayed in a loose and tangled bun at the base of my neck. If I was pretty at all, it was in an old-fashioned way, I knew that. Small at only five foot two, with large brown eyes, I wasn't the va-va-voom kind of beautiful that men whistled at. It was more of a pleasing beauty that could be enhanced if I tried, although lately I hadn't. But Bill? He was dashing, which he loved to hear, his Virginia Southern plantation ancestry adoring that particular word.

He tossed one leg over the other and gave that lopsided smile, the one Douglas had inherited, at me. "I'm going to the seven thirty AA meeting tonight. Are you coming?"

"Not this time. I think I'll stay home with the boys and finish mending their winter clothes."

Under the table I clenched my hands, waiting for the rebuke, which didn't come. I exhaled in relief. Bill stood and stretched with a roar that made Davy laugh before he walked to the entranceway of the kitchen. "I'm going to work now," he said. "Or at least try one more time."

"Okay." I nodded with a smile, but oh, how I ached to return to my own work. The editor of the magazine on the kitchen table had asked me for a series of articles on the Ten Commandments, and I was scarcely making headway. But Bill was the man of the house, and I, as he and society reminded me, was the homemaker.

The little boys ran off to the playroom adjoining the kitchen, bantering in a language all their own. I hesitated, but then called out, "Bill, C. S. Lewis wrote back to us."

"Well, it's about time." He stopped midstep out the doorway. "What has it been? Six months? When you're done reading it, toss it on my desk."

"I haven't opened it yet, but I know you don't have much interest in any of that anymore."

"Any of what?"

"God."

"Of course I do, Joy. I just don't obsess over answers like you do. Hell, I'm not as obsessive about *anything* as you are." He paused as if weighing the heavy words and then tossed out, "You don't even know what he wrote. He might request no more contact. He's a busy man."

I deflated inside, felt the dream of something I hadn't yet even seen or known collapse. "Bill, I can't let my experience mean nothing. It can't be discarded as some flicker in time. God was there; I know it. What does that mean?"

"I sure don't know. But do whatever you want, Poogle. Write to him or not. I must get back to work."

———

In my office, I shivered with the chill. If only our house were as full of love as it was books—now more than two thousand of them piled on shelves and tables and, when needed, on the floor. The house was drafty and again the coal had burned low. I would send Davy to bring more inside. Weeks before, we'd had to let the housekeeper go. I would write anything I could for the money just to get her back.

Things had to change and soon.

I held the letter in my hand and, pulling my sweater closer around me, settled into a threadbare lounge chair. I wanted my husband to understand the longing inside me, a yearning for the unseen world hidden inside the evident world. Lewis was seventeen years older than I—the experience and the searching well behind him. I wrote him seeking answers that would satisfy both my heart and my intellect.

I ran my fingers along the rise and fall of his words. The ink, obviously from a blue fountain pen, bled tiny lines from each character into the veins of the cotton paper. I lifted it to my nose and inhaled nothing but the aroma of cold air and dust. I slipped my finger under the sealed flap, eager to read every word, yet oddly I also wanted the expectancy to last—waiting and longing are often the cheap fuel of desire.

Dear Mr. and Mrs. Gresham,

it started.

Thank you for your long and elaborate letter.

I smiled. Long and elaborate indeed.
My eyes quickly scanned to the bottom of the page to be sure.

Yours, C. S. Lewis

He had written to us.
Of all the hundreds of letters he received, he had written to me.

CHAPTER 3

I have loved some ghost or other all my years
Dead men, their kisses and their fading eyes

"PRAYER BEFORE DAYBREAK," JOY DAVIDMAN

The day after Lewis's letter arrived, I listened to the wind whistle its wintry call. A pile of sewing sat on the far chair, and yet I ignored it to stare out the window. I missed my rambling walks through our acreage and the apple blossom–tinged air of my spring garden that lay dormant beneath the frost. Spring would come again; it always did.

I returned to my work, to the black-faced keys of the Underwood, blank paper in waiting. I had blocked that afternoon hour for my poetry: a gift to myself.

The fires are in my guts and you may light/A candle at them that will do no good.

I paused, sipped my tea, and tucked stray hair behind my ears. With eyes closed I searched in the depths of myself for the next lines. All my life I'd written from the knotted places inside me with a hope for the unknotting.

"Joy!" Bill's voice shattered the stillness.

The line of poetry was blown away by his voice, a fragile dandelion pod now empty and scattered.

"Up here," I called just as he appeared and leaned against the door-frame, a cigarette dangling from his lips.

"Not in the house." My words would do no good, but still I said them.

"The boys are at school." He inhaled a long drag and then exhaled two plumes of smoke from his nostrils before asking, "Didn't you hear the phone ringing?"

I shook my head, drew my sweater closer.

"Brandt and Brandt called. They want to schedule your author shot with Macmillan for the back flap."

My agent calling about my publisher.

"Thanks," I said, slightly annoyed I'd missed them and it had been Bill who spoke with them. "I'll call back."

"Are you okay?" he asked, walking closer and dropping ash into the trash can by my desk.

"I'm restless. And I can't find my words this afternoon, or at least not any that make sense."

"Why don't you call Belle to come for a visit from the city? She always cheers you up."

"She's busy with her family too. And we're both writing as much as we can. Phone calls must do for now."

"This path we've chosen," he said and drew his cigarette near his lips. "Being writers. Maybe we should have chosen something easier." He was joking; it was a kind moment.

"As if we could have chosen anything else." I looked to him. "I miss my poetry, Bill. I miss it terribly."

"We do what we have to do. You'll return to it." He kissed my forehead as he held the cigarette high in the air. "Now back to work."

He clicked on my little space heater and then shut the door. These acts of kindness eased the tension, reminded me of feelings that now felt like mere memories. I faced the typewriter again. But instead of poetry, I wanted to answer Mr. Lewis. It had only been a day, and though I didn't want to appear anxious, I certainly was.

C. S. Lewis:

Your spiritual search is much the same as mine has been. It's quite stunning to be pursued by the great Hound of Heaven, is it not? My first reaction was rage and terror. I wonder if you felt the same. I believe I have spent my years since that moment attempting to make some sense of it all. But are we to make sense of it? I'm not quite sure that is the reason for our encounter. Yet, still we try. It sounds as if you are caught in the mesh of His net—you have not much chance of escape.

It seems that my friend Chad Walsh has told you much of my life, do tell me about yours. What is your history, Mr. and Mrs. Gresham?

I paused with a desire to take this slowly, thoughtfully, not rush into it as I did nearly everything else, stumbling and falling and getting back up.

My history—that is what he had asked for. It had been too long since anyone cared for more than what was for dinner or if the laundry was finished or the schoolwork done.

Dear Mr. Lewis,

How very wonderful to receive your letter during the frigid cold of the New Year here in New York.

So now? How does one begin to articulate what is only seen dimly by the person who lives it? All my life I'd been seeking the Truth, or at least my version of it. If there was anything I'd always done with single-minded intent, it was this—seek means to soothe my troubled heart.

I'd believed in so much and so little.

I'd ruined myself and saved myself.

This is Mrs. Gresham writing in return. Thank you for answering some of our questions. Most astoundingly, you have knocked the props right out of my argument about longing being something we must battle—your assertion that if we long for something more, then surely that something more must exist (God)—rings as true as the sky above me.

But, by cats and whiskers, you're not asking me to argue or agree with you. You ask about my history.

I paused, took a breath.

Shouldn't I be funny and witty? A pen-friend he'd want to answer and engage with in intellectual pursuits? Intelligence was the one thing that had sustained me through the years. As my parents reminded me (and anyone else who would listen), I was not fully bestowed with beauty, grace, or charm. My cousin Renee encompassed that particular set of attributes. She was the pretty one. And wasn't I smart?

Masks are the hallmark of my life, my theme if you will, the history of Joy. The façade changes have been innumerable, but the aching and emptiness inside have remained steady, which I now believe is the longing that brought me to my knees.

Was this too serious?

No, he had asked.

It was my parents who gifted me with my first mask: a Jew. I was born Helen Joy Davidman. But I have always been called Joy.

I typed as if in a fugue state—pages dented with black ink, the staccato sounds of metal on rubber. When my sons' calls let me know they'd returned home from school, I typed the last of it.

After the profound conversion experience that shook me from my firm atheist foundation, my soul will not let me rest until I find answers to some of my spiritual questions—questions that will not go away, questions that have every right to nag at me until I find peace. Who is this God I now believe in? What am I to do with this

Truth? Was it real at all or have I deluded myself with another cure-all that cures nothing?

Yours,

Joy

When I finished, my heart stretched as if waking from a long and lazy slumber, and a secret hope fell over me. I smiled. Then I whisked the final page from the typewriter and folded the four pages into an envelope.

The winter afternoon howled with a coming storm; my sons played knights fighting for the maiden, my husband closed himself into his office, and I sealed a letter to C. S. Lewis, shedding all my masks.

I wanted him to know me. I wanted him to see *me*.

CHAPTER 4

And this is wisdom in a weary land;
ask nothing, shut your teeth upon your need

"SELVA OSCURA," JOY DAVIDMAN

Nineteen months later
August 1951

August shimmered thick with heat and rain as our old Impala, chok-
ing on fumes, pulled into Chad and Eva Walsh's Vermont summer
property. After I'd contacted Chad about his article, we'd forged an
intellectual and spiritual friendship through phone calls and letters,
and then finally his wife and four daughters visited our farm in upstate
New York. The Walshes had become dear friends.

Davy and Douglas bounced around the back seat, weary from the
long drive and hungry, as they'd eaten all their well-packed snacks
before we crossed the New York state line. Bill's hands were tense on
the silver steering wheel as we entered a lush landscape of craggy rocks
and moss-crusted trees, of thick, wild fields and a crystalline lake wink-
ing in the sunlight.

We'd both agreed, this trip to visit Chad and Eva held some promise of reprieve.

Yet even that morning Bill had balked. "Do you want to spend this
vacation with Chad because he's close to Lewis?" he asked as we packed.

"That's absurd." I stood at the end of the bed with my open suitcase
half full.

Bill opened a dresser drawer and then turned back to me. "He's the one who told you to write to Lewis in the first place."

"Bill," I said and stepped closer to him, "Chad is the foremost scholar on Lewis in the United States. He's a professor. And like us, he's a middle-in-life convert. He's a dear friend to you as much as to me. If you don't want to go on this vacation, we won't go. Just tell me now."

Bill kissed me dryly, missing my mouth to land on my cheek. "We need to get out of here. We need a break," he said. "Vermont might be just the trick."

Joy:

Mr. Lewis, I feel lost in what Dante calls a "dark wood, where the road is wholly lost and gone." Motherhood is selfless. Writing is selfish. The clash of these two unyielding truths creates a thin tight-rope, one I fall off of daily, damaging all of us.

Yet my garden has been sustenance. Has yours yet blossomed?

C. S. Lewis:

Mrs. Gresham, I have also been lost in that dark wood and felt the same, not about motherhood of course (which would be quite odd), but about my life and work. God promised us these times; darkness is part of the program. I find solace and nourishment in nature as you do, and on my long walks up Shotover Hill (one day will you come see this place and walk with us?). The only command nature demands of us is to look and be present. But do not demand more of her than she can give.

It had been a year and a half since that first envelope had arrived from Oxford, and I couldn't count the letters Mr. Lewis and I had exchanged. They flew over the ocean like birds passing each other in flight. I'd gather the tidbits of my day and save them like treasures. I wanted to share it all with him, to show him my life and read about his.

I was as eager for his letters as anything in my life, rereading old ones until the new one arrived.

The Lion, the Witch and the Wardrobe had reached our shores the year before, and I shared Mr. Lewis with my boys as I read it to them. Now *Prince Caspian* had been published and brought with us on the trip. Over and over I narrated, until Aslan and Lucy and Edmund were as familiar as family members.

C. S. Lewis:

Ah, yes, you see the medieval influence in my stories—it is above all my world view. Professionally I am mainly a medievalist with a desire for meaning and search for Truth, and I believe stories are there to delight and inform.

Joy:

Your Arthurian influences are deep within your prose. You must have found his legends early on.

C. S. Lewis:

I did find King Arthur at a young age, eight to be exact. The same age you decided to be an atheist, I see. And ever since then he's probably been influencing much of my imagination. Along with Dante, Plato and moorings in Classical Greek thought and of course many others. How can we know what has filtered into our work? This is precisely why we must be careful of what we read.

Out of the corner of his letters I experienced a different kind of life: one of peace and connection and intellectual intimacy, of humor and kindness, and I indulged.

Meanwhile in that year of 1951, the world spun on its axis: the Great Flood filled the lands of the Midwest, the nuclear bomb was tested at a private site in Nevada, the Korean War was taking our men's lives. Perry Como, Tony Bennett, and *I Love Lucy* attempted to alleviate our fears with music and laughter while Harry Truman fired General MacArthur.

But in our house a different battle raged. Fights with Bill grew monstrous. I was embarrassed by who we'd become and was resolute to change it, to heal our marriage.

Only a month before the vacation, drunk and throwing pages of a failed manuscript across the room, Bill had grabbed his hunting rifle and swung it wildly about.

"Stop!" I cried out. "You're scaring me, and the boys are asleep."

"You've never understood me, Joy. Not once. You got the house you wanted, the fame you desired, but what about me?"

"Bill, you're not making sense. You're drunk. Put down the stupid gun."

"It's empty, Joy. Stop being dramatic about everything."

He pointed the gun at the ceiling, pulled the trigger, and blew a hole in the plaster. In an adrenaline rush of fear, my heart a bird against my ribs, I bolted up the stairs, unable in my muddled mind to decipher where the boys' room was compared to the shot. Panic choked me until I reached the top of the landing and realized that the bullet had entered the guest room, a peephole now in the floor.

Bill ambled behind me, the gun dangling from his hand.

"Whoa," he said and stared at the splintered wood. "I thought the chamber was empty."

I closed the door in his face, dropped to the single bed, and shivered with rage. It was a weak response, but I hadn't known what else to do. I only knew to try harder. Pray. Do more. And turn to the letters that sustained me in my search for Truth and meaning.

C. S. Lewis:

My brother Warnie enjoys your letters as much as I do. He bellows with laughter at your stories. He will write to you soon also. He is deep in research for a French history collection. Have I told you that he is also a corking good writer?

Joy:

I am envious (that breaks a commandment, non?) of your closeness with your brother and how you live together. My relationship
with mine has been broken, and it is my fault. A series of articles
came out in the New York Post, titled "Girl Communist," where I
bared my soul and told stories of my past, how I had journeyed from
atheism to communism to Christ. I felt at the time that I was being
truthful about my journey, that integrity was my goal. But now I'm
not sure. Howie was embarrassed by the family stories I told; he
was mortified that I confessed my involvement in the party and had
confessed my youthful exploits. He's angry and hasn't spoken to me
since. It is a great loss. Don't you know that pain of baring your soul
in the writing and suffering because of it?

C. S. Lewis:

Yes, Joy, I know that pain well. When we write the truth, there
isn't always a grand group applauding. But write it we must.

On that first afternoon in Vermont, after I had unpacked and the
men had taken the children to the lake, Eva and I walked beneath the
bright summer sun through the long paths and beds of wild flowers
that ran beside the lake. She asked how our family was getting along.

"It's too much to talk about," I told her. "I try to be free and full of
laughter for the boys, Eva. I want them to be happy. We're thrilled to be
here. Let's not talk of the hard things for now."

"What hard things, Joy? I'm your friend." She plucked a black-eyed
Susan from the ground and stuck it behind her ear, the yellow petals
bright against her dark hair.

I didn't want to tell her everything; I didn't want to complain. My
thyroid was low again, pulling me toward a deep fatigue. Asthmas and
allergies for the boys. Bill with hay fever, phobias, and threatening a
nervous breakdown. Then the alcohol, always the alcohol. And deep
down I suspected that again there were other women.

I searched her sweet face before I asked, "Do you ever feel that there is *more*, that life holds so much more, and somehow we're missing it? I want to be part of the bigger world, make a difference, see it and feel it, engage in it. Don't you feel that longing inside you?"

She smiled prettily. "We are making a difference—by taking care of what God has given to us in our children."

"That's not what I mean, Eva."

"I know." She touched my arm. "I know."

"I want a life of my own—heart, mind, and soul, who I *really* am. I want my life to be my own, and yet I also want it to be my family's and God's. I don't know how to reconcile."

She laughed. "You want to figure it all out at once, don't you?"

"I do."

She shook her head. "Not everything is about logic, but you know that—I've read your poetry." She paused. "It's about surrender, I think." She shielded her eyes in the sun with a palm over her eyebrows, called out for one of her daughters. "Madeline?"

"We're in the lake, Mommy," Madeline called in return.

Eva grabbed my hand. "Come on, Joy. Let's go have some fun."

C. S. Lewis:

My saddest moment, you asked me? Of course it is obvious—my mother's death when I was ten years old. She withered away with cancer and it is the defining dreadful moment of my life, all stable happiness gone. It was as if the continent of my life sank into the sea. And by the by, please call me Jack, which is the name all of my friends use.

Joy:

Yes, don't our breaking points thereafter influence our life? Mine? Maybe there are too many to count, but if you must make me choose, it is the day I saw a young girl commit suicide. My senior year at Hunter College I was studying at my desk and looked out to see her fly like a bird from the top of a building across the spring green quad. When she landed, askew and bloody on the sidewalk, I knew I'd never be the same. When I discovered the cause was her poverty and hunger, I believe it was my first impetus toward communism— the unfairness of it all.

And yes, by the by, I am honored to be considered a friend, and Jack it is. Please call me Joy.

"What do you dream of when you dream of more than this, Joy?" Eva asked as we ambled down the hill.

"When I was very young, and for years afterward, I had the same dream over and over."

"Tell me." Eva stopped midstep and lifted her sunglasses.

"I'm walking down a road. It always begins in a familiar neighborhood, but as I continue, I round a corner onto a grassy path and suddenly I'm on unfamiliar ground. But still I walk and walk. I know I'm lost, but for some reason I'm not afraid. There are willow trees and oaks lining the walkway with high limbs that protect me. There are daffodils and tulips bright, just like my childhood parks. The grass is thick and emerald. It's too lush and familiar for me to be afraid. I continue onward until the path opens."

"And then what?" Eva was now interested.

"Doesn't just that image of the path make you long for something wonderful? Like I'm about to tell you the best story you've ever heard? One that will satisfy your heart?"

She laughed. "Yes, it does. Go on."

"The path opens into a woodland everlasting green with grand rocks and a forest floor full of small mushrooms and flowers," I said. "It's a place I call Fairyland. And when I arrive there, I feel that my heart is going to burst with happiness. Far off over the hill there is a castle, and its spires rise into the clouds. I'm not there yet, but I already know it's a place where there is no hate, no heartbreak. Anything sad or terrible is only a lie. All is well. Peace reigns."

"Do you ever make it there?" Eva asked. "In your dream?"

"No." I shook my head, and the old disappointment that often filled me when I woke from that dream returned. "I always wake up before I arrive. All I can do is see it there." I paused. "I told Jack this dream too."

"Lewis? You told him *that*? I didn't realize you two were so close."

I laughed. "We haven't even met, but yes. The amazing thing is that he has imagined the same place. He wrote of it in his *Pilgrim's Regress*, this Fairyland. Well, he calls it 'the Island,' but it's the description, the idea of a place where longing is fulfilled."

"We all want to believe something perfect lies ahead. That's heaven, Joy."

"I know. But here's the difference—I dreamt this when I didn't believe in anything greater than what our eyes can see. It was Jack's book that revealed to me what my dream truly meant."

"Does *his* pilgrim ever reach the island?" she asked as if this were the most important thing to know, and maybe it was.

"Yes, he does."

She exhaled as if in relief.

Jack:

You must become frustrated that I can't answer all your questions, Joy. Your mind is as quick and lithe as any I've known. But sometimes I have no answer but his, which is "Just follow me." Your marriage and your husband's infidelity sound like horrors, but you also sound resolute to love.

Joy:

Yes, with the questions that won't let me rest, it's best to remember your answer. Again and again I will turn to that: "Follow me."

Eva stopped as we crested the hill, spying Bill and Chad on a blanket with a picnic basket between them. All six children were at the lake's edge, splashing and calling one to the other. Multihued wild flowers, thimbleweed and liverwort, aster and doll's-eyes, bloomed in open-faced eagerness that made them seem desperate for attention.

"Look at this world," I said. "It's such a wonder, profoundly beautiful. I want to live in it that way—not as if life is one big chore." I leaned over and picked a flower, held it to the sun.

"That's a lovely thought. You, my friend, you are the most fascinating woman I know. I'm thrilled you're here." She hugged me with a tight squeeze before descending the hill to the men.

I stood still for a moment. The lake rippled with our children's splashing and swimming. Bill and Chad cast a handsome scene, leaning back on the blanket and laughing.

It was two lives I lived: the one right there, the sun extending its warmth toward us, the children calling with happiness, the cry of songbirds in the canopy of oak trees overhead, the splash of lake water. Then there was the second, parallel life: the one where my mind was preoccupied with how to describe this time and feeling to Jack. What would I take of this day to share with him? I was living a life with him in my mind while externally picnicking with my family. It was both disorienting and balancing.

I walked carefully down and reached the blanket where Eva sat, her face lifted to the sun, laughing so freely. I was envious. There she was, happy with her husband and four girls.

Chad, his dark hair plastered against his round and eager face, smiled at me. "Welcome, ladies." Mosquito bites welled on his freckled arms and he scratched absently.

Eva turned to him, and he leaned down to kiss her lips. "What are you boys doing down here?"

Bill sat up. "Poogle!" he cried in a joyous voice that suggested I had just arrived from far off. He too leaned over, kissed me with the sweet taste of Chianti on his lips, and palmed my cheek gently. "Aren't you glad we came?" He turned back to Chad. "How can we ever thank you?" Exuberant, he was up and off to run into the lake with the children. He swooped Davy over his head and ran into the water with him to squeals of delight.

Jack:

I have read your conversion essay, "Longest Way Round." I am quite in awe at your ability to explain what is almost impossible to articulate—the power of conversion and the realization that atheism was too simple. It is flaming writing. Not much in our world is as simple as it appears, and if you want to dig deeper, as you do, Joy, you must be prepared for the difficulty in that journey. Most are not. And I am honored that you mentioned my work in your essay. Thank you.

Joy:

In that essay I state that ever since that half minute, I'd been slowly changing into a new person. And for the first time in a long while, I can feel that change again—the transformation toward a new life with my true self.

Yes, of course I mentioned your work. Both *The Screwtape Letters* and *The Great Divorce* stirred the dormant parts of my spiritual life. It took a little while, but the stories moved inside me until I was ready. Isn't that the way with all good stories? But it was you, Jack, who taught me where I had gone wrong in my intellectual analysis. Your words were not the last step in my conversion, but the first.

Chad lifted a bottle of Chianti, poured some into a glass, and handed it to me.

Eva glanced at Bill in the lake and then lowered her voice as if we shared a secret. "I want to know how it all started," she said, returning to the subject of Jack. "What do you two write about?"

"Everything. Books. Theory. We have a running argument about birth control. Love. Mythology. Our dreams. Our work." I laughed. "There's no subject off limits."

Eva smiled. "There are learned men everywhere who would love to have Lewis write to them about philosophy and dreams."

"Eva, it's as if all the reading and all the writing I've done in my life have led me to this friendship."

"I don't feel that way about anything." Eva smiled at me. "Except my girls."

"And me, my love?" Chad asked and pulled her close.

"And you."

I glanced toward Bill at the lake's edge, throwing Davy from the far edge of the dock.

I wrote about the Ten Commandments, yet wrestled with their meaning in my own life. Yes, I was committed to staying married. I wanted to make it work with Bill, and yet my mind was consumed with what to say or write to another man and what he might say to me in return. This wasn't infidelity, but what was it?

Jack:

You asked about mythology. It was Tolkien (have you yet read his work?) who convinced me of the one true myth—Jesus Christ. It wasn't an easy conversion for me, but one of an all-night conversation at the river's edge.

Joy:

Of course I have read *The Hobbit* (and read it to my sons). It is extraordinary. As far as myth, I was once ashamed of my taste for mythology and fantasy, but it helped me make some sense of a world that made no sense. And I'm grateful for it now, as it brought me to your work, and to my beliefs. I found MacDonald's *Phantastes* at twelve, bored in the school library. Once I only believed in a three-dimensional world, but it was a fourth-dimensional world I wanted, and those stories gave it to me. It all seems one master plan in hindsight—each story a stepping-stone to where I am now.

Jack:

My! What a joyful coincidence—it was *Phantastes* that baptized my own imagination, and to wonder that it brought you to my work. What joy to have a pen-friend whom I admire and look forward to hearing from. I expect your next letter with great anticipation.

Chad rose to join Bill and the children in the lake. I took a long sip of the Chianti and let the warm haze settle over me. Far off, thunder clapped.

Eva groaned. "Not again with the rain." She rolled over to study me. "What has helped you get through this year?" she asked. "If there are so many ills?"

I folded my legs beneath me and set the empty glass sideways on the grass. "My sons. Writing. Drawing close to God, or what I know of him, as best I can. I still don't quite have Christianity all figured out as you seem to."

"I surely don't have it figured out." She propped her face in her palm. "None of us does."

"Do we ever? You've believed much longer than I have."

"I don't think so, Joy. It's an unfolding. A constant unfolding to new life—or at its best that's what it is."

"New life." I said the words as if I wanted to taste them.

Chapter 5

Love will go crazy if the moon is bright

"Sonnet III," Joy Davidman

From a hazy woodland sleep, Davy and Douglas's laughter along with that of the Walsh girls flooded through the open window. They'd woken me from a dream—what had it been?

Morning fell soft as cashmere through the open window, and I rolled over to glance at the other twin bed in the room—Bill had woken and gone. I snuggled back into the pillow as the familiar thunderheads drummed from far off.

The children's laughter turned to raucous roaring. In their sibling bantering I remembered my half-forgotten dream—it was of Howie and our midnight trips to the zoo. I missed our childhood closeness; I missed him with an ache below my heart. I closed my eyes, wanting for just a moment to remember when he loved me, that particular feeling elusive now.

I opened my eyes to the morning sun, to the children's voices and the new day. I wanted to be a different kind of parent for my boys than my parents were for me. Was I?

With these long, slow days of summer, I'd decided, with great fortitude, that my top priority was to look after my sons, my husband, my garden, and my house—all gifts given to me. I wanted to heal my marriage, ease into the early happiness of those first days together. I wanted to rest in the gentleness we found with each other in small moments—writing together, playing with our sons, making love. It would take radical forgiveness and grace, but these were my goals, and maybe joy and peace would show up with their accomplishments. *Here's for hoping*, I thought.

My cotton nightgown tangled in the sheets as I rose, and I laughed, slipping the gown over my head to change into shorts and a worn red T-shirt left over from Bill's college days. I pulled aside the red-checked curtain and called out the window, "Good morning, all you lovies out there."

"Mommy!" Douglas waved from the rope swing that hung from the lowest gnarled branch of an old oak. "Mrs. Walsh is making pancakes for breakfast. Hurry!"

Jack:

But what has arrived at our home, the Kilns? You sent Warnie and me a ham! Thank you very much. You can't imagine what this means during the days of food rationing. We are not short of food, but we are quite tired of the repetitive choices.

Joy:

You are more than welcome. I could barely tolerate knowing you were eating the same foods day after day. Here my summer garden is abundant! I've made jams and canned the beans; I've baked pies with the apples and pears from my orchard.

There in Vermont, the children ran through the forest as wild as the flowers themselves. I took all six children on long walks through the woods, stalking mushrooms, teaching them the names and tastes of all things wild. The boys teased the girls for being too frightened to eat what I picked from the soft earth. I knew they thought me eccentric, and I didn't mind.

Our summer hours with the Walshes were garrulous and inspiring. We walked and talked philosophy. We played card games and Scrabble. We discussed Bill's thoughts on Buddhism, and we both admitted that we'd had to scramble for money by writing articles and books we didn't always want to write. We talked about the atom bomb and how it might change our world.

Sometimes during those bright and truth-filled debates I felt the freedom and intellectual stimulation I had experienced during my four summers at the MacDowell Colony. In that community of artists and writers in New Hampshire, on acres of pristine woodlands, the combination of quiet for writing and the conviviality of peers had offered the creative backdrop for my best work. That was back when writing was all I did and all I talked or thought about.

Jack:

I'm sorry you're having trouble with your new work on the Ten Commandments. Do remember, Joy, that what does not deeply concern you will not interest your reader.

Joy:

Oh, Jack, it does concern me deeply. I am just finding theology more difficult to write about than I'd anticipated. Maybe I wasn't ready. But sometimes we must do what we aren't quite ready to do.

The rain was incessant, but I knew friends in New York were burdened under the heat, and there I was with foggy mornings and steaming soil. The earth was so soaked that the weeds grew almost overnight and yet the tomatoes never seemed to ripen. Thunderheads gathered like gray armies on the horizon, and the storms were both foreboding and magical.

I'd heard talk in town of people blaming the clouds and boomers on the atom bomb. "The end of the world," they murmured. I wrote and told Jack he could find quite the storyline in the American gossip of end days.

It was a moonless evening, the electricity shut off by a storm, when Bill, Chad, Eva, and I again talked about writing and publication. Eva said, "Oh, Joy, tell us how *Weeping Bay* is doing."

I cringed, and yet knew she asked from love. "False gods of all kinds are revealed in *Weeping Bay*, but that doesn't matter because it has not done well, my friend." I took a long swallow of wine. "A quite fervid Catholic boy in the sales department found my book offensive and buried it. You can hardly find it now. You can't know what it's like to pour your heart into a novel and have it discarded for its merits."

"What about its debits?" Bill asked in the Southern accent he turned on and off at will. He was right, the novel hadn't done well, and the reviews had been tough. "'Marred by obscenities and blasphemies,'" he quoted from the harshest critique of them all.

"Bill!" Eva's voice rang out. "I'm sure it's awful enough for her."

I clapped my hand against my leg. "Bill, why would you attack my work?"

"Ah, is this where you remind me that you have two college degrees and I have none?"

"I've never done that, Bill. You're the only one who brings that up." I looked at Chad and Eva. "But he's right about the book," I allowed. "Some of the reviews were wonderful, but others declared that the shortcomings of one main character fractured the story beyond repair. They're not wrong, but I wrote the story the way I wanted. The way I *needed* to write it." I pointed at Bill. "And one of my favorite characters, the whiskey-drinking preacher, is your contribution, so maybe be sweet about it." I tried to smile at him. How I wanted us to be sweet to each other.

Damaris, the Walshes' eldest daughter, called out from the children's rooms. "You are so loud out there!"

We all laughed and Eva rose to help settle her. She glanced at me with warmth as she left the room. "You worked on that novel for years, Joy. I can imagine how hurtful it must be to hear the negative feedback."

"Yes. I started it at MacDowell all those years ago. Before kids. Before Bill and marriage and articles written for money. Back when writing was done for the magic of putting sentences one after the other and making a story that made sense to my soul." I settled back into my chair, feeling melancholy bloom.

"Fiction must carry so much," Chad said. "I don't know how you do it."

"Jack and I have written about that."

Candlelight flickered across Chad's face, catching on his eyeglasses. He was a studious-looking man, appearing just the way a college professor might be imagined, yet his easy smile burst through the serious demeanor.

I leaned forward. "And how the gospels are *not* fiction. You see, fiction is always in a straight line, congruent if you will. But life isn't. This is how we know the gospels are real; they don't read like fiction."

"I've heard Lewis say the same," Chad said.

"Joy," Bill said in a quiet voice. "What do you mean? I thought we were talking about *your* work."

"I am talking about my work, and what fiction can do."

Chad nodded, his glasses falling down his nose in agreement.

Bill smashed out his cigarette on his piecrust. The ash melted with a soft hiss in the dessert I'd made that morning from freshly picked apples.

"I think I'm done for the evening." He stood and walked away, leaving Chad and me at the table where the leftover stench of cigarette settled between us.

Jack:

Warnie and I are planning our annual summer pilgrimage to Ireland for a month. Although we love the Kilns, we long every summer for our childhood land. It is there I visit my dearest friend, Arthur Greeves, my comrade since childhood. Back to the land of undulating green hills and the mountain views that remind me of some of the happiest days of my life.

Joy:

Ireland. Oh, how I would love to see that land one day, as well as Oxford of course. It seems these lands have shaped your internal landscape. For me, it has always been New York, except for the one soul-stealing year of screenwriting in Hollywood. Your descriptions are so lucid that when I close my eyes I can almost see the Kilns. I wonder if it is possible for you to send a photo from Ireland?

Yours, Joy

"You've become quite enamored of Jack," Chad said carefully.

I didn't answer at first, weighing my words with caution as the buzzy rivers of wine flowed through me. Chad knew Jack in a way that I never would—he'd stayed six weeks in his home in Oxford. He knew his routine. He'd seen Jack when he woke and when he worked and when he went to retire. He'd seen him teach and attend church and partake in the Eucharist.

"Yes," I finally said. "I'm enamored of his mind. He's become my teacher and mentor, as well as friend. Bill doesn't care so much anymore about God, and we don't always see eye to eye. I don't think one could ever get to the end of Jack, or to the bottom of his views at all."

"I think Lewis would tell you to follow Christ, not him," Chad said with a sly smile.

"Ah, but can't I follow both?" I paused before finding what I meant to say. "I'm not as traditional as Jack is, but then again he's not as traditional as others believe him to be." I let the next words settle on my tongue before I spoke them. "I wish *I* could visit him as you did. I can almost feel the cool green English world. The quiet. The libraries and cathedrals hushed with sublime beauty."

Chad clasped his hands together and tented his fingers under his chin, nodded. "It was profound, I'll give you that. Maybe there will come a day when you can do the same."

"It's easier for men," I said. "It's not fair, but it's true. Wives and mothers can't just up and go to England to research and write and interview. You can go for two months and study, leave your four children with your wife, but there's some invisible and unstated law that I can't do the same."

Chad's gentle smile told me he understood. "Maybe one day, Joy. Maybe one day."

"Jesus tells us not to worry about tomorrow. Do we believe him?"

"What ever do you mean?" Chad rubbed the bridge of his nose as if his glasses were too heavy.

"What if," I said and leaned closer, my voice lowering. "What if I trust that command? What on earth would become of me if I should ever grow brave?"

Chad nodded his head. "Indeed, Joy. What would become of any of us if we were to become so brave as to believe his words?"

We were quiet for a few moments until Eva's voice called for him, and he rose to leave. I sat alone as the storm raged.

After a while, with the house quiet, I slipped into the bedroom where Bill snored, in search of a sheaf of paper. I took it back to the kitchen, where I sat and vibrated with the thunder and began another sonnet. Although I no longer wrote poetry for publication, I could create for my spirit. Feelings that could not be acknowledged in the light of day or with the sound of voice—the ache of stifling desires, the pain of rejecting needs because they were unacceptable, the frustration of responsibility that hemmed me in as a woman—found their way out through the gateway of poetry.

I wrote in a tight script, and the first line of a sonnet appeared.

Shut your teeth upon your need.

CHAPTER 6

Coinsilver, moonsilver, buy me a tear;
I lost of all of mine in a bygone year

"FOR DAVY WHO WANTS TO KNOW ABOUT
ASTRONOMY," JOY DAVIDMAN

Winter 1952

"The moon goddess is Selene," I told Davy one dark winter night with a full moon hovering above. Six months had passed since Vermont, and the peace of that trip had fallen away like a waterfall, down a river far gone. My elder son and I lay still on a blanket bundled in coats and staring at the dome of sky above us, naming constellations. He wore glasses by then—my genetic gift of poor eyesight—and his eyes seemed to grow beneath the round lenses.

"I wrote a poem about her once," I told him. "About the moon. I imagined her dripping liquid silver."

"You write poems about everything," Davy said and shifted closer to me on the blanket. "Maybe you'll write one about me."

"I will do exactly that," I told him.

Davy was enchanted with astronomy. We scoured the library for books on the celestial objects. I felt closer to him in this desire than any he'd had in his short life. I could feel bits of myself pulsing in his small, frenetic body. As a child I'd also been enchanted by the sky and the stars. The firmament demanded nothing of me, yet offered everything. As with Davy, in the rare moments when he was not thrashing his way through the world.

Meanwhile, Douglas was immersed in the earthly world, whether in a fort he'd made or in the mud he'd plunged into at Crum Elbow Creek, which sliced through our property over moss-covered rocks and silver pebbles. Topsy, our rescued mutt, followed Douglas everywhere as he roamed our acreage, and it was there, in the natural world, that I found my connection with my younger son. He dug his hands into the dirt of my garden and roamed the orchard I'd planted. He seemed to be as I had been as a child—a loner, yet quite happy with his lot.

At night I knelt at the edges of my sons' beds to say prayers, tuck them under the blankets, and kiss their smooth cheeks. My precious boys, now seven and nine years of age.

Time fell away from me in the mundane dailiness of survival as I wrote and took care of them. "I love you," I always said as I shut off the light. "Sleep tight."

We spent the days together reading or playing outside. Color TV had come to our part of the world, but we didn't have the money for such luxuries even if we'd wanted them. As I read fairy tales and mysteries to my children, the dream of visiting England, of meeting my friend Jack, grew.

We were two years into our pen-friendship, and I looked forward to his letters as I did to the arrival of spring. I was hungry for them. Sometimes desperate.

Jack:

Waiting for the garden to burst forth here—the birch trees sprouting green above our heads. I believe spring comes later for us than it does for you. I hope this season brings you back to your poetry, as I know you miss it. Oh, and have you heard—Queen Elizabeth will now succeed to the throne at only twenty-four years old. At that age I didn't know my bum from my nose, and she will be the Queen of England.

Joy:

The primrose is poking above ground, red and yellow and shy. The tomatoes are so rich they burst through the skin as if impatient.

Some day I hope to see England, to see your garden. Yes, I've returned to my poetry, and I'm even trying my hand at sonnets. Oh, poor Elizabeth. At that age, I was a resounding atheist. I was active in the Communist party and the League of American Writers, writing my first book of poetry (*Letter to a Comrade*)—not exactly a queen.

I didn't hold back with Jack, and because of that I knew he truly saw *me*, even through the sharing of my most embarrassing gaffes and mistakes, my most humiliating reviews and blunders.

Late one January afternoon, bent over my typewriter, a torrid cough ripping a hole in my chest, I attempted to start a short story. The allergy medicine kept me jittery and awake, but still useless. I had dropped my head to the table when Bill appeared with a letter in his hand.

"Here is another delivery for Mrs. Gresham," he said. "From Oxford, England."

"At least it's not another bill." I tried to smile.

Bill dropped the letter on the table and paused. "What are we doing about dinner tonight?"

I glanced at him, weary to death of it all. "I don't know."

He walked out without a word, and I tore open the envelope that had traveled across the ocean from England.

Jack:

It is only in the giving up of ourselves that we find our real self. Giving up the rage, your favorite desires and wishes.

Joy:

Oh, how is that possible? I want to know.

My mother always wanted me to be someone else, comparing me to my cousin Renee and to the beautiful women on the streets. My father, well, I'd never be good enough for him, much less be understood. My parents believed criticism was a show of love. And Bill? He wants from me the kind of wife I cannot be no matter how hard

I pray or try. These hurts don't melt easily even under the "giving up" of a false self to find the real self.

Winter continued in its usual way in upstate New York, and the infection that had started in my lungs burrowed deep into my kidneys. Eventually the fever, jaundice, and vomiting sent me to the hospital for a few days. When I was finally sent home, it was straight to bed with doctor's orders to rest.

Illness had followed me all the days of my life, but always I'd rebounded. As a child I'd had everything from a radium collar for low thyroid to liver pills for fatigue. This last blow, however, left me bereft. In the bed, I stared at the ceiling as the walls closed in and the doors felt locked tight. No escape. I ran my fingers along the lump in my left breast—at least the doctor had said *that* was of no concern.

Dr. Cohen, the gray-haired family doctor with glasses as thick as windshields, visited the house one afternoon and sat at my bedside with his stethoscope dangling and his weedy eyebrows bending toward each other. He directed his words to Bill as if the illnesses had left me invisible. "Your wife must get some rest."

His wife. My definition now. I was the object of someone's life instead of the subject of my own.

A sudden thump emanated from the hallway, and then Topsy's bark and Davy's scream. Bill bolted from my bedside to the door.

"Bill," Dr. Cohen said firmly.

"Yes?" He turned with his hand on the doorknob, ready for escape.

"I'm very serious. Your wife will not recover from the next blow. It's too much. You both must find a way to get her some rest, even if it means going somewhere else for a while. I don't care where—but somewhere where she can heal. Her body cannot sustain any more illness in this state. Do you understand the seriousness of what I'm telling you?"

Bill nodded. "I do."

Douglas burst through the bedroom door with Davy fast at his heels, fists flailing, and Bill just as quickly ushered them out, slamming the door shut.

Dr. Cohen and I heard him shouting, "Both of you straight to your rooms and wait for the spanking. I've had enough of this."

I closed my eyes and spiraled into despair. What could be done? My body had betrayed me.

Hopelessness was my companion and fantasy my escape.

Jack:

Oh, my dear friend. If your husband is both drinking and being unfaithful, what choices do you have? Adultery is a monstrosity, a man attempting to isolate one kind of union from the sacred one. But sometimes, Joy, divorce is a surgery that must be done to save a life. Are the boys safe? Is it possible for you to take a holiday and come to visit England? We are praying for you, as always.

Joy:

Thank you for the kindness of your sentiments. I agree with your view and yet being gobsmacked in the middle of it all, it is hard to gain perspective.

Oh, Jack, a holiday? Yes, I dream of coming to England. I dream of so much.

The days were long and crammed with pain, the pills barely easing the throbbing in my kidneys. One terrible night there was a winter storm shrouding the windows in translucent ice, and Bill still had not come home. Memories of previous disappearances appeared as taunting ghosts. Finally, in the middle of that sleepless night, I heard him arrive. First his steps on the stairway, the *click-snap* of the old doorknobs inside their mechanisms, and then he stood in our bedroom.

His shadow fell long beside the bed, and his shape bent over to kiss me on the forehead. "Poogle, your fever appears to be gone."

The sticky, primordial aroma of sex overwhelmed my senses, making me dizzy. If only the pain meds could dull the pain of betrayal. "Where have you been?" My voice rose, exhausted but steady.

"Hey," he said softly, "don't be angry. This has nothing to do with how much I love you, Poogle. Can't you see that? A man's needs must be met, and you're in no condition to meet those needs. I'm just trying to be kind, give you a chance to heal while I recharge my batteries."

"Who was it this time?" My question was a whisper, a last breath.

"Oh, Joy, my love. Don't ask me what you don't want to know." He stood and backed away as if he had just realized his own scent.

Jack:

God of course does speak to us in our pains—his megaphone to reach us.

Joy:

If only I could hear what he says; usually that megaphone of pain drowns out all other noise and I can't understand anything else. In my moment of greatest weakness—my novel tanked, my health in disrepair—Bill decided that fulfilling his own needs would help.

"Oh, Joy," Bill said with that false Southern lilt in his voice. He lay down beside me, his body stretching long and his leg flopped over mine in a motion of love and familiarity. His breath smelled of rancid whiskey and cigars. "Rest. And heal. And when you do, we'll be better. Just you wait and see."

But I knew this would not get better. If I did not leave, I would die. I felt this as surely as knowing soon it would be spring, then summer, then fall, and then the cursed-iced winter again.

God, I prayed in desperation, *please help me. I don't know what to do.*

CHAPTER 7

Knew, in the lonely midnight afterward,
The terrible third between us like a sword

"SONNET II," JOY DAVIDMAN

February 1952

The mug of tea beside my Underwood had gone cold, yet still I took a sip, distracted by the Ten Commandments article I was writing. *He is the source of all pleasures; he is fun and light and laughter.* I was moving fast now, nearing the seventh commandment.

Downstairs lay a pile of sewing and mending for the boys. I would get to it soon. All the while I was slowly healing and sleeping better as I'd moved out of Bill's bedroom and into my own.

I wanted to leave him, how I wanted to leave Bill, but I saw no way out. And God help me, I did love him. Love doesn't disappear when it's supposed to leave; it doesn't shimmy away at the slightest provocation. If only it would.

There I was, writing about God's will, and at the same time contemplating divorce. Yet we didn't have enough money to split; there were sons to protect. And now, to add to the constraints, my cousin Renee and her two children were arriving. This little family would move in with us while Renee escaped her alcoholic husband in Mobile, Alabama. It had been a secret plan that involved my parents and hers plotting a pretend crisis in New York City, but instead she'd come to me, where her husband could not find her.

With a start, I heard the sound of a car door slamming. Were they here already? It felt as if Bill had just driven away to fetch them from Grand Central. I glanced out the window to see the three souls who would change my life: Renee and the little ones, Bobby and Rosemary. She was a moving picture of elegance as she emerged from the passenger side, touching a gloved hand to her black hat. I'd almost forgotten how arresting she was. A blue wool double-breasted coat hugged her lovely silhouette, and her long, dark hair fell over her shoulders in a shimmering cascade. Her children, ages six and eight, spilled out from the back of the car looking stunned and submissive. I rose to make my way downstairs and greet them.

Jack:

It is true, that if we are free to be good then we are also free to be bad. Yet this choice is what makes possible the love and joy and goodness worth savoring.

Joy:

Free to be bad. Oh, how I'd like to argue with God about this choice. But how could I? When I choose it all the time, and when I want the choice to be mine to make.

How odd, I thought as I descended the stairs to the front door, that Renee and I had both married alcoholics. And now she was running to *me* for safety, when she'd always been set forth as the example of the "good one"—a yardstick my mother had used to measure my inadequacies as a young girl when Renee lived with us.

Davy and Douglas had already opened the front door, and I stood in the entryway, shivering and running my hands up and down my arms. Snow fell in a haze of fat white flakes, luminescent. Bill was bundled in his long black coat, looking gallant as he eased the luggage from the back of the car and placed it on the snow-covered driveway. Renee leaned in to place her hand on my husband's and say something

I couldn't hear. She smiled; he laughed. Indeed he was charming, and at his best, kind.

When they reached the base of the steps, Renee's gaze caught mine, and she smiled so widely and gratefully that I almost ran through the snow in my socks. This was my cousin, my blood, and my dear friend. Davy and Douglas stood behind me, quiet and watching.

She rushed up the steps and we hugged. I brushed the snow from the soft shoulders of her coat. "Get in here," I said. "I'm so happy to see you."

"Oh, Joy, how can I ever thank you?" She placed one hand gently on top of each child's head. I looked down at them. Bobby with cropped brown hair squashed under a cap speckled in snow. Rosemary, a dark-haired child with wide eyes, dressed as if for church, her patent leather shoes so shiny I saw a brief reflection of the porch light.

"Get inside, Joy," Bill said as he stepped onto the porch, stomping the snow from his boots and weighed down by luggage. "It's bitter out here."

"Come in, come in," I said. And then I felt it as a tremor under my ribs: the subtle shift beneath the foundation of our home, the change that arrived with these three stranded souls.

We settled around the table in the warm kitchen, and I served them tea and grilled cheese sandwiches. I fussed over them and made small talk. Renee had draped her woolen coat over the ladder-back chair, and she pulled pins from her hair, unfastening the snow-sprinkled hat and placing it on the sideboard. Her tweed dress had crept up, and I caught a glimpse of the black nylons covering her legs. Sitting beside her, I was a reverse image in my men's corduroy pants and a button-down shirt.

I looked at my cousin's familiar face, nearing thirty-five but with something close to ancient clouding her eyes. It was pain one should only carry after war, an agony I saw in my husband's eyes. Yet there she was, a woman on the run, and her cat's-eye liner and mascara were intact: the perfect image of the fifties housewife in an Electrolux adver-tisement. She'd always pulsed with an inclination toward beauty, and in spite of whatever battles she'd fought, that hadn't left her. I tucked a stray hair into my bun and started chattering self-consciously.

The children stared quietly at one another, their shy looks flitting from one to the other like confused butterflies. As soon as they were full of food and thoroughly warm, they ran off to the playroom, Douglas at the forefront with his game ideas and unquenchable desire for more fun.

Jack:

The stories of your life: your cousin's arrival, your animals, and the farm amuse both Warnie and me. Oh, and Davy trying to catch a wild snake to keep as a pet. Please keep sharing with us.

Joy:

I doubt I could stop now.

Later, upstairs, Renee and I were finally alone, and I told her. "We'll share a bedroom," I said. "Just like the old days."

"You don't sleep with Bill?" She dropped her large black purse onto the wooden dresser and turned to me with wide eyes. "Even when things were at their worst at home, Claude would've never permitted me to sleep in another room."

"Well, that's the difference," I said. "Bill doesn't permit or not permit me anything. His last foray with another woman almost did me in." I wiped my hand through the air. "And look at you—you didn't just leave Claude's bed; you left him!" I winked at her.

Renee sighed as if she'd been holding her breath for years and sat on the single bed across from mine. "Thank you so much for letting us come here," she said. "I don't know what I would have done if you hadn't. I promise not to be a bother. I'll pull my weight."

"Stop that, cookie. We're family. We'll get through this together. And frankly, I'm thrilled for the company, for a girlfriend to talk to. I've been very . . . confused. It will be wonderful to have you close again." I brushed stray hair from my eyes. "Even if Mother did always say, 'Why can't you be more like Renee?'"

"Oh, Joy, she never meant that." Tears brimmed like snow on the windowsill. "I'm glad to be here. It's just been awful. We need something steady. All of us do."

"I know." I reached across the space between the beds and took her hands in mine. "Let's get you settled. We can talk later."

Joy:

Must the most awful parts of childhood always turn into unconscious urges that influence our life for all time? Why is it hard to overcome the past and fall into Greater Love, where our True Self can guide our life? It seems this should be the easiest thing in life. But ah, we return again and again to that word—surrender.

Jack:

And how do we feel about discovering we are not our own Master? Just when we believe we want our life to be our very own, we discover we can only have our life by surrendering our life to that Greater Love to which you refer.

After dinner, settling the children in bed, a round of Chinese checkers, and a few glasses of rum, Renee and I reclined in our single beds.

I sank onto the pillows, slightly buzzed and sleepy. I shifted my hands behind my head, knitting them together as my elbows splayed wide. "How did we come to this, Renee? How did we both fall in love with and marry alcoholics?"

"I've asked myself that many times, Joy. We did what was expected of us. And now look at this mess. Was it something in our childhood? Something we were unconsciously taught? I don't know."

"I think somewhat. We were taught to dim our light so the men might shine, or at the very least look good. We were trained to appease, to please, to dance to the tune of their needs. We were held hostage by my father's rage and expectations of perfection, always scared to be who we were, to be ourselves. And now—how could we have done any differently with our own men?"

"We will do differently now, Joy. We must."

"Yes." I sat and looked across the dark space between us. "There must be another way to live a woman's life—make it our own. I want to find out who I am beyond all these expectations that fold us into a neat box. I want to unfold. How do we do that?"

"I don't have any answers. I'm just trying to survive—and thanks to you, I might."

"It's not much better here, cookie. Bill is still on and off the drink. He wants me to be who I cannot be: a housewife, maid, and submissive spouse. He knew *me* when he married me. Now he wants someone different, as if marriage would turn me into a compliant doll. I don't want to make you hate him, but he has said and done terrible things."

"Has he hit you?" she asked in a whisper.

"No. It's not like that. He hits other things—like the time he smashed his favorite guitar over a chair or threw his rifle across the room. Usually it's just the screaming. The yelling. The irrational rage." I stopped. "Renee, he told a friend that he's not as successful as he could be because a writer needs two things, a typewriter and a wife—and they should both be in working order."

"What an asinine thing to say."

"I shouldn't complain. It's not as awful as your situation. My children are safe. No one is dying or ill. It's not all that bad, it just feels like it sometimes."

"I don't compare, Joy. There are many ways to be miserable in a marriage. Claude hit us and threatened to kill us. He threw us around and almost drank himself to death. But there are other things that can happen to make you feel like you're dying. At least you have your passion for writing. I have nothing."

"It does help," I said. "But, my dearest, now you have us, and your children have mine."

"Yes, I'm here now," she said.

As if she'd come to save us, and not the other way around.

CHAPTER 8

Yet I lie down alone
Singing her song

"SAPPHICS," JOY DAVIDMAN

Weeks passed, and I wondered how we'd all done without each other: how the children had not rolled around together like puppies, or Renee and I hadn't always sat up late playing Chinese checkers and drinking rum, talking of life and love.

It didn't take long for my cousin to take over many of the household chores, and she did it smoothly, as if this was what she'd been sent for. Her natural impulses were always toward neatness and elegance, and I welcomed this as a gift. We laughed, sipped, and helped each other with the children, who often ran wild through the house and gardens. The radio I'd kept off, Renee turned on, and it murmured with news of the outside world. Britain announced it too had atomic weapons. Albert Schweitzer won the Nobel Peace Prize. Herman Wouk was awarded the Pulitzer for *Caine Mutiny*. Each time I heard about a literary prize, my old dreams awakened inside, stretching and breathing life into my work.

With another set of hands in the house, I wrote later and slept in more often—one of the things I loved the best after long nights at my desk. The children ate a hot breakfast instead of cold cereal, the laundry was finished and neatly folded, and food lined the refrigerator shelves.

Joy:

How does one keep obligations when the will has grown weak? It's a virtue, I understand, and maybe it's only through a higher power. A giving up? Or a giving in? Somehow the secret is hidden in this idea.

Jack:

Let me tell you about Janie and Maureen Moore. Have I mentioned them as of yet? They lived with Warnie and me for twenty-four years as I fulfilled an obligation and commitment—that is indeed a virtue, Joy, and it's just as you're doing with your cousin, your niece, and your nephew. You see, Mrs. Janie Moore and her daughter, Maureen, came to live with us because I promised my wartime comrade Paddy Moore that I would watch over his family if he were killed, which horribly he was. Maureen moved out a while ago, but Mrs. Moore— Janie—lived with us right up until last year. Right now she is in a rest home—she left us raging and furious—and has not long in this world. The last many years it wasn't easy, in fact for a long while it's been quite miserable. Her exit set both Warnie and me free from a grievous burden.

Joy:

I had no idea you had two women living with the both of you for so long! Jack, you are an admirable and kind man. But I love having Renee here—it is my commitment to Bill that is tearing away at the fabric of my virtues.

I banged at the typewriter one afternoon when Renee ambled into my office with a pointed question. "If you're miserable, have you not thought of divorce? I can see that your heart is closed to Bill."

"I'm trying to make it work; I do love him." I pointed at my work. "I'm trying to keep these commandments here, cookie." I attempted levity and winked.

"*I'm* getting divorced," she said, her eyes as dry as her heart for Claude. "Is that wrong and 'unbiblical'? I have no use for a religion like that, if one at all."

"No," I said with warmth. "Claude beat you. And the children. That is not my situation. My heart is troubled toward a man who says he loves me even as he berates me: a man I love and now fear. And, Renee, I've come to see that there is a difference between religion and God. A *very* big difference."

Renee came closer with a softer tone. "Bill told me what the doctor said . . ."

My eyebrows rose. "Oh?"

"That you need to heal, that you might need to go somewhere to do so. We all need you, the kids especially, and if you're sick and exhausted you're no use to anyone. Not even yourself. And especially not your work."

"I know, but leaving feels impossible. How could I leave my children? I'm not sure I could survive that either."

"It may not be easy," she said, "but it's not impossible. I've done loads of things lately that I once thought impossible."

"I have thought of England," I said. "Of going there and getting some rest from these illnesses, of writing and talking to the one friend who might be able to help me. I've longed to see the English countryside, immerse myself in its history and literature. I have an idea for a book set there, but all I can do is keep trying to make things right here. Keep writing. Keep taking care of my family."

She crossed her arms over her chest. "If you dream of going to England, and your doctor suggests the same, then you should, Joy. We will be fine here."

I stared at my cousin with wonder. Maybe it was possible: all the dreams and the wishes and the imaginings of England's cool countryside.

"I don't know." I stared outside as if England rested on our Staatsburg acreage. "Chad went and it changed his life. When he came back he wrote his best work yet, and hasn't quit."

"It could change all of ours too, Joy. Maybe this is your one chance. Why not take it? I'm here to help."

She smiled at me with the kindness one might bestow on a small child and then stood to walk away.

When the room was empty, my thoughts returned to something I'd said to Chad not so very long ago in Vermont, *What would become of me if I should ever grow brave?* Well, I believe I was about to find out.

Jack:

How is the visit with your cousin? With our house claimed again as our own, Warnie and I entertained a guest from Ireland—my childhood chum, Arthur Greeves—and we are now resting for the weekend. Even being turned down for a new professorship at Magdalen cannot dim my cheerful mood. And last week I gave a speech about children's literature at the Library Association—I believe I shall take the speech and turn it into an essay; it contains much of what you and I wrote about in our letter—the good and bad ways to write for children. As has become the way: your words help to clarify my own.

Joy:

It's been nice to have a female friend in the house. It does bring old memories of childhood, though. Renee has taken a job in Poughkeepsie, therefore we have money flowing back in now; she is deeply worried about carrying her weight. I am writing like a madwoman—the King Charles II book has opened a crack in my creativity and the words are flowing once again.

Exciting news: I am making plans to come to England. There are some logistics to unravel, but I believe it can be done.

One humid spring morning I went to both Bill and Renee and asked them to hear me as I told them of my plans to save us all.

We sat in the living room, Bill and I on the sagging corduroy couch and Renee in the stiff Naugahyde chair across the low wood veneer coffee table. The room was as clean as it'd been in months—between Renee's ministrations and the return of our housekeeper, Grace, the dust and clutter had been temporarily excised.

"In April," I began, "I'll receive a check for my articles. I'd like to use that money to take a journey overseas." I paused. "To England."

Renee smiled at me, her eyeliner crinkling. Bill shifted, his back pressing against the armrest of the couch as if he was trying to get as far away from me as possible. "England," he said in a sentence all its own.

"Bill," Renee said in her sweet voice, "you know Dr. Cohen said she needed something like this."

Bill glanced at Renee and then to me. "Are you feeling sick again?"

"You know how I feel. My body hurts. *Everything* in me hurts. But that's not the only reason. I love you both and I love the boys, I know I do, but I feel numb to it, and lost."

"And how will you live?" His voice sank lower, the Southern accent nowhere to be found.

"I have the articles, and a royalty check coming from Macmillan any day now, and I'll finish or work on at least two books while I'm there." I shifted on the couch, took in a breath, set forth the words I'd practiced. "When I close my eyes, I see the deep green of it all. It's a place where we have friends I can stay with—Phyl is in London now." I looked at Renee. "She stayed with us last winter during a crisis in her life, and she's made it clear that I have a place to stay. And we also have a friend who might have some answers to help us all."

"Mr. Lewis," Bill said.

"Yes." I hesitated. This was where I could lose my balance. "I've started the novel on King Charles II, and I think it could be a real moneymaker. But I need to go to Edinburgh to the library there for research. I could also complete the Ten Commandments articles, which might make an appealing book, all compiled. And to boot, England's medical care is practically free. They don't stop tourists from using it when on holiday. I could finally get all my teeth fixed and some checkups I've been putting off because—"

"We don't have the money here," Bill interrupted, but then softened, moving closer to me and taking my hands. "Joy, we want you to get better, and I know we can't afford the medical care here. Do what you need to do. If you feel going abroad might help you, then you should do it."

"Whatever you need to be healthy," Renee agreed.

"I'm doing this for *all* of us," I said. "I can barely stand to think of leaving my boys, but I know they will have both of you. Everything will be better when I return. It's no different from one of your business trips," I said to Bill. "Whenever you come back, it's like you never left."

Bill kissed the inside of my palm. "We will be fine." He stood and sauntered off as if we'd just decided to have sloppy joes for dinner.

Renee also stood. She picked up a plastic dog-chew toy shaped like a bone from the floor and threw it into a basket under the coffee table. "We'll be dandy, cookie. Just fine. You've saved us, and I will do the same for you." She reached for my hand. "You get well so you can return ready for anything."

"Yes, ready for anything."

Jack:
> Warnie and I look forward to finally meeting our pen-friend. Please keep us apprised of your travel plans. Looking forward.

Joy:
> I sail from New York the second week of August and will arrive in Southampton on the 13th. I shall be staying with an old friend in London and will let you know when I arrive and have settled.

During those weeks before I left, my insides felt torn open in places that had felt numb for years, as if the decision itself had awakened the soul inside of me. I told my sons where I was going and what a grand adventure it would be. We made up stories of what England might look like. Davy drew pictures, and Douglas wondered if the forests were denser or greener. No one could count how many times I told them how much I would miss them, how the idea of being gone made me ache for them even as they sat by my side.

"Boys," I said when I tucked them in a week before my leaving, "I love you so much. As big as the universe."

"The universe can't be measured," Davy said with his new celestial wisdom.

"Exactly," I said.

"When you come back, will you bring us presents?" Douglas asked.

"Loads of them."

"Do you think Mr. Lewis will be as nice as the professor in his book?"

"Even nicer," I said. "I will write to you and tell you everything about him."

They fell asleep as easily as exhausted children can, and I stood over them, tears running down my face and into the corners of my lips.

When we arrived at the pier of the Hudson River docks that August morning, Bill stood tall and stiff as the dock's pilings. "Safe travels, Joy." He offered a weak hug.

I took his hands. "This is a trip for all of us. It will be a return to health, more stable finances, and vitality for our family. You see that, don't you, Poogle?"

He turned away, and Renee came to me. She held me longer, her hug tighter. She stepped back in her red sundress and wide-brimmed straw hat and smiled. "I will miss you, cookie. Come home safely and quickly." She kissed my cheek, and I knew there would be a bright-red mark from her lipstick.

A humid breeze carrying the pungent stench of smoke and gasoline washed over us as I held out my arms to my sons. Behind me the grand ocean liner waited, a mountain of a ship I would soon board. "Davy, Douglas. Come to me."

One son under each arm, I drew them in a tight circle and kissed their faces, every little inch. "I will be home soon. I love you so much." My voice snagged on the tears clogged in my throat.

"Don't cry, Mommy." Douglas patted my cheek. "You can bring us presents from England."

Davy buried his head in my shoulder and began to cry softly, his glasses falling to the ground. I lifted his face and held his chin in my hand to see his deep brown eyes fixed on mine. "Look at the moon and know that I'll be looking at it too. We will be under the same stars and the same sky. And it will carry me home. I promise you."

We clung to each other until Bill announced, "Let's not make this worse than it is. You must go now."

With two more kisses on my sons' cheeks, I watched as Bill took their hands and the foursome walked away toward Bobby and Rosemary, who stood waiting at the end of the sidewalk. It was only Douglas who looked back and waved. I didn't move one step until they were gone from sight, and then slowly I lifted my eyes to the ocean liner. She held firm to the docks with ropes as thick as trees, and she didn't move in the choppy waters, although all around her the water swayed, danced, and slapped against her hull. Tall white letters along her smooth ribs declared: SS *United States*.

Onboard, the wind was warm, and I could almost taste the sweet-salt middle of the ocean, where the heat would dissipate. I stood on the aft deck, my dress flapping like a bird that couldn't get off the ground, and I stayed there until the Statue of Liberty was as small as a toy in a gift shop, until the last of land faded from view and the vast sea was all that remained.

PART II

ENGLAND

"...you can't keep him; it's not
as if he were a tame lion."

THE VOYAGE OF THE DAWN TREADER, C. S. LEWIS

CHAPTER 9

Love is this and that and always present

"Sonnet III," Joy Davidman

August 1952

I stepped off the SS *United States* onto the Southhampton docks, squinting through my glasses at the unfamiliar country shrouded in fog and coal dust. The land, and what lush green glory it held for me, rested somewhere beyond.

I dragged my luggage, a sight I'm sure for all to see, because even with the smog and dirt, I had a feeling of such lightness and gaiety that the malaise I'd been carrying for years fell off like shed skin. I wouldn't have been surprised if someone had chased me down and bellowed, "You dropped something back there!"

I had left my family in America, and I knew there were neighbors and friends who didn't understand. Our church community scowled. Other women talked about me. And yet must not their souls die inside? Did they not feel the anxiety that comes when the inner light rises and cries out, "Let me live"?

Perhaps our Maker had stitched us each together in such a way that this was not true of all women. I could have kept on the way I was going, empty and jaundiced, sick and desolate of soul. I could have tried even harder to erase the stench of whiskey from my alcoholic husband, to scrub the floors cleaner, to quiet my troubled heart. Of course I could have, but what would it have cost me?

A complicated musical composition of accents—from Cockney and melodic Irish to sophisticated Queen's English—carried me along the sidewalk as if it had been written for my very arrival. I boarded a train and then disembarked in London to hail a cab. The city passed by with beauty: cobbled streets and red double-decker buses, lampposts arching over the sidewalks so majestically they seemed to guard the city. Men in suits riding bicycles, women in smart, waist-cinched dresses tottering on high heels along the sidewalks. Cathedrals with spires reaching toward the sky. Cherry-colored phone booths on the corners, the doors often swung open like a secret invitation. The taxi arrived at Phyl's flat on 11 Elsworthy Road, a road lined with silver birch and sycamore trees that beckoned like a secret passageway.

My sea legs swaying beneath me, I stood on the brownstone steps and knocked with the confident hope of a new beginning. Phyl threw open the door, and for a moment I didn't recognize her. The last I'd seen her had been at my house in Staatsburg, where she'd been suicidal and wan—but there she was, her cheeks flushed and her smile wide, full of vitality with a boisterous greeting and a grand hug. "You're here!"

Transformation. Yes! That was what I sought. To name something was to make it mine—transformation of my heart and body.

And it would all begin here in London.

———

Today I will meet Jack.

The thought awoke me with a smile in the guest bedroom at Phyl's. I'd been in England for a month already—wanting to become strong and ready to meet my pen-friend, as well as enjoy the peace and rest I needed. Today was the day.

I rose slowly to the whistle of a teapot.

In the past days I'd been seduced by England, and time had flown by with proof that it is relevant, that it moves quicker in happiness, fleeing away from me like water from the highest fall. I'd explored London with an awakened desire to learn and see everything I could in the nine-hundred-square-mile regal city. This journey, these days away from my little boys, must be worth the absence, and I set forth to make it so. As Phyl and I ambled through Trafalgar Square, she huffed, out of breath. "You've walked all of this city, I'm sure. Aren't you tired of it?"

"Tired of it?" I spread my arms wide and laughed. "Walking has always allowed me to slough off the darker parts of myself. And I'm stunned by this city's beauty." I sat on the edge of the fountain and motioned for her to do the same. "What's fascinating is the way I see the world now. It's as if in believing in God I was given new eyes—the world is full of possibility and fascination. It's no longer just nature, or just beauty—it's *revelation*."

She squinted into the sun and jostled me. "Looks the same to me."

"Oh, Phyl!" I held my hands to the sky. "Can't you see now that anything is possible? Anything. The world changes when you understand the Love behind it, over it, and under it."

"You love life by the fistfuls, my dear." She patted my knee.

We made our way home, and for the remaining weeks I was poked and prodded by the dentists and doctors I visited—healing was paramount in this journey. I also filled my days with reading and research, writing and traveling, meeting new friends and finding a writing group.

Loads of letters flew back and forth between Bill, the kids, Renee, and me. I wanted to tell them every detail of my journey.

Joy:

Oh Renee, how I wish you'd been with me at Trafalgar Square where I found a Spanish restaurant you would have adored. But I've realized this: Londoners must be half duck. If not for the crepe-soled shoes I'd have swum through the streets.

Bill:

I'm very glad to hear that all is "beer and skittles" for you, and that you are marvelously happy, but we are having a hard time here. Money is tight. Forgive me for not sending more this time.

Joy:

Dearest Poogle,

I am sorry money is tight. I will do what I can here to write and sell, to pinch the shillings. I think of you often—I wish you could have been with me when I went to an open-air theater where a huge thunderstorm shook the tent as if we were still in Vermont! I also took a trip to Hampstead Heath, where I bought three pieces of art for cheap-cheap, a watercolor for only thirty-five shillings. It's a wonderful place and full of all sorts of artists and writers. Maybe we should sell the house and move here. Love all around, Joy.

P.S. to Davy: The aquarium here has a five-foot grand salamander from Japan!!

Davy had written to me of the snake Bill had *finally* let him get—Mr. Nichols, he named him. I thought of my boys continuously, and when I went to the London Zoo I missed them fiercely and bought souvenirs to send.

I visited Madam Tussauds Museum and every chapel or cathedral or art studio open to me. Then there was my solo journey to Canterbury, which felt like entering a book I'd read as a child. I'd never seen a land that echoed my dreams—the seductive, rolling green hills in their variegated greens, lined with stone walls and dotted with cottony sheep.

I fell in love with England again and again. The shape of my soul was changing with every view; I wanted to be strong and steady before I met Jack in person.

I traveled through Kent, a country of short-horn cows and undulating golden hills. I tried to describe it in my letters, but how could I do it justice? Miles and miles of apple and pear and plum trees. Hazel thickets and rowan trees with red berries flaming like fire that didn't consume. Chestnut trees and fields of hops flew past like Renoirs. I filled myself with the views. The WWII bombed-out spaces revealed ancient Roman pavement and walls below—there was a story everywhere I looked. Oh, how America seemed provincial and boring in comparison.

Then there were the friends I found. Two days into my trip, at Jack's urging, I knocked on Florence Williams's door. Her late husband, Charles Williams, had dubbed her his "Michal," and although he was gone, the name had stuck. He'd been a poet, theologian, author, and an Inkling with Jack and J. R. R. Tolkien. And in a connection that made us both break into the laughter that binds friends, we discovered that Bill had written a foreword for one of her late husband's books—*The Greater Trumps*. Not only did we become fast friends, but she also introduced me to an author's crowd in London—a group of science fiction writers who gathered off Fleet Street on Thursday nights in a low-slung ceiling pub called the White Horse. They dubbed their group the "London Circle," and I ducked into their cluster and drew that circle around me. Over thick beers and bangers their stories, debate, and publishing gossip swirled around me. It was community I'd been after and community I found, as though I'd washed up on an island after being lost at sea.

Bill:

It's nice to hear you went to both the doctor and the dentist already. I hope you are healing. The boys are doing well but miss you more than they let on.

Renee:

Thank you for the Liberty scarf! I've been wearing it everywhere. Please forgive Bill for not sending much money; we are broke as we can be—sorry to be so down, but it's just the gosh awful truth: Bill is having trouble selling anything at all.

Joy:

Dear Poogabill,

I'm sorry you can't send money and that you actually are "broke as can be." I am writing every day and if I sell something, I will send some cash to you. Meanwhile I will scrape by—thank God for Phyl and a place to live. You'll be thrilled to know that I've found a writing group. Most of them are sci-fi writers, and many of them know your work. And guess who I met? Arthur Clarke! You know, the famous author who is a member of the British Interplanetary. As for my health, I've never felt better. Just you wait, Sweetabill, when I come home I'm going to be the nicest poogle you've ever known me to be.

"Joy!" Phyl's voice called from the hallway. "We must leave or we'll miss the train to Oxford."

I'd switched outfits and hats three times; I had almost chosen the black Jaeger wool jersey I'd just bought but changed my mind when I saw it might look dreary. I'd put my hair up and then down, and then pinned again in my regular bun. It was Michal Williams who'd told me that Jack liked it when women made an effort in their dress.

Phyl poked her head into the room and pressed her hands to her chest. "You look beautiful. I love that tartan dress."

"Oh, Phyl." I pulled up my stockings and snapped them into the garter that dug into my thigh. "I wonder what we'll all talk about. I'm not very good with new people. That's Bill's realm in the kingdom of our marriage—he's engaging and charming, he laughs loud and tells jokes, he plays his guitar and participates in games. I usually find myself in a corner debating politics or religion or books." I slid my glasses on and smiled at Phyl.

"But you already *know* this man."

"I do, I believe. He's bringing a friend, and there'll be four of us." I glanced in the mirror one more time, tucked my hair under the grosgrain hat with the blue ribbon. "Thank you for coming with me."

"It's no trouble," she assured me. "And I certainly want to meet him too. Plus Oxford—who doesn't want to take a sojourn to Oxford? You think you like London? Just you wait. And you'll adore Victoria's little guest room, both convenient and cozy."

I fetched my bags and straightened my shoulders. "Let's be on with it then."

———

Phyl and I sat side by side as the train lurched from the platform. She read a novel and I watched her face, her long eyelashes sweeping down and up, and a horrid memory flooded me: a terrible fight with Bill in December of last year. He'd taken Phyl in our old Chrysler to Pier 88 in Manhattan for her return trip to London. I'd been sick, miserable, cooped up, and suspicious after the previous nights of admitted infidelity, and I hadn't been rational. When Bill called to say the car was sputtering with trouble and he would spend the night at Hotel Woodstock, I accused him of seducing Phyl. I screamed and cursed and embarrassed myself. He in turn raged at me. I didn't remember the words that were said, but the gaping soul-wounds had cut deep and remained.

Phyl had proved herself to be the most loyal and uplifting friend; I wondered how I ever could have thought she'd take any such nonsense from my husband. And Bill had sworn his infidelity was over . . . but for a wife it is never over. Ever.

"Phyl," I said as the train exhaled coal-tinged smoke and heaved toward Oxford.

"Hmmm?"

"I'm nervous. Isn't that odd? Why should I be nervous about meeting a man and his friend at a restaurant? I've met a hundred writers in my day, and most of them not worthy of the awe I gave them."

"Because you respect this writer so much. I think you're quite afraid to meet the *real* man. Maybe he's not everything you've imagined him to be."

I laughed, too loudly as always, and two women a row ahead turned with disapproving looks. I offered them my biggest smile. Nothing like a little kindness to kill. "Oh, cookie," I said to Phyl. "Could you be any more blunt?"

"We might as well face the truth, my dear." She stretched and closed *The Great Divorce*, which she'd wanted to skim before meeting Jack. "There's no real use in pretending you don't care. Of course the butter-flies must be flapping all over your insides."

I thought for a moment as the landscape flickered by, green and gold. "It's not losing the respect for him that makes me nervous; there's no chance of that. It's the regard he might or might not have for me. You know, my dear, Jews aren't taken too kindly round these parts. Even ex-Jews. What if this ex-atheist, ex-Communist, Bronx-born woman appalls him?"

"Maybe appalled, but more likely a little enthralled. Like a good book unfolding, you'll just have to wait and see."

The checkered fabric-covered seats itched to the touch but I sank back anyway, lifting the shade higher on the window. Green fields passed by, wetlands and rivers, marinas and creeks. It seemed as if we crossed many rivers, although it might have been only one, snaking its way between London and Oxford. High on a knoll we blew by a small town where the chimney pots below looked like headstones. Then we passed through the coal-tinged Industrial Slough and onward through Reading. The rocking sensation of the train left me sleepy as I imagined a few opening lines for the moment I saw Jack.

It's an honor and a privilege.

You've changed my life.

I've adored you since halfway through The Great Divorce *when you stated, "No people find themselves more absurd than lovers."*

Hi, I'm Joy, and I'm a nervous mess.

But in the end I said none of those things.

CHAPTER 10

I'll measure my affection by the drachm

"SONNET I," JOY DAVIDMAN

The brick of the Eastgate Hotel, a grand dame of a structure in Oxford, was the tawny color of my cat's fur. I was, even after a month, still struck by the solid antiquity in England—the fashion in which structures were built as if they'd known their ethereal beauty would be needed for thousands of years. The windows were inset like sleepy-hooded eyes. The four steps to the front door were wide and curved. To our right was what one might believe was a medieval fortress but was really one of Oxford University's thirty-four colleges, Merton College, with the long stone wall that followed the curved street as closely as a lover.

"Phyl," I said, and we paused at the dark wood doorway, "although I miss my collection of poogles, I'm very happy to be here."

She gave me a calm and knowing look, her blue eyes squinting against the sunlight. "This will be interesting, my friend. Enjoy it."

I nodded at her and placed my hand over my stomach to settle the nerves. Dabbed my lipstick with a tissue. For years I'd hoped to meet Jack, yet doubted I would, and now I stood on an Oxford sidewalk outside the place he met friends for lunch.

We entered the hotel bar lobby, where he'd said he would be waiting. I called to mind the photographs in which Bill said Jack looked like a kindly old basset hound. In those images, Jack sometimes wore round black-rimmed glasses, and he always appeared in a suit and tie—did he wear these things on a regular day to eat lunch at a hotel? Or would he be in his teaching robes? A pipe between his lips? A cigarette dangling?

My thoughts winged everywhere—caged birds.

Did I look all right? Beautiful but smart? Kind but intelligent? I'd never admired my looks, per se, except for one very lovely photograph on the back of *Weeping Bay*. And every time I tried to reproduce that exact pose, I came up short and disappointed. I fiddled with my strand of pearls and glanced around the bar. It was full at lunch hour: men in three-piece suits and ties, women in pearls and hats no different from what I wore. The room was a haze of chintz and velvet, low lighting from lamps at dark wood side tables. The walls were covered in green damask wallpaper, the ceiling with dark wood gables thick as railroad ties. It was all very stately and noble, which caused me to stand taller, shift my shoulders back.

My gaze roamed the room until I found him.

Jack.

There he was, animated, in deep conversation with the man across from him. His smile was kind and curved as he listened.

I took stock of him as if I had eternity to stare without his noticing.

His hairline had receded, and what dark hair remained on top was slicked back with comb marks. His smile sparked with life. His eyes were shadowed by his sloping eyelids beneath rimless glasses, as if he'd just woken and was happy to have done so. He sat casually, with one corduroy-clad leg over the other.

There was something lit up about him, the way the landscape of his face was animated beneath his strong eyebrows. His lips and mouth were full. These attributes—his mind, which I knew in letters, and now the light of his spirit—combined into a singular word: *beautiful.* The birds in my mind moved to my chest, fluttering there in anticipation.

And then, as if someone placed a hand over his mouth, he stopped midlaugh. He looked to me as if my stare had tapped him on the shoulder.

Our gazes caught and stayed. He grinned, as did I.

I gathered myself and ambled toward him, came to a stop in front of the couch as he stood. Those brown eyes of his, they were sparkling as if lit.

"Well, well. My pen-friend Joy is finally in England." His voice was a song: part Irish brogue, part English. He wasn't quite as tall as I'd expected, perhaps five foot ten at the most, yet his charisma stretched to the beams overhead. He wore a ragged tweed jacket with brown leather patches on the elbows and a white-buttoned shirt with a bright-blue tie.

"And you," I said with a jittery smile, "must be my very famous friend, Jack Lewis."

He bellowed with laughter and thrust out his hand to take mine in a rigorous shake. "Famous? Infamous perhaps, in very small circles."

My voice sounded breathy and silly. I lowered it. "I'm really happy to see you. After all these years of friendship and an entire month here in England, finally we meet face-to-face." I held to his hand and we smiled at each other. For what was most likely only a few seconds, time paused. He let go of my hand as Phyl stepped closer. "Oh! I've forgotten myself! Please meet my friend Phyl Williams."

The man next to Jack lifted his eyebrows, and at once I knew what I'd done wrong—I'd spoken loudly in my New York accent.

Jack shook Phyl's hand and in that brogue stated, "George, may I introduce you to Joy Gresham and her friend from London, Phyl."

George nodded once at each of us and Jack explained. "George is a dear friend who was once a student of mine at Magdalen."

I glanced at George. "It's such a pleasure to meet you." I held out my hand and he shook it without a word. Nervous, I pressed my lips together, hoping the lipstick was still there and hadn't bled into the small creases around my mouth.

"Come," Jack said, "let's sit down. They've sorted a table for us."

The four of us wound our way to the low-lit dining room table reserved in the middle of the restaurant, where four cut-glass tumblers sparkling with amber liquid waited.

We settled in, shook open the napkins on our laps, as I quickly assessed George. He possessed a long face like a horse with a deeply etched forehead, a road map to years of furrowed brow. Large ears perched as if tilting toward his eyes, and his long nose ended in a rounded bulb from which he seemed to look down at me as he caught my eye. I looked away.

"Sherry," Jack said and raised his glass. "Welcome to Oxford."

We all lifted our glasses and together took a sip. "Hmmm," I said, "Lovely. In America we would've started with hard liquor and moved to wine and we'd be drunk before the meal even began." I shook my head. "Then I'd have felt the particular hell of a hangover before the food was gone. But everything here is very . . . civilized."

Jack laughed, and George gave me the furrowed brow look. I smiled my best smile. "Mr. Sayer, Jack says you were a former student of his? What do you do now?"

"I teach at Malvern."

"Oh, lucky you. This city of Oxford," I said. "It makes me wonder how different my life would have been if I had spent it in a place like this with men like you two."

"I daresay your life is much better spent around men other than us." George lifted his glass. "Boring as we can be."

"But the intellectual life here—what, nine hundred years old?" I leaned forward. "How stimulating."

"Yes," Jack said. "It can be, but then again it is also quite boorish at times, the tedium of teaching and grading and lecturing."

"Well, I would have liked to give it a shot."

Then Phyl told some joke lost to me in time, and we began to talk in circles and with laughter. We ate salmon mousse as light as whipped cream, and I lost track of the wine refills. Gaiety increased exponentially with the wine, and jokes were told badly and histories regaled with embellishment. We talked about the new queen's upcoming coronation, of the tea rationing. The long lunch felt but five minutes. Often Jack and I caught each other's eye and smiled, but shyly. We knew each other as well as any friends—he'd heard my secrets and my fears—and yet it was just now that our eyes could catch as our minds already had.

"How did you come upon our friend's work?" George finally asked as trifle was delivered for dessert.

"Like Jack, I was surprised by God. Both of us midlife converts." I smiled at Jack and then looked back to George. "When I was eight years old I read H. G. Wells's *Outline of History* and marched right into the family room to announce to my Jewish parents that I was an atheist."

George flinched. I saw it, and knew it was the word *Jewish*. Brits could claim they weren't anti-Semitic, just as white Americans could claim they weren't racist as they segregated their schools and neighborhoods.

"We've been writing about our spiritual journeys," Jack said to George and then turned to me. "And you have brought to my attention holes and missing links in some of my arguments. I must say I have rarely met such a worthy adversary."

Adversary? I wanted to be anything but.

George cleared his throat. "Well, do tell us what you think of England, Mrs. Gresham. You've been here a month now?"

"Well, I have fallen in love, Mr. Sayer. In mad, passionate love." The heat of a blush filled my face and neck. I reached my hand to my décolletage, grabbed onto the pearls I'd strung there that very morning thinking they looked elegant, and took in a long breath. "It is England I'm talking about, of course!"

George nodded, patting his lips with a napkin.

I continued as I often did when nervous, words pouring out. "I love everything about it. I've practically walked my legs off. I'm enamored with the golden light. And how can air be softer here? I have no idea, but it is! The kindness of strangers is unparalled. And oh, the pubs." I exhaled. "I adore the pubs. The dark warmth of them, the murmur of conversation, the music played by a man with a fiddle tucked away in a corner."

George burst out in hearty laughter. "You obviously haven't yet seen the bloody English fog. Just you wait; we'll see if you're still romanticizing our country then. Which, by the way, is jolly fine by me."

Jack lifted his glass. "When I first saw Oxford I wrote to my father and told him it was a place beyond my wildest imaginings, a place of the fabled cluster of spires and towers. I'm quite envious of *your* view of Oxford today. There's only that one first time."

We all fell silent and finished our desserts slowly, as if not one of us desired the parting that would naturally follow. I felt bereft by Jack's absence, even though it was merely an idea and had not yet happened.

Then he stood, wiped crumbs from his jacket, and smiled. "Why, let's walk to Magdalen and I'll show you around a bit, if you have the time."

If I have the time . . .

CHAPTER 11

Between two rivers, in the wistful weather,
Sky changing, tree undressing, summer failing

"SONNET VI," JOY DAVIDMAN

September in Oxford is a glory of color and silken air, of golden hues and ivy-covered hope. It was like being transported to the land of a fairy tale you'd forgotten you read.

I ambled next to Jack as he swung his walking stick with each step, his fisherman's hat settled crooked on his head. We crossed High Street for my first view of Magdalen College, which rested regally on the River Cherwell. I stopped midstep. "Stunning!" I stared at the college's stone tower with six spires reaching toward the bluest sky. A great fortress of walls and doors surrounded the limestone buildings. It was a painting, a diorama from a fantasy movie, the architecture medieval and mystical.

"My first view of it stunned me the same," Jack said. "It still does. It's just as beautiful as you draw close. Come."

"You know," I said, "after the bustle of London and the bombed-out spaces, this feels pristine and untouched."

A wistful expression passed over Jack's face, but then he turned to me and nodded. "Yes, we were spared the bombs—Hitler planned on making Oxford his own and he wanted to save it. We'd watch the planes head here and then veer to the left or right using the river as their guide."

I glanced up as if the planes were whirring overhead. "I'm so glad to be here."

"I'm quite happy you made the journey." He smiled at me.

Phyl and George walked ahead and through the great wooden door of Magdalen, leaving Jack and me alone. The yellow leaves formed a plush carpet under our feet while a few still clung to the trees by their fragile stems. Gravestones were as common along the sidewalks as benches or stone walls.

We ambled; I was in no great rush. We passed the gray weathered wooden doors to Magdalen, as grand as the castle doors I'd seen at Buckingham, and Jack motioned for us to first walk across a stone bridge. Halfway across he paused and we stood together, leaning against the ancient wall and absorbing the sight of the River Cherwell. We stood, our shoulders only a breath apart, as a line about rivers from Shakespeare's *King John* came to me. "'Trust not those cunning waters of his eyes, For villainy is not without such rheum.'"

With a sudden laugh Jack lifted his face to the sun and finished. "'And he, long traded in it, makes it seem like rivers of remorse and innocency.'"

Our eyes met, widened, and together we said, "King John."

Jack removed a case from his pocket and took out a cigarette, striking the match hard against the flint in a swift movement. He set the fire against the end and puffed until it was lit. This was all done slowly, carefully, as if he had all the world's time to complete this singular act on a stone bridge over a river. Below, punts were crowded against the banks, lashed together and held tight, waiting to be chosen. The willow trees swept downward as if to stroke the river, their branches waving with a breeze.

I broke the silence. "This river," I said. "It's very much like life."

"How so?" Jack turned to lean against the stone parapet, taking a long drag of his cigarette.

Well, that would teach me to speak without thinking. "The water flowing," I said decidedly. "It reaches its end at the sea no matter what."

He considered this. "I believe life is more like a tree. Each branch differentiating as it grows. Each an individual choice."

"Jack." I pointed at the river flowing beneath us. "*That* is the river of life. It's bound by its edges but still it is free. Do you sometimes debate for fun?" I asked with a laugh. "Just to see if I can keep up with you?"

"Ah, no—I am quite sure you can keep up with me. But the river, as beautiful a metaphor as it is, isn't right for our choices in life. We don't all meet in the same place, as rivers do."

His eyes were deep and rich brown, and I wondered what they saw in me—he knew how to hold kind attention, a presence.

"Choice." I bent over and picked up a handful of leaves, let them fall through my fingers. "What if we choose wrongly? Do we burn in an everlasting hell? You believe this?" I tossed a leaf at him. "As you wrote in *The Great Divorce*? You can't take any souvenir of what you love with you?"

He laughed. "I have enjoyed our correspondence, yet it is even better to be chatting with you."

"Yes." I took in a long breath and stated the truth. "Through the years my sluggish heart began to beat again with words, *our words*, and the very power of them."

Jack smiled as that golden English sunlight crested from behind a pleated cloud, resting gently on his face as if the light desired to touch him. For just a moment, no longer or shorter than the one on my knees in my sons' nursery, my body felt untethered from the earth, as if we were merely a dream fragment. My heartbeat fluttered in my wrists, in my chest, in my belly. A warm flush, timid but sure, flooded me.

Oh, Joy, be very, very careful.

He had captured my intellect, my mind, and my thoughts; I could not allow him to do the same to my heart.

I turned away from his smile, those teasing eyes, and together we strolled back from where we'd come, passing trees with birds' nests like tiny hats in the naked branches, till we were only a few paces from the entrance to Magdalen. When I first saw the college's name in print, I had said it incorrectly. I thanked the heavens that I heard the correct pronunciation before I met Jack—"Maudlin" it is. Yet still we didn't enter. Jack sat on a bench, crossed one leg over the other.

He held his cigarette between his thumb and forefinger, and the smoke circled upward. He spread his arms along the back length of the bench.

"It's not so much any souvenirs we want to take, it's our hearts we need to carry," he said. "They yearn for what I call the High Country, and we can't get there without abandoning the belief that this is all there is, and that we must get the most out of it, and take something with us." He looked at me then, silently, like a man in a debate who had just nailed his point.

"Oh, Jack," I said and sat beside him, twisting to face him. "Your High Country is my Fairyland. I've dreamt of it since I was a child. When I read *Pilgrim's Regress*, I knew you meant the same place—'the Island,' you called it." This repartee with a man whose mind I had come to esteem and value felt like water to a parched soul.

I continued. "You and I both had the same experience as children, that same thrill that nature brings, the knowing that sometimes the world evokes a feeling so full of longing that words can't capture it. And that longing hints at a place where evil can't exist and heartbreak can't abide. Even when we weren't believers, we still believed. It's as though we took the same path, and the High Country called to us both."

He nodded, and I almost believed he blushed. "*Pilgrim's Regress* was the first book I wrote after my conversion, wondering about yearning and what it might mean." He smiled at me slowly. "With the yellow leaves and the happiness of this afternoon, I long even more for such a place," he said. "Isn't it odd? That we can be happy here and yet want to go . . . there?"

"As if at our happiest, we want even more. Like this is the hint." I took a breath. "Jack, I look back at my life, and I understand the lure of atheism, but it now seems almost impossible. How could I have *not* believed when my heart always knew?"

"Maybe we were too simple."

I shook my head with remembrance. "I don't know; I think I just wanted my soul to be my own."

"Indeed." He nodded as if he remembered the same.

"Have you ever . . ." I paused.

"Ever what?"

"Felt another presence? Felt like the veil lifted for a minute? And I don't just mean in prayer."

"Tell me what you mean, Joy." He leaned closer.

"When my friend Stephen Vincent Benét passed away, I felt him. I think . . . no, I know I even saw his wraith pass by." I cringed. "Is that crazy?"

Jack drew nearer to me, and his tone lowered as he dropped the last of his cigarette. "Joy, I was devastated when Charles Williams passed; I was dazed and stunned. I went to the pub we frequented together—the King's Arms—and ordered a pint. It was then that I felt my friend. He was with me, and he passed by. No one will ever convince me otherwise. Tollers believes I am quite absurd, but I know it to be true."

We stared at each other then—another thread that bound us.

————

We strode through the archway to Magdalen, and the happiness I felt couldn't be measured as Jack turned tour guide, his voice deepening.

"You must know, of course, that Oxford is made of thirty-five colleges, and this is but one—Magdalen—and it is outside the gate of the medieval city."

"Nine hundred years old," I said. "That's what I've read. It feels humbling to be in the place of such deep history."

Magdalen's glistening white stone tower shot toward the blue sky, her six spires secured to stone buildings that splayed in every direction, a master of geometric precision. I pointed at the tower as we drew closer. "It's a phallic symbol for a male-dominated institution, ain't it?"

Jack paused, his eyebrows raised above his spectacles, then, with an exhale of laughter and cigarette smoke, he bellowed with delight. "You call them as you see them, don't you, Joy?" he said in a brogue so beautiful that my heart fell to its knees.

His voice, I thought, *is like an ocean in a shell.*

"I feel that I could never get enough of this place." I paused and ran my sight over the buildings and the ivy-covered walls, the thick pristine lawns with well-groomed pathways. "And that entranceway . . ." We were nearing the massive wooden door that was decorated with thick brass and sat protected under a stone archway. "It looks as though one of your magical beings should saunter out."

"The grand entranceway to the quad," he said. "Or the Ancient Door. It's fascinating seeing the familiar through your eyes."

The stone wall, Jack informed me, was called the Longwall, enclosing Magdalen—the dining hall, the Cloisters, the classrooms, the chapel, student rooms, dining room, library, and more. We entered, and the stone hallways and limestone alleyways were as numinous as any I'd seen, echoing with the past. Lichen grew along the pathways and in the cracks between the Headington stones. I joked about private and hidden rooms—a dungeon, perhaps. The Middle Ages clung to the air and seemed concealed in the hallways and thin stone stairwells.

In a perfect square, the hallways of the Cloister surrounded a green lawn. These walkways were pale-yellow plaster, the open archways to the quad garnished with corbels and carvings. We walked together, turning left and left and left to end up where we began, talking as though we'd never stop. After the second round we paused, both facing the green quad. Gargoyles peered down from the buildings that hovered over the Cloisters. "I can't decide if they are watching us or guarding us," I said and pointed up.

"Hieroglyphics." He pretended to cower beneath them with a feigned fright. "Now this way." He motioned forward. "Let's walk by the river."

I followed him out the hallway opening to a wide-open field. "A hundred and twenty acres," he said. And then we walked through a wrought iron gate and archway onto a smaller stone bridge, under which

ran a tributary of the Cherwell. "And this is Addison's Walk." The dirt
pathway was strewn with leaves of all hues, the trees so densely gathered as to crowd the pathway yet leave enough room to feel free and
protected both.

"The whole of this was first built in 1458," he told me, standing
with his arms spread out. "And this meadow"—he pointed ahead—"in
the spring, it is full of flowers of a purplish-green color that fills the
senses."

"*Fritillaria meleagris*," I said.

He laughed in that already familiar bellow.

"And are you a walking Latin nomenclature appendix?" he asked.

"My sons think so," I said. "I survived many a childhood day by
wandering the botanical gardens in the Bronx and memorizing the
genus and species for all the plants and flowers."

We stood together on that pathway, and I wondered if my eyes
would ever be able to see all the glory of that place; it was too much for
one visit. The architecture and the natural world melded together into
something so sublime it would take years or decades to see it rightly.

I turned back to him. "Jack, there's something I've been wondering."

"And what is that? What questions have I not answered as of yet?"

"Why are you called Jack when your name is Clive?"

"Ah!" He swung his walking stick up and then stuck it into the
ground. "Well, it's a bit of a story."

"Then tell." I set my hands on my hips and planted my feet. "I'm
ready, sir."

"All right then. When I was a young boy we had a dog named
Jacksie. On a warm summer day, when the world was good and right,
Warnie and I were walking to town when a car came roaring around
the bend and hit our dog. Killed him right there in front of us." Jack
shook his head. "If I could make a request of God it would be that no
young boy ever see his beloved dog killed." He shuddered and then continued. "Therefore I announced my name was Jack and vowed never to
drive a car."

"You named yourself after a dog, and you don't drive." I laughed, and he took a step forward with his stick, glancing over his shoulder to see if I was following.

"Now maybe you know all there is to know."

"I doubt that," I said as we caught up with Phyl and George.

"Darling," she called out and came to us. "I must be going if I'm going to catch the last train."

"And I," George said, "must return to Malvern. Today has been a pleasure." He bowed his head and tipped his hat before walking away.

I thanked Phyl, and once again Jack and I were alone. We talked and strolled through Magdalen's grounds until the afternoon sky's pink hues hinted toward evening.

Our parting was polite, and when I told him that I'd be there for ten more days, he smiled. And that man, when he smiled . . . it was the only thing you wanted to see. His face was so serious in photos, yet in person both animated and buoyant. He seemed continually prepared to burst into laughter if given the chance. I wanted to give him every chance.

I didn't know whether to embrace him or shake his hand. In the end I did neither, as he wrapped both his hands around the top of his walking stick. "My brother, Warnie, will be available tomorrow. Would you like to meet us here for lunch?"

"I would very much like that," I said.

"Where are you staying?"

"With a friend of a friend, Victoria Ruffer. Meanwhile I'll be taking full advantage of the city, walking and admiring. The autumn here might be the most beautiful I've ever seen."

"Yes, it's glorious. Autumn makes all things seem possible."

"It is spring that does that." I swept my palms open like a flower blossoming. "All that life coming back from frozen earth."

He gave a sly smile.

"What? Did I say something awful?"

"No." He shook his head. "But you certainly have your own opinion about everything. I knew this from your letters, but now I can see it's true all the time, isn't it?"

"Yes, I'm awful that way. I know."

"I'm not yet sure it's awful." He looked at me closely then, as if seeing me for the first time.

We parted ways, and I headed along the storyland sidewalks of Oxford, back to Victoria's. I knew what I would do the minute I shut the door to my little guest room: write a poem. What else was one to do with these emotions that seemed to say, like springtime, that the world was about to begin anew?

CHAPTER 12

Even the bells in Magdalen tower were ringing
Death to the drooping afternoon

"Sonnet VI," Joy Davidman

The second day in Oxford arrived, luminescent, the honey-hues of sunlight falling from the leaves to settle on the grass like spilled paint. The air was as clear as glass and soft as cotton. I rolled out of bed and into the day, expectant.

Lazily, I started a letter to home and also set my eyes for a quick read-through of my Second Commandment article before leaving to wander toward Magdalen for lunch. Fifteen minutes later, when I reached the college gate, I paused, the old fatigue threatening at the edge of my bones.

"No," I said out loud. "We are here in Oxford and healthy and well. We are going to see Jack and meet Warnie."

Something in the trees and the river breathed of holiness, and I said a silent prayer—*You've brought us together. Please be with us*—and then I eased under the ancient stone archway of Magdalen into the quadrangle. Men rushed past in black robes, open and flapping in the wind, like so many crows. The students wore their suits—boys dressed as men with their buttoned sweaters and rumpled suit jackets with only the top two buttons fastened. And the cigarette smoke—it seemed a fag sprouted from every mouth. This was a man's domain if I'd ever seen one. It reeked of leather and pipe smoke. I made it to the dining hall door with timid steps, my mask of bravado slowly cracking.

What was I doing?

Women of course weren't prohibited (except as students, fellows, or tutors), but I could feel in every nerve ending that here we were most welcome as appendages or footnotes. Pleasant company at best.

I wore a prim sheath dress fashioned of taupe tweed, and the double strand of pearls hung around my neck. My new nylons rubbed pleasantly against my thighs. A silk pale-blue Liberty scarf, one I'd purchased in London, was tied artfully around my neck as if I'd casually thrown it on, and yet I'd had to try the knots more times than I would admit.

I stood at the entranceway of the dining hall and waited, trembling. Doorways in this fortress were small and unmarked, almost hidden except for those who knew what they were. I entered slowly, blinking in the dim light. Dark paneled and cavernous, the room seemed built for men of knowledge, for fine literature and discourse of philosophy. Great oil paintings hung from the walls, portraits of men in robes with striped stoles around their necks, unsmiling and serious men. The tables were long and rectangular, set for lunch with white napkins tented at each place setting and sparkling crystal glassware awaiting the sherry. Dark brass chandeliers hung low, casting circles of light. At the end of the room a long table was set up on a foot-high platform, and there sat the dons in their black robes. The high table. Stained glass windows watched over the room, and a carved stone fireplace dominated the left wall.

I wanted this room to be mine.

I adjusted my dark-blue plate hat and smiled as widely as I knew how, but my thoughts were preoccupied with one thing: I needed to find a ladies' room. It had been a lovely but long walk from Victoria's guesthouse, and I shouldn't have had the last two cuppas before I left.

Jack spotted me before I did him.

"Good afternoon, Joy." He approached me with a smile that settled on me with warmth, as if we met for lunch every day. He wore the same tie as he had yesterday, and his black robe hung unbuttoned over his gray suit, his spectacles poking above the pocket of his jacket as if to spy what was happening.

"Thank you so much for having me here."

It was my accent that made the men turn from their plates to stare. Another man drew near. "Well, good afternoon. You must be Mrs. Gresham. How very much I've enjoyed your letters." The man was shorter than Jack, but I knew who he was immediately, his sincere smile and earnest eyes the giveaway.

"And you must be Warnie." I smiled. "I can't tell you how wonderful it is to meet you."

Warnie's face was much rounder than Jack's, and his chin seemed to fade into his neck, but his smile lit his features. He wore a similarly drab suit but without the robe. His tie was askew, as was his smile, and he was charming in his rumpled way.

"We're pleased you've come to visit," he said from under the hood of a bushy moustache.

And with that greeting, Jack guided us out of the main room and through the arched hallways to a private dining area where lunch was set for us. We settled into the warm stone room, the dark wood and towering bookshelves nearly making me forget the press of my bladder. The deep plush furniture seemed made for men to sit and light their pipes and read to their hearts' content. What did it say of me that I felt more comfortable there than in any ladies' sitting parlor?

Jack turned to greet another man, and I turned to Warnie. "Is there anywhere in this man's enclave that a woman might relieve herself?" I asked, slightly desperate by then.

Thank goodness Jack and his acquaintance didn't hear. As it was, Warnie blushed and averted his eyes. Women must not talk about the bathroom in this country.

He pointed me in the right direction and off I went. My low heels clicked against the cobblestones. Instead of feeling embarrassed, I experienced a flash of envy: I wanted to be a part of a place like this—a tutor, an academic, a writer of great import. I wanted so much. But I'd start with lunch.

In the wavy and dusty mirror over the sink in the lavatory, I stared into my own wide eyes, surrounded by horn-rimmed glasses. What did Jack and Warnie see? I swiped on red lipstick and smoothed my hair. Not bad at all.

I returned to have sherry poured into cut-glass goblets, and I drank mine too quickly, feeling the soft buzz that came with it. Far-off bells rang and then more, echoing upon one another's cymbal-sounding peals.

"It seems that bells never stop ringing around here," I said. "From your high pinnacled towers." I feigned covering my ears.

"Yes, our bells in the various colleges are off a few minutes here and there," Jack said and waved his hand toward the window. "Not as congruent as we'd like."

I allowed my attention to wander as I glanced around, pausing at the words etched on the Magdalen crest. "*Floreat Magdalena*," I murmured. "'Let flourish . . .'"

"You read Latin?" Jack asked me.

"Excuse me?"

He pointed to the crest.

"Oh. Yes. Latin, German, and French. I've taught myself Greek, but I'm a bit rusty. The Latin and Greek tend to flip over into each other sometimes." I paused, embarrassed, afraid that I sounded like a braggart. "My college roommate, Belle, spoke Russian, but I never could quite get the hang of it. But you know more languages than I do, Jack. Latin, Greek, French, and Italian. Probably some others as well."

Warnie's laughter echoed through the room as we sat to eat. "It seems there isn't much our American friend can't do."

"Oh, there's plenty," I said. With that I turned my attention to him. "Tell me, Warnie, what are you working on? What are you writing now?"

"I'm toiling away on a book about Louis XIV, the Sun King. Probably not of much interest to you, but an exceeding obsession to me." He sounded so like Jack that I felt a kinship I was not due.

"Not of interest to me?" I asked. "Well lordy! I'm working on a book about Charles II, and my Lord Orrery, whom I wrote my thesis about for Columbia, sat in the House of Commons at the very same time as your king."

And we were off into the world of history as if Jack weren't there at all. We talked about France and kings and battles. We chatted about research and how difficult it was to write history that had long ago disappeared and left only hints of its life for us to unravel.

Soon Jack joined in our conversation and we returned to the present. I reached to take another bite of my grilled sausages and tomatoes and noticed that Jack had polished off every bite on his plate.

"Am I a slowpoke?" I glanced at Warnie. "I'm sorry. Do you have someplace you need to be? I've been talking too much."

"No!" Jack stated with a loud voice, his hands held in supplication. "It is a problem of mine. I eat too fast. I blame it on Oldie."

"The horrid headmaster at your old boarding school," I said, remembering a story from one of his letters.

"You know?" Warnie asked.

"Not very much, but some." I glanced at Jack. Was I betraying a confidence?

Jack placed his fork over his empty plate, lit a cigarette. "We were in great trouble if we didn't finish our meals on time or finish at all. It led to this terrible habit of gobbling, which I've tried to no avail to break."

"That or he's just itching for his cigarette," Warnie said with a laugh.

"Well, I will savor mine." I took an exaggeratedly slow bite, the tomato juice dripping onto the plate.

They laughed, as I'd hoped. After a few moments passed and I pushed my plate away, Jack asked, "Shall we walk to the deer park perhaps?"

"That sounds smashing," I said with a terrible false English accent.

"Then off we go." The bells of Magdalen rang again, chiming out the hour, the rich ring of sacrament.

Enveloped in the soft buzz of sherry and companionship, Jack, Warnie, and I exited the dining room onto the great lawn. Men ambled past with pipes and cigarettes, books tucked under their arms. Grass leached its green to the coming winter, turning the brunette color of fine hair, and yet the leaves fell, adorning the lawn's nakedness. Students sat in clusters on blankets, books scattered around.

Jack pointed at a long rectangular building ahead of us across the lawn. "That is where my rooms are." He swung his walking stick and headed away from the building and under the iron archway we'd passed through the day before. The three of us sauntered slowly across the small stone bridge, a miniature version of the larger Magdalen Bridge across the street, and onto Addison's Walk and to the deer park.

Warnie walked next to me as a speckled fawn sauntered across the lawn, looking over her shoulder.

"My boys will love this," I whispered before I realized I'd spoken aloud, a prayer or incantation for the future. "Those eyes of the deer," I said. "As if they are looking at just us, so round and brown."

"Like yours," Jack said so matter-of-factly that it took me longer than it should to seize upon his statement.

"Mine?"

He didn't answer, as if he'd already forgotten what he said. He walked ahead of us with his walking stick in sway. Warnie and I caught up to him; I already felt the blisters forming in the shoes I'd worn for beauty, not comfort.

"In the forties," I said, "I spent a few months in Hollywood trying to be a screenwriter. The only screenplay that was nearly filmed was about fawns." I watched the little deer before us as it sprang forward into the underbrush. "I borrowed Kipling's white deer theme."

"How very clever of you," Warnie said. "Why was it never made?"

"Well, we had a director, but deer are mighty hard to find in Hollywood. If I'd known how to import them, I would have. But my powers have their limits."

They both laughed.

"What else did you write out there in California?" Warnie asked. "It seems a land a million miles away."

"You don't want to know. It was a terrible time. Except for the MGM lion—his name was Leo—whom I came to love as greatly as you can love any animal, it was a time I'd rather forget. But I had a dream to cast Tristan and Isolde in a love story at sea. It's one of my beloved myths of all time."

"Irish love," Jack said, "that ends in death."

"But *true* love," I said and paused at the edge of the park, lifting my face to the sky where layered white clouds were spread flat against an unseen barrier. "The kind that makes you notice every small thing in the natural world, bringing you to yourself."

"Oh, you're a romantic," Warnie said and lifted his hands to the sky. "You two will get along properly well."

Jack either didn't hear Warnie or didn't reply, because his next comment ended the afternoon. "Tomorrow we shall walk Shotover Hill."

"That sounds interesting," I replied without asking where Shotover Hill was or why we would walk it.

"Then tomorrow it is." Jack's smile fell over me. Swallows spun above and the song of skylarks filled the air.

With plans to meet in the morning, the brothers departed, one home to the Kilns and the other to tutor a student. It could have been the newness of it all, and how I tasted it as unspoiled as new fruit, but Oxford and the Lewis brothers had cast their spells; I was enchanted.

CHAPTER 13

The world tasted fragrant and new
When we climbed over Shotover Hill

"BALLADE OF BLISTERED FEET," JOY DAVIDMAN

Shotover Hill rose from Oxford like the breast of a woman in recline. Jack, Warnie, and I began our hike in silence, our conversation lulling and beginning again like waves. Through bracken-covered slopes we walked; blackbirds and wrens swept above us. The brothers swung their walking sticks in a step-step-swing-step rhythm, swatting at nettles and pushing rocks or debris from the path for me to pass. We climbed the hill and our breathing synchronized.

With the physical exertion, logical thoughts fell away, unspooling and leaving nothing but sensation and the bliss of nature's quiet. Jack had already told me that it was a mistake to combine talking and walking—the noise obscuring the sounds of nature. So through switchbacks and jagged turns, soft heather swept us forward. When we reached the top, all out of breath, we stood above the patchwork of valleys and rivers, ponds and forest, an area called South Oxfordshire.

"A land fashioned of someone's fairy tale," I murmured, out of breath as we reached the top. The sunlight settled on me with such warmth as I sat on the ground, my knees tented to rest my hands.

"Yes," Warnie said. "It does seem so from here, does it not?" He took in a deep breath and bent over to clasp his knees. "But it's just plain ole Oxford."

"Oh, Warnie!" I said, looking to him, his baggy cuffs puddling at his feet as he leaned on his walking stick. "There is nothing plain about Oxford."

"The eye of the newcomer," he said and straightened. "Let me look again." He squinted against the sun and leaned forward as if on the bow of a ship. "Yes, a fairy-tale land it is. You are very right, Mrs. Gresham."

"This land must be part of you." I inhaled the cleansing aroma of grass and soil, the blue sky above like the bowl of an alpine lake. "I want this landscape to be mine and the landscape to have me."

"Then you shall," Jack said. "I doubt there is much you set out to do that doesn't get done."

The brothers came to sit on either side of me, and we talked: of Warnie's new work, of Jack's students' upcoming Michaelmas semester exams, of the Socratic Club meeting he must attend the next day. We debated Winston Churchill's conservative views and his recent announcement that England had an atomic bomb. Would they test it? Where was it? We talked of how Prince Philip must feel with his wife becoming queen, and of course the tea rationing, which had all of England annoyed. We were three chums who'd been friends all our lives, or so anyone who came upon us would have believed.

"Even the Garden of Eden could not be as beautiful." I poked at Jack. "Although I know you don't believe there is such a thing at all."

Warnie put his fingers to his lips. "Hush, don't tell anyone that the great C. S. Lewis believes that Adam and Eve are a myth."

Jack made a snorting sound and stood to stretch. "I've never claimed to be a theologian." He shook his head. "Now let's walk off this hill to a decent pub. A beer is due us."

As we descended, Warnie piped up. "Where to next for you, Joy?"

"Well, I'm here for another week." I stopped at a switchback to catch my breath and ease the ache in my knees. "Then I'll travel to Worcester, where my king lost his battle at Powick Bridge. Then on to Edinburgh to dig into the library archives."

"Worcester!" Warnie turned to Jack. "Isn't that where the Matley Moores live?"

"It is," Jack said. "I'll tell them you're coming." He turned to me. "Dear old friends of ours who might give you accommodation."

"Oh, that would be simply wonderful," I said. "To save what little money I have."

"Consider it done." Jack nodded, and then we slowly walked down the hill, the sun at our backs warming us. We reached town and collapsed onto the hard benches of a nearby tavern, guzzling our thick brown beer eagerly. Warnie ordered pork pies, and we dived into them with abandon.

"Pubs might be the greatest invention of the English," I said, basking in the warmth and the smell of whiskey and fried food.

"You think so?" Warnie asked. "Not pork pies or the pencil or the electric telegraph?"

I almost sputtered against my glass. "The pencil?"

"Yes." Jack nodded seriously. "In Cumbria in the 1500s, or so Oldie told us."

"Then yes, the pencil is grand, and after that, the stories. What is it," I asked, "that makes British stories so much better? Or am I just being seduced at every angle?"

"You *are* being seduced," Jack said and reached his arms across the back of his chair.

Our glances caught and then slid away. I swore he blushed at his blunder.

"But what do you believe is the difference in the stories?" Warnie asked and motioned to the waitress for another beer.

"Your stories, the English I mean, contain magic. Mysticism. Our American stories are more realistic. You know, Tom Sawyer for us, Mary Poppins for you. That kind of thing. The day-to-day–ness in our American stories weaves a tale but doesn't transport. Nothing pragmatic about your George MacDonald and *The Light Princess*. And that extraordinary *Phantastes*, nothing like it in the world."

"*Phantastes* changed my life," Jack said simply. "I didn't know it at the time, but it did."

We'd written about this, but how much better it was to talk about it. There was no comparison.

"I felt the same." I slugged back another gulp of beer to dull the throbbing of my blistered feet. "Tell me," I said and lifted my drink too eagerly, splashing it onto my face and into my eye, causing both men to laugh.

"Oh, laugh at me, but look at *you*," I said and leaned forward to wipe a fleck of crust from Jack's chin.

Warnie coughed. "That's what happens when old bachelors live together. We don't notice when food has fallen onto our faces."

I nodded. "Well, that's what happens when a woman gets excited. She spills beer in her eye."

Jack smiled, falling back into reverie. "*Phantastes*. I found it in a bookshop at Great Bookham Station on my way back to school one lonely afternoon. One shilling and a penny was what I paid for it. I, who have no head for money, remember exactly what it cost." He wiped at his chin with his napkin, as if to make sure nothing remained.

In a gust of emotion, I wanted to travel with him to that train station. I wanted to be with that lonely boy when he found the book that baptized his imagination.

He smiled at me. "You weren't yet born."

"Not yet," I agreed.

He continued. "Only now do I know to call the experience of reading that book, holy. Books can help make us who we are, can't they?" Jack settled back in his chair. "What a treasure it is to find a friend with the same experience."

"MacDonald sees divinity in everything," I said. "But when I first read it, I would have just said he saw magic. You do the same in your work."

"Not like MacDonald. He was such a corking good writer. He so influenced me that I wrote my first poem in answer."

"*Dymer*," I said. "A poem you wrote at seventeen. It was Chad Walsh who showed it to me, and I loved everything about its allusions to a life of fantasy . . ." I paused and then quoted a line, one that had snagged long ago in the crevices of memory. "'She said, for this land only did men love; The shadow-lands of earth.'" I paused. "And to think you wrote that as an atheist—how beautiful. How profound."

Jack's ruddy face turned ruddier, his smile crooked and his eyes averted. "Thank you, Joy."

"Yes," Warnie said, and we both looked at him as if we'd forgotten he was there at all. We were deep in our cups, but Warnie, I realized, was sloshed. Adorably so, but sozzled.

For an hour, or maybe it was longer, I lost track of time. The three of us talked about our favorite books, what had influenced our childhoods and our minds, and most importantly what had ignited our imaginations. Our voices grew quiet as we drew closer and closer to each other.

When our yawns overcame our words, we rose to leave. Outside, rain thrashed the sidewalks, blurring the sky with a waterfall veil. Gray skies and bent tree limbs, leaves loosening from their final anchor and swaying to the ground, socked us in. Yet there was nothing in that moment that could dampen my soul. Water dripped into my shoes, filling them as if I'd waded into Crum Elbow Creek.

We bade a soggy farewell with promises of tomorrow. I made it to my little room and collapsed wet as a fish, exhausted but satiated. Before I allowed sleep to steal the memories of the day, I took pen to page and started to write "Ballade of Blistered Feet."

But my mind was restless. Away from Jack and Warnie, I was back in the guest room, where a letter from Bill sat on my bedside table. My other life rushed in like a tidal wave.

Bill:

Thanks for the story suggestions. I'm working hard to get something together. The boys are doing well and they have enclosed letters here. Davy now has turtles and Douglas is building a fort down at the creek. Renee is keeping us all together—I don't know what we would do without her. Right now she is mending the boys' clothes.

Joy:

Dear Collection of Poogles,

    I miss you! I wish you could see the complex splendor of this city. I could never, ever grow tired of Oxford and its towering buildings and moss-covered stone. I don't miss London at all but for the chummy friend I've found in Michal Williams. I pray every day for all of you and hope that things are getting better there financially. Bill, once you set your mind to it, I know you'll find the right story. You have always been talented this way.

P.S. Will you please send my thyroid meds, and a copy of "Longest Way Around"?

    As I readied for bed and thought of my sons, I sent a prayer to cover them with love. Oh, how I wanted them to see everything I'd seen that day, let them touch the heather that ran across Shotover Hill, have them feel the rain soft on their faces, raise a kite in the wind at the top of the hill.

    Putting the pen and paper aside, I gave up on the poem that memorialized the day. I drew the pillow close—all that was soft for me to hold.

CHAPTER 14

And yet, not too forlorn a memory:
Oxford, autumn leaves, and you, and me

"Sonnet VI," Joy Davidman

Oxford held ancient secrets, and if I leaned close enough and was quiet, I could hear its whispers, and then maybe even hear my own. In that place I started to feel the contours and edges of my internal landscape, a world that at thirty-seven years old I'd still never quite mapped.

I saw Jack and Warnie every day during that week and a half. When we weren't together I wandered Oxford, where I'd found a corner in Blackwell's Bookshop to read or write until my eyes ached for nature. In my letters to home I attempted to describe the landscape, but found myself giving up and walking outside, leaving the letters unfinished on my bedside table at Victoria's.

In New York I'd spent hours anticipating Jack's letters—the anticipation to see him now was no less than that waiting, just more pleasant, like being hungry but smelling the meal to be served in the very next room.

For days I'd walked the paths from my room in Victoria's house on High Street, a cramped room full of dark English furniture too big for the room, dusty and mildewy, but warm enough with her chatty companionship, to the staid elegance of Eastgate and around the green and flower-speckled perimeter of Headington. I climbed to the top of its hill and spied the hummocks and lakes below. Jack's home—the Kilns—was a three-mile walk along Headington to Kiln's Lane, but I didn't venture there. I hadn't been invited.

On Tuesday afternoon I wandered slowly to meet Jack in his rooms. Students spilled out from the heavy, carved door of Magdalen with books under arms, laughter echoing just as it had in the generations that had come before. Coasting as if I were on a punt in the Cherwell, I passed the deer park and imagined my boys, how they would run through it, battling with imaginary swords, chasing the fallow deer with the huge curved antlers. I closed my eyes and offered a prayer for my sons' safety.

Jack's rooms were on the third floor of the New Building, "new" meaning built in 1733. The building was a beige stone rectangle behind the quad of Magdalen proper. I strode under the arched entryways on the bottom level and then climbed the curved stairwell, worn smooth by shoes and time. I ran my hand along the cool stone wall and then found myself in front of his door—third floor, third door. *Mr. C. S. Lewis* stated the brass nameplate, *Tutor of English Literature.* I knocked timidly, and yet the door sprang open as if he'd been waiting with his hand on the knob.

"Joy!" He stepped aside. "Welcome." He stood there with his arms spread wide, that lighthearted smile on his face, his eyes steady upon mine. He wore a dressing robe, thick gray flannel with a wide collar and striped piping at its edges. It was tied around his waist with a thin rope, and below I could spy his suit and the blue tie loosened against his throat.

He noticed my gaze wander to his dress. "My robe." He patted his chest. "There's only coal for warmth here, and this keeps me warm. Come in. Come in."

I straightened my shoulders and smiled at him. "Seeing all of this is great fun. Thanks for the invitation."

"If only my students felt the same way. You might be the only one who has ever crossed the threshold of this room and offered the word *fun.*"

"I will do my best to be more solemn," I said and formed a serious expression, furrowing my brow.

"Ah, yes. Much more appropriate."

His rooms were a trinity—a cluster of a bedroom (closed door), office, and living area. I followed him into the office, which was covered in cream-painted panels rather than the dark wood I'd imagined. Books seemed to stabilize the room. A grandfather clock ticked nearby, and an earthy-colored oriental rug covered the floor edge to edge. His desk sat in the middle of the room—simple and dark wood, a chair shoved tightly underneath. A plush upholstered chair faced the desk askew, as if glancing sideways at the work in progress.

"Is this where your student sits?" I asked and pointed to the chair.

"It is."

"May I?"

"Please."

I plopped down and exhaled, wiggled off my shoes and stretched my feet. "I believe I have walked all of Oxford and Headington."

"Well then, I'm all the more glad to offer you a rest." Jack sat at his desk chair, bordered by the fireplace behind him. Framed photos of what appeared to be either the Irish or England countryside were lined along the mantle.

Jack tapped out a cigarette from the package on his desk, lit it, and took in a long draw. He rested his right arm around the back of his chair and with his left held the cigarette across his bent knee. "I know," he said, as if I'd rebuked him. "It's a terrible habit, but I started at twelve and there doesn't seem much to be done about it now."

"Twelve?" I laughed. "However did you get away with that?"

"I got away with a lot," he said. "Didn't you?"

"No. Not at all. I stayed out of trouble mainly because my most pleasurable activity was reading, and you can't get in much hot water doing that. And of course I was scared to death of my father—that helps one be good as one can be."

"Ah, fear as motivation."

"You know, right now you look like your photo in *Time* magazine," I joked with him. "Like you're posing all over again."

He adjusted the round spectacles on his nose. "I was much younger and thinner then." He sprang from his chair. "Which reminds me. I have something for you."

He walked to the bookcase, plucked a slim volume from the lineup, and extended it to me. I accepted it into my hands.

Mere Christianity.

My eyes flashed with tears, and I hoped he didn't notice. "This book changed my life," I told him.

"No. God changed your life. My book just jolly well appeared at the right time."

"Yes. At the right time." I opened the cover to the title page: *For my friend, Joy Gresham. C. S. Lewis.* I looked up. "It's a first edition. Signed to me." I gave myself away by brushing at a tear.

"Yes, it is."

I flipped to a random page in the middle of the book and read as if he'd highlighted the words. *When a man makes a moral choice two things are involved: the act and the feelings and impulses inside of him.* The words rang like condemnation, and I closed the book.

"I don't know how to thank you." I wanted to hug him, but instead I sat primly in the chair with the book clutched between my hands. My heart, I felt it bending toward him, our friendship as intimate as any I'd ever had in my life.

"No need for thank-yous," he said. "I'm honored the book has meant so much to you." He stepped closer, looking down at me gently, and if it had been any other man, I would have believed it was not only admiration that emanated from his eyes, but quite possibly more. But it wasn't any other man—it was Jack.

I pointed to his desk, where a thick pile of papers lay scattered among an inkwell, unopened letters, and a cup of half-drunk tea. "What are you working on now?"

"Oh hell," he said with a wash of his hands over his desk. "It's my nickname for the work that might be the very death of me. Sixteenth century—*The Oxford History of English Literature, Volume Three.*

O.H.E.L." He shook his head. "You see why I just give the bloody thing a nickname."

"Indeed." I crossed and uncrossed my legs in some attempt to find a comfortable position.

"Magdalen gave me a sabbatical to finish, but I'm covering over two hundred books—no sabbatical will do the trick." He moved back behind his desk, crushed his cigarette in an ashtray, and immediately, in the same smooth motion, lifted a pipe from his breast pocket and a bag of tobacco from his desk drawer. "I'm also working on a college edition of Spenser and finishing the seventh, and final, Narnian adventure."

"How do you work on so many things at once?" I asked. "My mind runs like a train with whatever project I'm working on, and I can't jump from track to track."

"What *are* you working on?"

"Seeing England," I said with a smile.

"Of course you are. But I know you have something brewing. Your mind and pen won't be stayed. How are those articles coming along?" As he spoke I swore his eyes glittered, the deep brown of them almost changing to dark green, the lushness of Oxford seeping into his spirit.

I glanced away to the window. "Right now I'm polishing the Fourth Commandment."

"The Sabbath," he said without hesitation.

"Yes. I'm calling it 'Day of Rejoicing.'"

"I'd like to read it when you're ready."

"Really?" I held my hand over my heart. "My goodness. I'm happy to have you read it, yet feel tremulous with fear to even think of it," I said in a splurge of honesty.

"Joy." He uttered just my name. And it was so simple that a warm rush of happiness flowed over me. "I've read some of your poetry, and of course your conversion essay. Why would you fear anyone reading your writing?"

"Sometimes I believe I'm a better editor and helper than I am a writer. I have two novels out in the world, and neither seems to have dented many souls." I paused in that truth. "But if you'd like me to read pages of O.H.E.L. or anything else, I'd be honored. When I'm not with you and Warnie, I'm quite bored at night in that little room, and I'll be traveling later this week." I took off my black grosgrain plate hat and set it on the side table, and as I did a pin fell from my hair and a lock fell over my shoulder.

Jack looked away as if my shirt had fallen off and was quiet as I pinned it back in place. When he turned back to me, he smiled. "Well, that is quite the offer, and I'll indulge if you allow me."

The dominating grandfather clock with three pointed bevels above it rang the hour in a sound of clashing gongs. We both startled, and Jack stood. "My, the time has flown from us, has it not?"

I glanced at the clock, a single-eyed monitor of the room, and wanted to tell its black hands to stop moving, to please allow Jack and me to sit longer, extend time.

He spoke as he tapped his pipe against his palm. "That happens between us, doesn't it? Time takes on a different measure when friends gather, I believe."

I donned my hat again, tilted it to the right. "Yes."

"Well, it is a Tuesday, and I must be off to the Inklings." He paused as he removed his robe to hang it on a hook next to the bookcase. "I have hesitated to ask, Joy, but I feel I must. Your eyes give away some sadness. Has your marriage healed at all? Are things at home improving?"

It was a subject that had to be addressed. I had written to him about the awful mess, and we couldn't sidetrack it anymore.

"My eyes?" I asked, blinking with a meager attempt at humor.

He didn't smile but kept his own sight steady on mine. He would not allow me to wiggle free of his question.

"No, Jack. It is not any better. I'm praying for healing and peace on this journey. What is it that King David asks?"

"'Create in me a new heart.'" Jack stated the prayer with reverence. He took another step closer to me. "What do you say to your husband during these troubled times? When he comes home from another woman or erupts?"

"He can't hear me, Jack. When I get upset, he asks if I'm on my period or if my shoes hurt. And then he launches into his ten million excuses."

"Joy, I'm sorry for your troubles."

"There's this gap, Jack. This opening between the story it is and the story I had wanted it to be—that's where the pain is, and that's where God came in and where I now hope transformation can happen."

"For too long we avoided that gap, didn't we?"

"Yes. I turned away from it with every preoccupation known to man. But no more." My heart opened. When had there ever been anyone I could talk to like this?

Jack donned his tattered gray fisherman's hat, retrieved his coat from the rack by the door, and placed his hand on the doorknob. "Whenever you'd like to talk about it, you know our friendship is big enough for even the sorrow." He opened his office door to the stone hallway.

"Thank you." I stepped into the hall. "Please give Warnie my regards."

I walked away, and as with each time I departed, I felt I left a piece of my heart in his hands.

Back at Victoria's, I tweaked the poem "Ballade of Blistered Feet" (merely a way to relive that glorious day on Shotover), organized a folder of King Charles research, wrote another letter to Bill, wondering why he hadn't written back in so long, and drank a long hot cup of tea. My mind circled back again and again to Jack's rooms, to his bright eyes and easy manner, to his laugh and his wit, to each subtle compliment or connection. I lifted the book he'd given me and ran my finger over the inscription of my name in his handwriting.

Eventually I lifted my own pen. Some had journals; I had sonnets.

I'd been writing them for years—it wasn't a new way to release my pent-up emotions. Through those many years the faces of "love" had changed—the sonnets weren't meant for one man, but for the amorphous feeling of being loved and loving in return, for that moment of connection and intimacy. And yet, that night in Victoria's guest room, the sonnets began to pulse their sentiments, like a heartbeat that had quickened, toward Jack.

Even as I wrote about the commandments, *the beast in the heart is always the self* and how God was a *being who demanded your whole heart,* I knew to protect my heart. The monster that seduced me to break the very commandments I wrote about lived and seethed inside of me. And there was no Wormwood to cast my blame upon.

"No," I said out loud to the empty room. I would not descend into that impossible fantasy of being with Jack.

Yet reason and emotion never wedded well in me. As Blaise Pascal stated, "The heart has reasons that reason knows nothing of."

CHAPTER 15

Or fill your eyes and ears with any loud
Mere thanks—until I am no longer proud!
"BREAD-AND-BUTTER SESTINA," JOY DAVIDMAN

The sights and sounds of Oxford during those ten days soaked into my skin and settled into my bones. I walked for miles, ignoring the dull ache in my hips. I crafted sonnets about longing, but for what? I wasn't sure, but understood it had something to do with Oxford and how I felt a kind of freedom I'd never felt before.

I wrote letters to Bill and Renee and the littlest poogles while ignoring the nagging sensation that something was amiss at home. It was probably irritation that I was still gone, too many kids underfoot with too little money in hand. I would make up for it when I returned home.

That last afternoon I sat in Jack's rooms after he'd given me some pages of O.H.E.L. to read on my journey to Worcester. I'd handed him the rough draft of the "Day of Rejoicing," and there we sat, each other's work in hand. I eased slowly to stand and walked to the window, looked west to the deer park where elm trees shed the very last of their gold. The croquet lawn was empty of players that day, but I could imagine how it looked when the weather warmed and it was full. "Let's walk along the river?" I asked.

"Yes." He stood quickly and his pipe fell to the ground, ash scattering across the carpet. He brushed his trousers but didn't even register the mess on the floor, which only made me smile.

I tucked the pages he'd given me into my bag while he plucked his hat from a hook on the wall and settled it on his head. It landed crooked, and all the more charming. With a swoop of his hand he retrieved the smooth walking stick that had been leaning against the wall and then locked his office door behind us. "Shall we?"

We wound our way along the pathways of Addison's Walk to the river's edge as the sun burst through a cloud. My breath caught in my throat. "This," I said. "This is the place you wrote to me about—where you walked all night with Tolkien and Dyson. This is the place you came to believe."

"Yes." He tipped his hat in response.

"It's like walking into one of your stories, to see a place once only imagined. To see where you were convinced of the one true myth."

"That God is the storyteller and Providence is his own storyline." He stopped and exhaled.

"I wish I'd been here for that discussion, to have someone like you to talk to, or have just listened in."

"Ah." Jack laughed and leaned on his walking stick with that twinkle in his eye. "You think you could have just listened?"

I smiled and shook my head. "I'd like to think so . . ."

"It would have been a better conversation were you included."

"It's odd, isn't it? One minute we don't believe at all. In fact, we are a bit snobbish about those who do believe. And then we know it's true. We just *know*."

He stared at me so intently I almost looked away. "It seemed sudden, didn't it? But we know it's not. It had been creeping up on both of us all of our lives."

"Yes," I said, and a tremor rumbled under my chest—to be seen like this by a man, to know he felt and sensed all that I did.

He began walking again. "Yet even as I believed in God, I wasn't sure if I believed in Christ."

"When did that happen? Here also?" I imagined the air remembering, the trees and the flowers and all the company of heaven remembering the conversation Jack Lewis had on this very walkway, the one that changed his life.

"No." He laughed. "I was in the side car of Warnie's motorcycle on the way to the zoo. Somewhere between the Kilns and the zoo, I believed in Christ. I don't know where it happened on that ride, but it did."

"In a side car on the way to the zoo. God does have a sense of humor." I fell silent a moment, watching the flow of the river. "I can see why God would reveal himself here. It's achingly beautiful. I would come here every day if I could."

"I do."

With each dropperful of our lives that we dripped into our conversation, the closer we became. It was a quick flutter inside my belly that told me to *be careful*. I'd ruined more than one friendship with the wrong kind of love. This was a friendship I would never sacrifice.

"Tell me about your average day, Jack," I said brightly.

He swung his walking stick in a circle and then popped it onto the ground. "It's not so thrilling. Maybe you'd rather imagine."

"No." I shook my head and my hat fell over my eyes; I pushed it back with a laugh. "Bore me."

"On the nights I stay here in my rooms, I'm awakened at seven fifteen by my page bringing me tea. Then I walk down here." He tapped his walking stick on the green earth and looked directly at me. "To Addison's Walk. I linger for as long as I can. I pray and allow nature to bring me to silence."

"The beauty that brings us to peace and whispers that there's something more."

"And every square inch claimed by God." He gave me that look I'd come to know—that we agreed and there was nothing more to say. It was just enough.

"Then at eight o'clock we have Dean's Prayers in the chapel." He pointed toward the quadrangle. "Then to breakfast in the Common Room, and by nine in the morning I'm in my rooms, reading correspondence and answering as bloody much as I can. My students then arrive until about one in the afternoon."

"Since I've been here I've barely been up before nine," I said. "And there you are with half your day done. And structured. I believe I need more of your order."

"I'm quite sure your life has more excitement," he said. "And variety."

"Well, go on," I urged, hungry for more of his everyday-ness.

"Some afternoons I give lectures on High Street. But usually after my students leave, I walk or catch a bus back to the Kilns, three miles from here. Once home, I sneak my way into the fourth dimension." He leaned forward conspiratorially. "My nap. Then I'm back here by five for more tutoring. It's the evenings I enjoy most—full of readings and guests and conversation in the Common Room at Magdalen."

"It sounds wonderful. A life full and stimulating."

He drew a pipe from his breast pocket and filled it with dark leaves of tobacco from a small pouch, lighting it with a match that took four efforts to strike. He did this all in such a slow ritual that I wondered if he'd forgotten I stood next to him. Then he looked at me and puffed, his cheeks like small bellows, until the pipe lit and smoke plumed upward.

"Since I've handed over the pages of O.H.E.L. to you, I feel concerned about how you see the work."

"Concerned?"

"To be found the fool." He set a hand on the back of an iron bench and leaned forward, his pipe dangling from the corner of his mouth. The wind rustled his hair and the yellow tie that hung from his neck. "Yet all seems right from this angle, doesn't it? One of those moments when bother fades away."

"Yes." We were standing so close that our shoulders almost brushed. "Being here right now, I feel that nothing in the world could be wrong."

He turned to me then. "But it is, isn't it." His cheeks rose with his sly smile, patient and waiting for my honest answer.

"Yes." I pulled my coat closer, buttoned the top button to stave off the chill I felt coming. "The letters from home feel off. Bill is being hedgy at best."

"Hedgy? There's something he's not telling you?"

"Yes. I think so."

"I've never been married, Joy. How can I give you advice? But I can say that letters don't always give the full rounded truth of how someone might or might not feel."

"Not between you and me," I said. "I understood you."

"Yes." He nodded and tapped his pipe on the edge of the bench. "Not between us."

I stood in the comfortable moment, its ease, and wondered if I could take it with me wherever I went. "I'm not asking you to say anything, Jack. Or give advice. But suffice it to say that it's been a terrible few years and I've lost my steady sense of self in it all."

"Why do you stay, Joy?"

"God's will, I hope, but maybe safety. Not wanting to give up on my family. I want to do the right thing." I wrapped my arms around myself, rubbed my arms to get warm as the wind above rustled the nearly naked trees.

"Sometimes it feels as if God's demands are impossible, does it not?"

"Impossible." I nodded. "Love. It's a complicated endeavor, Jack."

"I've attempted to write about it—over and over—drafts of a book about the subject, you know. We are the only ones who have but one word for it. In Greek we have *storge* for affection, *philia* for friendship, *agape* is God, and of course *eros*. But even words, Greek or otherwise, can't hold the truth of what it is or isn't."

Jack's smile was then replaced by a look of such caring warmth that I wanted to throw my arms around him.

"Your first love?" I asked, tentative and with a smile.

"Poetry." He paused. "Or Little Lea, my childhood home."

"You know that's not what I meant." I jostled him slightly.

"I worked on the poetry for years until I realized that I would never be good enough."

"Good enough?" I laughed so loudly that he startled. "I've read your poems. They are more than good enough." I shook my head. "I left poetry for publication and money. And you left it because you believed you weren't meant for it. Either way, we both left our first loves."

"But it led us to the prose and to the now," he said.

I folded my hands behind my back, stared off. "You know what I believe?" I asked, but didn't wait for his answer. "It is poetry that is rooted in the sacred. The prose is good and well, but the poetry is something else."

"Yes."

"Sometimes I believe it is only the paper and the words that understand me. I wonder what I haven't tried—from screenwriting to essays to book and movie reviews."

He was quiet, as if we had all the time in the world to watch the sunlit water move in waves, yellow and russet leaves riding the current. "A sestina," he finally said. "Have you written one of those?"

"Oh, maybe not since school, if then."

"Try it." He stepped away from the edge of the bench.

"Before I leave for Edinburgh," I said, "I will write us a sestina about these days."

"Now *there* is something I'd want to read."

A voice behind us called out Jack's name, and a man in long black robes approached through the film of autumn sun. I wanted to shoo this man away.

"Good afternoon, Lowdie." Jack greeted him with gusto.

He introduced me to his colleague, and I felt the shiver of knowing that I often ignored—it was time to take my leave. I departed with promises to meet Jack and Warnie for bangers and mash at the Eagle and Child that evening. I was anxious to enter its doors, settle into its corners, and be another part of Jack's life, the very place where the Inklings—his group of fellows and writers who met to indulge in a pint or two while quipping about philosophy and writing—met on Tuesdays. No women allowed, of course.

As I wandered off I wondered what might have happened if right there on the banks of the river, as we talked of poetry, I'd told him of all the other poems I'd been writing—love sonnets naked with yearning, so quivering with need that he might jump into the river in fear of me. If they weren't about him directly, they were most definitely about the feelings he disturbed inside me.

No, I would never show them to him.

Never.

CHAPTER 16

What I am saying is that I have nothing
To give you that you possibly could want

"Sonnet XII," Joy Davidman

It was my last night in Oxford, and eventide fell across the city's architecture as I left Victoria's house to walk the lamppost-lined sidewalks. Men rode by on bikes, their coats streaming behind them. Women strolled, pushing children in prams. In England I felt a sense of fragile joy, as if everyone was stepping into the sunlight yet still waiting for the sirens and overhead whir of aircraft, hesitant after the horror of the bombs and gunfire of World War II to believe in peace.

In my little clutch I had tucked the sestina Jack suggested I write. Forever I would be able to read it and summon our time as clearly as if it played on a screen. I planned to give him the carbon copy that night.

We'd had such grand times, and I knew he admired me as I kept up with him, whether it was speaking in Latin or quoting Shakespeare or poetry. But did he more than admire? If so, he kept it hidden well beneath his banter. He'd not so much as touched my sleeve; his comment about my eyes was the only physical attribute he'd ever mentioned. Yet he praised me for my writing or my wit or my intellect. He made plans for us to see each other every day.

I'd never been around a man who looked at me the way Jack did, and talked to me as he did, and yet never once made a pass. I expected a touch in the natural pauses between man and woman, but he kept an armor about him invisible as air but impenetrable as iron.

He was fifty-four years old, and he'd never married. Was it past the time to think of women as anything more than friendly companions? As many times as these thoughts prodded, I shoved them away. The theological quandary I found myself in was nearly laughable. I was a married woman trying quite desperately not to fall for a man whom I'd made an idol as I wrote about the commandments of God.

Instead of changing my emotions, I needed to surrender them. Maybe I could find a way *not* to indulge them, but the company and the walks and the intimate talks didn't lessen the longing that flourished deeply in the places of me that had been lonely for a long while. After I left, would the emptiness inside be deeper? I was willing to pay that price.

My bags were packed—the next day I would head off to research King Charles II and try to forget *my* life by delving deep into another man's. It would be a long journey to Edinburgh by train, through Worcester. Jack had, as he'd promised, arranged for me to stay in a cottage with some old friends of his, the Matley Moores, and I wondered at the fact that we'd become such grand friends he'd make arrangements for me with others he cared for.

I walked two more blocks toward the pub to meet him, my musings keeping me company. The woman I'd become in exploring England, and in spending time with Jack and Warnie, felt like who I *really* was. The real self, Jack would say, in God. I'd been covered so long in the coal soot of my home, buried in the laundry, silenced by the screaming of my children and the berating of first my parents and then my husband—it wasn't until England I saw who I could be: a brilliant light, cherished for who I was.

I stopped at the corner of St. Giles and Wellington and allowed a red double-decker bus to pass. Across the street was the Eagle and Child. It was a whitewashed three-story building on St. Giles Street, its paired windows set beneath gables with a matching pair below. The sign that hung above the dark wooden door showed an eagle in full flight against a sea of blue, carrying a baby in his wings. That explained the loving nickname: the Bird and Baby.

Crossing the street, I opened the door and stood, letting my eyes adjust to the dim. The pub was divided into smaller rooms, the ceiling hovering close. I entered the "Rabbit Room," with its arched opening like a church window. Jack stood before the fire there, poking it back to life. There was a scarred wooden table set with worn stools. But it was the corner banquette, clothed in burgundy, where the Inklings usually sat.

If that august group had been there, I wouldn't have entered the room, no matter how brave I was feeling. But it was a Friday night, not a Tuesday, and I'd been invited. Just two men sat in the corner, one being Warnie.

The bar glittered in the lamplight and the space was warm. I shed my coat and flopped it over my bent arm, then smoothed the front of my best dress—the one I'd worn the day I met Jack.

He didn't see me at first, his attention intent on the fire, but Warnie called out my name. The other man looked up; his white hair sprouted in many directions, and a pipe dangled from the edge of his mouth. There was no mistaking him: J. R. R. Tolkien.

I wasn't ready.

I wanted more time with Jack before someone he dearly valued arrived to judge me. A near panic fluttered under my chest. I walked toward them, hoping that the soft glow of the room might make me look pleasing to Tolkien.

"Good evening, Joy, there you are!" Jack hung the fire poker on a hook and hurried toward me, gesturing to Tolkien. "I'd like you to finally meet Tollers."

Tolkien stood, but when I held out my hand to shake his, he merely nodded. "Good evening, Mrs. Gresham." He lifted his hat an inch as bushy eyebrows towered to meet a deep line between his eyes. Freckles scattered and blended across his face, and there were deep furrows on either side of his mouth, rendering a look of disapproval or judgment.

"It's a pleasure to meet you. I've heard so much about you." Nerves flared under my ribs; I felt young and unsure. I grasped for surety and flashed a smile. "You've had a profound effect on my friend here."

I sat and Jack joined me. This was the bench where the Inklings sat on Tuesday nights. I didn't believe their genius could rub off on a slab of wood, but I nestled in farther just in case.

"As he does me," Tolkien replied and sat with his attention firmly set on Jack, as if I were a specter.

"Is your wife here?" I asked, wanting a woman's companionship, another buffer. "I should like to meet her."

"My wife is home with the children. She does not frequent pubs."

Suddenly I was ten and Father was telling me my grades were disastrous. I was twelve and my mother was telling me Renee was more beautiful. I was thirty and Bill was telling me I was a horrible wife and he needed to recharge his batteries with another woman.

It was Warnie who spoke up. "Mrs. Gresham here has two sons and a husband in America. She's a writer doing research on our King Charles II, and she's also toiling away on a book about the Ten Commandments. A crocking good writer indeed, and an even better poet."

Jack nodded in agreement. "Her writing is flaming."

Tolkien nodded at me as if acknowledging the Lewis men's assessment. "Why are you here in Oxford?" he asked.

"Don't worry, Mr. Tolkien." I stiffened. "I'm not here to collapse the walls of your men's world or beg of you to let me become an Inkling. I'm only here for the fun of it all, and for Jack and Warnie's friendship." I paused. "Now where is a whiskey when you need it?"

"On its way," Warnie said. "Along with a good heaping of pork pie. Sadly, it's your last night."

"You're leaving England then?" Tolkien asked with an air of satisfaction, leaning in with a long puff of his pipe, short bursts of potent tobacco wafting toward me.

It reminded me of when I'd first met Bill. I'd thought him debonair with his pipe and his drawl, his guitar flung across his lap. Look how that had turned out.

"I'm not leaving England, not yet," I said. "But I'll be off to Edinburgh and other sites tomorrow. Then back to London. Of course

I'd love to return to Oxford before America, but we shall see how the days unfold."

"Of course you must return here before you leave," Jack said. "There is no question about that."

"Yes," Warnie agreed.

The relief they offered was like a warm bath after the chill of a rainy walk.

"Mr. Tolkien," I said, "both of my sons have read *The Hobbit* and were enchanted. I want to hear more about your work. Jack tells me it is brilliant."

"I never said such a thing." Jack laughed into these words and banged his hand upon the table. "Don't let him think I said such daft nonsense."

"No, then," I said, "*I* say your work is brilliant. When Jack tells me of your conversations, I'm envious. There was a time when I believed that religion was not something nice people talked about in public. What a relief to be able to discuss and debate and it not be an argument. Do you believe that I used to think that people who believed in God were mundane and ignorant? And now I can't get my fill of the bottomless discussions. Isn't that a thing?" I was talking too fast; I could feel the words bubbling up in nervousness.

"What do you find the most fascinating about what I believe, Mrs. Gresham?" Tolkien asked, his hands wrapped around his nearly empty mug of beer.

"Your views about fairy stories," I said.

"And how do you know my views on fairy stories?"

"I was fortunate to befriend Michal Williams in London. She's been a bright light in that city that seemed enchanting until I found Oxford, which is a million times more so. But anyway, she loaned me the volume of essays that should have been presented to her husband. It was a lecture you gave—"

"I know what it was," Tolkien said.

"How you began your essay 'On Fairy-Stories,'" I said, "about the perilous land and stars uncounted and how a fairy cannot be caught in a net of words."

"Well, well," he said. "You must have the most photographic memory."

"I confess I do," I said. "It's helped me through the worst of school-days. But with your essay, I didn't just memorize. I digested it. And it seems your views have rubbed off on Jack here." My hand lifted without thought, and I touched Jack's shirt sleeve in what must have seemed a gesture of ownership. I withdrew my hand quickly.

Tolkien sipped the last of his beer and pushed back on his chair. I could see he was ready to leave, and the fear that I'd sent him away made me try one more time.

"What is it about fairy tales that we all love so much?" I asked.

"You've said you read my opinion."

"It is the consolation we want," I said. "When you wrote of the sudden joyous turn of events, the grace, the happy ending. I think we love our fairies and their stories and their lands because through all the hardship, there is the consolation of a happy ending."

Tolkien slipped his coat on and settled his tweed hat onto his head before looking at me. "There you have it." He nodded at Jack and at Warnie. "I'm late for supper at home. See you chaps tomorrow."

The pork pie, usually comforting, tasted like cardboard in my mouth. Had I offended Jack's best friend? Warnie excused himself to greet a friend across the room and left Jack and me alone with the fire burning bright behind us.

Jack watched Tollers until the pub door closed and he was gone. Then he leaned back to light a cigarette and smile at me. "He can be a bit gruff, I fear."

I nodded, but directed my attention to Warnie, who stumbled and grasped on to the back of a chair, laughed it off, and strolled to the bar. "Is he all right?"

"I think so, yes. But if he's not, this won't be the first time I've had to pour him into a taxi. I'm sorry you must witness it."

I held up my hand to stay his words. "Jack, I've lived through this. Not with someone nearly as wonderful as your brother, but still the same. If you should ever want to talk more about it, I hope you know that you can."

Jack nodded, and a sadness he usually kept cloaked beneath his smile overshadowed his face for a moment. Then, just as quickly, he turned his attention back to me. "Did you enjoy Tollers?"

"I can't yet tell," I said. "I do want your friends to like me."

"Ah, but Mrs. Williams likes you bloody well—blinding, I think she said."

"We've gotten on quite well and laughed so much, which is important, don't you think?"

"To get on well or to laugh?" That twinkle in his eye, and it was a twinkle.

"Isn't it the same?" I asked.

"Yes, it is." He leaned forward. "What draws people together is when they see the same truth. As we do."

"But your Tollers does not approve of me. He set his eye on me as if I were here to steal you into the night and never let you return. He bristled."

Jack laughed with that merry bellow. "I don't think Tollers is quite worried about me running off. But he *is* married with children and maybe doesn't understand the friendship that can grow between a man and a woman." He stared off for a moment. "Tollers separates family life, academic life, and pub life each into its own sequestered box. And what matters of it anyway? I don't bristle."

"If you did, I'm sure I wouldn't know," I said. "We all have two faces. I wrote about it—"

He interrupted me. "In 'The Longest Way Around.'"

I smiled. Toller's apparent rejection was losing its energy. "Yes. My false face. It can get in the way. I don't see God as magic; you know that. I wanted my conversion to escort some change into my life, but sadly I think I'm essentially the same. Only with God. My masks remain.

Anger still bursts out before I can stop it. I built my masks readily and with such skill that I believe they lock into place when I'm unaware and nervous. It can be blisteringly difficult to show one's real face."

"Perhaps it's a lifetime's work." He covered his face with both hands and then peeked around them to make me laugh.

"What do you see?" I braved the question.

"A brilliant mind," he said with force and slapped his hand on the table. "Take a gander around, Joy. There's none like yours. Maybe some men can't admire you for your manly virtues the way I can. Your intelligence and forthrightness."

His words were concrete on my chest. "My manly virtues?" Tears sprang to my eyes, and there wasn't anything I could do to stop them. "Jack, how would you like me to extol you for your womanly virtues?"

His face fell, his jowls seeming to settle farther over his tight collar. He removed his spectacles and rubbed his forehead. "It's not exactly what I meant. I can be a bumbling fool."

"You can't see me as a woman, can you?"

"It's not so easy as that, or as simple, Joy. The book I'm working on . . ." His voice trailed off.

"It's always the work with us." I took a deep breath and softened it. "Don't talk about your work. Tell me how you *feel*. Even in *Screwtape Letters* you didn't include emotions—just will, intellect, and fantasy. What are your feelings?"

He bent his head, considering. "Like you, I find my way through such things on paper. But how I feel is that there are four kinds of love. And you and I are the luckiest kind."

"Yes," I said. "Philia."

"From storge to philia—we are indeed blessed." Then with a great laugh he leaned forward conspiratorially, as if we were in on the same joke. "And no matter my feelings, Joy, you are married." He paused before adding with a smile. "And I prefer blondes anyway."

It was a joke meant to soften the blow, but it did not. "I don't believe you always know your effect on others." I settled back in my chair. "Or maybe you don't want others to affect you as you keep up that armor of words and wit."

"I don't know what you mean."

"Did you know that *Vogue* magazine called you the most powerful force in Oxford? They wrote of your huge following and your large crowds. And you sit here and act as if your words have no impact."

"I don't read *Vogue*." He tried to smile. "And I don't intend to be callous, Joy. I was aiming for levity and missed by a few miles."

I was saved from further humiliation as Warnie returned to our table. I attempted to be light and playful. Finally the night grew darker, and I said, "I have an early train. Here we must say bye for now."

The three of us stood, and Warnie made me promise to return. Jack strolled outside with me. Facing each other in the darkened night, he slid his hand into his coat and withdrew a book.

"I have something for your boys." He held out to me a first edition of *The Lion, the Witch and the Wardrobe*. "I signed it to Davy and Douglas."

I eased the book from his hand and clasped it against my chest as if it were a warm ember. "Jack, this is such a generous gift. They will adore it. I've read it to them more times than can be counted, and I know that Douglas especially wanders into the woods and hopes to find Narnia."

"Then maybe he will find it," Jack said.

A light rain began; the mist glazed my cheeks with a chill that would settle into my bones until I crawled into bed with the hot water bottle. "When I think of Oxford, I shall remember so much, Jack. But the rain will always be a part of it." I stuffed the book into my bag, protecting it.

"Remember Oxford? As if you won't return?"

I wiped the wetness from my face and manufactured a smile, hiding the sadness of leaving.

"You must come back," he said. "Warnie and I insist. We'd like you to join us for the Christmas holidays, if you don't mind staying in a bachelor's home with rattling pipes and inadequate heating. But we do have a roaring fire and books to your heart's content, and Oxford at Christmas is quite charming." Jack opened a black umbrella and held it over me as the rain quickened. "Or will you have sailed back across the pond by then?"

"I'm waiting on a late royalty check from Macmillan, and then I'll book my ticket. Soon, I think." I hoped the word *royalty* disguised the embarrassment in my voice, but I didn't think I could ever fool this man. I never wanted pity from anyone, and definitely not from him. I would sleep on Phyl's kitchen floor before I allowed pity to come between us.

"Then Christmas it is," he said. "Now get on out of this dodgy rain or you'll catch your death before your journey to Edinburgh. We'll make arrangements as the time draws closer."

"Wonderful," I said. "Let's send our critiques and pages back and forth. Between now and then we shall get as much work done as we can so we may enjoy the holidays." I held my arms around myself in the same way I'd have held him if I could.

"Yes, we will. We have much to look forward to, and I do have a lecture in London in November. So I shall see you soon. London is not far away, you know. Give us a bell when you return." He handed me the umbrella and tipped his hat. "Cheerio and take this with you."

I started to step away, shifting the umbrella to protect my face from the rain. "Oh, Jack. Wait."

He'd already placed his hand on the brass door handle of the pub.

"I almost forgot." I reached into my bag and plucked out the folded paper. "The sestina I promised you."

He took the paper from me and raised his eyes to mine. "Wonderful."

And with that, he was gone.

CHAPTER 17

I just wanted to see what would happen if . . .
"Apologetic Ballade by a White Witch," Joy Davidman

The train to Worcester pitched forward and my suitcase flew from my hands, sliding down the aisle. I didn't want to leave Oxford, and yet the train was moving me away. In other heartrending times in my life, I'd used writing as an escape, and I was hoping to do the same again. I was restless and it felt an awful lot like panic. But what was I afraid of? I had no idea.

Or perhaps I did know my fear: that I'd never know *real* love.

Must I settle for the trouble that was mine? A life of disappointment and anger, alcohol and despair with Bill.

After stashing my valise under a seat, I walked to the dining car and ordered a gin. A tall woman came and sat next to me, and she was elegant in the way I would never be, like Renee.

"Hello," she said and settled into her seat, crossed her legs daintily. "Are you headed to Edinburgh also?" She swung her fashionable bob of shiny hair.

"Worcester and then Edinburgh," I said. "I've never been to either."

"Oh, you'll be charmed, unless you stay too long," she said with a laugh. "You know, like a man you think you love until you have to live with him."

I joined her laughter and then added, "Love. It's never what we believe, is it?" I sounded like a bitter old woman at the end of her affairs.

"Never," she said. "But isn't it great fun—the falling into it?"

And it all spilled out. "I feel as if I'm falling in love. And I mustn't."

I felt the weariness bearing down on me, the way it arrived, bone deep. I pushed my drink away and thought I might sleep for the entire train ride and forget everything.

"Oh, I'm *always* in love," she said with a gay sound as tinkling as ice falling from the trees. "Well, where are you from? It sounds like maybe New York."

"Yes." I was conscious again of my difference. I would never be like these cultured women with their painted nails and English accents and tiny waists.

A gray-haired man in a suit who smelled of too much cologne sidled to the bar and greeted her. She smiled at him in that secret way women know, and he ordered her a drink. I rose from the barstool, feeling quite awkward, and returned to my seat to collapse. I had just told a stranger that I was falling in love, as if I'd *had* to say it out loud to know it. I closed my eyes, but sleep was as elusive as Jack himself.

Sunlight poured through the square window as the train skated along the tracks, the scenery a blur of every green. I took out a pad of paper. Who else could I possibly confide in?

The page. It was always the page.

If I looked backward at my loves, perhaps I could rearrange the *now*, summon the ghosts to this train compartment and reconcile them so they could no longer influence my future. I didn't want to ruin this friendship with Jack. I needed to go back, start at the beginning of my ash pile of love affairs.

As far as other men, they had paid me no mind until college—my sicknesses, awkwardness, and absences in high school hadn't led to a social life of any kind. And whom did I choose to first seduce? I was young, only sixteen, and it was my married English professor in college. Dark curly hair, a deep voice that resonated in my chest as we talked about books and history. His eyes so piercing blue they seemed painted on. I'd thought in those days that sex would be enough—that conquering him would satisfy me. But it was never enough. The quick ducking into small rooms, the furtive glances and our bodies coming together in frantic need—remembering it now was shameful. His body had seemed the answer to all my questions and needs. How could I hold Bill's indiscretions in high-horse judgment when I had done no differently? There had been a wife at home. I'd known that and yet I'd grasped at him all the same, my desire fierce, disguised as love.

For it wasn't love; it was obsession. The compulsion to own him along with a clawing need to prove I was worthy of such notice. I'd wanted him to sacrifice his life, his wife, to be with me—proof that he loved me. I was as much acting against my father as I was *for* myself.

Then the next love—a writer at MacDowell Colony. Four summers I'd spent there, the balm of my early writing years. I'd found another writer; he too was older. And I had pursued him as if he were a savior of my own making, proving a fool of myself as I banged on his door in the starry night or waited outside his cottage to see if he'd emerge, seeking me. Was that love? Or avoidance of my own work with obsession? I'd tangled him together with MacDowell, confused the feelings for the place with my feelings for him.

I'd sought lovers to still the spinning sadness inside. I'd sought lovers to quell my pain. I'd sought lovers to fix what could not be fixed. Even when I found solace in another body, even when I'd conquered, still my soul cried out in loneliness. It was never enough to fill me. And still I'd pursued men with embarrassing voracity.

Then there was the movie star—the worst of all embarrassments. Oh, it had been anything but love during those lonely, miserable months in California, trying to be someone I could never be. How I'd pursued him, even as he ran. When he was cast in a show and moved to New York, I stalked him, once even boarding the train he took home to his family merely to catch a glimpse of him.

Obsession and possession again confused with love.

Then, of course, there was my husband. How desperately I'd been trying to verify my worthiness to him, and how long he'd been telling me I wasn't worthy. I never would be. And still I tried, over and over, expectantly, as if I were bringing Father my report card.

All of my loves had been lost causes, and yet some wrecked part of me kept reaching for more.

My pattern of pining came into view as if I'd stared at the stars until the astrological signs were clear as drawings. My design needed men who could not and would not have me, especially older men.

Who was this needy false self who believed that a man could fix the gaping wound inside my soul? What terrible dance was this? This fox-trot of straining with the inevitable result of failing? Was Jack just another man who couldn't love me no matter how charming, smart, or witty I was?

I had to stop caring or I had to stop trying. I could never stay Bill's drinking or his rages or his affairs. I could be near perfect and still it wouldn't stop. But could I love him as he was? Just exactly as he was? Was acceptance the answer?

This I knew—I could not take this decayed form of loving to Jack. I would indulge in our philia without the push for more.

God was now meant to be my primary relationship. On my knees that night in my children's nursery, I'd promised him so. But there I was, repeating a prototype that had begun the day I wanted my father's love and didn't attain it.

Perform, Joy. Do better. Be smarter.

As the years passed, those commands had changed. Now it was *Seduce.*

Anything for love.

With Britain's countryside flashing by the windows, my mislaid lovers hovered like a banshee warning of death. How could I ache for something I knew nothing of but only read about in stories?

What a fool I was.

Throughout these doomed affairs, I'd poured my brokenness into poetry—from passionate to melancholy to possessive; it had become the vessel holding all need and unmet desire.

I felt empty as any woman who takes stock and sees the futility of chasing love she can never catch.

CHAPTER 18

Instead you put my hunger on a ration
Of charitable words, and bade me live

"Sonnet XXVII," Joy Davidman

Cold bit to the core of me, soaking through my coat and boots. Northern England was a land of moors and limestone, stone abodes and quaint churches, a place where kings rose and fell. I wanted to engross myself in 1651, in the catastrophes of King Charles II instead of my own, so there I stood on Powick Bridge overlooking the muddy and sluggish water of the River Teme. This was the location where my king had wanted to avenge his father's execution, and at first he'd watched the battle from the safety of Worcester tower before running into battle with his men. His Royalists lost this last battle in the English Civil War, and Charles eluded capture to escape and hide in Normandy. I stood on the bridge of his failure, with the imagined smell of musket smoke, the thud of running feet, and the stomping of horses' hooves.

Yet it was present time, and the triple-arched bridge over the Teme felt more like a place for Jack's creatures than for a battle. Ivy clung along the edges in a thick mat that rustled in the wind like rain. The banks of the river were brown with winter and didn't offer even a hint of the white flowers that would burst open in spring. Far off the Worcester Cathedral was almost a mirror of Magdalen College tower, its spires reaching to the sky. I took some notes in a damp notebook, wanting to remember the particulars of the land. Crossing the bridge, I walked into the thicker forest to the very place Charles had fought, and the thud of sadness came clear: I wanted Jack with me. I wanted to talk to him and show him all of this.

No.

I was there to heal, and to take home that healed woman to her family.

Joy:

Dear Bill and Renee,

Forgive the sloppy handwriting; I have no typewriter on this trip. I'm staying in the moors with Jack's friends the Matley Moores. They spoil me rotten and I've eaten enough of their rich food to burst at the seams. He is a fellow of the Royal Society of Archaeologists, and he's given me invaluable research books as well as taken me to Powick Bridge! Please tell me how everything is at home.

No response.

Joy:

I am about out of money, Bill. I should have a royalty check from Macmillan in November, you can send that. And why haven't you written to me? I can't book my ticket home without a bit more cash. Ulp.

And Unconquerabill, I believe I am beginning to understand our life together, but it is not a cheery understanding.

After a few warm, convivial days and grateful cheerios to the Moores, I boarded the smoking train to Edinburgh, where I rested my forehead on the window as the train staggered through the backcountry around Lancashire and Birmingham. Through pastures and bracken fields, I watched it all go by: the heather and broom bending to the wind of the passing train; far off in the distance, the rolling hills. Sheep with mud-stained bellies grazed on the rich and undulating fields of green.

Shaggy moorland ponies looked up with lazy stares, bored with the passing of yet another train.

We passed Cumberland, where lakes dotted the landscape like fallen pieces of the blue sky. And ever present was the stone—always gray: the cottages and dikes and churches. Falling always was the glorious golden light I'd come to revere. We moved from Carlisle across Cumfries and Fenmark, bunnies and grouse rushing off in flashes into the moors, until I finally disembarked in Edinburgh.

It was Bill I thought of as I trudged across the platform to hail a taxi. The few letters he'd sent overflowed with depressing news of all the problems at home, but what niggled at me more was the insight I was beginning to have about our life.

I didn't see a cure for us. God help me; I didn't see a cure.

In Edinburgh, I found a room in a nice enough hotel and warmed myself with thick blankets and whiskey. After some sleep, a cuppa, and hot soup, I entered the wide-street city. I fell under the spell of Edinburgh, and my panic eased. It felt airy after London, the houses ordered and the yawning store doors welcoming.

Have you ever had this in your mind's eye when you told your stories? I wrote to Jack. *A fortress city made of stone and lichen, bowing down in reverential worship to Castle Rock above.*

The towers of Edinburgh thrust toward the sky, with the churches and buildings stepping-stones that climbed ever farther up and up into the hills. The great clock watched over the city, a timekeeper. The fountains gurgled over sculptures so finely wrought, I felt the mythical creatures in them would surely come alive.

I didn't feel a stranger, and I never once became lost. Hope arrived—this King Charles II book could become something I could write with passion. It would keep my mind from the uncoiling of my life as well as offer some financial freedom for all of us.

Libraries are sanctuaries, and the one in Edinburgh was a sacred space, with its soaring ceilings and hovering lights dropping circles of gold onto tables and floors. The open center, an aisle of desks and chairs, winged to reveal the second floor, which soared above me with an iron railing like black lace. I stood in the middle, my neck hinged back to stare up. The Corinthian pillars and dark, scarred wooden desks beckoned me to my work. I settled in with books and pad and pen and began to write. I exhaled with relief: now this was a place I could work, not like Staatsburg at all.

I was only half a day into my notes when again the dark fatigue settled around me, and I realized I hadn't felt this tired and worn since my last bout with a kidney infection. I craved nothing but sleep.

The fever came on slowly, and it was with sorrow I realized I was sick with something awfully near the flu. Shortening my trip, I hurried to pack and return to London.

Joy:

Dear Unconquerabill,

I am terribly sorry for all the grief at home. I have been derailed with the most awful flu I've ever had—I thought I might die. But it led, as pain often does, to a great spiritual awakening. And I know I must get my emotions in order.

Bill:

I'm sorry for your illness. Here we are well. Renee has become dear to all of us, and especially to me. Maybe it really is over between us—you and me, other than our abiding friendship and being parents to these spectacular children.

Joy:

I must be happy for you that things are well there; that Renee is as dear to all of you as she has always been to me. The bad time is over on this end, and I can now tell you the truth: October was a Dante's inferno of a month in low-middle-class London, where I've moved in with a woman named Claire I met at my Tuesday night sci-fi boys meeting. No man—no matter how wonderful, as you are—is worth dying for with lovelorn languishing. I'm better now and today I'm going to watch the queen's procession to open Parliament. We will save all discussions of our future for when I return home.

Love to all,
Joy

CHAPTER 19

Oxford is cold (and I'm not warm!)
The blizzards drive upon sea and shore

"Apologetic Ballade by a White Witch," Joy Davidman

November 1952

"Joy!" Michal's bright voice rang out across the foyer of the Mitre Hotel in London. Near Hyde Park, the bar was warm and rich feeling, with damask wallpaper and leather furniture. In an hour Jack and Warnie would join us, but for now it was just us ladies. Michal waited for me at a corner table, and I hurried to her.

"I've missed you," she said. "This flu has kept you away from me for far too long." She gave me a warm hug. Her heart-shaped face, long bourbon-colored hair, wide red-lipstick smile, and jaunty accent comforted me.

"Oh, Michal! It's so good to see you. I feel on the mend now, and I'd like to forget that October even happened. Can one do that?"

We sat together, and her laugh fell across the table like nourishment.

"Yes, like editing a book? Charles used to say that to me when he was editing. 'Ah, if we could only do this to life.'"

"Yes." I banged my hand on the table. "I would delete the pages of this month. Put them in the rubbish and then light them on fire."

"But you can't get here without being there." Michal slid off her stylish red coat and set it on a hook behind the chair. "Would you like me to take your coat?"

"I think I'll keep it on for a bit. I just haven't been able to get warm for so long now."

"Oh, poor Joy. You are so brave and yet so hurt by life." Michal made a motion for our drinks, and when they arrived we lifted them to each other before taking our first sip.

"Yes, my friend. I believe I may be both, but let's not talk about me. Tell me what's happening with Charles's manuscripts." I eagerly placed my hands around the glass and inhaled the deep scent of the sherry.

I had broached the most sensitive subject—her husband, who'd passed away unexpectedly just six years before, and still his estate was in chaos. I knew the pain lingered.

I continued. "The last I heard from you, his executor hadn't given them over."

"He doesn't seem to care that they were left to me." She glanced around the room as if someone might hear her. "Joy, Charles's manuscripts are everywhere. He gave them to other women also."

I reached my hand across the table. "Oh, Michal."

I didn't have to ask, because I saw the pain in her eyes. I'd felt the same betrayal—the knowledge that your man had been with and given something of value to other women. It was a knowing that wounded the soul.

"And the entire Oxford set has snubbed me since his death. All except Lewis. So I can't reach out to them for help. And what would it matter if I did? Maybe I don't want to know what those women have or know. Perhaps it's best if I just let it go."

"Just let the sleeping women lie," I said. "Let them keep their papers and their souvenirs."

She leaned closer. "I think you're right, Joy. I don't know what letters are out there either."

"It's horrid. Men can be absolute animals," I said. "Others see them as heroes, while we're the ones who live at home with them and are expected to tolerate their infidelities and peccadillos."

"Yes." Her head bobbed in agreement.

"Not Jack." I glanced toward the door as if my voice might hurry him to us.

"You think he's different? That once you lived with him he wouldn't have the same proclivities?"

"I *do* think he's different."

"Oh, Joy. You might be right. But how could we ever know? How could any woman but Mrs. Moore—God bless her soul—know? She's the only one that ever lived with him, or probably ever will."

"You might be right." I took a long sip and felt the warmth of the sherry fill the cold crevices inside. I wanted to ask more about Mrs. Moore, things I wouldn't ask Jack, but I stilled those inquiries and smiled at Michal.

"Joy." Her voice was soft. "Tell me what's troubling you. I want to help if I can."

"Am I that transparent?" I lifted my glass in salute.

"To me, yes, you are."

"It's hard to pin down, but it's Bill. Something seems really off. He's not answering me, and he's not sending money. I'm busted. I know I could ask Jack for money, as he's offered, but I'd rather cut off my ear." I pulled my coat tighter around me. "I've asked Bill for my thyroid meds and some food and a few books, and yet he's sent nothing."

"I'm sorry. What can I do?"

"You don't need to do anything. Just being here, being my friend is enough. I've given Bill so many ideas of what to work on—we have half-finished projects that he could delve into." I rubbed my fingers against my thumb. "Right now I don't even have the money to buy a ticket home."

Her eyes glazed with tears—for me! The empathy felt as comforting as the blazing fire at the far end of the bar.

"I sound like I'm complaining," I said. "I know that. But I'm going to write like crazy. I'm going to finish this project and then I'll make everything right at home."

"Where are you with your Ten Commandments?"

"I'm almost done—only five more articles to go, and I have them outlined. And I've found a title for the book: *Smoke on the Mountain*."

"So your work is chugging along, but you don't seem yourself, Joy," Michal said, catching me staring off to the front door.

"I believe I might be a bit homesick," I said. "I don't much want to talk about it. What else has gone on in London while I've languished?"

"You've heard about Charlie Chaplin, right? He sailed here for his *Limelight* premiere and he's decided to stay."

I laughed and felt warm enough to shed my coat, setting it across the back of my chair. "Good for him. If all Americans came here, I believe they'd stay. And I don't think you want that."

Michal waved her hand. "Well. Do you know what beats all? The tea rationing ended yesterday."

"It ended? Well, thanks be to God." I pretended to cross myself, and she clasped her own hands in false prayer.

"Oh, the sacrilege," she said. "We might be struck any moment."

Our conversation flowed easily. We caught up on what we'd been reading, and she told me that her son Michael had found a job. I told her that I'd been working on O.H.E.L.—and Jack had sent me edited pages of the Ten Commandments manuscript.

"Well, you and I will have some grand times with the days you have left, Joy. You must come over for dinner, and we'll go to a vaudeville show, and of course we'll enjoy our White Horse boys."

I took her hand and held it in mine. "I'm thrilled you've come into my life," I said just as Jack and Warnie entered the lounge. Jack saw us waving at him, and together they joined us, shedding their coats and hats.

With greetings all around, Jack turned to me first. "How pleased I am to see you. We must hear everything about your travels. We have missed you."

"Yes, we have." Warnie beamed at us all, tipping his hat.

Jack sat next to me, and I caught the warm aroma of him—tobacco, wet flannel, and rain.

"I've written about everything to you," I said. "And poor Michal here has had to listen to me for an hour now."

Jack slapped his hand lightly on the table. "Then I shall start with this—I want to proclaim here in front of our dearest friends that you have written a divine sestina."

"I'm glad you think so." My smile broke through the words. He loved my sestina. And if he didn't love it, he certainly liked it.

"What have you ladies been talking about and drinking?" Jack pointed to our half-empty glasses.

"You know how it is with Joy," Michal said. "We've been talking about everything."

Life flowed back into me. I smiled at Michal in true gratitude. "It is Michal who brings the interest. She's like water in the desert."

We were interrupted as the server, a young girl in an apron and a long braid down her back, brought two beers for the brothers. They took their long sips; Jack patted his coat pocket for his pipe, a habit now familiar.

"We miss your husband," he said to Michal. "You know it was at the Mitre in Oxford where we celebrated after his first lecture there."

"Ah yes." Michal nodded. "And wasn't that the same place you met T. S. Eliot? The good ole days."

"Yes, indeed. When Eliot told me I looked older than my pictures."

I blurted out, "What? You do no such thing. He was trying to get under your skin, because in real life you are younger, more vibrant than any photograph." The blush began below my collarbone, and the heat of it rushed to my face. Why didn't I think before I spoke?

Jack smiled, his eyes wrinkling. "Well thank you, Joy. I dismissed his insult, and together we worked on a revision of the *Book of Common Prayer*." Then his attention turned to Michal. "Charles's absence in my life and among the Inklings is profound. We miss him every day."

"Thank you, Jack."

"I wish you could have met him," Jack said as his attention again turned to me. "Charles was what I called 'my friend of friends.'"

"Even though I never met him, there is an odd tie between us," I said. "My husband wrote the preface for Charles's book *The Greater Trumps*."

"He did?" Jack paused midway through the sip of his beer. "I didn't know that."

"See?" I lifted my glass. "We're connected everywhere. Even before we met, we were all of us tied together with these funny little threads. I love those small hints that God brings people together and says, 'Here you go. This one's for you.'" I smiled at Jack. "Each chapter in Bill's novel *Nightmare Alley* opened with a tarot card. So the publisher must have thought that he knew enough about it to introduce Charles's work."

"Fascinating," Jack said. He leaned back in his chair, folded his arms across his chest, and drew out his pipe.

Warnie chimed in and stared off into space where he might see the long-gone Charles. "His work lives on."

"That's what we hope for, right?" I lifted my sherry in a toast. "That our work will live on."

"Indeed," Warnie said.

"Indeed," Jack echoed, and we all lifted our glasses to Charles Williams.

The afternoon was spent with warm food and even warmer conversation. I was so content to again be near Jack's friendship that I felt no need to be anywhere else. I had missed him and denied even to myself that very feeling, as if by pretending one doesn't feel an emotion, it will dissipate.

Eventually and too quickly for my taste, Jack and Warnie bid us cheerio, as Jack had a lecture with Dorothy Sayers that afternoon. Before he departed, he leaned across the table. "Joy, next week I'll be speaking to the children at the London library. Children make me nervous. Please be my guest? It would be smashing if you would go with me."

I promised to meet him there. I would have promised to meet him anywhere.

Bill:

Dear Joy,

I have reread *Weeping Bay* and it is very good but depressing. Where you went wrong is in the tone-scale strategy. If tragedy is to be popular at all, it must have that Gotterdammerung quality, which you don't have. I think when you read through it again, you'll see I'm right. Meanwhile, I've been working on a few carnival pieces and with Renee's help I haven't felt this energized and full of creativity in years.

P.S. I am very impressed with the sestina you sent me!

CHAPTER 20

Your pity and your charity; indeed
If I had courage, I might ask your love
"WHINE FROM A BEGGAR," JOY DAVIDMAN

The London public library loomed over the landscape like a castle, as if London understood better than Americans the regality of story. With its arched windows and gables, its stone façade and rich wood inside, it was a haven. That afternoon the reading room overflowed with young children sitting cross-legged on a thick brown carpet, jittery and bored while their teachers told them to hush and be still.

In the back conference room, amid books piled for reshelving and chairs stacked against a wall, Jack and I waited together for it to be time for his speech. I wore my new wool-lined boots and a beige tweed dress (with a scalloped collar) cinched at the waist, feeling as lovely as I had in some time. I'd started knitting again, and I wore a scarf I'd made from a fine blue sheep's wool.

"Joy, must I face the firing squad out there?" he asked as he paced the room.

"You write for them," I said with a smile. He paused in front of me, and I reached out to straighten his tie, pat it to his chest in a familiar movement that seemed to surprise us both.

He clasped his hands behind his back. "Ah, but that is not the same as speaking to them."

"They will love you. They will be gobsmacked." I teased him with a wink.

Jack shook his head, his jowls caught in the tight constriction of his pressed white shirt and knotted tie. "I don't care if they love me, as long as they don't rebel and mock." He smiled, though: all that Irish charisma even among nerves.

"Today is Douglas's tenth birthday. How I wish he were here with us to hear you, to be with me."

Jack drew closer to me and took my hand. "I shall pretend he's in the audience."

I nodded just as the librarian organizing the event, Edith was her name, came to my side with hushed voice. "Do you have children here?"

This was her insufficient attempt to figure out who exactly I was in relation to C. S. Lewis.

"No, my children are in America," I said. And then wished I hadn't. A flow of excuses burst forth from me. "I'm writing with and helping Mr. Lewis. I'm researching—"

Jack came a step closer and addressed Edith. "Mrs. Gresham here is a renowned American author and she's here for research. Now, are we ready to talk to the children?"

"Ready." She tottered off in her pencil skirt and high-heeled shoes, tight-waisted jacket, and hair stiff with spray that smelled like wet paint.

Jack and I walked into the main room, and I eased into a chair at the side of the lectern as he approached it. The room quieted. Many of the children held copies of *The Lion, the Witch and the Wardrobe* in their lap, opening and shutting the pages as if Aslan might leap out and join us.

The boys wore caps and little suits, their jackets buttoned and their pants pressed. The little girls wore dresses and polished Mary Janes with little white socks tight about their ankles, their hair in pigtails and ribbons. They all appeared to me as mini-adults, ready for tutoring.

"Good afternoon," Jack said with a great bellowing voice, the one that made him the most popular lecturer at Oxford.

A few children startled, but most just stared at him in awe. He glanced at me and I smiled, waved my hand at him to go on.

"I'm here today to talk about stories, and most particularly the one most of you seem to hold in your laps, the one full of talking animals and imaginative children and a great Lion."

The children were frozen like statues at the White Witch's castle, and Jack showed not one sign of being nervous save the clasp of his hands behind his back, his thumbs worrying back and forth against each other—a "tell" no one else would know.

"I had the idea for Narnia long before I wrote the first book," he continued. "From the time I was a very young boy, I imagined a faun walking through a snowy wood with an umbrella. I kept that picture in my mind, not knowing what to do with it. Then during the horrible bombings of World War II, three children came to stay with me in the countryside of Oxford where I live. They were escaping London, this very place you live now, which was once very dangerous. I don't have children of my own, so I did the only thing I knew how to do to keep them occupied—I told them stories."

He paused, and not one child made a peep; he cleared his throat and continued. "One of those stories was about children who were sent to live with a professor in an old musty home in the country. I wanted to make them into kings and queens, far different from the frightened children they were. And *that* is how Narnia began. But"—he let out a long sigh, as if remembering the wasted time—"it wasn't until years later that I sat down to write it."

He stared at the silent, wide-eyed children and kept on talking, enthralling them with stories. Eventually he reached the subject most of them had been waiting for.

"Aslan," he told them, "just bounded onto the page. I hadn't planned on him at all. But for many nights I dreamt of lions, and then I knew I had to put him in the story."

A young girl let out a mewling sound and blurted out, "Not planned on Aslan?" Her sweet English accent made Aslan's name a symphony of sound.

Jack laughed with such joy that the children joined in. He then chattered on about Edmund and Lucy, about Mr. Beaver and all the rest of his Narnian books, which were set to be published year after year. "I'm just finishing the last one now."

A small boy in a tweed cap raised his hand.

"Yes, son?" Jack asked.

"How do you make a book? I want to make a book."

"First I try to write the very books that I want to read. I see my books in pictures. I watch them unfold, and then I write about it. I tell what I see, and then I fill in the gaps."

"Who shows it to you? Who shows you the pictures?" the boy asked quietly. "I want to know him."

Jack leaned forward on the lectern, that twinkle in his eye. "The Great Storyteller, I believe."

The boy stared at Jack for some time and then seemed to dismiss him as a silly old balding man.

Jack continued. "When I was just your age I started making stories with my brother, Warren. We imagined a small country full of walking, talking animals. We called the place Boxen. Many of those creatures, the very ones I imagined when I was just the age of all of you, found their way into Narnia. There is no limit or age for making stories. Begin whenever you want, and stop whenever you please." Jack's charm—an indescribable quality that emanated from him like light—brought the children under his spell. It was the cadence of his voice, the manner in which he leaned forward as if he were telling them a secret, the twinkle of his eyes, and the hint that he might just burst into laughter at any moment.

When it was all over and we'd left the library, Jack and I met Warnie, who'd been lingering in an old pub, hunkered in a corner booth. Jack let out a long whistle.

"Well, that was a blooming disaster. I should best stick to writing for the little ones and not speaking to them."

I watched Jack with wonder. How could this man, the most revered, have such little personal pride?

"Jack, you held those children completely in your thrall. They sat motionless, mouths open, eyes unblinking. When children are bored, they fidget and move about like little worms in a bucket. You captured them in your net of stories."

"You believe so?" he asked.

"I know," I said. "You are *very* good with children. You enchanted them."

"I actually feel rather shy around children." Jack squinted at me in the low light. "I do believe I forgot to tell you—I wrote back to Davy. He sent me the most accomplished letter. He told me all about his new snake."

"What?"

"You didn't know about the snake? Have I gotten him into trouble?"

I laughed and rested my hand on his sleeve. "I know about Mr. Nichols. I meant I didn't know that Davy wrote to you. Bill told me that he wanted to, but . . . What did you write in return?"

"I told him that I was working on the last Narnian adventure and I hoped he'd love it just as well."

Jack wrote to my son.

A peculiar warm happiness fell over me as if I'd awoken to discover it was spring and my garden, which I'd planted in the desolate winter, was in bloom.

Warnie broke into the conversation. "How are those science fiction boys doing? Do you still go to Fleet Street?"

"It's my only real social hour, at least until I see you two or meet Michal for a show. But even with the writers, it seems I can't escape you Lewis brothers. They are quite enthralled with *Perelandra*. And they can't believe I'm friends with the two of you."

Jack lit a cigarette and paused before his next inhale. "Oh, I know there are those in that crowd who don't like my stories. I've received their letters. I believe there are probably some there who would like your husband's stories more."

"I met a woman the other night who nearly fainted when she

discovered I was married to the man who wrote *Nightmare Alley*." I stared off for a minute. "It's odd. For all the pain, when I think of the man who wrote that book, I'm quite fond of him."

"But he's not the same man now?" Warnie asked.

"No, he's not." I shook my head and changed the subject.

Eventually, as with every gathering, we said our farewells. I wandered away from them as they hailed a cab to the train station. In a cocoon of contentment I spent that late afternoon on Regent Street, where I bought a cheap wool jersey for a mere five guineas that fit me for the weight I'd lost during the flu. In a great fit of missing my littlest poogles, I also wandered the aisles of the huge two-story toy store and with the last of my shillings bought Douglas a globe and Davy a long plastic snake that slithered when shaken.

The afternoon dwindled to evening, and by the time Jack and Warnie would have been at the Kilns, I'd wandered back to the bus station to ride to Claire's cold house and boiled parsnips.

The dismal month behind me faded away, for there were more days to come with Michal, with London, with my White Horse boys, and with Jack and Warnie. Those times seemed to hold secret and as yet hidden rewards, waiting patiently for me to arrive.

Happiness was the greatest gift of expectancy.

CHAPTER 21

Here I am, and what have I deserved?
Here I hunger, waiting; I am cold

"SONNET V," JOY DAVIDMAN

I awoke slowly one morning, my bones creaking with the cold but my heart eager with the realization that I was headed to Oxford again. That day I would travel by train to hear Jack lecture on Richard Hooker. This was his first of the semester and would be my only chance to see him properly in his element.

I'd moved away from Claire and her vegetarian diet and cold house. My new room in the Nottingham Hotel was a dingy fourth-floor walk-up, but I'd spruced it up to keep my spirits from flagging—red and gold flowers from the market, a cheap India-print bedspread, a glazed and chipped pot, and a floral tablecloth with a small stain on the lower corner. I hung the three little pictures I'd bought that first month in Hampstead Heath when I'd thought the money and the good cheer would last. As shabby as the room was, at least the location was good—in the middle of the West End with lovely shops and easy walking.

Meanwhile, I worked diligently on anything that could make us some more money—I finished *Smoke on the Mountain* and continued to outline my novel. In the lulls, I read and edited the work Jack gave to me. Bill sent a few dollars now and again, and I scrimped the best I could.

Socially, I was making the most of things. Just a few days before,

I'd had lunch with Dorothy Heyward, who was staying at the most decadently gorgeous hotel—the Cavendish. She was a dear friend from MacDowell, fragile and in a steel brace from a car wreck, but still thrilled with how the opera *Porgy and Bess* (based on her husband's novel and produced by the Gershwins) had done in its London premiere.

She leaned forward with that shake of her curls and said, "No one wants to tell you how it was my idea, how I helped DuBose adapt the book to theater."

Of course I was able to sympathize. "Why is it we are often left at the wayside of their creative lives?"

Together we lifted a glass to our own imaginations and creations.

If the old anxieties laid claim to my heart, which sometimes they did, I walked through London to absorb the medicine of the roses and chrysanthemums, the iris in full bloom, the winter jasmine vines with their yellow flowers hanging from wrought iron flower boxes along the sidewalks.

It was time to set out for Oxford. I poured water into the flower-pots and made my bed. I straightened the small piles of work next to the typewriter on the kitchen table and then locked the door behind me.

With my purse clutched to my chest, I waited at the Victoria Coach Station on Buckingham Palace Road, a name that sounded so regal for a place that was just another station, dirty and thick with smoke.

Yet for the gladness of it all, still my belly churned with disturbance. Bill's letters still weren't arriving as they once had, and even when they did, he never addressed anything I'd written to him or answered my questions. Had he received the boys' Narnian book? Could he send some copies of *Weeping Bay*? His cool tone startled me, and yet what more could I expect? There I was in England, and there he was with four children and Renee, both doing the very best they could.

But soon I'd go home—I'd finally scraped together enough money between a few dollars that Bill had finally sent and a small royalty check to make a stop at the travel agency and book my journey home on the RMS *Franconia*—a six-day journey departing on January 3. The ship wouldn't be as lovely, fast, or as well appointed as the SS *United States*, but she would take me back to America.

Even with the expectation of hearing Jack's lecture, I couldn't shake the deep dread of Bill's lack of communication and cold tone. The bus was delayed, and I found an iron bench where I sat and dug into my bag for stationery. I began, with a surge of pent-up emotion, to write in a furious scribble.

Joy:

Dearest Poogabill,

You have always known how to hurt me by omission, by leaving off what matters so that I must guess at your feelings. Maybe I have done the opposite, been too forthright with my opinions.

In loopy and desperate handwriting I filled six pages. I found myself needing to connect with him, with my family, and to do this I felt I must repent of my own sins and not focus on his. I admitted that I'd wounded his ego by leaving, and that I understood it must be difficult to forgive me. It wasn't his fault that I had tried to be Superwoman and had failed miserably, and then blamed him. And I missed my sons as if part of my body had been amputated. The healthier I had become, the more I missed them.

Joy:

I will never be without my boys again. That much I know. No power from heaven or earth will keep me from them.

Just as the red double-decker coach pulled to the curb, its somnolent smoke trailing behind, I shoved the letter into an envelope and placed a stamp on it. I needed these sentiments to fly across the ocean to my family.

As if the words had emptied me of energy, I slept on the bus ride and only awoke as it rattled to a stop. Bleary-eyed, I glanced out the window at Oxford with its now familiar scenery: bikers, the lampposts and brick streets, the limestone buildings and bustling walkers. I spied Victoria waiting on a bench, bundled in her coat and scarf, her long brown hair hidden inside a blue wool cap. I knocked on the window but she didn't look.

I blew out the door of the bus, and she jumped from the bench and hugged me.

"You're back!"

"Are you not tired of me yet?" I asked.

"Not yet." She smiled coyly. "You are, after all, taking me to hear the great C. S. Lewis."

I looped my arm through hers. "Onward," I said.

The few minutes' stroll down High Street was familiar enough to make me feel as if I almost belonged.

"Does Mr. Lewis know you're coming?"

"I told him." I squeezed her arm tighter. "We'll see. He might be too busy to even notice us."

"How many people could possibly come to hear a lecture on Hooker?"

"With Jack as the speaker, I suspect many."

We strolled down the leaf-strewn pathways to one of the other colleges in Oxford—Christ Church, fondly called "The House." We only had to ask two students where the Senior Common Room was before we found it—a cozy, dark room where the dons went to smoke. By the time we arrived we realized we wouldn't be able to see Jack. There wasn't enough space even to enter. Disappointment swamped me.

Victoria stood on her tiptoes to peek and then nudged at all five feet two of me, who couldn't see over anything or anyone. "Guess I was wrong about how many people want to hear this," she said.

It was then that the crowd, like a wave, began to move toward us. "Excuse me," a short bald man in a black robe said. "We're moving to the lecture hall."

Buoyed then, Victoria and I trailed behind the crowd into a larger room with a pulpit at the very front. I felt like a student, and rather liked it. We found seats in the back row and settled in next to each other. Murmurs filled the room, conversation rising and falling until Jack appeared.

It was difficult to see him beyond the group of large, bearded men in front of us, but Jack's image was with me, everything from his smile to the glimmer in his eyes to the tap-tap-swing of his walking stick to the jacket with the worn elbow patches.

Another man in a robe (they were all beginning to look alike) stepped to the lectern to introduce C. S. Lewis and his subject: Hooker, the great Anglican theologian of the 1500s who had broken away from the theology of predestination.

Jack stood, as I'd now seen him do a few times, with his hands behind his back, where I was certain he would be worrying his thumbs back and forth. His bright eyes behind his rimless spectacles moved across the room as if taking it all in, one face at a time. I watched with fondness, marveling at his warm familiarity, at the sheer wonder of how we'd become friends. Who was he looking for? Then, with a great surge of delight, I knew for whom he searched—because when his sight rested on me, his smile burst into such a sunbeam that I felt its warmth. I gave him a little wave, and he nodded.

In that moment, all sense of rejection crumbled like ancient armor. Certain emotions can be hidden, but a smile like that can't disguise a heart—he was as connected to me as I was to him—friendship of the highest order.

Victoria leaned over to me and whispered, "He was looking for you, wasn't he?"

"Yes, I believe he was."

She made a soft noise that sounded like a hum and squeezed my hand.

Jack stepped to the podium and cleared his throat. The lecture was informative and witty, and I hadn't expected anything less. When

Jack used his Oxford lecturing voice, I could almost forget he was a Belfast man. But then he turned on that charm, and the Irish in him was unmistakable as he captured the room.

When it was over, Victoria and I sat still, allowing the people to move past us. As the crowd thinned, Jack slowly wound his way to the back of the room to greet us. Our talk was pleasant, quick and interrupted by men who needed his attention. But it didn't matter what he said; it was his smile I'd carry with me through the rest of the day.

Once back in the hazy, cold air of Oxford's November, Victoria and I walked to town. It was always in the smallest moments that I understood larger truths, if I paid attention. And as we walked in rhythm side by side, the sunlight falling thin and straight through the naked branches, I burrowed into this happy feeling, asking myself what it really was about.

Acceptance.

The word winged its way toward me. And I realized that I could live a better life without the ill-rooted feelings of dismissal that slithered within me, without the curdled knowledge that I wasn't or couldn't ever be enough. Those were lies I believed. It was Jack's smile that broke me free, if only for that moment, and I would carry the remembrance of it always. I would tack that brightness to my heart as a placard.

"You're in an awfully good mood," Victoria said as we ambled the sidewalks of High Street.

"I am." I laughed as I pulled her into the Bird and Baby, where we drank whiskey, talked, and laughed until I needed to catch the bus back to London.

All would be well, I believed. As Jack's favorite mystic Julian of Norwich told us: All will be well. All manner of things shall be well.

CHAPTER 22

I made my words the servants of my lust.
Now let me watch unwinking, as I must

December 1952

A rustle outside my Nottingham hotel room stirred me, and I rose from the kitchen table where I'd been working on edits in O.H.E.L. to see that a white envelope had been slipped under the doorway. I wrapped my robe tighter and shivered. The frigid air that felt as if it went bone deep was the only thing that caused me to shudder at England. I bent down to retrieve the paper: *finally,* a new letter from Bill. I smiled at the expectancy of a witty correspondence with news from home and maybe a little money to eat more than boiled potatoes and canned soup.

I put the kettle on, tipped a tea ball into the china cup, and opened the envelope. I glanced at the pile of other letters I'd received since arriving in England. Chad Walsh. Marian MacDowell. Belle Kauffman. My publisher, Macmillan, and my agency, Brandt and Brandt. My Davy and my Douglas. A life in letters, a stack of them wrapped with twine. Of course there was only one letter from Mother. I had expected nothing more, but hope dies hard. Alongside the letters sat the mound of my work—both my own writing and Jack's—as if all my life were made of words typed on a page.

I sat to read.

Bill:

Dear Joy,

I admit to my cool tone.

Ah, I wasn't crazy.

Then he wrote of money troubles, but how much he'd been working through it with Renee's help in the house. The kids, they missed me but were doing well—neighborhood parties and outdoor activities.

Then the proclamations were set down, one after the other in quick and unrelenting succession.

I must tell you the truth of our lives here also—Renee and I are in earthshaking love. We are blissfully happy and feel that we are more married than in our marriages. I know this must come as a hurt and a shock, but you and I both know that willpower cannot make you love me or me love you. Being writing partners and having a companionable friendship does not make a marriage work.

And to state the obvious, Poogle, you don't much want to be a wife. You will never be anything but a writer. Renee cares about the things I do—making a home, taking care of all the children and her man. You could promise to try harder or attempt to be more like Renee, but we both know you would go insane.

Bill was both blunt and articulate, as if writing an appendix for his novel. His words were like a great bludgeoning hammer.

He suggested that I find someone to fall in love with in Staatsburg, and then we could live near each other and raise the kids together. Oh, he was even so kind as to suggest that he could wait to marry Renee until I too fell in love, of course with someone convenient and near.

And, could I believe, he didn't see anything sinful in "attaining the maximum love with Renee"?

Nausea boiled. The cold felt colder, the bare floor rougher. How had I held this understanding at bay? Maybe I hadn't. Maybe the past weeks of anxiety had been nothing more than this knowing breeding inside.

He ended by telling me not to feel "forsaken and unloved, Poogle." But what the blazing else was I supposed to feel? I was a teenager and overweight, and my mom forbade me to wear the dress that made me look fat. I was in love with my professor, and he slept with me and went home to his wife. I was standing outside the circle of beautiful girls in college who knew how to giggle and flirt. I was reading a horrific review of my novel. Jack told me of my manly attributes and joked of his love for blondes. I relived all these moments in one fell swoop of the grand forsakenness Bill told me not to feel, each memory rising to join anger and rejection. My cousin? My beautiful cousin and best friend?

I slammed my hand on the table, typewritten pages of O.H.E.L. falling to the floor.

Bill ended the letter with the announcement that he wouldn't carry my sons to the docks to pick me up in a few weeks, but they were excited I was returning home. The end of the letter was filled with chatter as casual as if he'd told me he loved a new car or book, not my cousin.

I sank to the kitchen chair and wondered what the annoying high-pitched scream above me could be when I realized it was the kettle. I rose in a daze and mindlessly poured the boiling water over the tea ball, bounced it up and down, dropped in two cubes of sugar, and took a sip. I cradled the cup and drank, tears as hot as tea rolling down into the corners of my mouth before I knew I was weeping.

If I went back to bed, I wouldn't get up. I had to keep moving. Maybe I should have never left to pursue anything other than what I'd been given at home. Was I being punished? Did I even believe that God punished?

I glanced at the pages scattered across the tiny kitchen table: my notes, work, and research. It all seemed futile. I tried and I worked and I tried and I wrote and I did what I thought was best—and now my cousin was sleeping with my husband? She wanted to claim my family as hers?

My emotions spun out of control—I blamed myself, blamed Bill, blamed Renee, and then of course blamed God himself. Bill was despicable. He wandered through life fulfilling his needs and then settled on my cousin? Rage coursed through my body like fire.

I finally dressed and with haste pulled my hair up, wrapped myself tight in a coat, and burst outside to find my breath.

I walked the streets like the dove from Noah's ark in search of mooring but finding only water, endless miles of ocean and nowhere safe to land. It was of course all my doing, the ruin in which I found myself. What did I think would happen if I left Bill with the perfect Renee? What did I think would happen if I chased peace and health across an ocean?

I had destroyed my own ark.

For hours I wandered through London—the first city I'd ever really loved—twisting through alleyways I'd never seen, around squares that ended where I started, in parks of deep green. It was late afternoon by the time I paused on Westminster Bridge over the River Thames. The sunlight both rosy and golden, the bloated and magnificent moon hanging in the sky behind me while the false moon of Big Ben loomed before me. When darkness began to filter through, evening leaking into the edges of the river, I walked with determination to the Abbey. The arched windows of the sand-castle cathedral glittered in the twilight, their stained glass beckoning me to view their glory inside. It would close tomorrow to prepare for the June coronation, and I needed to find refuge before the doors shut me out.

I slipped in. A service had just begun. The sanctuary surrounded me like a Gothic forest, the buttresses winging down over the crowd of over five hundred people. I took stock: altar boys in white carrying burning candles, priests in black at the front of the altar, and the black-checkered floor leading me toward a pew on the left side.

"The Lord be with you," the priest said from the front of the church, his words echoing with a reverberating bellow.

"And with thy spirit," we responded as one.

I stayed, and the service felt both familiar and cleansing, a ritual that hadn't changed in hundreds of years, a sanctity. When the lights were shut off for the homily, only candlelight and torches and twilight saturated the sanctuary. When the Eucharist was over I was the last to linger, alone in a pew with thoughts that would not settle. Eventually I rose to return home and collapse into bed, the grief as heavy as concrete.

I wept for all the loss I had never acknowledged, all the pain I'd held in reserve: my marriage, my dreams, my career, and my health. To acknowledge their demise meant to mourn them, and I hadn't been ready.

The next morning I began my wanderings again, prowling through the city like a stray cat. I didn't want Bill back. Not now. Almighty, no! But the betrayal in my own house felt as sick as any illness that had sent me to bed.

It was unseasonably warm, the sky a cloudless and intense blue. I draped my coat over my arm and put one foot in front of the other. I couldn't write. I couldn't read. I could merely walk and feel.

This time I found myself at St. Paul's perched on Ludgate Hill, the highest point in London, where I might be closest to God or myself or whatever great sorrow moved within me. It was an Anglican church, and I'd seen the old black-and-white photos of it surrounded by smoke from the bombings of the 1940 blitz. The great dome of the cathedral built in the 1600s, a round mountain of man's tribute to God, had survived. Men had stood all night, passing water buckets and fighting to save what now stood as my sanctuary, and I climbed to it with knees shaking, entered with the remnants of my torn life trailing behind.

This time the church was empty, my footsteps echoing under the vast dome as I approached the altar. The English baroque style was a sharp contrast to the Gothic spires of the Abbey. There was too much for my eye to absorb—gold and winged archways, jewels and embellished carvings, and stained glass everywhere as the scenes of Christ's life unfolded before me. Sunlight spilled from the windowed dome overhead, falling upon me, the floor, the pews, and carved statues. Ropes held me back from approaching the gold and marble altar, three candlesticks on top—Father, Son, and Holy Ghost. The dark wood pillars on either side were twisted, leading my sight upward, past the arched stained glass of Christ on the cross, higher still to the dome, where marble angels looked heavenward as if to remind us we were being guarded and loved.

I'd once heard Jack say, or had I read it, that sometimes a soul would cry out, "Thy will be done" to God and other times, with fury say instead, "Fine, have it your way."

I knelt on a padded bench and uttered the latter.

What could I have done differently? I begged the tortured Christ in stained glass.

My parents had warned me—*Why can't you be softer, nicer, and kinder? Prettier? More like Renee?* Why couldn't I? Was this my punishment for such self-will?

I stayed for I don't know how long, until finally I grew restless. I rose and made my way to the stairs that led to the Whispering Gallery, where I could climb to the dizzying top of the dome itself, as if maybe there I might finally reach God. Higher and higher I climbed, counting each of the 257 steps. The dome itself reminded me of Davy and his intense interest in the constellations, and a poem unraveled in my mind.

"I'll make a magic to ferry you soon," I mumbled out loud. I would rescue my sons from the sickness of Bill and Renee. I would build a new life with them.

The Whispering Cathedral was so named because one person could stand against the ornate golden wall to whisper, and another, standing far away but holding his ear to the same wall, could hear what was said. Even in all my confusion, something in it summoned my deep connection to Jack, and I wondered if I murmured something here and now, in this sacred space against these walls, he might somehow hear me.

Instead it was Jack's words that came to me, an echo from one of our letters. *God did not love us because we were lovable, but because he is love.*

I wandered to a window and felt in the deepest part of me that I would return to England, but with my sons by my side. Fantasy? I didn't know. Maybe. But in that moment it felt true. The city below was shrouded in mist, and from there I could see the cavernous abscesses of earth blasted by bombs dropped from on high, the ruined churches, remnants of World War II and the same horror that had sent the children to Jack's house.

I left the hallway and followed a stairwell down to enter a library and trophy room, where I found a verger in robes.

"Good afternoon, ma'am." He bowed his head down and then up. "Welcome to St. Paul's."

"It is glorious," I said, my voice full of the shed and unshed tears of the past two days.

His face softened, as if he could see my pain shimmering around me. "I urge you to rise to the belfry as they ring the one o'clock hour with one hundred tolls of the bell."

"Yes." I nodded at him. "Can you show me the way?"

"Follow me, please."

We reached the top of the bell tower, where a group of people were clustered expectantly, awaiting the great ringing. A young woman with three children clinging to her hem leaned toward me. "Those bells up there weigh seven tons," she said. "Isn't that marvelous?"

I smiled at her. "Marvelous indeed."

"They say it is the largest ring of bells in the world." She pointed, and I cranked my neck back to see the bells and wheels above me, feeling dizzy.

"A ring of twelve bells," the friar stated.

The room was warm: a circular space with pale-yellow plaster walls and photos of the grand cathedral framed and hung. Twelve men entered the room to stand on foot-high wooden platforms. Their muscles bulged from their tight shirts as if to burst as they grabbed the ropes hanging from the plaster ceiling and at once, in unity, began to pull.

One resounding ring after the other filled the tower. In a great stationary dance, the men pulled and grunted, they swung and moved, as the bells tolled. Of the ten people there, most ran from the tower, but others only covered their ears. I did neither. I stood still and allowed the reverberating air to swallow me whole.

I stayed and felt the enormous noise vibrate through my body. Chills ran through me, and I shivered with the unceasing sounds, which were cleansing me, coursing through my veins, through my mind and my spirit. The tenor and the fifth ringing together, not synchronized or in harmony but in perfect sublime sound. My boundaries dissolved; transcendence enveloped me. God was with me, and always had been. He was in the earth and the wind, in the ringing and in the silence, in the pain and in the glory of my life.

Those bells rang for a full five minutes, but an eternity in my soul.

The scabs of my ego fell off in large chunks of acceptance: *Bill doesn't love me.*

When it was over I stood in the resonating air with a sense of emptiness and relief, of calm and cleansing. I was as pure as if I'd partaken in the holy act of Communion on my knees.

One by one the crowd wandered away, and soon the ringers were gone also. I stood alone in that tower, my hands over my heart, tears wet on my cheeks. God might not fix things for me, but he would be with me in whatever waited ahead, that was clear. I knew nothing of the future, except that in two days' time I would arrive at Warnie and Jack's to spend Christmas at the Kilns.

And in the new year I would return home to a new kind of family.

CHAPTER 23

I brought my love obedience; cupped my hand
And held submission to his thirsty mouth

"SONNET VIII," JOY DAVIDMAN

December 15, 1952

Oxford slumbered under a freeze, but I didn't bother about the weather at all as the taxi careened on the ice toward Kilns Lane. I only cared that I would have two weeks with Jack and Warnie. Back in London, thick fog carrying the smoky remnants of coal exhaust had consumed the city, killing thousands (they were still counting) and sending Parliament into a tizzy until Winston Churchill finally declared he would implement new laws to protect his citizens from the poisonous smog. I'd been hiding in my room with a cloth over my face, and I was thrilled to be away from it all.

I stood at the end of Kilns Lane as the taxi drove away with a few of my last shillings. I'd left most of my belongings in London, as I'd return there for a few days before boarding the ship home.

Silver birch trees formed a long path to the brothers' home. The lane was thin and muddy, frost and ice at the edges.

"The Kilns," I said to the air and the birds and the naked trees, with a great love for everything that was to come. I lifted my suitcase and took a few steps to the fork of the lane, where a ramshackle shelter, possibly a garage caved in on itself, stood with a sign attached that pointed the way down the lane. *The Kilns*, it said in crooked letters with an arrow.

Two thick green hedges bordered the path to the house by the back way. I carefully stepped forward, keeping my eyes on the ground so I wouldn't slip. When I reached the end of the lane I glanced up to see the rambling cottage, smoke rising from a roof chimney pot, and a rush of expectation ran through me.

The house spread out as if stretching. Built of deep-red brick and creamy stucco, the dormered windows sprouted like bugs' eyes from the russet-colored roof, where three chimneys stood staunch guard over the gardens and property. I walked under a brick archway and through a small iron gate that creaked with rust as I pushed it open. I reached the green front door of the house in only a few strides. The white porcelain doorbell was pressed into the doorframe and bade me PRESS in a small white sign. Which I did.

Many others had visited here. I'd heard Michal say that Jack frequently took in strays—both animals and humans. Maybe I was one of them, but a stray I would be.

It was quiet all around, and then came a barking dog and a woman's voice, and the door flew open.

A balding woman, whom I had to look down at to see her face looking up at me, was wearing a dirt-smudged apron. "Well, well, you must be Mrs. Gresham."

"I am," I said.

"Well, don't stand out there in the freezing cold, my dear. Come in, come in!" She moved aside, and I stepped into the dimly lit entry hall to set my suitcase on the brick floor. Beside me there was a long bench that ran the length of the wall. I set my purse on it.

"I'm Mrs. Miller," the woman told me.

"I'm Joy." I smiled so widely I could feel it reach my eyes in a wrinkling at the edges. Her thick English accent and my New York one made it sound as if we spoke altogether separate languages. Already I felt we looked at each other with certain camaraderie—women in a house of men.

"The brothers are in the common room. Follow me."

We took only a few steps down the dark-paneled hallway before turning left and emerging into a room so covered in books that I believed they must be holding up the roof itself. I took it all in: papers scattered around, a half-finished Scrabble game on the table, comfortable chairs, and the aroma a soft amalgamation of fire, cigarette, and pipe. The walls were painted a hideous mustard yellow, and the window decor was obviously left over from the war—curtains made of army blankets. A fog seemed to fill the room, and I took off my glasses and rubbed at the lenses with the edge of my cotton shirt.

Jack stood from his chair, a book falling from his lap, and gave a boisterous bellow. "Good afternoon, Joy! Well, well. You must have sneaked into the house like a cat." He shook Warnie's shoulder. "Look who's finally here."

They both came to me and vigorously shook my hand.

"No use cleaning those glasses of yours," Warnie said with affable humor. "It's the fug in here. We wait until the room is unbearable and then out we go for fresh air."

I laughed. "I'm so happy to be here," I said, "I don't even mind the fuggy-ness."

"It seems you've met our housekeeper, Mrs. Miller. Let's show you around and get you settled," Jack said. "We've given you the best room, but you'll have to share a bathroom with two old bachelors."

"I'm not worried about sharing anything," I said.

Awkwardness settled over us, and I wanted to shoo it from the room. It would take a little bit, getting used to sharing a home.

"This way," Warnie said and waved his hand toward the hallway.

I followed, Jack behind, until we reached two doorways.

"We added these rooms as soon as we bought the place," Warnie announced and opened the bedroom door. "This was once my room, but I've moved upstairs since Maureen moved out. This will be yours for the weeks." He waved his hand to the door next to it in the hallway. "This is my study. But I'll try not to disturb."

I peeked into his chaotic study, books and papers and a little bronze

Buddha sitting serenely in lotus pose on his mantle, staring at the mess. My room was small, with a single bed in the corner, a dresser tight against the wall, and a washbasin. The bed was made with what must have once been a white bedspread, but now was gray and faded. On the walls were pictures of trains and steamships, framed in dark wood and hanging crooked. Without thinking I walked over and straightened a photo, then turned to the men.

"Favorite trains?" I asked.

"Well, you know Jack's very first toy was a train," Warnie said with authority and a laugh.

"First toy? No. That I did not know." I smiled at them both. "How nostalgic. I'm honored to share a room with them."

"Not exactly plush, but comfortable." Jack dropped my suitcase into the room and pointed down the hall. "Bathroom that way."

"Now let's get outside and show you around the grounds," Warnie said.

"Well, Warnie, let's allow her a little time to settle in."

"No, I don't need that." I smiled. "I want to get outside. Let's go out and see it all."

The house sat on the outskirts of Headington Quarry, settled on rolling lowland. To the south lay a lake and a wooded area that slowly rose into Shotover Hill. The three of us set out as Warnie began his tour speech.

"The house was built in 1922," he said as the frigid wind whipped our faces. "We fell in love with it the first time we saw it in 1930." He stopped a few yards into our walk and pointed to two conical-shaped kilns shooting from a brick structure like overgrown funnels. "This was once where all the bricks were made for the city. Thus . . ."

"The name of the home," I finished.

From there we ambled off, and I comprehended the extent of the property: I would need hours to search it on my own, to soak in the acres of beauty, though most was hidden under winter's caul. We passed chestnut, mountain ash, and oak. I ran my hand along the bark of a slanted fir tree, its arched branches and needles being all the green in the landscape.

"It's like Narnia," I said. "I'm almost able to see the walking trees, not ambling along as we do but as you described, wading through the forest floor."

Shivering, we eventually reached the pond and stood at its edge next to a little red punt with ice filling its center and crusting its edge.

"We should have chosen a warmer day to show you around." Jack pointed at the frozen pond. "It's a dirty little thing, a flooded clay pit where they once dug out the mud to make bricks in the kilns, but surprisingly you come out quite clean when you swim in it."

"Are there fish?" I asked, peering over their shoulders.

"Perch and pike. But poor things get eaten by my two swans."

"Swans?" I craned my neck, looked past Jack and into the reeds.

"You'll see them surely enough," Warnie said. "They'll want to know who you are and why you're here."

"I'm Joy Davidman," I called out over the pond, using my maiden name, my writing name, my *real* name. "And I'm here to celebrate Christmas with two old bachelors."

Great bellowing laughter carried across the water, and Warnie shook his head. "Well, you may have scared them off for good." Then he became quiet and reflective, his expression serious. "This place is more than Jack and I ever deserved. In spring the primrose and gardens burst forth. In autumn we have the windless sunny days . . . it's a veritable Garden of Eden."

I smiled at Warnie's sweetness, his almost childlike admiration. We rushed through the remainder of the outdoor tour until we passed a lilting shelter, a small almost-house. "This?" I asked.

"An air raid shelter," Jack said. "Paxford built it during the war."

"Who is Paxford?"

"Ah, you'll meet him soon enough. He's our gardener and landskeeper."

"The war." I pointed at the bomb shelter. "How can it all seem so far past when it just happened? Maybe because the bombs themselves never reached my shore." I ran my hand along the concrete walls, moss growing thick along its edges.

We continued on until I paused at a dormant garden. "Oh, Jack. You have room to grow so much! I can almost see the vegetables and flowers."

"That's Paxford's territory," Jack said as a dog came loping into the garden. I dropped to my knees to greet the dark lion, a flopping pack of fur.

"Who is this?" I buried my face in its neck, memories of the midnight hours with such animals coming back to me with pangs of nostalgia: the lion at MGM, the lion of my childhood Bronx Zoo, Aslan, and this animal.

"That's Bruce III."

"He's magnificent," I said.

"You like dogs," Warnie said. "That's a good thing."

"I have two at home. Four cats. A whole cast of animals."

I rose and Bruce III followed; we walked silently for a while until we reached a gathering of crouched and freezing trees.

"Jack, Warnie!" A voice flooded with a Cotswold accent so thick that their names were scarcely recognizable.

Then there stood a great tree of a man, the cracks in his clothes caked with dirt. He dusted his hands, one against the other, and smiled at us. His teeth were yellowed and crooked, his lips chapped, and his face wrinkled like a sheet from the wash.

"Paxford," Jack said. "Meet our American friend, Mrs. Gresham."

He was quite rotund. His chin . . . there must have been three of them. His stomach was so round, one could place a glass on top of it. A cigarette was firmly set in the corner of his mouth, and his white hair was slicked back. It was his nose that was incongruous with his face, so large it looked as if it were a replacement.

"I knew you were coming, and it is jolly good to meet you," he said.

"You've done some wonderful things on this property," I said. "I can't wait to see your garden unfold."

Paxford's eyes grew wide. "You will be here in the spring?" He pulled up his shirt sleeves to show his forearms, hairy and thick.

Silence stretched into discomfort, until far off a single bird let loose a torrent of a song. "No," I said. "I won't be, regretfully."

"Well," Warnie said, always the one to smooth the awkward moment. "Let's get ourselves inside to warm up. You have plenty of time to explore the acreage."

Once our coats were hung on the hooks in the back hallway, we settled into the common room, and Jack poured us all a sherry as we each settled into a chair.

"Blackout curtains." I pointed at the windows. "You still worried about the German invasion?"

Warnie and Jack both laughed, and Warnie told me, "We're lazy old bachelors. It might just be bloody time to take them down."

The fire crackled, dwindling. Jack turned to Warnie as he must have done a million times during their thirty years of cohabitation and said, "Your turn to stoke."

Warnie rose, and Jack spoke around his cigarette. "Joy, it's difficult to believe your journey is nearly over. You had so many writing projects. Did you find the time that you needed?"

"I did. As you know with writing, it's never enough. But"—I leaned forward—"your edits on *Smoke* have been invaluable."

"As have your notes on O.H.E.L. I feel I've found a treasure in you."

Warnie returned to the room with a load of firewood and dropped it into the fireplace, stoking it with a brand and jumping back from a litter of sparks that landed on the carpet. Neither Jack nor Warnie rose to put them out, and I jumped up.

"Oh, don't bother," Warnie said. "Not much else can be done to this rug. It's a disaster."

And he was right—it was dirty and full of holes, ash scattered here and there. "I wouldn't have noticed," I said.

"Tollers's wife won't even allow him to visit us anymore—says he comes home a mess and muddy." Warnie shrugged. "Wonder if she'd be willing to come clean it up for us."

"Well, housekeeping ain't one of my best attributes. Just ask Bill."

"Ah, your husband." Warnie sat again, settling into a slouched posture of comfort.

"If one can call him that at the moment." And the fresh pain rose again in my belly.

"And why wouldn't you call him that?" Warnie's question was hesitant, wary.

"I've just received a letter," I said and glanced between the two of them. "He is in love with my cousin and wants to marry her."

Jack and Warnie exchanged a glance, both seeming to flinch as if I'd picked up the hot poker Warnie had just laid beside the fire with my bare hands.

Jack leaned forward, his hands set on his knees. "Perhaps you misinterpret his meaning. Letters can be waffling and misleading sometimes. I know that. Sometimes I'll receive an argument against something I've written that I didn't write at all."

I stood slowly, my knees and hips aching from travel and the walk through the grounds. I limped to my purse on the side table across the room and took out the letter. "Here," I said. "You tell me if there is anything at all to misinterpret."

Jack was silent as he read, and Warnie sat quietly in his chair. The fireplace flames rose wildly, smoke wafting upward, fire licking the black walls.

"'You will never be anything but a writer'?" Jack spoke Bill's words aloud and glanced at me. "What a cruel thing to say."

"That's the least of it," I told him. "Go on."

Jack's eyes fell to the page until finally he spoke. "'I have never yet known determination and willpower to make a go of marriage,'" he quoted and then asked, "and you are returning home to *this*?"

"My ticket is booked," I told him. "My children are there. They're my family." I leaned forward and pressed my fingers into the corners of my eyes.

"Bill has not given you a choice, Joy. You mustn't stay there."

I glanced up, ready to receive any advice he had. "But how can I desert them?"

"This is not your doing. These are his choices." He gazed intently at me. "What did you answer in return?"

"I told him that we'd discuss the issue when I returned home." I smiled and shrugged. "What else was there to say? I'll be home in two weeks, and what good would another letter do? So many letters. So many words. What good?"

"Yes, what good?" Warnie mumbled.

"I try very hard to believe in God's best for this," I said. "It is a newly acquired habit that I sometimes forget to employ." I laughed to alleviate the darkness I'd brought into the room.

Jack stared at me with gentleness. "Maybe you aren't doubting that God will do the best for you, but wondering how painful the best might be."

"You are very right, sir," I said.

"But to return to abuse isn't anything God would demand of you. Of any of us. His commandments aren't meant for that. You know that as well as anyone." He paused and the fire popped. "What you've tolerated at home isn't about being a good wife or about obeying God. You must know that."

I stood and walked to the fire, facing the flames. I rubbed my hands together. "I do know, but I forget. When I'm in the middle of all the chaos and arguing, I feel like such a failure, so demeaned, and then I blame myself for not being able to be someone else, someone better."

"You blame yourself for not being who Bill wants you to be?" That was Warnie, blurting out the question with a frustrated voice.

I turned around to face them both again. "Yes." The absurdity of it felt simple, a fact overlooked. "In your words it's all so easily seen. You take a truth and boil it down to its essence."

Jack eased to stand. "It's easier to do when you aren't in the middle of it. My heart isn't blistered and mangled by his abuse. That privilege is yours, it would seem."

I walked toward him then, wanting to reach across the space between us, to touch him, to wrap my arms around him, allow my head to rest on his shoulder the same way my heart was resting in his words. "How do I ever thank you for this kind friendship? It sustains me."

He nodded, his cigarette ash falling to the carpet.

I exhaled and brushed my hands through the air. "But I'm here to celebrate the holidays, not to bring doom and gloom. Let's play some Scrabble and forget this affair for now." I pointed to a half-finished game on the table a few feet away.

"Yes," he agreed.

"Can we use Latin and Greek words too?" I inquired.

He laughed, that low rumbling sound. "Any language. If it's been used in a book then it is fair game."

"German? French?"

"Anything at all," he said.

"The best way to play," I replied. "Warnie? Will you join us?"

"Not tonight." He rose but smiled at me.

Jack and I moved to the table and sat, bowing our heads over the board. It was a game he must have started with Warnie. I scanned my row of letters in their tray and chose five squares to spell *verti* against his word *article*, and scored a triple. Jack leaned back in his chair and bellowed loud enough to make Warnie poke his head back into the room.

"I've met my match."

CHAPTER 24

How the wind
Whips all our talk and laughter out of mind,
And time, far more than Thames, has power to drown

"SONNET VII," JOY DAVIDMAN

I awoke slowly in that cold room in Jack's house and pulled the covers to my chin. A pounding came from inside the walls, like someone trying to escape from a stone-walled dungeon. The plumbing, ancient and groaning like one of Jack's fictional frozen statues come to life.

The house bustled around me, doors opening and closing, Warnie's voice calling out to Mrs. Miller. A man's low voice, must have been Paxford, and then Jack's reply, that rumble of familiarity.

I stretched and rolled over to glance at the clock. Already nine. They must think me lazy, but I didn't mind. At home, this one thought—*lazy*—would have made me nervous, the jittery feelings overcoming me as I thought about Bill being angry that I'd slept in.

After I dressed and finished my morning routine, I entered the common room to find Jack reading the Bible, a Latin version that morning.

"Good morning," I said quietly.

His pipe bent down from the corner of his mouth and he startled, sending it to drop onto his lap. He brushed the ashes onto the carpet as if they were crumbs from breakfast and smiled at me. "Good morning, Joy."

He didn't move to stand but held his finger fast to the spot in the Psalms. "Mrs. Miller has some breakfast in the kitchen if you'd like some. We were gifted a few extra eggs from the neighbor." The war was over but egg rationing wasn't, and Jack always managed to finagle a few extra.

"Thank you," I said, suddenly a bit shy. We were no longer at a pub or on a hike or in his Oxford rooms. This was his home, and he had his routine.

I spent some time in the sunny warm kitchen with Mrs. Miller, satisfied with tea and a biscuit when Jack joined us.

"My correspondence is done for the day, and Warnie is off to work on his Sun King. How's for a walk, just enough to get the blood flowing for the day's work?"

A smile was my answer.

Once we bundled and left the house, the wind came in great gusts as if the sky were holding its breath and then exhaling. I wrapped my scarf tighter around my neck and moved as close to Jack as possible. We were headed to the Headington Quarry's Holy Trinity Church, a half-mile walk on sidewalks and then down a frozen-mud lane. A high stone wall with bits of broken bottle capping the top like a crown bordered the narrow walkway to the church. Jack walked ahead of me, only room for one at a time, and I followed quietly. As we neared the churchyard he opened a wrought iron gate to enter a graveyard with a stunted forest of headstones.

I turned away from the irrefutable proof of death and instead focused on the church. It appeared as old as the land on which it sat, a limestone building with a bell cote and two bells on the west end. A slate roof sloped toward the ground and then seemed to take an abrupt halt at the building's edge. White and stolid, the church spread east and west, its doorway hidden under a portico of stone where a cross was mounted, another engraved in a circle above the doorway.

"Anglican," I said.

"Yes." Jack surveyed the church with a proud stance. "Are you?"

"If I defined myself as anything, it would be Anglican, but I'm hard-pressed to be put into a category."

"I don't believe you need a category," he said, and it sounded very much like a compliment.

"It's very medieval looking," I added with a shiver, closing my coat tighter, "like something out of one of MacDonald's stories."

"I'm quite sure that's what the designer was after; he'd be flattered to know you think so." He put out his cigarette in a puddle. "Let's see if it's any warmer inside." He opened the doorway of the church and then stepped aside to allow me entry.

The pews, dark wood and shining in the dim light, were lined to face an altar and stained glass window of Christ with his hands spread wide. The simplicity of this church compared to the grand cathedrals in London brought my heart to humbleness. White plaster walls surrounded us. To the left a white curtain hung, separating the sanctuary from the back hall. Candlesticks sprouted from pews' ends, and wan sunlight washed through the stained glass windows in multicolored hues, a nimbus on the angels and saints, the pews and floors.

"That's beautiful," I said and pointed to the window above the altar. "So beautiful that I wish I possessed a better word."

"Words," Jack said quietly. "The joy and art of them. Saying exactly what you mean."

I pondered for a moment, staring and then closing my eyes. "Sublime," I whispered.

"Yes! That's it." He paused. "That window was installed just last year as a memorial to those who died in World War II."

"I wonder sometimes what those days were like for you. For all of you."

Jack ran his hand across the back of a pew, and his sight seemed far off, as if those wartime days danced on the altar. "There was a time I believed that they'd invade and we would belong to them," he said. "I threw my pistol into the river off Magdalen Bridge because it was rumored that the SS would find me for all the Royal Air Force lectures I'd given, and that a gun would be my demise." He shook his head at the memory.

"We felt the fear in America," I said, "but nothing like that. I'm not sure that the fear of invasion would have been something I could have tolerated."

"You tolerate what you must when it becomes your reality." Jack pointed to a pew on the left-hand side about halfway back and walked that way; I followed him.

"This is our pew, Warnie's and mine." He sat and I joined him. "Not exactly ours, but where we prefer to sit. We started coming here all the way back in . . . I don't know, 1930 or thereabout? I like the eight a.m. service. The organ music in the other services grates on my nerves." He lowered his voice as if the organ might hear his insult.

I leaned close to him. "I don't much mind organ music; it's the eternal sermons I can't stand."

Jack laughed and pointed to the Communion table. "It was here during the Eucharist, during World War II, that I thought of Wormwood and his story."

"Oh, Jack," I said. "Tell me. I love hearing where stories began."

He turned slightly in the pew to face me. "I'd heard a speech Hitler gave over the radio waves, and I was easily convinced by him, if only for a moment. I started thinking what it would take to convince one of evil, just as the sermon that morning was trying to convince one of good." His voice was quieter than usual. I didn't want him to stop talking; I wanted him to unload his heart into mine.

"While the preacher spoke of temptation, my mind wandered. How would a head devil instruct his underlings on such things? Would he do it in the same but opposite manner as this preacher?" He paused and smiled at me. "I had almost the entire book in my head before I returned home. And then I believe I wrote the whole thing during the Battle of Britain with airplanes overhead. Young children were sent to live here. Hitler was on the radio with his fierce voice. And during all of that, my mind was churning with the idea."

"I'm envious," I said. "You just decide to write a book and then you do it." The church was growing warm, or I was. I removed my coat and laid it gently in my lap. "You have tapped into something others have not."

"Don't admire me in that way, Joy. I write stories just as you do, one after the other. People believe I spent years studying for Screwtape and Wormwood, but the idea and words came from the wickedness of my own heart." He rose from the pew and motioned for us to leave.

I sat for a moment longer. "Maybe they are the type of stories we think of during war—the devil and his works. *Paradise Lost* was written during the English uprising." I stood and followed him.

He opened the door to the outside and wrapped his coat tighter. "I read that when I was nine years old and fancied myself a critic." He paused. "And how do you come to know these things, Joy?"

I donned my coat and squinted into the sunlight. "Because I'm writing about King Charles II. It was his father who was executed during that time. I retain the oddest information, Jack. I can't quite remember to pay the bills or buy a new button for my jacket or answer a letter, but I can remember a piano score after seeing it once and little facts like Milton writing *Paradise Lost* during that terrible war. Those obscure things burrow themselves into my brain. But ask me to catch a train on time?"

He laughed. "No one really knows you, do they, Joy?"

"I wouldn't say no one."

With a few tentative steps back into the courtyard, Jack spoke. "That's what Tollers says about me also. But I don't believe he says this with great affection, merely annoyance."

I laughed. "Tell me more about Tollers. How did you become such grand friends?"

"We met in 1926 at a Merton College English faculty meeting." He sat on a bench in the courtyard, and I joined him. "I thought him a pale little chap, but soon found that we had the same mind about many things. From poetry to English literature. We've been each other's first readers, and we haven't always liked what we've read." He paused before telling me, "He's not a big fan of the Narnian stories."

"What does he know?" I said, obstinately horrified.

"Oh, he knows very much indeed. As with any good friend, we have many of those moments when one turns to the other and says, 'You too?'"

"Like?"

"We don't like politics. Neither of us has bothered to learn to drive a car. Dante. Theology."

I nodded, but felt envious also.

"But there are our differences also. He's the don of linguistics and language. Not a literature fan as I am. Yet what draws any two people together toward friendship is what drew you and me—that we see the same truth and share it. For example, there was this moment in an Inklings meeting when we both agreed to this—if someone won't write what we want to read, then we shall write it for ourselves." Jack paused. "For now he's working on a sequel to *The Hobbit*. I'm quite astounded at his ability to create another world."

"You've done the same."

"I try, at least."

"Let's always do so."

"Indeed." He nodded with that smile, and we stood to head down the path.

Once home, Jack retreated to his room to "enter the fourth dimension," and I took his O.H.E.L. papers into the common room and began to read with a pencil in my hand. For many pages I had to pretend this was not his work on which I wrote, to feign that I wrote marks on any old paper, and not become muddle-headed with admiration, forgetting to be honest.

A new twist but plenty good, I wrote in the margin and continued.

The fire puttered out, and Mrs. Miller came in to stoke it. She turned to smile at me, and I thanked her.

"'Tis wonderful to have a nice woman in the house," she said as she hung the poker on the hook.

"Was there a not-so-nice one here before me?" I asked cheerily, not expecting an answer.

"Oh, not-so-nice is a kind way to describe her." And with that, Mrs. Miller was off to the kitchen, not allowing for any more questions.

I closed my eyes as the fire reignited and a flood of gratitude and grace filled me. How very blessed I was to be there reading Jack's work, warming by the fire after spending a morning in his church. But, oh, how many women had Mrs. Miller seen come and go in this house?

I wasn't sure I wanted to know.

CHAPTER 25

Why, you may call the thing idolatry
And tell no lie; for I have seen you shine

"SONNET X," JOY DAVIDMAN

Jack awoke early in the mornings, which wasn't in my particular bag
of tricks, and began returning letters to his wide array of correspond-
ents, some fantastic and some boring. It occurred to me that maybe
his morning letter writing greased the wheels for his stories. He spent
hours doing this, bent over his desk, a cigarette burning a long dry ash
before falling onto the carpet or into the ashtray, his spectacles perched
low and his brow furrowed with thought. He read the Bible every day,
not from beginning to end, but wherever his eye fell. Sometimes he
perused it in the original Greek and other times in Latin.

It was his upstairs office where he worked, and I adored it—
crammed from corner to ceiling with books, stacked and lined up on
floors and tables and bookshelves. There were two upholstered chairs,
one in which he bid me to sit many times when we were working on
separate writings. The desk, large and dark wood, had belonged to his
father and was set for Jack to see out the front windows to the garden
and beyond. To the left of his desk was the door to his bedroom, always
closed and bolted. He didn't even unlock it to go through the office
and down the inside stairs to use the downstairs bathroom, but instead
used the door in his bedroom that led outside to the metal staircase
that descended to the side door of the kitchen. He'd then enter the
kitchen and use the only bathroom in the house. I wanted to ask why

he had this funny little habit, but bathroom behaviors didn't seem quite right for discussion.

In his office Jack didn't just read; he went deep inside the work his eyes fell upon, taking apart the sentences and themes. And while I was nearby, he would often call my name.

"Joy," he'd say, "what do you think . . ."

Off we'd go into a theological or thematic discussion. Sometimes I feared I would wake and be back in the rambling, falling-apart house in Staatsburg, Bill stumbling drunk down the hallway smelling of sex and whiskey, and find my time with Jack had only been a dream. But instead I sat in the armchair of his office at the top of the staircase discussing the meaning hidden in stories.

With rain lashing the windows of his office one morning, I looked up from my pages. "You're fortunate that you are deeply seeded in one place—that you were a student at Oxford and now a tutor there. It's home for you, I can see that. I wonder if Oxford has any idea how very fortunate they are to have you."

"They don't quite give me the reverence you assume." He didn't look up from his papers, his fingers tight around his fountain pen.

"I don't believe that." I eased to stand and padded to the window, glimpsed the property shrouded in the downpour.

"I was just recently turned down for the Professor of Poetry at Oxford," he said, his voice dropping away from the usual joviality. "A horde of English teachers didn't want me to have the position." I turned back to him, and he set his pen in the inkwell. "It was political, but still disappointing."

I leaned against the windowsill. "I'm sorry, Jack."

He laughed and shook his head. "My dear Joy, whatever would you be sorry about? It all comes with the academic life."

"But your poetry; it's brilliant," I said. "How could they not . . . ?"

"Yes, *you* think so, but most of it was published under my pseudonym, Clive Hamilton, so some never knew of it. I wasn't quite posh enough."

"I don't understand," I said and felt the regret for him as if I were the one they'd turned down.

"It isn't my first disappointment with Oxford," he said. "And it won't be my last."

"Not your first?"

"Just two years ago, when the Merton Professorship of Modern English Literature became available, Tollers believed I would be best for the slot. He gathered the forces and suggested that the two of us could split the title. But it seems I wasn't quite up to snuff. To the electorate, I didn't have nearly enough published scholarly works." He smiled at me, but I sensed his sadness.

"For goodness' sake, how many publications did they need?"

"It wasn't the number, it was the kind. It seems that my most popular works were my novels, and this was not what they wanted."

"Did Tollers take the position?" I asked.

"Yes, he did. And it was my old tutor, Wilson, who took the slot I was to have. It is told that I would have discredited their great reputation."

"That's absurd."

"Well then, if only *you'd* been on the committee." He again dipped his pen into his inkwell.

"I don't know if it helps to say this, but I believe the world would rather have your stories than your titles."

He nodded. "Well, enough of academia. Let's get back to our work."

I often watched Jack write when he believed I was working myself. He wrote with a quill, dipping it slowly into the inkwell and then bringing it back to paper. He said it "allowed a thought to form between well and paper." I imagined stories and fantasies unfolding in the slow dance of pen to ink, back to paper and then again to ink. When I offered to type those written words for him, he took me up on it straightaway.

But that day he wasn't writing, he was marking on my Ten Commandments manuscript. A nervous flutter rose in my throat until he looked up, feeling my stare.

"If you'd like me to write the preface, I will," he added. "When it is time for the British edition, you let me know."

"Like you to write the preface? Well, whiskers and cat's ears, of course I would," I said. "Thank you so much."

Then we both bent our heads back to the page.

In those mornings, we worked; in the afternoons, we walked and we drank and we ate and we read.

One late afternoon after a nap, I opened the bottom drawer of the dresser in my room looking for my favorite green sweater, one I'd knitted before coming here, which seemed to be missing in action. Instead I found a pile of drawings, childlike drawings. I withdrew them and knew what they were: Jack's and Warnie's childhood drawings of a country called Boxen. Pencil drawings of anthropomorphic creatures—there was a cat wearing a tuxedo and a top hat, smoking a cigarette and having drinks with men. A frog in a suit and a bird in formal wear. I smiled and felt a bit like I was in a dream and waking in the attic of Little Lea, his childhood home, where I knew these had been sketched and imagined.

I carried the drawings with me, just two sheaves, into the common room where Jack and Warnie sat at the fire reading. They both glanced up with smiles as I entered the room.

"What have you there?" Warnie asked.

I stood there, barefoot, not yet having put on my house shoes. My hair fell over my shoulders, and I brushed my free hand through it, suddenly quite self-conscious. "I found these. I'm enchanted."

Jack rose and walked to me. "Are you sleepwalking, Joy?" he joked and took the papers from my hand before letting out a laugh. "Oh, Warnie, it is Viscount Puddiphat."

Warnie came to us also, holding his drink in one hand and stroking his moustache with the other. "Indeed it is. Look at him visiting us from Little Lea. I don't believe I've looked at him since we stored him in that dresser. No matter how long we were cooped up in the little end room of that attic, we had our paper, pencils, and paint boxes."

"And your imagination," I said.

"Yes," Jack replied. "Always we had that. How else could we have survived? We made a whole world, didn't we, Warnie?"

"I believe we still are," he said.

I brushed my hair off my shoulders. "The world should see these. They should not be hidden in a drawer." I looked back and forth between them. "It's as if you imagined Narnia even then. As if you always knew what waited."

"How could we ever know what waited for us?" Jack smiled at me. "Who could have known *you* would be here with us?" He took the papers from me and wandered off to his office without another word.

It was during these times when Jack left us that Warnie and I came to know each other. We talked of history and book ideas.

"Joy," he said to me as Jack disappeared with Viscount Puddiphat, "how would you feel about a collaboration with me?"

"A collaboration? Cat's whiskers, Warnie," I said, sitting in the chair next to him and leaning forward. "Anything. What's your idea?"

"Madame de Maintenon, the wife of Louis XIV. She has never been written about, and she is as fascinating a character as any in that court."

"She was from the West Indies, right?" I asked. "And wasn't she married to someone else first?"

"Yes indeed. It's a modern-day Cinderella," he said. "And I know you can do it justice. She was the king's governess for his illegitimate children and then he fell in love with her."

"More," I exclaimed. "Tell me everything."

Then Warnie and I were off and running on *Queen Cinderella*, as I called it, and we began to throw ideas at each other as if we'd been a writing team for ages. Warnie had already written an outline and done most of the research—I would write the story. It was a match made in heaven: the Lewis men and me.

Or so I believed.

At night I returned to my sonnets. If there would ever in some far future come a day when someone read them and set them against my letters to home, would they feel the disparate and divided parts of my self?

What Bill's letter had set loose in me, what I'd hidden from my conscious admissions, what my sonnets had been hinting at all along, could no longer be denied. I didn't just love Jack; I was falling *in* love with him.

CHAPTER 26

You are not God, and neither are you mine

"SONNET X," JOY DAVIDMAN

I awoke on Christmas Day and for a long while lay still in the bed thinking of home, of my boys waking with Renee and Bill. I imagined the Christmas tree and wondered if they put it in the galvanized bucket as I'd always done. I imagined Topsy tearing through the wrapping paper, and I almost smelled the bubbling cider on the stove. I'd practically handed my family over to Renee, and here I rested, in an empty bedroom in Oxford.

The fog had rolled back days before, and there was both ice and snow along with wicked gales. Yet every day these men still bundled up and, taking me with them, walked for miles—into Oxford to the Bird and Baby or Blackwell's Bookshop, up Shotover Hill or into Magdalen's parks. We walked and how we talked. And laughed so deeply and richly that if it had to last for all my days, I could make it stretch beyond its time.

Two nights earlier we'd gone to a Christmas pantomime, where Jack had sung at the top of his lungs and I had reveled in the silly display like a child.

Still in bed, I could hear the men gathering wood for the fire, murmuring to each other, a sound now familiar.

I rose and dressed, taking time with my appearance for Christmas morning. From my suitcase I withdrew the two gifts I'd bought and wrapped for them—both books—and entered the common room, already warm and smoke-filled. Both men rested in their chairs, Jack reading a book I couldn't see and Warnie resting with his eyes closed.

We'd decorated over the past week with my urging to chop down the smallest fir from the acreage. Paxford had cut it down for us and hauled it into the room, dropping it into a bucket, temporarily transforming the aroma from smoke to evergreen. We decorated it with popcorn strings and pinecones, making up the silliest songs about the holiday.

"Merry Christmas," I called out and bent over to put my gifts under the tree.

They both startled, and Jack rose with a stretch. "Feliz Navidad, Joy!"

He went straightaway to the tree and retrieved a package wrapped in brown paper with a red string ribbon. "For you."

"Wait," I said. "I have something for you also."

"Open yours first," Warnie said and rose to stoke the fire.

I stood for a moment, taking in the room and the Lewis men I had grown to love with such depth. Soon it would be over. I wanted to hold this moment close, tuck it into my heart, because I would need it when I went home.

I took the package from Jack, and then sat in the ragged chair I'd come to think of as mine and opened it slowly. It was a copy of *The Great Divorce*. I opened the cover to find a quote written in Jack's now-familiar tight cursive handwriting, the fountain pen ink bleeding into the cotton paper.

There are three images in my mind I must continually forsake and replace by better ones; the false image of god, the false image of my neighbors, and the false image of myself. And then his signature, C. S. Lewis.

I held the book to my chest. "I cannot tell you how much this means to me," I said. "Where is that quote from?"

"A chapter I never included," he said with a nod.

"There's more," Warnie announced.

"Wait, it's my turn to give." I placed my new book on a side table.

From under the tree I brought out gifts for the men. For Jack, *The*

Illustrated Man by Ray Bradbury. Inside I had written a line from G. K. Chesterton's *The Ballad of the White Horse*, but slightly altered for my own influence on the line: *And men grow weary of green wine and sick of crimson seas.*

For Warnie, a new book of French history from Blackwell's Bookshop. *To Warnie, With great love, Joy.*

There aren't two men who would be more content with such gifts. They perused the books immediately and thanked me as if I'd given them a second home in Oxford.

After a long moment, Jack handed me another gift. This time it was not his own work but *Diary of an Old Soul* by George MacDonald—the author we'd both loved in childhood. I stared at the red cover with calligraphy letters spelling out the title, and tears welled in my eyes. I reached under my glasses and wiped them away before opening the cover to see that George MacDonald had signed his name on April 27, 1885. Below George's signature Jack had written *Later: from C. S. Lewis to Joy Davidman. Christmas 1952.*

He had gifted me his personal signed MacDonald and signed it to *Davidman.* Not Gresham.

A flood of gratitude poured through me, settling into the cracks of my pain. I might have been reading signs where signs weren't meant to be, like the ancient Greeks who believed that the Nine Muses hidden behind the golden cloud influenced their writing and creation. But read the signs I did.

I took a chance I had not yet taken and I went to Jack, put my arms around him, and hugged him tightly. I held to him for longer than he did me and then drew slightly back to look at him, my hands on his shoulders. His eyes, wet with unshed tears, felt like they bore right into my soul.

"Jack, I don't know how to thank you."

"You're welcome, Joy."

I let my arms drop to my sides but kept my eyes fixed on his. "You are precious to me. *You* are a gift."

He smiled and touched my arm for just a moment. "As you are to me."

I turned to look at Warnie. "And you too, Warnie. I don't want to leave you or this place."

"Don't think about that now," Warnie said. "It's Christmas. There's much to celebrate."

Jack flicked ash off his trouser legs and straightened his jacket. "Let's gather our things and begin the walk to Trinity," he said. "The Christmas Eucharist begins in thirty minutes."

I clutched MacDonald's book to my chest and sent a prayer for my family at home. I felt it rise to the heavens. Then I opened my eyes to Jack and Warnie and all the day might hold.

It was after we returned from church that Jack stopped me in the hallway. "Joy, I must tell you how much your edits and work on O.H.E.L. have meant to me. I'll be dedicating the book to you."

"To me?"

He nodded and smiled as if he'd just offered the most beautiful Christmas gift—frankincense or myrrh. And he was right. It was a gift of immeasurable value.

When the men had wandered off for their nap, I found myself alone in the common room. I walked about, picking up framed photos in an effort to glimpse the Jack-of-the-past: the boy, the adolescent, the soldier, the atheist, the man. Seventeen of his years had occurred before I even entered the dingy world of the "Jewish ghetto" in New York City.

There he was—a boy wearing knickers and knee-high black socks, a dress shirt with a triangular white collar, a white whistle lanyard looping down and into his top left pocket. I picked up the photo, ran my finger along the grainy black-and-white of the boy with a mother who loved him and had not yet fallen ill. Then there was another—a young boy, maybe eight years old, standing with his brother in the Irish countryside, both in suits and knotted ties, holding onto their bicycles, staring almost blankly at the camera. Then the soldier with a pipe in his mouth, a roguish smile on his face as if he knew he would survive and that God was fast on his heels. The posed photo of a man of maybe twenty, sitting in a three-piece suit with a book on his lap, gave me quite the thrill. Goodness, he struck such a handsome pose, so trim as he looked directly into the camera, his grin the same, impish and ready for trouble. I loved that young man I never knew. A far-reaching yearning bled backward in time, to a world that existed with Jack in it while I was still young and an ocean away. I pined for the time lost, something and someone I never could have had even then.

I set the past aside and entered the kitchen. I'd volunteered to cook Christmas dinner and half expected the men to retire to the common room or their offices while I bustled about the kitchen. Instead they planted themselves at the wooden kitchen table, regaling me with stories as I basted the turkey and simmered the cranberries, as I lit the stove and chopped the potatoes.

In the lull of another story about Warnie and his childhood happiness at Little Lea, I spoke.

"I once believed that it was Christianity that would finally make me happy."

"Oh, the history of man looking for something to make himself happy." Jack smiled.

"Well, I don't know if I've ever been happier than I've been today, even with the melancholy of missing of my little boys."

"If you're looking for a religion to make you happy, it wouldn't be Christianity," Jack said with a laugh. "A bottle of port might do that, but Christianity is rightfully not here to make us comfortable or happy."

"Cheers to that," I said and lifted my glass. "Tell me another childhood story." I poured a cup of burgundy from Magdalen's wine cellar into the gravy and stirred.

"Wait!" Warnie stood. "You pour wine into gravy?"

I stopped midstir. "You've never seen such a thing?"

"Never," Jack said.

"Well, I'm here to educate you on finer cooking."

Warnie scoffed with laughter. "Oh, don't you let Mrs. Miller hear you talk of any finer cooking than hers."

"I won't let her hear me, but my goodness, of course there is."

Silence settled for a moment, and then it was Warnie who answered me first. "My favorite times were the ones when our family would go to the seashore. It was where I fell in love with the ocean. With ships and with mariners."

"When Mother was alive," Jack added, in a voice so tender it took great self-control not to put down my whisk and sit before him, take his soft and beautiful face in mine, and kiss every corner of it.

"Let's not talk of this on Christmas Day," Warnie said firmly. "Look at that huge turkey. I'm not sure where you found one that size, but in anticipation, let's imbibe immediately."

"What we need," I said, "is some champagne."

"Oh no." Jack placed his burgundy glass on the table and lifted his hands in surrender. "Anything but champagne."

"Who doesn't like champagne? That seems nearly impossible."

His brow furrowed between his spectacles, his eyes going distant in the look I'd come to understand meant his mind's eye had been cast to the past. "It was the Battle of Arras in 1915," he said, but then fell silent.

This was the first time I'd heard him talk of his time in the First World War. I knew from his writing he'd been a commissioned officer in the Somerset Light Infantry and he'd reached the front line in France on his nineteenth birthday. I could barely imagine his fear, yet he not once had spoken to me of it. That May he'd been injured in the Battle of Arras—these were the facts, but I knew nothing else. I set my wineglass on the counter in a silent urge for him to continue.

"It was during an artillery barrage when I'd taken my men over the parapet." He shook his head. "A debacle. It was my sergeant who died instead of me." He blinked slowly, as if all these years later, it still cut deeply in his psyche. What the public saw was a mask, just like any I wore. Behind it was a man who still trembled with sorrows and pain:

the death of his mother, the harsh bringing-up at boarding school that had tortured him as a young boy, two wars, his failures at Oxford.

Humankind's cruelty in its entirety.

"The shrapnel buried into my body and sent me to the hospital. While the cries of other men echoed in my ears, they moved me behind the lines. The only liquor available was champagne, and I swallowed rivers of it. I've not been able to abide the taste of it since."

I stepped closer to him. "I'm sorry for that," I said. "Blast the champagne then. We shall break out more wine!"

"It's all in the past," Warnie said.

"Except when it isn't," Jack replied, and they exchanged a look, the kind that only those who know your innermost spirit can read.

"I wish I could scrub the horrid parts of the past clean for both of you." I paused. "For all of us."

We were silent for a while longer until I served the food and Warnie lit the candles, and we all began to sing the verse from the Christmas pantomime we'd gone to a few nights before.

Jack first: "Am I going to be a bad boy? No. No. No."

Warnie next: "Am I going to be awful? No. No. No."

And then finally my tone-deaf voice joined in: "I promise not to pour the gravy over baby's head." And with that I poured the Magdalen burgundy gravy over the turkey and we sat to eat.

We prayed over the meal and lifted our glasses to Christmas Day. Before he took his first bite, Jack reached over and took my hand. "Merry Christmas, Joy." He ran his thumb over the top of my hand in a motion so innocent and yet intimate that my limbs loosened and my breath was lost.

"Merry Christmas to you too, Jack."

CHAPTER 27

A thing to move your laughter or your loathing;
Still, you may have my love for what it's worth

"SONNET XII," JOY DAVIDMAN

The morning of my leaving I stood in the hallway of the Kilns, its friend-
liness holding me one last time. My valise and suitcase were packed and
waiting by the door, and I glanced at them with scorn, hating them for
what they represented.

Jack and Warnie were bumbling about in the back of the house; I
heard their footsteps and the water running fierce through the pipes.

The kitchen was empty. The copper pots hung clean from their
hooks where Mrs. Miller had put them, but there was no leftover evidence of our frivolity or deep conversations. When I left, the house
would resume its natural rhythms.

I'd become at home in the kitchen, and I took a frying pan from
the hook. It clattered as it hit the stove: iron on iron. The black market
eggs huddled in a bowl on the counter. I took one and cracked it open
against a white porcelain bowl. The yoke remained whole and floated
in the globular whites. I lifted a fork and punctured that yellow dome,
watching it spread and stain before I stirred it. Somewhere in the back
of the house Warnie called Jack's name, and then there was laughter
and a closing door, shuffled footsteps.

I dropped a dab of butter into the warming pan and inhaled the
comforting aroma as the butter spread and melted, sliding to the edges
of the pan. The lump of fear about going home lodged beneath my

throat. I poured the eggs into the hot pan and began to stir them as they cooked. A sprinkle of salt, and I whisked the eggs to finish.

"Good morning, Joy." Jack's voice startled me, and the spatula clattered to the floor.

"Jack." I turned and pasted on the smile, lifted the utensil from the ground, and wiped it off on a towel.

"Today you leave us." He brushed his hand across his unshaven cheeks, staring out the wide windows to the garden outside.

"Yes, today," I said. I placed my scrambled eggs on a plate and sat at the kitchen table. Jack joined me. "I have a story I want to tell you."

"Please!" He leaned back in his lounging clothes and worn slippers.

"When I was a child," I said quietly, "my brother, Howie, and I would sneak out at night to go to the zoo. We'd slink through the dark streets of the Bronx, holding our hands so tightly together it hurt. We'd slip through a hole in the fence, and the first thing I would do was run to the lions' cages."

"You as a child." Jack smiled tenderly. "I would have loved to have known that little girl."

"Oh, you do," I said and laughed. "She's here also."

He folded his arms across his chest, his eyebrows raised in curiosity. "Go on."

"I would call their names, Sultan and Boudin Maid. They were Barbary lions, and they would come to me. To *me*. Sometimes I would feed them small bites of meat and always bury, if only for a moment, my hands in their manes. Those golden eyes, I don't know how to describe those eyes. It was like falling and falling into another world where anything was possible. Time stood still. It was forever and not long enough. It was everything to me when that animal paused and let me touch him."

"Ah, the magnificent beasts," he said. "You weren't afraid?"

"Yes, I was."

"But you touched them anyway."

"I had to. There didn't seem to be a choice."

"What absolute wonder," he said, shaking his head.

I continued because I knew where I wanted to take Jack, what I needed him to see and feel in the cold morning of my leaving. I wanted to understand what we might be becoming; I wanted to hear his heart.

"It was a wonder, Jack. Years later, I opened *The Lion, the Witch and the Wardrobe*, and again dug my hands into the mane of a great lion. I felt that Sultan had followed me through all of my life, gone to visit you and then returned to me."

Jack's gentle eyes were moist, and his eyebrows fell down into a V. He leaned closer to me. "That's a lovely analogy. A graceful way to see the past."

"It's not an analogy, Jack. Can't you see? It's grace, the kind that hunts us down and doesn't let us go. It brought us together. The grace that keeps planets in their orbits and causes lilies to open their faces to the sun." I dared to meet his eyes with mine. "It's love."

He folded his hands in his lap. "Philia, yes. We must love that way. It grows not once but over and over and then again over. I value ours beyond measure."

"Real philia," I echoed, my eggs now cold and congealed on the plate. Yes, that is what he thought of us; this vibrating connection and kindness was nothing more than deep friendship. Then why did it feel more than that one word? Why was I confused?

He took a raspy breath and continued. "It is difficult for Warnie and me to think of you heading home into that mess. We hurt for you. I do wish there was some way to help you, something more we could do than send you on your way with our prayers. If you decide to return, we will be here. We will always be here for you."

But like the lion behind a cage, I couldn't free myself to offer what I was in no position to give—my freedom to be with him.

"These have been some of the happiest days of my life," I said.

"These have been happy days for us also, Joy."

"Thank you for taking me in and allowing me to spend Christmas with you. Thank you for my gifts, and for the warm nights, the games, the long walks, and the conversation."

Underneath all of this simmered so many unsaid words, so much unexpressed emotion. How was I to leave them?

Warnie entered the kitchen, coughing into his palm to shake off the cold morning. His eyes were red and his cheeks thick with three days of stubble. "Well, good morning," he said upon seeing us.

"You must get to the doctor, Warnie," I told him, "before that settles deeper into your chest."

"I will," he said. "I have dialed Doc Harvard and made an appointment."

It was in that moment that the honk of a taxi startled us all. Jack and I stood.

"I must go," I said. "Back to London and to the docks and then . . ."

"We will miss you, Joy." He nodded, his spirit closed to me. I couldn't discern—was he sad or frustrated? Angry? "Please write to us."

"I'm going to miss you both terribly."

Warnie came to me and also hugged me. "Joy, we aren't going anywhere. When you return, we will be here."

Tears gathered in my chest and then found their way to my eyes, falling before I could catch them. "I don't know how I'll find a way to return, but if I can, I will."

They nodded at me in agreement and I turned away, walked out the painted-green door of the Kilns and into the taxi waiting outside.

I'd offered my heart, and now I would pay the price—I always did.

Part III

AMERICA

January 1953–November 1953

"Courage, dear heart," said Aslan.

The Voyage of the Dawn Treader, C. S. Lewis

CHAPTER 28

Saying I must not love him any more;
But now at last I learn to disobey
"SONNET OF MISUNDERSTANDINGS," JOY DAVIDMAN

January 9, 1953

The farmhouse shimmered, ice and snow covering it like a veil. I stood on the front porch like one entering a prison. I had willfully submitted myself to the sentence and would find the willpower to face the disarray. Claim my part in it. I would take care of my children and write furiously and completely. I would be brave.

I entered the house, and an odd stillness surrounded me, a waiting silence like that right before a battle begins. The children were in school. The hallway overflowed with shoes and coats, schoolbooks and mittens, in organized piles or hung on hooks. Family life, one I'd always wanted and needed, seemed a mirage. Renee had taken my place, and yet this was *my* place. My heart was at the Kilns and my body was here, and nothing at all in the world made any sense.

Bill strode down the stairs and, not having heard me enter, was surprised to see me standing in the hallway in my coat and hat, my suitcase and trunk at my feet. He wore pressed blue jeans and a black sweater I'd never seen, but his grimace was familiar.

"Joy," he said flatly. "You're back."

And I hated him. That suddenly and that completely. All resolve and all promises to be the nicest girl washed away as finally as if a flood had come through the front hallway and swept me away. "That's right, Bill, I'm back. Back to your little love nest."

It was vitriol. It was the sin I'd placed before God more times than any other: my anger and my acidic tongue. But it was the truth, and my spirits had been rubbed raw and open. This was the blood of it all.

He bounded down the last few steps and grasped my shoulders, his face contorted with rage. "Don't you come in here and ruin the peace and love that Renee and I have built."

"Renee and you?" My voice rose to a high screech of pain. "You are a horrid person, Bill Gresham. You're a sociopath, and she has no idea who you are and what you're capable of. You've seduced her so that you can have the life you've always wanted, one of adoration while you write your pitiful stories alone in your room."

In an instant, like a snake's strike, his hands closed around my throat. I stood perfectly still, my eyes a challenge. If he was to choke me to death in the foyer of my own house, it was a better ending than to live with him. His fingers pressed into the flesh above my collarbone, anger an electric current flowing through his hands. Despair buried me, black as any grave.

"You are disgusting," he said and flung me from him as spittle flew from his lips. I rocked back, my head banging into the wall behind me.

I steadied myself to find my footing before stepping toward him. "You don't frighten me. What a cheating, lying man you are. I'm not one bit fooled."

"You know nothing," he said. "If I ever loved you, and I doubt I did, it wasn't even close to the way I love Renee."

A small mewling sound came from the top of the stairs, and I looked for my cat; instead I saw Renee standing with a basket of laundry in her arms, tears falling freely down her pretty face.

"Stop." She dropped the basket, and a full burst of clothes fell down the stairs: socks and underwear, children's shirts and pants. "Both of you stop it! Not here. Not now."

I picked up one of my suitcases and pushed past Bill to climb the stairs, kicking laundry clear of me with each step. I couldn't even look at the room Bill and I had once shared. I stormed instead into the bedroom I'd once split with Renee. Her personal belongings cluttered the room. Her hairbrush sat faceup on the dresser, long strands of black hair caught in the bristles; her perfumes and makeup organized in a straight line; her clothes folded neatly on the bench at the end of the bed. Her bed was made and her pillows fluffed and sitting upright.

I grabbed her belongings, one by one, slowly and deliberately throwing them into the hall. Her clothes. Her makeup. Her shoes and finally her pillow. Only then, when the room had once more become itself save her cloying perfume, did I slam the door and fall onto the single bed, the one I had lain on only months before, confiding in my cousin my husband's cruelty and betrayal.

Hot tears rushed from me, and I shuddered with their release. If only I believed God would come down to fix it all. If only hurt could leak out of me with tears. If only I knew what to do or how to do it. If only I could run to Jack, crumble upon him, and start a new life.

But instead I curled, exhausted, on my bed, pulled my pillow close, and closed my eyes. Somewhere from far off in the house a phonograph played Nat King Cole singing about love. My boys would be home from school in a few hours, and I would pull myself together for them, and for myself.

Bill had wanted a Southern home. He wanted to pretend he was a modern-day Rhett Butler. Well then, I could pretend to be a modern-day Scarlett O'Hara. I would think about what to do . . . tomorrow. Tomorrow was another day.

I rolled over and picked up *The Screwtape Letters*, which still sat on my bedside table, and opened to a random page. *Suspicion often creates what it suspects.*

I slammed shut the book. Words weren't going to help as they once had; they weren't going to cure me. A book wasn't going to save me, and neither was its author.

I needed to save myself.

Yes, God saved my soul—was drawing me slowly out of my self-centered world view—but only I could pack up my things and leave, only I could protect my heart and my sons.

I rose to place my things in their spots as if I'd never left. I hung my dresses and thought of each place I'd worn them with Jack. I set my books out, one by one, on the dresser where Renee's beauty creams had been only moments ago.

Soon the front door slammed, and the sweet and familiar voice of my younger son rang through the house. "Mommy?"

I bolted from the room, charged down the stairs, and answered that call, the one I hadn't been able to heed in months, the call of being a mother.

Davy and Douglas stood in the hallway, their books in their arms. Davy straightened his glasses as if making sure it was truly me, then dropped his books with a resounding *thump*. His little body slammed into me, setting me off balance. Douglas was close behind, and I laughed and dropped to my knees, taking them both in my arms with a cry of pure delight. Their bodies against mine, breathing them in; the aroma of snow and earth from their walk home, their damp hair smelling of soap, and their chapped cheeks waiting for my kisses filled my senses.

"My poogles," I said, drawing back to look at their faces. "I want you to show me everything right now. I want to meet Mr. Nichols the snake and see your schoolwork and all of your Christmas presents."

"Mommy," Davy said and touched my face as if making sure it was real.

"Yes, my love?"

"Are you staying?"

"I will never leave you again. I missed you with all my heart."

"Me too," Davy said.

I stood. "Now let me take a closer look at you." I took a step back. "Douglas, you have grown a hundred feet tall. And you, Davy, you look like a grown man about to go to your job in the city." I playfully yanked at his buttoned coat.

"Renee fixed all my clothes."

"Well, good for her," I said, and yet I smiled. "Let's go for a walk through the acres. I have missed my gardens and our creek and my orchards."

"But nothing is growing now, Mommy," Davy said in the mature, concerned voice of the older child.

"I don't care what is or isn't growing. It's all hidden under there waiting to come out." I held out both my hands. "Let's go and see."

I donned my coat and scarf, yanked on my mittens, and ignored Renee, who had come into the foyer with a dishcloth in her hands. With precision, my boys grabbed each of my hands and we walked into the bright winter sun.

Right there, I began to reclaim my life.

I couldn't know what might happen next, but I could take one step at a time with my work and my sons by my side.

CHAPTER 29

The best of me is merely commonplace,
And I am tired, and I am growing old
"SONNET XII," JOY DAVIDMAN

The train to Manhattan smelled like rotten fruit, a stench that permeated the car. I stood unsteadily and moved to another car as the train rocked toward New York City. I found a seat, closed my eyes, and imagined that I was sitting with Phyl on an entirely different train from Paddington Station to Oxford. But it was no use.

It was February, and winter held us in its grip. The house was filled with misery. Renee hid and wept in the extra room where she'd moved. The children were confused and anxious and tiptoed around the house. Rosemary and Bobby acted like skittering mice, afraid to be stepped upon.

Sometimes I felt as if my anguished prayers of uncertainty were received into the hands of great Love, and other times I sensed that they hit the ceiling and landed flat in my lap, dusty, withered, and useless. I started to see that faith was something akin to understanding that it didn't matter so much how I *felt* but was closer to what I believed.

Meanwhile, Bill and I fought as if our lives depended on the next ill-mannered word. If I held these times in my mind against Oxford, against the smoke-filled peace of the common room at the Kilns or the ivy-draped stones of Headington or the silver-birch-lined lane to Jack's house, a despondency swept over me that felt both complete and irreversible.

Joy:

Dear Jack,

It's misery. Renee and Bill sneak off to be together, while Bill tries to convince me to stay and raise a family, but also allow them to be happy in their love. How disgusting can one man be? I must get divorced. Can it be God's will? I don't understand how it could be his will that I stay, but . . . And the children. I don't know how to find what God wants of me—how does one ever truly know?

Jack:

Tearing apart what was meant to be "one" is brutal but sometimes required. I am with you, Joy, and hold you in prayer all the time. Here, Warnie is on the drink again and I believe he must go for treatment. It breaks my heart. Look at us, my friend, both devastated by the drinking of those we love.

Oh, dear Joy, how do we know what God wants of us? Imagine you are a house and he has come to rebuild you—yes, some things must be torn down and cast away. Faith, patience, and bravery, dear—more than you dreamed possible.

When an invitation for a MacDowell Colony reunion in New York City arrived in January, I clutched at it like food for the starving. The first thing I did was ring Belle.

"I'm coming to see you," I said. As my best friend, roommate at Hunter, and confidante through the years, Belle, so beautiful then, had been kind to her New York roommate with the sickly pale complexion, who walked around in a red hat and tried to reinvent herself all those years ago. I longed to see her.

When the train arrived, Belle waited for me inside the arched majesty of Grand Central Station. The painted constellations swayed above her wavy black hair, which was pinned in lovely victory rolls I could never achieve. Her smile was wide on her broad face. When I'd first met her in college, her beauty had caused me to withdraw. Comparison was the devil of self-esteem. But her friendship had thawed me. Now she stood there in her prim suit, buttoned tight around her tiny waist. As much as her high heels would allow she ran toward me and then threw her arms around me.

I held to her longer than she might have expected before stepping back to take her in after all this time. "I've missed you so much."

"I've only been a train ride away," she said with her Russian lilt, a trace that remained even though she'd moved to the United States as a child. While my parents had supported me in college, she'd sold books from a basement book division. She knew me during the heady days of sexual exploration and adolescent narcissism. She knew me when I'd married and had children. She knew me when I'd found God, or more aptly, he'd found me. There wasn't much she *didn't* know, and to have someone like her still in what felt like a tilted world was ballast holding me steady.

Together we'd once scribbled our notes and poems, poured our hearts out onto paper. She'd published her first poem about the same time that I had—hers had recounted her hungry, atrocious childhood in Russia. When my novel, *Anya*, was released, I'd wanted her approval more than almost any other. Later both Belle and I graduated with master's degrees from Columbia, believing that our life would overflow with literary honors, parties, and publications.

There in Grand Central we linked arms and headed into the city for lunch, chattering without pause until we sat down at a prim white tablecloth in a room full of chic businessmen drinking martinis and eyeing Belle. I ordered a sherry, and the waiter looked at me with raised eyebrows. Belle ordered a glass of white wine.

"Sherry?" She laughed. "Are you a true anglophile now?"

"I believe I am," I said. "Which doesn't quite match with being a housewife in upstate New York."

"You've never been a housewife," she said with deep laughter. "Even when you were, you weren't."

"Sadly, you're probably right," I said with a small sigh.

"Oh, Joy, tell me how you've been since you returned home. I loved your letters from England. They were full of happiness, adventure, and interesting people."

"I'm going back," I said.

"What?" She slipped off her coat to reveal a beautiful V-neck black wool dress hugging her breasts. Men passing by our table glanced and then glanced again.

The waiter arrived with my sherry in a beautiful cut-glass goblet, and I sniffed it with my eyes closed before taking a long gulp. The aroma took me to the Eastgate for my first meeting with Jack, to Magdalen's dining hall, to the Kilns common room and the sweet, soft feel of autumn in the golden air.

I opened my eyes and looked right at Belle. "I didn't know it until I just said it out loud. But it's true. I *am* going back. And I'm taking my boys with me and starting a new life."

"You can't."

"Yes, I can."

"Who are you, Joy? What is happening to you?"

I poured it all out to her, wine from burst skins, flowing over the table. I told her of Bill and Renee and the miserable pain in the house.

"This is a nightmare," she said. "Why doesn't he just move out with her? Why don't you just get a divorce?"

"We're stuck, Belle. Stuck. We have no money to get a divorce. They have no money to live somewhere else. I'm waiting to sell something, anything, and then get the hell out of there. My poor boys . . ."

"Can you take them away from Bill? He'll allow it?"

"I don't much care what he will or won't allow right now, Belle."

She nodded.

"I know I sound cruel, but I'm repulsed by him. For the sake of all that is true, he's trying to make himself into a magician now. He wrote a nonfiction book called *Monster Midway* about the carnival life, and now he's trying to be part of it. It's like living with a disgusting adolescent boy who wants to eat fire for a carny act. The hate is eating at me."

"What can I do?"

"I don't know. Sit here and drink with me?" I smiled at her. "Bill asked me, actually *asked me*, if I would just agree to be a threesome with Renee. A threesome!"

"Oh, that is horribly distasteful." Belle shuddered. "And meanwhile you've fallen in love with England."

"Yes, but not just the country—also the friends and the land and the Lewis brothers."

"Let's remember that I've seen you in love many times, Joy." She paused and leaned forward as if someone were eavesdropping on us. "Are you *in* love with C. S.?"

"No." I took another sip of sherry. "I'm confused. I miss them both as if I'd known them all my life, but it's more than that . . . About Jack, I don't know. This time it's not just about some physical need. For goodness' sake, the man smokes sixty cigarettes a day and then his pipe in between. He's seventeen years older than I am. But he still has this great gusto for life—for beer and debate and walking and deep friendship. Christianity most definitely has not turned him into a dud. This isn't some lust-fueled fantasy. It's the connection between us. The discourse. The empathy. The similar paths. This isn't an obsession with getting something, Belle. It's the feeling of finally coming home. It's confusing at best."

Belle leaned back in her chair, patted at her lipstick with a napkin before taking a sip of her wine. "I don't want you to make a huge mistake that will destroy your family for good."

"Destroy my family? As if that isn't already done?" Heat rushed into my cheeks, a fiery determination. "I know my past mistakes, Belle. Even in my marriage I see my mistakes. This isn't all about blame. And I'm not sleeping with Jack. I just love him, and his brother also, but in different ways. We feel like a family. It's a fact as inescapable as breathing."

"But that's what I mean. I'm not being cruel. You know I love you. But you fall in love passionately, and then you don't listen to reason."

"Does love have any reason?" Tears rose easily, and I almost longed for the days when I wept only with rage.

"No, it doesn't. But *you* do. Why would anyone leave New York?"

"Belle." I leaned forward with the urgency to make her understand. "My husband is sleeping with my cousin. He is 'in love.' He is 'more married' to her than he ever was to me, he says. For so long I've been required to subvert who I am to be who men want or need me to be, and in England, with those friends, that isn't true at all."

Belle's eyes filled with tears. "I wish I could have been there for you."

"You've always been right there with me. Always. Remember the night I won the Russell Loines Award? When a thousand dollars seemed like a million? It was this great triumph, and I was haughty because Robert Frost had won the same award several years earlier. I took you to the awards ceremony and got so deep into the cups I could barely speak at the microphone. You took care of me."

"I do remember," Belle laughed. "Of course I do."

"And you were there to help me celebrate when I came home from the inferno and infestation of Hollywood. You remained friends with me during the days of Communism, inviting me to your parties and your house. Remember when I got in a screaming match with your pal Kazin? You've seen the worst of me, Belle. And I'm trying to tell you that I'm the *best* of me when I'm with Jack."

A waitress with bright-red hair arrived, and after we'd both ordered the salmon, Belle rubbed her hands together and then folded them as if in prayer. "I want you to find peace without running away."

Fortitude rose in me. I glanced around the dining room and lowered my voice. "I'm not running away. I'm running *toward*. It's a quiet and intellectually stimulating life I want to make there. I know I sound irrational. But there is a life to be had in England, in London, and it's a life I want."

"Your sons?"

"They will be better off for it." I gave it one more try. "Belle, for some reason I've believed that I needed to withstand the infidelities and furies, that it was my job and duty as a wife. But that's not true. I have my faults, no doubt about that. But my faults do not mean I must stay and endure his."

"That's as solid a truth as I've ever heard you utter." Belle's curls bounced with her acquiescence.

I steered away from the subject and turned my attention to her life. "How is your writing?" I asked. "And how are Jonathan and Thea?"

"Oh, like yours, the kids take buckets of my time. But I'm still writing articles for *Esquire* and working on a novel about an English teacher in New York City. I've titled it *Up the Down Staircase*. Sounds exciting, right?" She rolled those beautiful eyes and laughed that beautiful laugh. "It will probably never see the light outside my writing room."

"Anything you write is enthralling. I still remember the pangs of envy when I read your poems in our dorm room."

She smiled and reached across the table for my hand. "I don't believe I'm the one who won the Yale Younger Poets prize or had my first book of poetry published at the age of twenty-two. I believe your envy is misplaced, my friend."

"None of that seems to matter now," I said. "Those things I thought would bring eternal happiness are dirt in my mouth." I looked away to see the waitress approaching and then placed my attention back to Belle. "How is your marriage, Belle? Tell me it is wonderful, so I can believe in real love."

"It *is* a good marriage." She picked up her fork and we began our lunch, filling the remainder of it with literary gossip, which she still heard in New York. *The Crucible* by Arthur Miller had opened on Broadway; Saul Bellow and Ray Bradbury had new books coming in the next months, and they were whispered to be the best they'd written. And Belle had become enamored with Halley's *Seven Years in Tibet*, reading it twice already.

When we polished off dessert—crème brûlée we split—we walked the streets of Manhattan, window shopping and pretending we could have whatever we put our gazes upon.

"I remember when I believed I'd be rich enough to buy anything I wanted," I said as we passed Bonwit Teller. "That our literary success would bring the world to our feet."

"Honestly, Joy, I don't even like writing nearly as much as you do."

I stopped and stared at her, bundling my coat closer. "I couldn't live without it."

"I don't believe I could either, but I also don't love it as you do. I live for the one moment when it works. It's like a high I search for again and again, and rarely find."

"Better than the kinds of highs my husband is after."

Belle squeezed my arm. "You always cover your hurt with jokes."

"I know," I said. "But it's better than dragging you into the lousy gutter with me."

On the corner of Fifty-Second and Park we sat on a bench, the icy wind whipping past us with the aroma of burned chestnuts and the cabs along Park Avenue honking incessantly.

"Has Mr. Lewis ever been in love?" Belle asked quietly, as if the question itself might hurt me.

"I don't know." I twisted to face her on the bench, lifting my hand to shield my eyes from the wind. "I haven't asked. He's never married. And I've read his views on sex, and they are *not* provincial. He's not a man who has been celibate all his life." I suppressed a smile. "And he hasn't always been a Christian, a man so devoted to his virtues."

"So why has he never married?"

In quiet tones I told Belle all about Mrs. Moore and Maureen.

"Do you think . . . ?" she asked, her question trailing off.

"I don't know. I do wonder." I sat back and tried *not* to imagine what Belle was intuiting. "Remember all those years we were obsessed with Freud's work and believed everything had to do with either our mother, our father, or sex?"

"Yes!"

"Well, if I had to guess, Mrs. Moore was a mother substitute for him as well as a promise he fulfilled. I haven't asked . . ." I cringed with the thought of it.

"You must ask!" she said with a laugh, and then she jumped up. "There's an empty taxi." She lifted her arm, waved, and whistled, and the yellow cab squealed to the curb. It was time for me to catch a cab to the Columbia Club for the MacDowell Colony party.

I hugged her, holding her tightly "I love you, Belle."

"I love you too, Joy. Be safe."

I climbed into the dingy back seat and waved good-bye to my best friend. I didn't know when I would see her again, but even her words would not keep me with Bill or in New York for very much longer.

CHAPTER 30

Sir, you may correct me with your rod.
I have loved you better than I loved my God

"SONNET X," JOY DAVIDMAN

In the following months in New York, I wrote as if sentences were blood, as if they would save me. I pressed out articles and short stories, anything to find enough money to leave. Yet none of my work sold. I poured out my life's hours for nothing.

In private, I emptied sonnets from my heart, missing England and Oxford and yes, Jack. Sometimes I wrote these poems to God, sometimes to myself, and sometimes to lost love. The old Underwood clacked so long and harsh I heard it in my dreams, as if even my sleeping self typed in vain.

If I had known all my life that some place like the Kilns and some men like Warnie and Jack existed, I would have been able to bear burdens with more ease. Surrounded by the ragged warmth of old furniture, stained rugs, and walls made of books, it was like living in a land of stories. I couldn't help but believe that I should have been there all along, that I was meant for it.

I gathered the memories like wool to keep me warm: Walking Shotover with Jack and Warnie. Listening to their childhood stories. Awaking to the English countryside beyond my window, the sunlight luxuriant even in the icy cold of winter. The miniature whitecaps on the lake during a wind, and the stark hibernating gardens of the Kilns.

The pubs. Eastgate, where we'd met and then gone numerous times

for a pint and a grouse. Ampleforth and Headington. The Bird and
Baby. The quiet evenings and the songbird mornings. The smoke-filled
common room and the chatter of men's low voices wandering down the
hallways of the rickety house.

In the first weeks after arriving home I checked the mailbox even
when I knew the mail had not yet been delivered, afraid that Jack would
never write me again, frightened that I'd delivered the final blow to
our friendship with my abject need when I left. Then a letter arrived,
and with it the ache of our misunderstanding at my departure slowly
dissolved.

Joy:

Dear Jack,
    Maybe this pain is punishment for the things I've done in my life.

Jack:

It is dangerous to assume that pain is penal. I do believe that all
pain is contrary to God's will. You must leave Bill, Joy. There is no
reason to stay with such misery.

Warnie:

We've had the flu here, but we are both working jolly hard on
our new books. How is your work on our little project? Is our Queen
Cinderella coming alive?

One night I stood in front of the mirror and attempted to see what
Jack must see: my brown (not blonde!) hair was beginning to thread
with gray; the lines on my face were etched deeper by the day. I leaned
closer and looked at the downward turn of my lips, the thin lines resis-
tant to all moisture creams, the extra fold on my eyelids, the half spider
web that seemed to be sewn overnight from the far corners of my eyes.
There was nothing to be done about any of this, what time took from

me, and despair again grasped my hope in its hand and squeezed it dry of life.

I sank to my desk, and in handwriting tight with heartbreak, poured out my sorrow into yet another sonnet.

You have such reasons for not loving me.

A knock came to my door; I closed my eyes, girding my heart to deal with another blow dealt by Bill's hammered words. But it was Renee who entered.

"Joy," she said, "I can't live this way anymore." She took one hesitant step forward. "My heart is breaking, and our shattered friendship has destroyed me."

"Can we stop this then?" I asked. "I want a divorce as badly as you do, Renee. Can we work together to bring this hell to an end? In the name of family and peace?"

"Yes." Her eyes were swollen with grief, and her pretty face contorted. "You don't love Bill anyway. You love someone else—I can tell. How can you be feeling hurt?"

I stood from my desk, and the pen clattered to the floor as an exclamation point. "How? My dear cookie, how could I not? First my mother loved you best, and pointed out to me all the ways you are dearer and sweeter and more beautiful and thinner and kinder. And then you come into my house so my husband can say the same in a kind of repeated nightmare? So I can hear what I already knew?"

"It's not like that, Joy."

"Yes, it is. I won't delude myself so that I can stay safe and be loved in inferior ways. Mother loved you best. Bill loves you best." I choked on the truth, feeling the burn of it in my throat. "You can have him, Renee. But I don't understand why you want him."

"Why are you grieving? If this is okay with you, and you can help me, I don't understand."

"My life is falling apart, Renee. There is no sorrow in that? Are there rules about what I can and cannot be sad about?" I removed my glasses and rubbed at my face. "Do you know what Bill told me?"

She stood silent, bit her bottom lip, waiting.

"Along with all the hurtful words you saw in his letters, and the verbal assaults on my character, he's now lectured me and told me that if I was really a Christian, a true one at that, that my charity and grace would be happy for both of you. He told me that I was preventing you two from enjoying this wonderful new love."

"I'm sorry, Joy. I'm sorry he said those terrible things to you, but you've said horrible things to him too."

"You defend him." I placed my glasses back. "Of course you do. You're in love. What about his asking me to be part of a threesome with you? To live here in a bizarre situation so he can keep his money? What do you think of that?"

A prick of blood appeared on her lip where she bit too hard. "I think it's Jack you mourn, not this life."

"It's more than that." I stepped closer to her. "Look at me, Renee. I am not Helen of Troy. I am just Helen Joy Gresham. I've never been celebrated for my beauty. If I'm pretty, it's a common kind, and now age creeps up on me, stealing what little I have left. What is there for a man to want or love? If there was anything at all in the beginning."

"Stop that nonsense, Joy. You *are* beautiful, and smart, and in your best moments kind and giving and funny. You drink from the cup of life with words and laughter wilder than that of anyone I know. Remember when you would drag me to the zoo and the lion would come to you? The lion—he came to you! That's how you are. Life comes for you, fast and roaring, and you take it all in. I'm not like that, Joy. I must take what little I can find and make the most of it."

"It's not about finding another man, Renee. It's not about anything at all but saving my sons and myself. In the long hours alone in London I saw the truth." I leaned forward. "Bill uses his authority to soothe his anxiety; he offloads his pain to feel better. And I took it all in because I desperately wanted to be the good wife and then, in the last years, a good Christian." I laughed, but the sound held no mirth. "As if I understand what that even means—but I know now what it doesn't mean: subjugating myself to abuse."

"I don't understand." Her face was a blank slate.

"He passes on his pain so he won't have to feel it or deal with it. It's his way, Renee. Be careful." I sank back into my chair and glanced at her trim beauty. "I'll find a way to get this divorce, and you'll both have the life you ask for. But I *am* taking my sons. I will never leave them with you again."

"Where will you go?"

"Back to England," I said.

"You can't take Bill's boys away . . ." Her voice trailed off, already knowing that this wasn't true. I could and would take them away from him.

"Yes, I can."

Jack:

Dear Joy,

We miss you here. If you could have seen Warnie negate Tollers at our meeting yesterday you would have roared with the laughter of approval. And you must see the garden where you advised Paxford on the flower bed—it is arriving in full fanfare. I am sorry for your troubles there. I hope you can find some peace soon. Please let us know if you plan to return—we'd like that very much. I am praying for you and I hope you are doing the same for us.

Joy:

I dream of long walks on the moors, of warm fires in the common room, and thick beers at the pub. I reminisce about the golden air and long walks, about Shotover Hill and its view of Oxfordshire. Here spring has brought the sloggy earth to life, and there is delight in that. My pears and apples, my vegetables and flowers have been born again. I've made jam and canned the beans. I miss everything there—including you and Warnie.

All my love,
Joy

On an early-spring morning in late March, I started for the garden to take note of the daffodil buds that were beginning to poke their shy faces from below the earth. If they had survived the winter, I could also, even *thrive* the same as their yellow-gold goodness.

"Joy." Renee's voice called to me as I reached the edge of the garden.

I turned to her. We'd found ways to avoid seeing each other in the house, but now she was calling for me. I stood still, waited for her to reach me.

"I came to tell you that I'm leaving." Her eyes and lips were set with determination. "A friend has given me a place to live in Miami. Bill will put Rosemary and Bobby in a boarding school near here, and then when I'm settled he will send the kids to me." She took in a long, deep breath. "I've told Bill I want him to join me."

"Okay, Renee." I nodded.

She waited, but I didn't know for what. I had nothing left to say to her, or to Bill. I saved all my best words for my work, for my children, for Jack and for Warnie, and for my prayers.

CHAPTER 31

My mirror says. A woman gets destroyed
In little ways, by the slow little years
"SONNET XII," JOY DAVIDMAN

"Joy!" Bill's voice called out from the top of the stairs only two weeks after Renee moved out. I came from the kitchen, wiping my hands on a dish towel, and glanced up. There he stood in a ridiculous get-up meant for a carnival—a pair of wide-leg pants and a shirt with flames of red paint leaping from his waist.

I shuddered. Renee was gone, and now he needed me.

But this is what it had come to: repulsion.

He descended the stairs and stood before me with a huge smile. "Poogle, I've had a revelation." He paused for effect. "We can fix this. Make a go of it. We can start over, now that it's just the four of us again. I've found a little work, and you're writing. Let's give it a try." He reached his arms out for me.

I stepped backward with such speed that I tripped over a basket, righting myself and looking at him with confusion. "No."

"We can do it. I know we can."

He tilted his head for me to follow him into the living room, where we sat facing each other on the threadbare couch. Topsy saw a chance to join us and get warm; he bounded up between us. I buried my hand in his dirty fur, the stench of skunk on my hands preferable to Bill's touch.

"Please, Joy. I can't stand for you to leave here and take our sons. I'll do anything you want as long as you stay here and don't take them from me."

"Love cannot be had or felt with willpower," I said. "Remember what you wrote to me?" I shook my head, feeling the low-grade ache in my temples that hadn't left in weeks. "If we had any money at all, you'd have been gone to Miami with your lover by now. I know that. And the boys are terrified of your rages anyway. No, Bill. I won't stay."

"They aren't scared of me." His face blanched, and for one moment I felt sad for him.

"Yes, they are, Bill. Maybe by taking them away they'll remember only the good things about you."

"Listen to me, Poogle. I've written to Renee. I've told her that I want to make a go of it here. We have a family. There is still enough love between us to make it work. I believe that."

"Love?" I scoffed. "No, Bill. There isn't any love left between us. And what about Renee? You made her a promise. Are you going to break that too?"

He shrugged. "Things change. That was back when I was neurotic and you were gone. How can you expect a dynamic personality like mine not to change his mind now and again?" He attempted a flirty look, a wink.

I shuddered in disgust. "Poor Renee."

Anger twitched beneath his muscles as I stood to leave.

"Do not walk away from me," he warned.

Enough damage had been done, and I wouldn't allow myself to listen to one more word of rebuke. It was all enough.

And yet, even as I left our living room and opened the front door to escape to the orchard, I could recognize one thing—Bill was the father of my boys. There was no room for reconciliation today, maybe not for many days to come. But the old pull to appease didn't die easily. It was only courage that carried me forward now.

Renee:

Dear Joy,

I am devastated by Bill's decision to stay there with you. I don't know what to do.

Joy:

Dear Renee,

Do not be sad, cookie-pie. We have both been played the fool. I did everything I could to make him go to you. Now there is nothing left for me to do but console you with the fact that I too have been his victim. Remember, most men are not as bad as he. I have a favor to ask of you. Will you please sign a piece of paper and admit to an affair so that I may file for divorce with cause?

The days dragged as I fought not to believe Bill's threats and insults. I knew by then I didn't have to stay and tolerate the abuse. I had a choice; there were other ways to live. And those were choices I would make, as difficult and awful as they might be. Maybe by the rules and laws of Leviticus, I was drowning in sin, but in the same way God was with me that night in my sons' nursery, he was with me in the agony—not fixing it but always near.

By April I'd gone to the lawyer and filed for a legal separation. On my way home I stopped for a checkup with our family doctor, Fritz Cohen.

I told him of our woes.

"I believe he's a psychopath, Joy." This is what the doctor who had known us for years told me.

"I think, Dr. Cohen, that he's merely a louse. But it doesn't matter; I just want my freedom."

The checkup showed me healthier than when I'd left, but still with low thyroid and aches the doctor claimed were middle age.

"Middle age is thirty-eight?" I asked with a sad smile.

He patted my leg. "Please take care of yourself, Joy. Your living situation is most likely adding to your ill health."

The time passed in slow motion, and I saved money. Bill eventually took a job that carried him out of town for most of the week—traveling with a PR firm as a press agent. When he was home he endured the days with sleeping pills and tantrums. His fits now ended in crying jags, and I often felt like I was taking care of an adolescent trying to decide what he wanted to be when he grew up.

In May and June, my two articles in *Presbyterian Life* came out back to back, while Chad Walsh advised me on what publisher might be best to bring out the entire series of articles as a book. I was close to having enough money for tickets across the sea.

Although I missed Jack and anticipated a reunion, the decision wasn't about him. I wasn't leaving *for* him, because there was no going *to* him. I was leaving for my soul and for the souls of my children.

Joy:

Dear Jack,

I have filed for separation. It's been a living hell and sometimes I believe I have ruined our lives. But courage will carry me forward now.

Jack:

You will get over this, Joy, for you are strong. You can't go on loving someone you don't respect. Do not think of yourself but of the boys. Do not believe that you've ruined your life. You are but a spring chicken at only thirty-three years. Life is ahead.

But ah, I was thirty-eight years old by that time. I didn't correct him. "Life is ahead," I said to Davy and Douglas when I told them of our impending move to England.

Life is ahead, I told myself.

Life is ahead, I mumbled inside my mind as Bill berated and blustered and bellowed and slammed doors.

By July Bill started traveling with a carnival. Without him in the house, my nerves calmed and I began to think straight again. I slowly shifted from terror to pity. Although he'd taken the car and I had to hitchhike into Poughkeepsie for errands, the peace we found without him in the house was worth being stranded.

I held Douglas and Davy close in those days, reading books at night, mainly the three Narnian chronicles already out, *The Wizard of Oz*, and *Charlotte's Web*. I tried to take them into the fantasy that might sustain them until our new life started.

When Bill came home for the weekends I made myself scarce.

One August afternoon while he was gone, together my sons and I hung the FOR SALE sign, nailing the black-and-white placard to a post.

"So that's that," I said, taking their hands in mine. We stood in a line staring at that sign as if it had grown from the earth.

"Do you think someone will buy it?" Davy asked.

"Of course they will," Douglas said, as if he were the older and wiser. "It's the best house."

"If it's the best, why are we leaving it?" Davy released my hand and pushed at his brother.

I squatted down and took Davy's face in my hands. "Because we are going to have a grand adventure in England. A brand-new life."

"I like *this* life," Davy said.

I'd run out of assurances and promises, so I took him in my arms and hugged as tightly as I could for as long as he let me.

Through the next weeks we watched as couples and families roamed through what had once been my dream. The farmhouse sold quickly, and the furniture with it. We owed so much in back taxes and mortgage payments that most of the money went straight to the treasury department.

It was a lovely couple who bought the house—Sara and Wade, and

I could never remember their last name. They roamed the grounds with their two young daughters and fell in love with all I had once fallen in love with: Crum Elbow Creek, the orchard and wild flowers, the plotted garden, and the front porch that seemed to offer lazy afternoons sipping a cold lemonade while the perfect family ran through the yard with glee. For me it had been real, even when it had become an illusion. Losing it hurt as any death would.

As movers and trucks came to dismantle my life piece by piece, I felt I was crumbling along with the rotten wood on the porch. But it was the piano that broke me open to tears. I hadn't played it in years, and yet when they came to load it, I sat on the bench before my Steinway and began to play Beethoven's Moonlight Sonata. My fingers remembered the score and fluttered over the keys, heartache thrust upon the ivory and ebony as the music came alive. My sons watched with clenched fists, as if they would fight someone to keep the instrument.

The movers, two large men sweating in the late-August heat, watched me too and didn't move.

"Ma'am," one said, "would you like us to leave this?"

"It can't be taken on a ship," I said. "It has to go."

"Mommy?" Davy came to sit next to me on the piano bench. He wiped my wet face with his small hand. "Don't cry. Remember that story you told us? The one about the man waiting in the forest? Think about that instead."

Oh, the wisdom of small children.

One sad night after the house had sold, I'd told them a story of two young children lost in the woods who stumbled upon the house of a shepherd—an ivy-covered cottage that very much resembled the Kilns, a pond that very much imitated their lake, and an old man who looked very much like Jack. It had been my way of telling my boys that yes, we were lost and scared, but we would find our way.

Now it was my son who comforted me with the same story.

As Jack had written to me, *the world holds a long sordid history of man searching for happiness in everything but God.*

No more would I do so—or at least that was my intent, an intent I would again and again forget and again and again remember. I gently closed the piano top and then stood. I turned my back to avoid seeing the men take my Steinway, and we set off to the creek. The boys fished for carp, and I picked apples from the orchard for the last time.

Joy:

Dear Jack and Warnie,

I have done it. The house is sold and we shall be in London come November.

Jack:

This is jolly news, the best I've heard in weeks. Between sinus infections and examinations and student demands, I have been fathoms deep. We shall see you soon. And as you know, if there is any kind of help that you need, Warnie and I are here for you.

In October my sons and I moved into a boarding house on the winter-whipped bay in New Rochelle, New York, where we shared a kitchen with other women, bided our time, and waited for our departure on November 13.

I prayed fervently, out loud, silently, all day. Whatever kinds of prayers there were, I prayed them. Begging. Repenting. All of them to carry us toward a new life. While my boys played on the sandy beach, foraging for shells and discovering sea life carcasses as treasure, I prepared for the journey. Bill had finally ceased fighting our leaving, exhausted in his own right as I was, and he promised that money would be waiting for us at Phyl's house.

It seemed impossible, but my entire life's belongings had been distilled to this—four trunks, three suitcases, and tickets to England on the SS *Britannic* for an eight-day journey to London.

PART IV

ENGLAND

November 1953–July 1960

ASLAN

"Safe?" said Mr. Beaver. "Don't you hear what
Mrs. Beaver tells you? Who said anything about
safe? 'Course he isn't safe. But he's good."

THE LION, THE WITCH AND THE WARDROBE, C. S. LEWIS

CHAPTER 32

I wish you were the woman, I the man;
I'd get you over your sweet shudderings

"SONNET XXXVII," JOY DAVIDMAN

November 1953

England embraced us with cold, foggy arms. Douglas had turned eight years old on the *Britannic* in the midst of a gale fierce and wild. He'd clung to me and wondered in dramatic fashion if we would make it to the port alive. Well, we did. Alive and bedraggled and quite nervous.

Life is ahead.

Whatever dreams or fantasies I'd formulated of our romantic arrival in England evaporated in the soggy air as Davy stood on the dock and declared, "I don't like it here. It's ugly and cold."

I'd arranged for us to stay at Avoco House Hotel, near Phyl and her son, Robyn, in the convenient London neighborhood I'd already come to know. When we arrived, Davy clung to me in fear and Douglas was wide-eyed with hesitant wonder. My sons hid behind me as we entered the boarding house, seeking tea and biscuits on our first morning.

"Mommy, I want to go home." Davy's voice cracked under the exhaustion and unfamiliarity.

"Davy." I cupped his chin in my hands as the clerk came to check us in and give us our key. "This is home."

"No," he said. "Our *real* home."

"Love, sometimes we ache for what is familiar even though there is something better out there for us. Just give London a chance."

"What about school and friends and Crum Elbow Creek?" His eyes overflowed with tears, and my own rose also. Would heartbreak ever end?

"We will find a new school and new friends. And wait until you see the pond behind Mr. Lewis's house. You know what he told me one time? That sometimes we want to stay and goof off in a mud pit when God has an entire seashore for us to play in. England is our new seashore."

I dangled the Kilns like bait for my little fishes, but I too was scared to death as I wondered what I had done.

Life is ahead.

That first week hit us all hard. We'd rushed straight from the hotel to Phyl's house to discover that Bill hadn't sent the money he'd promised. Because of the Aliens Order of 1920, I needed to register as a foreign national, which meant I couldn't job hunt until I heard from the government. In my mind I calculated and recalculated the money I had and how long it would last: *not long* was the answer. Had I been too impetuous? Had I left America too soon?

I shoved fear from my mind, stretched food as far as I could, and didn't let on that I was as terrified as I'd ever been. Was I as big a fool as Bill said I was? No. It had been change or die—and I'd decided there was too much to live for.

When I saw Jack the next month I could ask him for money, but I was loath to do so. I wanted so much from him, but none of it was material.

I filled our time, the boys and mine, with sight-seeing and a forced cheerfulness to try and help them adjust. We trounced through Westminster Abbey, and I remembered the atrocious afternoon when I'd gone there on my knees, repenting of my sins and wanting to go home and fix what remained. That had been only one year ago. As the boys trailed along behind me, I stared at the stained glass window where Jesus peered down at me. Silently I asked him, *Did I do right by all of us?*

No answer came.

Buckingham Palace with its statues and gardens fascinated both boys, and they stared at the Queen's Guard—soldiers in red with their furry black hats—motionless and statuesque.

"They're like the statues at the White Witch's castle," Douglas whispered.

"But not frozen," I countered and tugged on his earmuff hat to pull it down.

"They look frozen to me."

"But they aren't," I told him. "When their shift is over, they walk off just like you or me, to their homes and their families and their beer." I laughed, catching the sight of a soldier, and swore I saw the corner of his mouth move the tiniest bit toward a smile.

It was in Trafalgar Square that a pigeon landed on Douglas's shoulder, and he shrieked. We collapsed, laughing, and sat on the curb. The fountain in the middle of the square, larger than most swimming pools I'd ever seen, sprayed water, and Douglas asked if anyone ever jumped into it.

"Try it," I said.

"You first," he joshed in return.

Davy noticed the grand carved lions—four of them—on Nelson's Column. "Oh, look," he said, pointing to one. "Aslan."

"Nope. Just another lion. But I can tell you a secret I know about this one," I said. "The Nazis were going to take it back with them if they won the war. Lions are beloved that way."

"The war," Douglas said with a low voice. "It was really here."

"It really was," I told him. "It wasn't just something you read about in books."

It was later that day when Davy asked what must have been niggling at him. "What will we do about school? Don't we have to go? All we've done is play. Not that I mind very much." He was right—we'd been to the zoo and the museums, the aquarium and the parks.

"I've been thinking quite a lot about that, darling, and I think boarding school is what is best for you both. Here they call it public school."

"No, Mommy," Davy said. "I don't want to leave you again." He set his fists on his waist, looking like such a man in his buttoned jacket and furry hat.

I shifted his hat on his head. "It's not leaving me at all. You come home for all the holidays and all the summer. Any school I choose will only be a short train ride away. Tomorrow we're having lunch with a woman whose son went to one of the schools I'm looking at. Mrs. Travers." I ran my hand through Davy's hair, straightened his crooked glasses. "She wrote *Mary Poppins* and she has a son your same age, nine years old. I bet he can tell you how wonderful it all is."

He stopped moving and looked pointedly at me. "I won't think it's wonderful."

I kissed the top of his head, which seemed to be the only answer I had lately.

When we returned home that evening, worn-out and hungry, the innkeeper of Avoco House entered the kitchen. Mrs. Bagley had her hair wrapped in a bright-red handkerchief and her robe buttoned tight with a belt pulled into a knot that looked too strained to hold.

"Good afternoon, Mrs. Gresham," she said with her crinkled smile that had become familiar in a homey way.

"Good afternoon to you in return." I slipped off my coat and hat to smile at her as the boys and I sat at the small oak table for afternoon tea and biscuits.

Mrs. Bagley sat with us. Her double chin bobbled up and down with her smile and nod. Her warm brown eyes, set deeply in the folds of her eyelids, seemed to see right through me. "You must be very tired, my dears, from all the travel and adjustments."

"I can't even begin to tell you," I said and exhaled, relaxed. "But there's much to be done, and honestly, Mrs. Bagley, I don't believe I can afford to stay here at the inn for much longer."

"Tell me, dear, what is your situation?"

I paused in embarrassment, but then relinquished the truth to her kind eyes. "I'm going through a terrible divorce and can't yet lawfully

search for a job. Right now I'm a single mother without enough money."
I glanced at Douglas and Davy and didn't elaborate.

Mrs. Bagley's downcast eyes filled with understanding. "I have been
in your spot." She rubbed her face as if the memory itched. "Almost
thirty years ago I was alone with a young daughter and baby son. I'm
here to tell you that it was most awful, but we rose from those ashes and
were better for it." She punctuated her remarks with another firm nod.
"Listen, Mrs. Gresham, I have a townhome annex for twelve guineas a
month. Would you like to see if it is satisfactory for you?" She smiled at
Davy and Douglas, who moved closer to my side.

I calculated in my mind: that was thirty-six dollars. It was less than
what I paid now and a tad more than I could afford. But I could find a job.
Bill had finally sent sixty dollars, and if I stretched I could make it work.

"Yes," I said. "Please. I have searched, but no one wants to take in a
boarder with two young boys."

"I know," she said. "I do know."

The brief walk to the annex was cold and rainy, an omen I ignored.
But when Mrs. Bagley opened the doorway to the rooms, I was flooded
with relief. I remembered, with such remorse and melancholy, the first
time Bill and I had walked into our house in Staatsburg, chock-full
of dreams with our babies and our money and our optimism. But as I
walked through the front door of the Avoco House annex, my dreams
had tapered down to the most simple: peace, safety, and rest in God.

I walked through the front door and into the square living area with
high molded plaster ceilings, a room the same size as our living room
in Staatsburg. And it was furnished! There was a woman, short and
bundled in a coat, her hat pulled low over a weary face with a broad
smile, standing at the far end of the room. I startled and jumped back
before I ripped into laughter. I pointed. "I thought that was someone
in the house." The image pointed back at me from a floor-to-ceiling
built-in mirror surrounded by ornate trim.

Mrs. Bagley laughed also. "Yes, that has happened before."

"This is a beautiful duplex." I exhaled in relief.

"Well, let's show you around."

We walked to the far side of the room, and my attention shifted as my hand flew over my mouth, stifling my cry. "A grand piano."

"Yes," Mrs. Bagley said. "We can have it removed if you'd like."

I didn't answer but went straight to it, lifted its cover, and ran a quick scale, the out-of-tune instrument rising to life beneath my hands. "No," I said. "Please leave it here."

"We will have music," Davy said to Douglas, serious and sure.

Mrs. Bagley smiled. As we walked down the hall she told us, "It's heated by gas. No shoveling coal here."

"What a relief that will be," I said quietly.

"There is daily housekeeping from the inn with linens and bed making. Breakfast and lunch are across the street at the main, and you have a small kitchen, which you share with the other residents." She pointed to a door. "Down there—that's where the shared bathrooms are as well."

Off the side of the living room sat a small table and a counter with a gas ring for light cooking if I didn't want to venture to the kitchen. There were two bedrooms, one for the boys at the front of the house and mine in the back. Davy walked into their room first, running to the high bed and turning to me with laughter. "How does a boy get into this bed?"

"Why, I think he has to jump." I feigned a crouched position.

With a laugh, Davy jumped onto one of the wooden four-poster single beds with its cream bedspread and single pillow.

In one fell swoop, I imagined our life in that house. I saw the boys' clothes and books scattered around the bedroom with its high ceilings and windows facing out to the street. I heard the piano music and laughter. I saw us cuddled together reading and talking.

"This way to your room," Mrs. Bagley said.

Davy jumped from the bed and Douglas followed, down the hallway with its white paint and detailed moldings. I walked into a bedroom where a queen-size bed dominated the center of the room. A brass chandelier surrounded by an ornate and gilded medallion was lit by only one bulb; the other four were out. There was a dark wooden dresser with six drawers and a cracked mirror hanging over it. I imagined framed photos of our new little family, of London and Oxford, sitting on it along with my hairbrush and bottles of cosmetics. I was already living in the bedroom I hadn't yet moved into.

Back in the main room, I spied the French doors that opened to the backyard, or what might pass for a backyard but was merely a courtyard of dried and deadened plants. But that didn't matter. I knew how to plant a garden; I knew how to make it more than it appeared. I turned around to face Mrs. Bagley with tears puddling in my eyes. I reached to take a swipe, knocking my tortoiseshell glasses off my face and onto the floor. Davy picked them up and handed them to me.

"I don't know how to thank you," I said. "This is a home. And we three most desperately need a home."

She took both my hands and held them in hers. "You are welcome," she said. "I once needed the same, and we must all help one another."

The boys and I moved in the next morning. We unpacked our things and then settled into our bedrooms for naps. We all fell into a sleep so deep and dreamless it was as if we'd been waiting for it. When I awoke, the boys were still facedown in their clothes with the roar and honk of London traffic outside their windows.

I let them be and settled down at the tiny kitchen table, where I started a letter to Bill. I had agreed to rent this annex, but I also knew the facts: I didn't have enough money to make it if he didn't send money or I didn't make some myself. We'd made it this far: the house sold, the divorce moving forward, the ocean crossing with my boys, and now a place to live. One step and then another and then another.

I would be brave enough; I must.

Dear Bill,

You cannot do this to your boys. You must not deprive them of your money to punish me. I've decided that they must go to public school here . . .

I lifted my pen as a rustling came from the front room.

"Mommy?" Davy's voice called out.

As I jumped up, a shot of pain from my left hip sent me crashing into the table. I shook it off and ran to his voice.

"Yes, my dear?" I asked as I entered, the late-afternoon sun rushing into the room in the evening of foggy London, all muted and gray flannel.

"Where am I?" He sat in his little bed, rubbing at his face.

Douglas, in the bed next to him, stirred also and sat, looking around. "We're in our new room in London."

"Yes." Davy dropped back onto his pillow. "I just forgot."

I hopped onto Davy's bed. He snuggled into my softness. How had I left them for even a moment? The curdling conscience and anxiety I'd had last year had not been for missing Bill. It was for my children.

Douglas thumped down from his bed and wandered to the window, pulling aside the damask curtain to stare out at the streetscape. "Does it stay foggy all the time?"

The disappointment in his voice made my heart squeeze tight.

"No, darling. In fact, I only saw it once when I was here last time. When it clears, and spring arrives, you will think you are in a land of fairies. It is the most beautiful country in all the world."

"You can't know that," Douglas said and turned to me, dropping the curtain to fall back over the window.

"Oh yes, I can." I laughed and jumped from the bed to hug him close. "Just you wait and see."

"Mr. Lewis's house will be like that too," Davy said.

"Yes, yes, it will," I agreed.

Douglas walked toward us and rubbed his stomach. "I'm hungry."

"Well then, I have some mulligatawny soup. We can heat it on our new gas circle."

"I don't like that stuff," Davy said in a defiant voice. "I heard you tell Mrs. Bagley that we don't have money and you can't get a job yet. Do we have enough money for something else?"

"The money will come, Davy. We *will* find a way. We always find a way. God is with us; I know that."

"How can you know that?" His face tightened.

I closed my eyes; I reached inside for the calm, centered space—around the corner from my ego, bypassing my grasping need and fear, and then opened my eyes to look directly at my son. "I can't *know*, not like that. But I trust."

CHAPTER 33

Saying I must not love him any more;
But now at last I learn to disobey

"Sonnet VIII" (previously titled "Sonnet of
Misunderstandings"), Joy Davidman

December 17, 1953

The small courtyard at Avoco House was but a miniature and dirty
replacement for the gardens and land outside our Staatsburg house, but
it was better than concrete. That December morning my sons played a
game of their own making outside the open door while I packed for our
first outing to visit Jack. I placed sandwiches in a basket, a thermos of
hot tea, and blankets.

It had been a year since I'd seen Jack and Warnie; anticipation
swooped in my chest, down and under, up again. A year since I'd written the "Sonnet of Misunderstanding" on the RMS *Franconia* as I
returned to America—all about leaving Jack and what he must believe
about my feelings, how he seemed to send me away with an indirect
command not to love him in any other way but philia.

"Boys," I called out to the courtyard, "I'm getting dressed, and to catch
the train we must leave in an hour. Please don't destroy your outfits."

"Okay, Mommy." Davy didn't glance toward me at all but continued
in his invisible sword fight with Douglas.

My heart swelled. I was in London with my sons. Starting a new life was never easy, I reminded myself. There would be bumps along the way.

I'd decided on Dane Court school for the boys—only a half hour away by train, and it allowed parents to visit as much as possible. As soon as the boys settled there in January, I would find a job and start writing again. A life could and would be built.

My courage couldn't flag now.

"It's odd," I'd told Michal over drinks the previous night. "One would believe that being a Christian would keep me in my marriage, but it is the trust in God that allowed me to start a new life."

She'd laughed and shaken those soft curls. "Being a Christian isn't what most think it is—all rules and regulations." She clinked her glass with the red lipstick stain on the rim against mine. "It is all trust and surrender and transformation, at its best."

In my bedroom, three outfits were spread across my bed. The tweed dress with the cinched waist that showed off my best assets. The flannel trousers with a wool jacket and a white collar. And a gray wool skirt with a matching jacket. I shivered in the cold and snatched up the dress, packing the remaining two outfits in the valise.

I slipped on my girdle and rolled the parts of myself I wished I could hide into the thick fabric. I fastened my bra and slid the dress over my body, letting it fall around me, and then turned to the mirror. I added a blue chiffon scarf I'd splurged on during my last journey to England. What woman would Jack see now?

The three of us locked the doors, and soon we arrived at Paddington Station, each carrying our own bag and me one long box with a Christmas gift inside for Jack. Although we weren't staying Christmas Day, I wanted it to rest under his tree.

I held my sons' hands under the grotto of smog-stained steel and glass towering over us. Douglas leaned his head back to stare at the ceiling. "It's so dirty," he said.

I pointed up with my gloved hand. "If you squint away the smoke, you'll see it's beautiful. Look at the intricate scrollwork and arched windows."

The sun filtered through the Victorian filigree decorations and glinted against the metal and open iron in snowflake patterns onto the concrete floor. Men and women, children and crying babies in arms, swarmed like fish in a closed pond, moving in circles and vying for position.

Douglas straightened his head and stared at me but didn't reply, and even if he had it would have been drowned out by the tinny, high-pitched voice over the loudspeakers announcing train arrivals. Baggage trolleys wheeled by with frantic travelers while other passengers sat reading or chatting on the S-shaped benches as if they had all the time in the world. The police with their bright-red hats hovered over the crowd, eyeing everyone with suspicion. This was my new world.

"The 144 to Reading and Oxford, now on platform 6," a voice bellowed over the speakers, and together, a little bundle of three, we hustled across the concrete floor to the double-sided platform.

Our one and two halves third-class tickets in my hand, I shepherded the boys onto the train.

"I'm a half," Davy joked as I placed our suitcases on the leather luggage netting overhead. It didn't look strong enough to hold the bags.

I settled into a seat, the boys on either side of me, and Douglas took my hand.

"Mommy?" he asked in a quieter voice than usual.

"Yes?" I brushed his hair from his forehead.

"What if they don't like us?" he asked. "They don't have little boys, and they are so famous. And what if they don't want to talk about Lucy and Peter with me, and they get mad that we're there?"

The memory of Bill rose like bile in these moments, a raging ghost. My son had known years of ire, and he was expecting more of the same.

"The Lewis brothers aren't like that, Douglas," I reassured him. "They are kind men. And even if they didn't like us, which isn't possible because you are the most lovable boys in all the world, they would never be angry or mean. You'll see. Everything is different now."

He settled closer to me and folded his hand into mine, our fingers winding together, while Davy drew small circles on the window with his palm, as if he could wipe the outside fog away. In a moment Douglas was sound asleep as only young boys can be, completely and instantly. Davy dug into his pack until he retrieved his tattered copy of *Prince Caspian* and opened it to a random page.

"What part are you on?" I asked as the train chugged forward, hesitating and then picking up speed as we hurdled toward Oxford.

"Peter just challenged Miraz to fight." Davy placed his little finger on the page and looked to me. "Do you think Mr. Lewis just imagined them out of nothing or did he know someone like them?"

"Why don't you ask him about it? He'll tell you. He's kind that way."

I shifted to allow Douglas's head to fall onto my shoulder, and I watched the passing countryside fly by. The industrial scenes gave way to fields of heather with stone churches reaching for the foggy sky and villages huddled under the smoke of chimneys. When we stopped in Reading, I pointed out the Huntley and Palmer Biscuit Factory outside our window and explained that they would soon know exactly what those biscuits were, and for all their life they'd have their fill of them. The boys nodded lazily and fell back to sleep.

When the train finally drew near to Oxford, it halted with a shuddering grind and they both awoke.

"Where are we?" Douglas rubbed his eyes and pointed at a cemetery out the window.

"The train always stops at this cemetery for about ten minutes," I said to him. "I don't know why. No one seems to know why."

"Maybe the conductor's mommy is in there," Davy said very seriously.

"Maybe." I kissed the top of his sweet head.

Once in Oxford, we stepped onto the platform and blinked in the sunlight. It was a simple country train station compared to Paddington, and I adored it all the more. I straightened the boys' ties and smoothed their trousers, fiddled with their wool hats until they sat upright. We boarded the bus and rode on the top deck to the Green Road round-about, along High Street, and then out to Headington.

Rested now, the boys were rambunctious, wiggling and switching seats, gaining annoyed stares from other passengers. Finally we tumbled out together onto Green Road to walk to Netherwoods Road and then Kilns Lane—it was a path I knew well in both memory and dreams. The white birch trees and naked branches sang of winter, but as the Kilns appeared in front of us, it told of renewed life. The story I'd told of wandering in the woods, boys lost and finding a shepherd's warm cottage, was silently between us.

"Look," I said, kissing them on the cheeks, then wiping off the red lipstick marks I'd left on their faces. "We're here."

CHAPTER 34

My love, who does not love me but is kind,
Lately apologized for lack of love

"SONNET XX," JOY DAVIDMAN

We stood, a bedraggled group, in front of the Kilns, its thatched roof a russet-colored welcome mat rolled out for our return. Smoke curled from the chimney, as if imitating Jack's pipe. Ivy, even in winter, grew along the brick walls, and the front door, green and cheerful, was closed to us. But inside I knew what waited.

"I'm hungry, Mommy," Davy said. We'd eaten our sandwiches on the train.

"Mrs. Miller will cook us something warm and wonderful," I told them.

"Then why are we standing outside?" Douglas, always pragmatic, pulled at the hem of my sleeve and we moved forward, under the arbor and along the gravel walkway where stones crunched under our feet. As we reached the door, the boys lagged behind me, suddenly shy.

I rang the bell, the one that appeared in my dreams and placed that smile on my face, and waited. Mrs. Miller opened the door. Her stolid figure covered by her work dress and apron made her look all the part that she was: guardian of the house.

"Well, look who's finally returned." She bustled us inside, and the boys looked at her and then at me with expressions that seemed to ask if we had arrived at the wrong house.

The entryway felt warm and familiar, with its dark wood filigreed bench and coat hooks on the wall. Mrs. Miller took our coats and hung them on the hooks and informed us that she would chivvy along and prepare lunch.

"You're here!" Jack's voice bellowed from the back of the house, and then suddenly he stood before us.

His accent, easily forgotten in letters, returned to my heart. He smelled of pipe smoke and dusty books as he greeted me with a hug and then bent down to introduce himself to Davy and Douglas, not waiting for me to do the honors.

"Well, what do we have here? Two American boys in England. Welcome," he said.

Davy held out his hand and shook Jack's, but Douglas stared at him with an open mouth, dumbfounded. "You can't be Mr. C. S. Lewis," he said in a small voice.

"My boy." Jack stood straight with his hands on his waist. "You expected Aslan, perhaps, and for that I must apologize. I'm merely a short, balding man with tattered clothes."

I looked at Jack through Douglas's eyes and laughed: a bed-rumpled man wearing gray flannel trousers with worn holes at the knees. A wrinkled collared shirt once white, now almost gray, and house shoes bent at the heel from walking without slipping them all the way on. Small flecks of tobacco had fallen onto his collar, and his glasses were crooked on his face. For me, this was a man of such warmth and charisma, such light and tenderness . . . but to Douglas, this was not the man who could write of Aslan, of Edmund and the White Witch. This was . . . well, just a balding man with yellowed teeth and a bellowing voice.

Douglas moved behind me and pulled my skirt around him like a coat. He spoke from his hiding place. "Not Aslan, sir, but maybe . . . I don't know . . ."

"Oh, Jack," I said.

"It happens all the time," he said in his good-natured way. "I write a story to give them a fantasy, and then I ruin it all with reality. Come now," he said and leaned again down to Douglas. "Let's eat some lunch and then explore the woods. Who knows what we will find there."

"Mr. Beaver?" Douglas asked with a shy smile.

"You rebound well, son." Jack patted him on the head as if he'd had ten of his own sons and knew the language and warmth involved, and I loved him all the more.

Mrs. Miller moved about us, fluffing her skirts and talking of food and wanting to show us our rooms.

"Look there," Jack said to my boys. "You got her all in a kerfuffle."

We laughed, but the nervousness in the pit of my belly began again, rising in a delicious and devastating mixture of love and yearning.

———

After the boys had been shown around the house, Jack announced, "I must pick up some papers at school. How about your first outing to Magdalen?"

"But I want to see the pond and the forest," Douglas said with such petulance that I felt a hot blush rise in my cheeks.

"Oh, you will have plenty of that. We have four days ahead of us," Jack said. "But first things first."

"Because," I said with a deep voice and a terrible imitative British accent, "you can't get second things by putting them first."

Jack smiled. I'd quoted a line from one of his letters. A moment of understanding passed between us—we were okay. All was well. The closeness and intimacy returned as if I'd merely left that house a fortnight ago.

"Then let's go." Davy pulled at my coat.

Warnie joined us and greeted me, clasping both of my hands. "It's as if my sister has returned."

Soon the five of us were trampling the paths and sidewalks to Oxford. Jack with his worn flannel pants and overcoat, his old fisherman's hat low on his forehead. Warnie the same. With every step they poked the ground with walking sticks and then suddenly, every fourth or fifth step, swung the stick both up and back before letting it sweep onto the ground again. I wondered if they knew their own rhythm.

I heard Douglas's voice float over the air.

"Mommy said I could ask you something."

"What is it, son?" Jack's walking stick clicked against a rock and he stopped to face Douglas, just as I imagined he would a graduate student with his thesis.

"Is it true that your gardener is Puddleglum?"

Jack's laughter startled Douglas, and he jumped. "It is true only that I made Puddleglum very much like Paxford. But Paxford is just Paxford. Wonderful in his own way."

Warnie and I lagged behind and talked of his Sun King book, the help I'd given him with the appendix, and how much we had left to do.

"It must be the travel and the getting settled into a new life, but I'm exhausted," I said. "Look at them up there, practically running."

"You've been through so much, Joy. Be gentle."

I smiled at him, and we continued in amiable silence as if I'd never left, as if it were another day of many we'd been together. In my mind, London and Oxford pitted themselves against each other, the war-torn remnants of London still as yet unmended while Oxford's nature and hills shimmered in their wintry mix. We made our way toward Magdalen campus, and my heart hammered in my chest.

Davy and Douglas, red-faced and full of laughter, ran to my side.

"Mommy," Douglas said, and pointed to the sky and Magdalen tower as we drew closer to campus. "Mr. Lewis said we could climb the tower to the very top. You must go with us."

"Must I?"

"Yes, you must," Jack said.

Warnie stayed below, and the rest of us climbed a narrow staircase with marble stairs smooth as silk. We walked in a single line, and still the stone walls were close. Jack climbed ahead of me. I would only have to reach forward and touch his hairline at the back of his neck to know what his skin felt like on my fingertips. I couldn't stop the first thought, but I could stop the second, or whatever came next. And I did.

We reached the top, out of breath, only to find a little ladder that still must be climbed. Gingerly, step-by-step, up the ladder until we reached the top overlooking all of Oxford. Warnie stood below us on the lawn peering up with a smile.

"Hello down there," Davy called out.

Warnie couldn't hear, but waved as if trying to take flight. The boys then pointed outward at the expanse of grass rolling toward the river.

"What is that?" Douglas asked.

"The deer park," I told him.

"Deer park? Deer live in a park?" Davy placed his little hand over his brows to squint into the winter sun.

"Yes," Jack said. "They are fallow deer and will come right up to you."

Douglas nearly jumped a step closer to Jack. "They will come right to *me*?"

"Yes, they will."

"Let's go!" Douglas was already moving toward the ladder down.

"Let's stand here for a moment and look out," I said. "Make it worth the climb."

"Oh, Mommy," Douglas said, as if I were the child. "We can just climb right back."

Jack glanced at me, and together we laughed heartily. "Yes, Douglas, we can just climb right back," Jack said.

Yet off they ran, my sons, around the tower to view the campus from every angle: the river as it curved to give the illusion that one was standing between two rivers, Addison Walk and the scrolled iron gates. Puffs of cold breath came from the robed professors bustling through the grounds, as if from invisible cigarettes. My sons craned their necks to spy each stone gargoyle and angel that bolstered the grand buildings. The other colleges appeared as miniature countries, each with its own castle and tower. Far off in the distance, the Headington hills rose and undulated like waves in the sea we'd just recently crossed.

Jack and I were alone for the first time. "Your letters," I said. "They gave me both sustenance and courage."

"Yours do the same for me, Joy."

"From the very beginning; from the first one." He lowered his eyes. Such raw emotion always a thing he looked away from.

"Are you writing now?" Jack asked as the boys passed us for the fifth time.

"Between the move and the boys underfoot and finding a decent place to live in London, I haven't had much time for the writing itself," I said. "I was just talking to Warnie about helping him with the index for his Sun King. But first I must get the children settled."

"Dane Court, you decided?" Jack asked.

"Yes. I'm hoping to find enough money from Bill when I return to London in a few days. Thank you for your suggestions. I chose the school partly because it's the only one that doesn't whack the children. Not that I haven't whacked them a few times myself." I smiled with a tinge of regret.

Jack laughed as the boys whizzed past us one more time, this time grabbing at my coat to pull me toward the ladder. "The deer!" Davy said. "Let's go see the deer."

"I cannot imagine how anyone could become aggravated enough to whack these boys. They are full of beans."

"Exhausting, aren't they?" I asked.

His smile and a tip of his hat was his only reply.

Together we walked down the winding staircase, and instead of taking my breath, this time the stairs slaughtered my knees, but our voices continued in conversation.

"Joy, I have an education fund for children who can't afford the public schooling. The Agape Fund. If you're in a bind, I'm here to help." His voice echoed off the stone wall, rolling down the stairwell.

I stopped midstep and turned around to face to him. "That is generous and kind, but I'm not here to take your money."

"Joy, I have reserved it for children's education—it's already there.

You aren't taking anything that I haven't already given. It will be used for the same purpose, whether your sons use it or not."

I placed my hands over my heart. "Thank you, Jack. If Bill doesn't come through, that gives me tremendous peace of mind. But know I won't use it unless I must." I continued on down the stairwell, holding tightly to the rail.

We made it to the bottom and then to the deer park, where Jack opened the gate to let us all in. Warnie joined us again.

"Do you miss home?" he asked quietly as we watched the boys drawing close to a fawn with Jack.

"I don't." I pulled my hat lower and my coat closer around my body. "No. I don't miss New York at all."

"We're glad to have you here," Warnie said. "And your sons. They'll bring life to the house."

"The Kilns," I admitted, "feels more like home than anything in New York has for a long time."

"Well, Joy, it's ours to share with you."

"I hope they adapt well." I stared off, watching them run. "I took a chance bringing them here—it might not work. But it was one I had to take. I had to try."

"That's the best we can all do," Warnie said. "Try."

CHAPTER 35

To be rejected, O this worst of wounds.
Not for love of God, but love of blondes!

"SONNET XX," JOY DAVIDMAN

The sunrise had barely lit the trees when the boys were full of Mrs. Miller's sausage and eggs and bundled up, their ear-flapped fur caps drawn with tight strings beneath their chins. Off we went into the day, interrupting Jack's normal slow morning of Bible reading and correspondence. But his buoyancy belied any annoyance if he felt it at all.

Once deep into the forest, ice tinkling in the trees and crackling under our feet, Jack crouched down as if peering behind an oak tree, his jacket flapping in the wind and the faint smell of tobacco wafting toward me. "Keep a lookout for Mr. Tumnus," he said to Douglas.

"He isn't *here*," Douglas half whispered.

Davy plodded on, not seeming to want to be a part of the fantasy, still weighing the merits and deficits of England in his ten-year-old way.

"But how can we know they aren't here?" Jack asked Douglas, his hands resting on top of his walking stick.

"We can't know for sure." Douglas peered at the ground.

"And what about giants?" Jack asked in a low voice.

Douglas stopped and glanced upward as if expecting to see one as real and obdurate as the birch tree with its silver bark glistening in the winter frost.

"Giants can't hide, though," Douglas said, his words echoing in the winter quiet.

Jack pulled his old fisherman's hat lower and stated with authority, "Oh, Douglas, my boy. How could you know? You would only see his foot and you might think it a tree. If you don't pay attention, you might miss it." His laughter bellowed and off they went, the two of them on a hunt for magical creatures.

I saw the forest and pond, the guesthouse and the gardens, through my sons' eyes, and then through those of Jack, the storyteller. Yes, a White Witch might ride on her sled down the path leading to the pond. Tumnus might prance under this very snow-clad forest with his umbrella. And the pond, padded at the edges with tall grasses, could very well shroud a talking beaver. And of course Aslan could come plummeting through that forest, crashing his way toward the children or carrying them on his back to safety.

This man, with a mind as sharp as any I'd known, could become as childlike as my sons, imagining a world so intense and full of color and myth that it became more real than reality.

As we reached the pond, Douglas asked Jack how to cross it with the old punt, which bobbed against the rickety dock.

"You see that old stump sticking up in the middle?" Jack asked.

Douglas squinted against the sun, took two more steps to the edge of the pond, where thin ice cracked when a ripple moved against it. "Yes! I see it," he said.

"When it's warm, that is where I tie the punt and dive in. Swim to our hearts' content." Jack smiled as if he could already see the next sunny day when leaves would rest on top of the murky water and he would dive into its chilly depths.

"Let's go." Douglas took another step forward.

"Not now," I told him. "It's freezing, and if you fall in, I'm not the one to save you. I'll have to let you both sink to the very bottom of that muck."

"I'm so cold," Davy said and moved closer to me. "I want to go back to the house and play chess with Warnie."

"No!" Douglas cried, and I put my fingers to my lips.

"Shhh," I said. "You'll scare off Mr. Tumnus."

With that both Jack and Douglas burst into laughter.

I grasped Davy's hand. "Look. I'll take Davy back, and you two follow along when you're ready."

Davy and I began to walk back, skirting fallen branches and patches of ice. Far off a loud crash sounded. Davy looked skyward. "There's not really giants here, are there?"

"Only if you want there to be," I said.

"I don't want there to be." He drew closer, and his head banged against my ribs. "Mommy?"

"Yes, sweetie?"

"There's a really awful noise in the wall where me and Douglas sleep. What if the giant is in *there* instead of out here?"

"The giant, if there is one, is not in the walls."

"Well, there was a terrible banging."

"Maybe the sun bangs for you before it wakes." I tried to joke with my son, to lighten his somber mood.

"No, Mommy. That can't be true or I would have heard it before."

"I'm being silly, sweetie." I squeezed his hand. "I heard the same noise when I stayed in there. It's the water in the pipes. It's an old house, and they haven't done much to fix it."

"And it's very cold," Davy said. "Except by the fire."

"You don't like it here?" I asked.

"I *do* like it." Davy stopped before the green door and lifted his thumb to obey the sign PRESS.

"We can just go in," I said and opened the door.

Mrs. Miller must have heard us approaching because there she was, kerfuffling around us, taking our coats and brushing ice off Davy's cap. "I have tea for you," she said.

"Thank you so much, Mrs. Miller. I know that three extra guests right before the holidays is not something you much looked forward to. And two little boys to boot."

"It's lovely," she said in her thick brogue. "Absolutely luvvly-jubbly. The house seems to wake when you arrive, Mrs. Gresham."

I took this admission and let it warm all the cold doubt about my place in this new world.

———

That night, as Warnie taught Davy chess as promised, and Jack and I read by the fire, Douglas came bursting through the door carrying an armload of wood.

"I cut all of this with Paxford," he called out and dumped it on the hearth. "Mommy, there are real kilns. That is why this house is called 'the Kilns.' There is even an air raid shelter by the pond."

"I've seen it, Douglas. Isn't it marvelous? Except if you'd had to go there during the war, of course."

"Except that," he said and fell, covered in wood chippings, into a chair. It was only moments later that he fell asleep, all that energy expended, his mouth slack. He was as spent as were we. I imagined Jack and Warnie had not had this much activity since the war itself.

"Boys," I said, "it's time to hustle off to bed."

Davy groaned. "But I'm almost done winning."

"And that he is," Warnie said. "But you have saved me from the disaster of losing to a ten-year-old who has never played before. So off to bed with you."

I gently shook Douglas. "Bedtime, son."

He roused himself, and both boys stumbled to the back bedroom where they'd been sleeping with the framed steamships above their heads. They settled into their little room off the kitchen, warm water bottles tucked into the beds to stave off the cold. Piles of blankets covered their little bodies as I tucked them in.

"Nothing here is the same as home," Davy said as I kissed his cheek. "I don't like it like I thought I would."

"I'm here, and so is your brother. All will be well. It takes time, my love."

"I like it," Douglas said from the next bed. "But I wish we could just stay here at the Kilns with the pond and the big forest and the guest cottage full of little creatures and the garden and Paxford . . ."

I knelt at the bedside for nighttime prayer, closed my eyes, and told the truth. "Me too, son. Me too."

Four days passed too quickly. Paxford and Mrs. Miller took to the boys as if they'd known them all along. Warnie rang a gong for lunch (only he was allowed to ring the small treasure from his time in Hong Kong during World War I), and Mrs. Miller cooked for us. Paxford showed the boys all through the property, giving them jobs and teaching them about the land. While Davy looked to the stars and wanted to know every constellation, Douglas touched each plant and wanted to know its name. In their individual ways, they were both trying to find their place in the world.

On the last night I approached Jack in the common room. "I have a gift for you," I said.

"Oh, you do? Is it a ham?"

"The ham! I sent that all those years ago." I laughed and found myself in a coughing fit—the cold settling in my chest. I shook my head. "No, not a ham." I held up my finger. "Wait here, it's in my room."

I returned quickly with the long box I'd carried from London. "You can save it for Christmas under the tree or—"

"Open it now," he interrupted and ripped the top off the box.

And there it was—an antique Persian sword I'd found in a flea market in London the week before. He pulled it from its sheath, and it shimmered in the light of the fire.

"It reminded me of your stories, of the magic in them," I said.

"Joy. A shamshir—a magical sword from all fairy tales. It's exquisite. I shall hang it right above the fireplace, allow it to remind me of you, our friendship, and your boys fighting with their invisible swords."

He ran his hand across the top of the metal sword, and then his finger slipped ever so slightly. A thin line of blood appeared on his fore-finger as he withdrew his hand.

"Oh, Jack." I took his hand in mine and bent to kiss the wound, a quick and natural reaction to injury.

He withdrew quickly and with such deft sureness that my lips landed on nothing but air. He put his finger against the wool of his coat and laughed. "I'm such a clumsy bloke. It's no wonder they never let me play sports."

Red heat filled my chest. He turned to place the sword on the mantle, and the structure of his chin, the lines of his smile, caught the firelight. A line of poetry surged forward in my mind: *the accidental beauty of his face.*

I was dangerously close to allowing this love to become what it must not.

He set the sword on top of the fireplace mantle. "Thank you, Joy. Look at it up there, so stately."

Together we sat on the chairs and stared into the fire, the quiet stretching into sleepiness until I shifted in my seat. "I've been meaning to tell you about a book I just finished. It really *must* be your next."

"Tell me."

"I think I've told you of Arthur Clarke. He's one of the sci-fi boys in London. He's written a book titled *Childhood's End.* He's sold so many copies, hit the jackpot if you will."

"Jackpots aren't always the best things," he said. "But it will be my next read so we might talk about it." He leaned forward, his eyes catching the shadows of the fire. "It is jolly well one of my favorite things to do—talk about stories with you."

"And I, you." I glanced around the room. "Where has Warnie gone?"

"He fell asleep in his chair when you tucked the boys into bed. I helped him upstairs." Jack's voice held the anxiety and grief I knew well—that of loving another who is destroying himself with alcohol.

"I'm sorry, Jack. I know how you feel."

"Just when I believe he's kicked it, he hasn't. It's the war. It still lives in him, and he tries to quiet it. I'd rather not speak of it. But thank you for your sympathy. It's a hell of a thing."

I did reach for him then, across the space between us. I touched his skin, the small space between his shirt sleeve and wrist. I ran my finger down to the knuckles, a gentle trace, and then gave his hand a squeeze of sympathy. This time he didn't withdraw.

"You love Warnie deeply and with such devotion. If only everyone in the world had such love."

"He's my brother," Jack said, as if that answered all doubt. "When Mother died, I would have also if not for him."

I withdrew my hand from his wrist and settled back into the chair. "Jack, have you ever been in love?"

He laughed, and in his way scattered the question across the room like ash. "If I ever find the beautiful blonde I've been looking for all my life, I will let you know."

His joke, so like him to deflect, hurt no differently than if he'd taken down the sword from above the mantle and swiped it across my heart. But I tried to laugh. "I will keep my eyes out for you." I smiled.

"Of course I'm being cheeky, Joy."

"Your humor, Jack, you use it to hide your heart, an armor to keep anything from touching it. I know because I do the same."

He was silent for a long moment, and I wondered if I had crossed a boundary. When he spoke it was with his face set to the roaring fire. "Do you know the German word *sehnsucht*?" he asked.

"Yes," I answered. "The idea of an inconsolable longing for what we don't understand. You believe that longing is for God. Or heaven. And that we can confuse it with longing for someone or something else."

He leaned forward, and for a moment I thought he might touch me, but no. "This deep and abiding friendship means more to me than I can say."

"Yes." I bowed my head. "It means more than we can say."

———

The morning came bright and clear, the fog lifting for the first time since we'd arrived. By the time I appeared in the kitchen after a restless night's sleep, the boys had already gobbled down their breakfast and set off into the woods to say their farewells to the pond and the kilns and the forest itself. I dropped our packed bags by the front door. Jack sat at the wooden kitchen table still in his lounging clothes, a cigarette already lit. "You must eat before you leave," he said.

"I'm not hungry." I patted the packed bags. "I'll eat when I arrive back at Avoco so I don't get travel sick."

The boys then burst back into the kitchen, a whirling cyclone of my sons.

"Well, boys," Jack said. "I have something here you might enjoy."

They stopped dead still, bundled in their coats, and looked at him.

"What is it?" Douglas asked eagerly.

Davy adjusted his crooked glasses and leapt forward.

From the side table Jack produced typeset pages. "This is the newest Narnian book, set to come out this year. I've dedicated it to the both of you. It's called *The Horse and His Boy.*"

Davy removed his gloves and took the pages from Jack's hands and held them against his chest. "No one has read it yet?" he asked with wide eyes.

"Only my publisher, and your mother, who typed some of the pages for me. And I'll tell you a couple secrets about it, if you please."

"Yes!" Douglas's enthusiasm could not be bound. He, like his mother, could not hide what bubbled below the heart.

Jack lowered his voice and placed his hands on either side of his full mouth as if telling a grand secret. "I wrote it before *The Lion, the Witch and the Wardrobe* was released. The events happen before *The Silver Chair.*"

"What's it about?" Davy asked, looking down at the treasure he held in his hands.

Jack sat up and resumed his normal voice. "After the last chapter in *Wardrobe,* there is a battle in Narnia."

"What happens?" Davy's voice dropped.

"I won't tell you what happens, but I *will* tell you my favorite part."

"What is that?" Davy asked.

"The battle cry." Jack paused for great effect until the boys were straining forward. "Narnia and the North!" he said with great gusto and lifted his hand to the sky. "Narnia and the North!"

"Where home is," I said softly. "North."

"Yes, *true* home." His kind eyes held such a look that I would have believed it love if he had not told me otherwise in every possible way.

"Home?" Davy asked as if just remembering we didn't truly have one. "Where will we spend Christmas if we don't have a home? What about . . . Santa?"

I switched on my brightest voice. "Oh, Davy, we do have a home. Avoco House. We'll get a little tree and I'll cook turkey and Mrs. Bagley and some other friends are coming to eat with us. Jack." I turned to him. "This is too kind. Dedicating the book to them."

"I could not think of any two boys more worthy." He smiled at them.

"Early Merry Christmas," Warnie said as he entered the kitchen. I hugged him and breathed the stale whiskey and sweat, and that very aroma punched a hole in time: I thought of Bill coming home late, this same smell wafting through the house like evil. I released Warnie and stared at him, grounding myself in the present, in England, in Oxford, at the Kilns.

With lavish good-byes and promises to return, my sons and I strode with the new manuscript in the opposite direction of the Kilns.

Somehow I felt that we were a new kind of family. Who was to say there was only one way to love someone? I knew he loved us; words didn't have to be spoken. And this, for now, would be enough.

CHAPTER 36

And yet the horror is a woman still;
It grieves because it cannot stroke your hair

"Sonnet XXI," Joy Davidman

April 1954

My first spring in England was like the first day of being alive in the world, a deaf woman's first chord of Beethoven. Daffodils, tulips, and blue primroses the color of sky filled London in wild bursts. The anemones and bluebells and star-faced daisies were overwhelming in their intricate beauty. Like the Greek goddess of spring, Persephone, it arrived in a slow seduction. First the cherry trees, scattering their pink-white petals through the air like snow, then the currant bushes with their fiery blossoms. Gardens erupted with earth's desire to create a torrent of color and aroma.

It was now April, the boys were home from school for the holidays, and soon we would leave for the Kilns. I would again see Jack, his smile turned up at the corners, eyes crinkling under his spectacles, cigarette ash falling onto his lap.

I allowed the boys to sleep a little longer before I roused them for our journey to Oxford.

It had been late January when I'd dropped Davy and Douglas off at Waterloo Station with a tall, Adonis-like man they called a head-master. Other little boys in uniform, clean and buttoned, gathered like a herd of baby lambs around the man, who, in his bowtie and jacket, drew my sons to him as if he'd known them all along. This, I thought, was the exact right decision. Though the boys had said they didn't want to go, I could see the goodness in it. I would miss them, and yet I felt a sense of relief. They would be educated, well, and taken care of, and I could work again to provide for us.

January then birthed a winter so fierce and frigid that I'd given it a name—*Fimbulwinter*, after the great Norse winters that came right before the end of the world. I wrote like death was knocking at my door and my work could convince its dark specter to depart. It's not the best way to write—in a panic of poverty—but it was all the inspiration I had. In four months I'd finished a novel called *Britannia* and also written at least twenty-two short stories, which I sent to my agent at Brandt and Brandt.

Nothing sold.

I had also ripped away anything in *Smoke on the Mountain* that sounded "American" and then sent it off to the English publisher, who wanted it because Jack had agreed to write the foreword. In it he'd said, *For the Jewish fierceness, being here also modern and feminine, can be very quiet; the paw looked as if it were velveted, till we felt the scratch.*

Is this about my work or about me? I wondered, but didn't ask.

I even took out my mentions of Ingrid Bergman and Ginger Rogers, as the publisher was fearful they might sue me for using them as examples of breaking the Ten Commandments.

I worked on King Charles and tinkered with Queen Cinderella. From afar my life might appear not so much miserable as difficult; one might believe that my choice to leave America hadn't worked out very well. But non! No matter the dingy and damp basement job at European Press, where I used Dexedrine to keep myself awake, or the poverty, or the sleep deprivation, I felt I was becoming—in some way—my true self. As I told one of my sci-fi boys, "For such a long while there was a breach between the woman I mean to be and the woman I am, and now that gap is closing, slowly. It just ain't so pretty in the becoming."

Meanwhile, I'd taken Jack up on his offer to pay for the boys' schooling through his Agape Fund. I hated to take his money, and I'd been skipping lunches, making things stretch as far as I could, with the intention of paying him back—I had every intention of all my writing paying off. I also begged and nagged and pleaded with Bill for more money, but one could not squeeze water from a stone. He was out of work again, and I highly suspected he was back with Renee, although he wrote to me that it was only friendship. But this was the same man who had married me days after his first divorce was final, which ours was not yet. It was ekeing along as slowly as a snail in mud.

The month before I had awakened one morning to a man's face on the pillow next to mine: Harry Williams from the sci-fi crowd. His soft snore let me know he was still asleep. We'd flirted for a few weeks, and then one night when the whiskey and the thick beer had done their intoxicating job, we admitted that we both needed some love, and not the permanent kind or the I'll-take-care-of-you kind. Just the variety that warmed the last of winter's chill from our bodies.

It didn't last long, this brief, tepid affair, but it was enough to quench a rising hunger for touch and skin. It was only Jack I wanted to be near, but it was Harry with his jolly Cockney accent, deep belief in aliens on other planets, and large soft hands who slept next to me that morning and a scattering of others.

This was a sin. I wasn't a fool; I knew the commandments of my religion. I wrote about them. Still I fell. And repented. And fell again. Maybe I always would, but somehow grace felt big enough, sturdy enough as I stood again, resolute to do better. Meanwhile, I wrote my sonnets. I eased the pain and loneliness by forging sheaves of poetry no one would ever read.

My friendship with Jack and Warnie grew—we wrote back and forth as always, our conversations pausing and beginning again, making plans to meet in London or Oxford. On rare times we chatted on the crackling phone in the hallway.

My most pleasurable hours were either with the writing crowd on

Thursday nights or typing Jack's biography, both critiquing and editing as he'd asked. *Surprised by Joy*, it was titled. He was coming to depend on me with his work, but alas, the title had nothing to do with me! Slowly I ran my eyes over his handwriting, able to decipher even phrases he couldn't read after he'd written them from his inkwell.

During these hours of typing *Surprised by Joy*, my emotions swung wildly. His words, the means by which I had first come to love him, now told me of his childhood and life, and it only made me love him all the more. I read much of what he'd already told me: the pain of losing his mother when he was ten years old; the horrific boarding school; the war and its horrors. I also spied parts of our relationship in the telling of his story, or did I only see what I desired? Whether it was the description of his conversion sounding similar to mine, or the phrasing of a thought he'd voiced on our long walks through the moors, nettles stinging our ankles and laughter following us high into the hills.

And my sons—on Sundays I would worship at St. Peter's Anglican Church, where I had once been cleansed by the one o'clock bells, and then hop the train to visit them in Surrey. Those visits were the life-blood I needed to begin another week.

As spring arrived, the trees covered in milky mist as they moved toward green, I walked for miles and miles through London. I sat in Primrose Park with a notebook and ball pen overlooking Hampstead and Belsize. I spread an inexpensive orange blanket I'd found in the market on the thick grass to write and revel in earth's rebirth: the May trees, the roses everywhere, the rhododendron and elder trees competing in a beauty contest. It was there that I plotted *Queen Cinderella* with Warnie's outline as a guide. I felt like she could be a real moneymaker, something to free me from begging Bill for money or depending on Jack for the boys' education.

I also planted a small garden behind our Avoco House room, and by April the vegetables were just beginning to sprout from the ground. Sometimes I would imagine a green bean or tomato busting forth and be taken back in a rush to my garden on Staatsburg. But by then another family lived there, other children ran through its acreage and splashed in its creek. I hoped they were happier than we'd been.

Do you miss it? Jack had asked in a letter a few weeks before.

I felt inside myself, poked around for the answer. *No,* I'd written. *I mourn what it could have been. I feel sad for what I wanted it to be but it never was. Maybe I miss the idea of what I wanted for all of us. But no, I don't miss what was.*

Never had a man been such an integral part of my life without also being in my bed. It was taking some getting used to, and included some heartache to boot.

But on this April morning, instead of typing more of Jack's biography or forging another sonnet (now numbering more than thirty), I took the quiet time to mend my boys' frayed clothes and sew name tags on their new shirts and pants. My little calico cat, Sambo, curled in my lap, and I worked around his soft, purring body.

The boys awoke without my prodding, and soon they came running into the hallway, their traveling clothes buttoned and ready. Sambo flew from my lap, and Davy tripped, landing flat on his bottom. Douglas roared with laughter, staying on his feet with a deft move.

"Stupid cat," Davy screamed, and Sambo was off, hiding beneath the couch.

"I'm ready, Mommy," Douglas said, and his voice contained the tiniest hint of an English accent, the *mommy* sounding a bit like *mummy*.

"Douglas, my poogle. You're starting to sound like a proper English boy," I said.

"I'm practicing," he said. "American accents can get you beat up, you see. Other boys can go barmy with it."

"Barmy?" My voice held restrained laughter.

"It means crazy."

"I know what it means, Douglas. It sounds quite proper coming from you. I like it." I placed my forefinger on his chin and tilted his face to mine. "Are you getting beat up?"

"No, Mommy." He glared at Davy. "And neither is Davy."

Davy stood by quietly, back on his feet with an angry look.

"Are you sure?"

"Yes." Douglas stood taller.

"Well then, are you both ready to go to the Kilns?" I asked.

"Very," Douglas said. "I wish we could just live there. Let Mr. Lewis teach us instead of going back to that school."

Davy poked at Douglas with a closed fist against his arm. "It ain't so bad." He glared at his brother.

Douglas beamed then. "I'm going to help Paxford plant some fir trees and new green bean stalks."

"Then we best be going to Paddington Station," I said.

We arrived at the welcoming green door and pressed the same thumb latch to be greeted by the same Mrs. Miller. The same bellowing voices came as Jack and Warnie arrived in the back hallway.

Without the need of coats and bundling, we were off into the spring-time land of the Kilns before our suitcases were even unpacked. The boys ran into the woods and out of sight, leaving me to stand in the newly sprouted garden with Jack and Warnie. I touched the very tip of a tomato plant, its tiny frond just sprouting from the earth. "The earth is waking up."

Warnie laughed and dug his foot deeper into the damp soil as if planting himself. "I think Paxford is trying to show off for you. On your last visit you gave him advice and now he wants to prove that his garden is worthy."

"Worthy? Cat's whiskers indeed. This land could go without a man to tend it. What rich soil." I bent down and scooped a handful into my palm, allowed the dirt to run through my fingers. Looking up, I approached the next subject gingerly, with care.

"Jack, when you describe joy in your biography, I realize that some-times I can't feel that emotion, as if it's left me for good. But right now, with the garden just about to burst wide open, and the boys laugh-ing out there in the woods, hearing them and knowing they're here, I believe I feel it again."

Warnie let out a sound very close to a sigh. "Jack's first taste of joy was in a little garden."

Jack nodded, and he too bent down and picked up a handful of dirt, cupped his other hand overtop and shook it before releasing it to the ground. "Yes," he said. "Have you come to that part yet? When I was sick as a child and couldn't leave the bed, Warnie went outside and made me a little box, a little fairy garden as it were. Inside a biscuit tin he set twigs and moss, tiny flowers and grass, even pebbles. It was a veritable world as small as a hand. And I felt it, the simplest *joy*. It was a mystical quality, and I've spent most of my life looking for it ever since." He smiled. "It is a feeling that jumps up under one's ribs."

"And here you have it," I said. "Joy." I pointed at myself in jest; a great smile spread across my face.

"Yes, indeed we do." Jack released that laughter I loved.

"But honestly," I said, "the way you describe it is palpable. It's a word that barely has a description, but you find a way—how it is a reminder."

"And isn't it odd," Warnie said and slapped his walking stick to the ground, "how he states that misery feels much the same as joy at first feels?"

I nodded.

"Quite," was all Jack said. He seemed embarrassed that we talked of his work as he stood there. He fell silent and ambled a few feet ahead of us, swinging his walking stick. We traipsed along the soggy path toward the pond, where the boys' cheers echoed. The air smelled of lost rain and fetid earth, of green and of birth. I inhaled deeply.

When I drew closer to Jack he looked from the ground to my eyes. "And what have you thought of it so far?"

I touched his coat sleeve and smiled at him. "When I type your words and read your work, I know this: our experience is alike, from the surprising mystical quality of nature to open our hearts to the reluctant conversion. How could I have anything but wonderful things to report?"

He nodded.

"And I think you're right about the misery," I said. "There's a certain pleasure in the acuteness of that agony, in the piercing of the heart. It's not the same as joy, but isn't it?" I paused. "As you wrote, 'joy is different than happiness or pleasure and it is never in our power.'"

"'Surprised by joy—impatient as the wind,'" he said, quoting Wordsworth, the poem from which he took his title.

I replied in same. "'I turned to share the transport, Oh! With whom but thee.'"

"Indeed," he said quietly and then took me in with his gaze, steady and still. "Nothing is ever wasted on you, is it? I believe more than anyone I know, you are enchanted by this world and its sentiments."

I couldn't respond to this compliment, to the vision he had of the woman I was and always had been. Had anyone ever known me so well? I allowed the intimacy to linger between us for a moment before I drew a breath and kept on. "If people are expecting you to reveal secrets of your life in this biography, they're going to be disappointed."

"It's meant to be a story of conversion, not a tell-all," he said.

"Of course. You aren't quite the tell-all type." I tipped my imaginary hat to him with a laugh. "To me it feels like the story of a conversion that is ever unfolding, as if you could write this book for all your life. But there is something I want to ask you," I said quietly, so Warnie would not hear.

"Yes?"

"I see parts of *us* in your work, pieces of our relationship and our discussions." I swallowed. "Is this true?"

"Of course it's true. How could you not be part of it? But if anything has crossed the line, you must point it out, because nothing would be said or done without your permission, or if plagiarized."

"No, Jack! Nothing like that. But when you describe your conversion, for example, the way it sneaked up on you, the 'reluctant' conversion, it's like my essay."

He shook his head. "Your description rang the same bell as mine."

I didn't feel he was stealing my words, and I didn't want him to think so either—he'd started this book long before he met me. I wanted him to see that we'd landed on the same shoreline after two disparate shipwrecks, that our love wasn't merely intellectual, but also spiritual—I pointed at our inevitability.

We reached the pond's edge, and Douglas ran to Jack. "Mr. Lewis, can we go out in the canoe?" He pointed to the red punt sinking into the new-soft spring earth. "Please? It was too cold last time."

"Of course you may, son, but don't go scaring my two ducks. They aren't used to such exuberance. They're accustomed to two old men piddling about."

"Old men?" I said. "Ha!"

Jack bent over to help my sons drag the punt from the mud with a great sucking noise. With effort, and merry laughter, they launched from the dock with a paddle. The boat shimmied and rocked and then settled on the lake, ripples radiating outward, a circle of misplaced water that reached the shore's edge to dance with the tall grass.

We stood watching until Jack roared out to the boys, "Narnia and the North!"

"Narnia and the North," they cried in unison, raising their fists as they paddled to the far edge of the pond.

Jack then turned to me with such a serious expression I at once thought something wrong. "I would like to talk to you about something, Joy."

"Anything. What is it?"

"Warnie," he said and turned to his brother, "would you mind very much making sure those young chaps don't drown while I return to the house with Joy? I'd like to ask her opinion on Cambridge."

"I believe it is a task I am fit for," Warnie said and smiled.

Settled into the common room at the Scrabble table, Jack took his lovely time tamping tobacco into his pipe and lighting it with a match. Then he looked to me, smoke curling from his lips, the sweet aroma of the rich tobacco filling my senses.

"Joy, I've been offered a job at Cambridge and I've turned it down, but now I'm having my doubts. I've talked to Tollers and wondered if you too would delve into the problem with me."

"Problem?" I asked. "Aren't you honored?"

"Of course. It's Cambridge." He drew on his pipe. "And they've created a position just for me. Professorship of Medieval and Renaissance Studies."

"Oh, Jack. That's simply wonderful." I leaned my elbows on the table, avoiding the tiles, and told him, "When I first visited it last year, I wrote to Bill and told him how much I loved it, how it is more compact and harmonious than Oxford, more Old World. But that I love the architecture better in Oxford. It's a glorious city, Jack."

He was silent as he set a word on the Scrabble board between us, as if it helped him think. He was beating me. I then placed my four tiles, the *z* on a triple score—*zeal*. "Looks like the game isn't quite as over as I thought," I said.

His laughter caused him to sputter smoke. "Do you mean my career or this game?"

"Both," I said. "Tell me everything. This offer must feel like redemption after Oxford's pass-over."

"It does, but here's my concern: how could I leave here, Joy?" He spread his hands across the room. "I've been at Oxford for thirty-five years."

I nodded. "Yes, that's a long time. A little less than a lifetime for me. But maybe change is good. And Cambridge is only a couple hours away; it's not another country."

"It's Magdalene College there also. Only one letter difference."

"Interesting. Would you stay here? Move? What does it all mean?"

"I could not leave Warnie. Or this home."

I took four more tiles from the pile, placed them on my rack but didn't look at them. "There must be a way," I said. "If they want you that much, enough that they created a position just for you, then they will help you find a way to live here and work there."

"Yes, they will." He took a puff of his pipe and closed his eyes. "But maybe I'm too old to make a change."

In this statement I heard his reticence of all things new, of all things that might unsettle his peace and quiet. He had built a safe life, and anything that rippled it as the punt had just done to his pond was to be avoided.

"Jack, forgive me for my impudence, for possibly offending you with my analysis of this, but I love you, you know that. And I can see parts of your heart that others can't, that sometimes you can't either. Your fear of change is palpable. You hide all the turmoil and pain of your past life inside of you: the loss of your mother; whatever happened in the war; the boarding schools. And Paddy and Mrs. Moore. And now here you are, at peace in your Garden of Eden with your brother and your acreage and your students and your Inklings and your friends and your quaint town. All these things both inspire and protect you. But a change might be in order. Not a change that disrupts, but one that expands." I paused. "Let new things touch your soul."

He stared at me for too long, so long that I believed I had overstepped. But he blinked once before stating, "You're right. And Tollers said much the same—that I could use a change of air. He believes Oxford has not treated me well. And the new job is three times the pay with half the work. But the problem is that I've turned it down twice now with very eloquent letters." He shook his head. "Or I believed them eloquent. It would seem absurd, would it not, to tell them that I would now reconsider?"

"Jack, they created the position for you! Why would it be absurd to change your mind? Sometimes we have to mull things over, pray about them, talk about them, and then our eyes are opened to the best path."

"And perhaps they'll allow me to live there only four days a week so I can be here as much as possible."

"You know how to work and sleep in trains. This job is made for you."

"You know what tells me I should go?" He paused and smiled. "I have already begun lectures in my mind."

"Then let us go from imagination to reality," I said.

"Yes, I think you're right." He nodded at me. "I shall write to the vice chancellor today and tell him I'd like the job, if it's not too late." Then he placed his tiles, forming the word *mischief*.

I shook my head. "How will I ever win again?"

Jack set down his pipe on the edge of the table and leaned forward. "Thank you, Joy. I always feel clearer and invigorated after talking things through with you."

Joy, that elusive concept that Jack coveted, enough to make it the title of his biography, washed over me for a blessed moment. It was as he'd written in his very first chapter, *It is not happiness but momentary joy that glorifies the past.*

If ever I would glorify this day, and I knew I would, it would be that moment where he asked me to sit with him to discover what next to do with his life.

CHAPTER 37

The monstrous glaciers of your innocence
Are more than I can climb

"SONNET XXXVI," JOY DAVIDMAN

Along with my divorce decree that had arrived from Bill's attorney across the pond, summer arrived with rains so unceasing that London announced 1954 as the wettest summer in almost fifty years. The earth was soaked and spongy beneath my feet, the flowers outrageous in their glory, raindrops settling in the cups of their raised faces. It was cold too. I was still wearing my wool socks and sweater when Jack came to visit me at the Avoco House that June afternoon.

This had been happening for months now, ever since our last visit when we discussed Cambridge—Jack now came to London for no other reason but to see me. Surely he fabricated other reasons, but they were only excuses. We'd pore over the pages of his biography and spread the papers across my little desk, rework and rearrange. We'd walk to the pub for a drink or stroll into Blackwell's Bookshop to wander aimless and content. Any second I half expected him to reach over and touch me, pull me close. But it never happened, consistently leaving me expectant and yearning, and mostly confused.

What was happening was happening to us both—we missed the other when we were gone from each other. More and more I wanted and sometimes needed to show or tell him what I'd perceived or accomplished in that moment or during that day. I wanted, as did he, to share every moment and thought. Did this describe love? And if so, what kind?

"Do you believe love fits neatly into your categories?" I'd asked during a wild thunderstorm while we huddled in the shared kitchen and I cooked mutton and vegetable soup.

"Fits neatly?" He shook his head and leaned casually against the counter, sloughing off his jacket to toss it over a kitchen chair. "I don't believe anything fits neatly into anything, but we must at least try, or what else is language for?"

It was true—we had to try, but I very well knew that our love was a fog or wind that could be more felt than seen, slipping in and out of the cracks of Jack's Greek-word categories. There was no pinning it down, and if I forced him to define it, or us, I was afraid I would lose the magic altogether. I reveled in the unfolding, and I kept guard as well I could over my own heart, watching carefully for the interlopers of fantasy, for the thieves of obsession and possession.

That afternoon the weather had lifted and we sat in my tiny garden, the tulips I'd planted months before bent and subdued by the morning rain. I'd wiped off the two metal garden chairs with a kitchen towel, and we sat with tea.

"To be outside again," I said. "It might be the cure for all ills."

"Quite possibly." Jack pointed to a folded rectangle of paper in my hand. "Is that for me?"

"Well, it's not *for* you, but I want you to read it."

"Ah, I thought it more corrections to my work. I'm not sure I could stand much more of them."

"Cat's whiskers, Jack, I don't correct but improve. Part of me is worried that I was meant to be your Max Perkins instead of an author myself."

"Foolishness," he said and held out his hand. "A poem?" He took the folded paper from me.

A quick-flash image of offering him my sonnets set me back; my breath caught in my chest.

"No," I said. "It's far from a poem, but maybe a grand piece of fiction."

Jack opened the folded paper, which had arrived days before from Miami—where Bill had moved to be with Renee—to Belsize Park, London. It's one thing to know of one's divorce—agreed upon with full custody for me and visitation for him, along with sixty dollars a week in alimony and child support—and another to see a sheet of paper that reads *vinculo matrimonii* (dissolved marriage). Bill and I had written to each other, agreed upon the terms, and yet the accusations inside the decree were disgusting and heartbreaking. I hadn't expected them, and all the more it socked me in the gut.

Jack read slowly, adjusting his spectacles, and once in a bit his eyebrows rose above his glasses. Every line or two he would burst out with a sentence.

"'The plaintiff alleges the defendant has been engaged in literary efforts and has a desire to be an author or writer and is overwhelmingly ambitious and desirous of furthering herself in this field.'" He seemed to spit the words, Bill's words, into the air. "Is he writing a complaint or spewing envy? Hogwash."

He continued reading, and then his head lifted with moist eyes. "Joy, this is rubbish." He glanced down again to read out loud. "'She continually and continuously indulges in alleged excitable and ungovernable displays of temperament and apparently lives in an artistic dream world.'"

"Yes," I said and sipped my tea. "I obviously live in an artistic dream world as I raise our children, write, and work." I pointed at the paper. "It gets worse, if you can believe it."

"I don't know if it can." His eyes shifted down to the paper.

While Jack read my divorce decree, I watched two red robins settle on my bird feeder and peck away at the seeds.

"And then there's this." Jack's free hand slapped the edge of the chair. "'The defendant feels that her artistic career is much more important than her domestic career, life, and duty to her husband and family.'" His hand was so tight on the document it began to crumple beneath his fingers. "How did you live with this? It is degrading."

"Yes, it is and it was. But I'm here now, Jack. Right here."

His cheeks grew redder, his mouth tighter. "Joy. He states here that he begged you to live happily with him and the children but that you refused to do so."

"Well then, there it is," I said, lifting my teacup. "Now who lives in a dream world?"

"This is such drivel and so smarmy. All wind and piss."

I leaned forward, my hands on my knees. "I should have done the filing, and then I could have lodged *my* complaints. But I know he's missing his sons, and I'm sure he's lashing out at me." I exhaled and felt the tension twist below my belly. "I don't think I can trust his child support and alimony unless I hire my own lawyer to ensure he makes good on it."

"Then you must." Jack lifted his teacup, a dainty flowered one I'd found at the flea market, but he didn't take a sip before setting it back down. A swallow spun above him as if circling in curiosity and then flew off.

"And these accusations," I said. "It's all because I was once such a submissive and acquiescing wife." I tapped my finger on the divorce decree. "He doesn't think I have it in me to fight, or he's forgotten. But I won't buckle under his rhetoric. I've done it for far too long. I feel as if I've jumped into a time machine and I'm back there, and Bill is drunk and the boys are cowering. I feel myself shriveling and scared, nervous and hopeless. I never want to feel that way again."

"You shan't," he said and almost, God help me, almost took my hand. But he didn't. He leaned back and lit his cigarette, a motion so familiar. "You have the strength, Joy. You always have. I don't know anyone stronger." His words carried such force that I believed him. He folded the divorce decree and handed it back to me. "As I said, rubbish."

"Yes," I said. "But freedom . . . a blessed release."

"Freedom," he echoed, and beamed at me as if we'd just decided to jump into the pond on the first day of spring, a mischievous look. "Think of your new life, Joy. Courage has brought you to a new place."

"My sons and me."

"Speaking of your sons, talk to me about Davy and Douglas. How was your visit to Surrey yesterday?"

A new energy rushed through me. "Simply wonderful," I said. "I saw them play cricket and I met some more of their teachers. Davy is getting personal tutoring in math. It's honestly more than I could have hoped for. Someday I'll pay you back."

Jack stood and held out his hand to lift me to stand. "Let's take a walk. A slow bimble to the park? It's finally warming."

I allowed him to pull me to stand, and then he released my hand. The dull ache in my left hip sent me to quickly sit again. It was one of my favorite things to do—walk with him, ambling slowly through gardens, but I couldn't. "Jack, I'm so sorry. My hips are acting up again. I have no idea why. Rheumatism, they say. I'm hoping it will clear whenever the everlasting rain leaves us."

"There is no need for apology." He smiled. "It's nice to sit still for a while."

"I'll make us more tea and bring out the stories we started to read yesterday."

"No need for stories today, Joy. If we want to read some jolly good fiction we could just reread the divorce decree." He laughed that hearty laugh and patted his breast before removing his pipe.

I laughed in return so fully that we both bent forward to clasp our knees, leaning toward each other face-to-face. It was there we paused, close, only inches. It would only take one of us to close the gap, and finally our lips would touch. But for now, it was only our smiles that met across the inches of space between us.

How, I wondered, does one make oneself *not* fall in love? Not destroy the most sublime philia?

As usual, I didn't have the answer.

CHAPTER 38

Do not be angry that I am a woman
And so have lips that want your kiss

"SONNET XXXIX," JOY DAVIDMAN

August 1954

"Warnie had the most awful binge." Jack said this with the twist of pain in his voice. "He's off to treatment, and that means I'm with you and the boys for a couple weeks. You must tolerate my company also."

Jack and I sat together in the Bird and Baby, which was as stifling inside as the August weather that simmered across Oxford. It was finally summer break and we had come—my sons and I—to spend a month at the Kilns. A month!

"Tolerate?" I laughed and shook my head at him. "That's not the right word. I'm sorry about Warnie. You know how much I love him, and I wish I could help. But by golly, I'm happy you'll be here with us."

He lifted his beer in salute.

"Is it over?" Jack asked quietly. "Are you legally divorced?"

"Yes indeed. I'm single." I allowed the simple statement to shimmer between us, watched carefully for the change those two words might bring, but found only the same kind smile. "And do you know what Bill did? He married the very next day. He married Renee the very next day." I shook my head. "But how could I have expected any different? Where we start is where we end, or so it seems."

"How do you mean?"

I cringed and, feeling peevish, told him what I never had. "Bill was married before me. He didn't have children, and it wasn't very real as far as marriages go—that's what he told me at the time. He married me only days after that divorce was final. How could a tiger ever change his stripes?"

"Well, it's over," Jack said and lifted his house cider, as yet untouched. "Here's to the forgiveness of sins."

I smiled and lifted my own cider. "And here's to Bill and all the pleasure he may find."

We clinked glasses, and our eyes met and held. He hadn't believed a word written in that lie-soaked decree. He knew my heart and my mind; he understood the harsh and the cruel, the soft and the vulnerable.

"How is Warnie doing at the hospital?" I asked when we set down our glasses.

"Not very well, Joy. I'm worried near to death. This binge was the worst yet. The doctors believed he might not make it, but he's recovering."

"I know the pain of watching someone you love destroy himself with drink. It seems there must be something to do, but then they off and binge again, breaking your heart. Breaking their own hearts. You know I've been through this, Jack. If you'd like I can tell you some of the AA steps and theories. They really do work. They *are* very spiritual, all about surrender to God."

"Thank you." Jack lifted his own glass of cider. "Of course drinking itself isn't a sin. It's the too much of it all. It's temperance. Going the right length and then not any further than that."

"*Mere Christianity*," I said. "You said that in there."

"Did I? What a fool, repeating himself in a bar. Ignore me. I'm knackered."

We talked a bit more of Warnie and how to help him. I suggested bitter ginger at the end of the night, which tasted like liquor but was not.

"However would I do without you now?" he asked me as finally we rose to set off and walk Shotover with Davy and Douglas as promised.

"I hope you'll never know." I jostled him as we walked out the door.

———

Shotover Hill had become as familiar to me as the curve of Jack's neck. My first long walk with him had been on this hill, the thick, tufted grass like patches on a bald man's head, punctuating the pathway. For each season I'd hiked it since, the flowers and trees had shown new faces. In fall, the leaves dropping one by one until the trees bared their skeletons, the acorns plopping to the ground like footsteps. In winter I'd crunched over frosted grass, seen the white landscape of barren trees crystalized with ice. A season later I'd swatted at nettles and memorized the woodland flowers, multihued, their faces lifted to the spring sun. Now summer, the heat and breeze mixing in an intoxicating scent of new grass and damp earth.

The white-balled flowers of the marsh valerian lined the pathway, wandering up the hill to join the scaly fern in nature-marriage. The orpine flower, its burgundy flower head, stood proud and tall. The bark of the gnarled sycamore enchanted, and the rain of white and pink petals from the cherry tree covered the ground.

Gratitude flooded me with warmth and chatter.

"Remember in *Phantastes*, each little flower had its own fairy?" I asked Jack as Davy and Douglas crested the hill to see Oxfordshire. My breath caught in the back of my throat, the hellish exhaustion pulling me down when I wanted to be up. I leaned over, balancing my hands on my knees, and then picked a round-faced daisy. I stood and handed it to Jack. "My favorite was the daisy fairy. The way MacDonald described it as a fat child, a cherub."

"The ash tree in that book frightened me," he said and pointed to an ash only four feet away, its bark corrugated and emulating small rivers. "For years I looked out my window to see if one was coming for me with its bloody knobbed and twisted hand."

"The things we remember about stories," I replied with a laugh. "If you had to choose only one, flower or tree, which would you keep in the world?"

"Trees," he said. "The ones that hold steady."

"Agreed," I said. "I think about those snake roots below the ground, reaching and reaching and never seeing the light."

"Just like all humans," he said with such a grin. "A hidden life."

"We all have one, don't we? But with friends maybe we can show a little bit of it, let it see the light, even though the trees don't have a choice at all."

"Not with *all* friends. But with someone like you, Joy, that's possible. It's only in friendships like this that I've ever been able to discuss the deeper questions—probe at the hidden life."

With someone like me. I took those words and I placed them on the altar of my memory. Then I bent over to take another breath.

"Are you okay?" Jack asked.

"Just a bit tired, I suppose." I stood to face him. "Well, more than that, actually. I went to see the doctors in London."

"And?" He glanced at my boys and then back to me, concern in his eyes.

"First I saw the dentist, who told me that the last London dentist—the one I thought had given me such a fantastic deal—had botched the job. Six more teeth needed to be pulled. Then I saw the doctors, eight of them, Jack. What a fiasco. Who needs eight doctors? The poking and the prodding and the needles and the X-rays, all to tell me what they'd always told me—my thyroid is low again."

"Can they help?" he asked, concern as softness in his voice.

"They increased my medicine," I said. "I had the radium collar when I was a child, and they were quite concerned about that, telling me they don't use it anymore as it causes burns and cancers and all kind of horrific problems. I told them it was too late to be worrying about all of that nonsense. All we can do is go from here."

"Sounds awful." He leaned on his walking stick, both hands wrapped around its top. "Perhaps the medicine will help?"

"Yes, I think it will. But there was a bright spot in that long day," I said. "I whiled away an hour talking to Dr. Greene, Graham Greene's brother. I told him I had just read *The End of the Affair*, and we were off and running about the literary London world and its gossip. Our chatter took my mind off illness. We gabbed about Dostoyevsky until they stuck me with another needle and brought in another doctor to stare at me like a specimen."

He shook his head, his jowls moving too. "Dostoyevsky at the doctor. Only you."

What I didn't mention to Jack was the actual hell of pulling all those teeth. I'd had so many removed and with such violent pain that only codeine had eased it. I didn't dare talk about it for reliving it. Nor did I tell him of the lump in my breast, which they once again dismissed as nothing but a cyst.

"You stay here a moment, rest." Jack took a few steps toward the boys and glanced over his shoulder, lifted his walking stick to me. "I'll catch up to them. You push yourself far too much."

"All right then, go on," I said.

I watched Jack with my boys on the top of Shotover. They'd lugged a folded kite to the top of the hill, and now they unfurled it. Bright stripes of red and blue shuddered in the wind, not taking flight but landing on the ground crooked and hard. Davy ran to it, picked it lovingly off the ground, and brushed it off to hold in his hand.

"I'll run," he shouted into the wind to Douglas. "You keep it up."

Davy ran forward, lifting his ten-year-old hands into the air with an offering of kite to wind.

Jack trotted alongside him to lift the kite until the fabric caught the wind and flapped like a bird, a slapping sound in the sky.

It was simple—a kite in flight. It was also a miracle, a grace.

"Ay up," Jack yelled, and the scene filled my heart.

Gold light fell upon him, and they all laughed about something I couldn't hear. Jack was beyond my greedy and needy hands, on top of that hill, and I could still be grateful for all he was to me, and to my sons.

Before I could climb to meet them, the three joined me and we ambled back to the Kilns. The boys chattered endlessly about plans for the orchard with Paxford, about cleaning the canoe, about visiting the deer park and punting on the Cherwell.

"Mr. Lewis," Davy asked as he threw a rock across the tufted grass expanse, "when does our book come out?"

"Our book?"

"*The Horse and His Boy*? The one you dedicated to us?"

"Ah, that," Jack said and lifted his walking stick before setting it down with his answer. "This fall."

"What's next after that?" Douglas asked.

"I just sent off *The Magician's Nephew*, where we see Aslan create the world, and we find out how the White Witch got there, and"—Jack whispered—"we discover that the Professor had seen and known it all from the very beginning."

Douglas stood on his tiptoes as if reaching for the sky. "I want to read it *now*."

Jack laughed. "Then you shall."

Davy and Douglas were gone in an instant, and Jack stopped at a large tree trunk, as round as a table, gutted in the middle and set up in the shade of a fern glen. "This," he said in a conspirator's whisper, "is a soaking machine."

"A what?" I raised my eyebrows and fiddled with my glasses as if attempting to see a machine somewhere in the thick green of the forest.

"It's my name for a place so private that I'm free to be alone and sit idly and do nothing, or think away a puzzle, or write with a notebook and pencil. A place to be free outside and sheltered. That, Joy, is what a 'soaking machine' is."

"Well then, here's to a lifetime of finding soaking machines." I drew back a step or two. "In fact, let's find another one now."

We were soon at the back door of the Kilns. Far off, Douglas's voice rang out with Paxford's name, and Jack looked over his shoulder as if he might be bowled over by one of my sons.

"They're exhausting, aren't they?"

"I'm glad you're all here. It would be morbidly sad without Warnie in the heat of summer." He opened the back door and we entered the house, Mrs. Miller arriving in her swirling apron and chattering inquisitions about our day and our well-being.

"Tomorrow," Jack said over his shoulder as he headed to his room to rest, "we'll go punting at Cherwell with some friends. The boys will enjoy it."

"Jack, your friends don't seem keen on me. Maybe you'd like to go without us."

"Hogwash," he said and came back down the two stairs he'd already climbed. He faced me.

"What did Moira and George have to say about me?" I asked. "I hadn't seen George since our first meeting in Eastgate, and when we had tea last month he was cold and clammed up. His wife looked at me like I was naked at the table."

"Moira is quite proper. Maybe she didn't like that you could talk circles around her. Or that you drank whiskey while she drank tea. I suggested *Childhood's End* to them based on your suggestion, and they both loved it."

"I don't want your friends to avoid me; I have plenty of my own."

"No one is avoiding you. And even if *they* were, I most certainly am not." Jack smiled at me and then took the stairs to his room, leaving me to stare after him with an almost irrepressible urge to follow him uninvited.

While Jack napped, I wandered outside to the garden, where Paxford had planted the tomatoes and beans I'd suggested. I closed my eyes, allowed the golden sun of Oxford to press gently on my head and body. I'd celebrated my divorce with a pint of cider and a hike with Jack and my boys. I couldn't have hoped for such when that first letter arrived in my Staatsburg mailbox over four years ago.

Even as Jack withheld his body from mine, he pressed his heart and mind as close to me as skin to bone. No, I thought, *love has never quite succumbed to my sense of timing.*

CHAPTER 39

Yes, I know: the angels disapprove
The way I look at you
"SONNET XXXVIII," JOY DAVIDMAN

I tucked Douglas and Davy into bed in the cozy side room off the kitchen, pulling the sheet tight under their chins and kissing them each before reading a chapter from the unpublished Narnian chronicle. I hadn't yet typed it, and the story spread before us in Jack's cursive quill and ink handwriting.

"What will this one be called?" Douglas asked, eyes already at half-mast.

"He hasn't decided. Maybe *The Last King of Narnia*. Or the other title he likes is *Night Falls on Narnia*. Warnie and I suggested *The Wild Wastelands*."

"Just read, Mommy." Davy pulled the covers up to his chin.

With a low voice, I began. "'There is a kind of happiness and wonder that makes you serious . . .'"

My sons rested in bed as I read, but I knew their imaginations were elsewhere, in a land through a wardrobe where a false Aslan reigned.

"Go on, Mommy," Davy said. "One more chapter."

Always one more chapter.

I kissed them good night before joining Jack in the common room, the words ready on my tongue to tell him how the boys were enthralled with the new story, but on my way out of the room, I paused beside a photo in a tarnished silver frame that sat on the hall table. I'd passed it many times and turned away—an older woman with white hair and a look of scorn upon her tight mouth. Beside her sat a younger girl with lush dark hair. Bruce II, the predecessor to Bruce III, sat upon their laps in what appeared to be the backyard of the Kilns. Janie and Maureen Moore. I don't know what caused me to pause that evening, or why it seemed time to dig into the past with a shovel when I had let the dirt on top of this phase of his life rest long enough.

After the intimacy of the past days, for the first time I attempted to imagine Mrs. Moore and her daughter, Maureen. But my mind failed me—I had no reference to see two other women in the house. Jack and Warnie, as undefended with me as an eternal hallway of flung-open doors, had never once discussed the two women who had lived some twenty-odd years at the Kilns.

Twice her name had come up in casual conversation, and twice Jack had changed the subject, and a cloud, a dark cloud, had passed over Warnie's face. I was adept at ignoring things—I'd done it for most of my marriage. I knew the drill: if it was too much or too difficult to look at, you just turned away, pasted on a smile, and went about your day.

But we'd come too far now, Jack and I. I had to ask. I entered the common room to see him, his spectacles sitting atop the end of his nose, as his head had bobbed down while reading. He wasn't asleep, but he wasn't awake either. I'd try. Just try.

"Jack." I said his name in a whisper. If he opened his eyes, I'd ask. If he didn't, I wouldn't try again.

"Yes?" His head rose slowly, his forefinger pushing his spectacles back to his eyes.

"Am I staying in Mrs. Moore's room?"

He ran both hands across his face and sighed. "We were to talk of this one day, weren't we?"

"Yes, I suppose we were." I sat before him and leaned forward, my hands on my knees so I could be closer, look closer. What I cared most was that this relationship had possibly soured him on true love, on the sensuous pleasures of a body pressed against his—as if it were wrong or in the end must be paid for with great and heavy duty.

Had Janie ruined it for me? For us? Or was I merely and always looking for a reason that we were only friends?

Jack stood and moved to poke the dying fire. "Joy. I fulfilled a promise, and whatever emotions or leftover feelings I have about how it all . . ." He turned to me, his hands clasped behind his back as I'd seen him do when he was nervous. "I don't believe Mrs. Moore's situation has much to do with us."

"But it does."

"I made a choice. I was young, and my friend Paddy had been killed in the war. I made it out; I was alive. Whether it was foolish or prudent or sensible, it matters little now. I promised Paddy I would care for his mother and sister." He drew closer to me, looked down as the firelight behind him created a nimbus around his body.

Then he moved, only half a step, and the angelic countenance was gone; what remained was a man battling the words he needed to say or not say about the nature of his relationship with a woman who had died years earlier: a woman who may or may not have been his lover, but had definitely been his obligation.

"Please, Jack."

He cleared his throat. "Now it is only a historical question; I fulfilled my responsibility, and, Joy, she is gone. The decisions I made as a young man, hedonistic and believing my actions right and true based on feelings I carried then, are regrettable now."

It was all he would say. I could see that, but of course I wanted more. Did he love her? Was she a mother replacement? Was she a lover? Deep down I knew the answer, of course—she was *all* of those things. There was no separation in these matters—no either/or; nothing was truly black or white.

Jack took a breath and said, "When I submitted to God's will, I changed, but my obligation remained. That is why she lived here. It is Warnie who has held on to the anger. He says his private life was hardly ever at peace with 'that senseless woman in the house.'" Jack imitated the slightly stronger Irish brogue of his brother. "Warnie believed her to be a horror. He is adamant that I could have written much more without her here. And I do believe he is right. But we've avenged that; there's no need to hold on to the anger as he does."

"What does that mean? Avenged?"

"It's over." He opened his palms to the ceiling. "Look at what we have been given, Joy. See the happiness of our life now?"

I did see, but the vengeful part of me wanted to find Janie Moore in the past and throttle her for whatever damage she had done to the man I loved. And again I saw a comrade in Warnie, another who felt the same as I did.

Frustration overwhelmed, and the words blurted from the deepest part of me. "You keep your heart hidden very well. You close that door and make sure no one opens it even a crack to see what is stored inside."

"I don't believe I do, but it might very well be that I can't access feelings as easily as you do. You feel so much and so deeply."

"I do, but I wouldn't change that. There's much I would change, but not that."

He cleared his throat and stated simply, "I don't want you to change anything at all."

And with that, he lifted a book to read and the conversation was over. I sank back into the chair—I'd heard from Jack most of what I needed to know, if not everything. And it would forever be something I would hold private. Janie Moore was a love affair and one he regretted, ended, and also paid for with pounds of flesh and servile actions.

How I wanted to redeem his idea of love, his idea of what true desire might cost.

But who was I to redeem anything at all?

CHAPTER 40

(Love) You can be very sure it will not kill you,
But neither will it let you sleep at night

"SONNET III," JOY DAVIDMAN

I saw the letter from another woman on his desk, and all propriety and
all goodness told me not to read it, but my eyes could not turn away. I
don't know how I couldn't have read it, although it had been a full two
blissful weeks in Oxford with Jack and my sons, and I had no need to
go ruin it.

The four of us had been a kind of family—we traipsed around
Oxfordshire and took a train out to Studley Priory, a country estate
that had been both a nunnery and a sanatorium—what a combination! We'd gobbled clotted cream and biscuits while the boys rampaged
about with the animals, from Dalmatian puppies to hamsters.

Through those summer weeks, the house became an author's
workshop—Jack and I toiling away on all of our projects. My work
was still as important to me as it had always been, and I fit it into the
open spaces of our days.

We worried about Warnie, and Jack called the facility to check on
him every day, hoping for the news that he was sober and well enough
to travel. Meanwhile, the boys turned the Kilns acreage into their
personal playground—playing cricket on the lawn, picking fruit,
building forts, fishing in the pond. Shotover Hill became their conquering lands. There was chess at night, and walls and piles of books
to peruse.

It was a rainy evening when I found Davy reading a French trans-lation of *Prince Caspian*, muttering out loud and slowly—French words in a part American/part English accent.

"I'm proud of you, Davy. Greek and French and Latin all there in your brain; you're brilliant." I hugged him so tightly that he had to push me away.

The time passed in this pleasant way until it was midmonth and the news arrived that Warnie was being released from the hospital and was healthy enough to travel. Jack was to launch off to Ireland the next day. I'd slept in later than usual that morning and wandered upstairs to look for him in his office. So why I felt I must wreck this peaceful bliss with my nosiness, I'll never understand.

The room was empty but for the things of him: the papers, letters, notes, and manuscript pages written in his tight cursive handwriting; the pipe tobacco and ash-scattered rug. I went to the desk checking for pages to type. The letters he'd answered that morning were piled to the left. The sealed letters, his answers, were stamped and stacked to the right.

He tossed letters after he answered them. I knew this because when I'd asked if he still had my first letter, he'd told me, "No. If something were to happen to me, I'd never want a greedy chap to come in here and gather my personal correspondence. People write to me of the most personal things."

"As I did," I'd said.

"Yes, as you did."

I lifted the morning pile of correspondence—it was from a wide array of people on varying subjects: Oxford-related news, dinner date requests, notes from the publisher, a letter from Dorothy Sayers, another from the Socratic Committee from which he'd just resigned. There were authors soliciting advice, children who asked if Aslan was real or if they might find Lucy in London. And every morning Jack rose and read this pile and answered nearly every letter.

I glanced to the right and saw the one unfinished answer in his handwriting—it was to Ruth Pitter. He hadn't finished or sealed this one yet.

I knew who she was, of course—a renowned poet and a friend of his. He sometimes visited her garden; he'd told me as much. Was it wrong for me to look? He'd written to Ruth on the stationery I'd given to him as a thank-you gift after the last visit: thick cotton paper with his name and the Oxford address on the top right corner, the emblem of Magdalen College stamped on the top middle in gold filigree. I'd spent an hour picking it out, designing the paper at the custom stationery store in London with the last few of my month's shillings.

My Dear Ruth,

No "Miss Pitter," or any other formal name. "My"?

I am writing to you on this fancy stationery given to me by the American.

"The American"? Bloody hell.

Your poetry collection is brighter each and every time I read it: drunk or sober, it's always a delight.

I wanted to look away, to wrench my attention from the private letter, but I could not. Wormwood had hold of my eyes, setting them farther down the page.

Surely you shall come to Oxford one day soon? Whether for the books or the shopping? If so, let us lunch together.

I glanced to the bottom of the page.

Yours, C. S. Lewis

It was in the same fashion he wrote to me, no different. No better. No worse, yet still it hurt. Her poetry a delight? A bright light?

My throat clenched; my stomach sank and swooped up. This was jealousy, and I knew well its taste and its vertigo. I turned away from the letter and searched for a sheaf of her poetry. I could not help myself. But as much as I wanted to read the rest of the letter, the goodness in Jack seeped through the office. If it had been Bill's papers, I would have torn through them, reading every word to find some infidelity, some betrayal. To invade the privacy of a good and decent man seemed far worse even if logically I knew it to be the same.

On the side table by the sitting chair were sheets of her poetry. I glanced at only three: "Early Rising," "If You Came," and "As When the Faithful Return."

And I was sad, O my true love, for the love left unsaid.

This was clearly a woman poet, brilliant and clear-minded, lucid and soaked with longing, expressing her love, which was subtle and meant to be discovered. This was *his* kind of woman—aloof and sedated. Not me—open and outspoken. Nothing was left unsaid with me.

He was right—her poetry was a delight. A bright light. And an *admission*. She loved him; I had no doubt. But did he love her?

She was willing to hint, while I was too eager to admit.

She hoped; I reached.

She was coy; I asked forthright.

Dizzy with envy, I finally turned away from Ruth's poetry. Tears hung on the edges of my lower eyelids, blurring my vision.

What if I placed one of my sonnets on top of Pitter's poetry? What if Jack saw my growing need for his touch? If he glanced down and expected her "bright light" and instead saw my words, "I take you for my pleasure," or even "Forever the tingle and flash of my body embracing you." What if he read *my* poetry about bodies coming together, of its ecstasies, of the ways I'd loved other men? Would he want to read of this?

I shuddered.

What if the reason he didn't love me as I was growing to love him was because he loved another?

———

"This is all yours for two weeks." Jack spread his arms out wide in his Magdalen rooms. "I want you to make yourself at home. Write to your heart's content while I'm gone."

"I don't know what to say." I walked to the open window facing the deer park. A long whinny, which sounded more like a horse than a deer, echoed across the grass. I turned to Jack and removed my glasses, wiped at my eyes. "First you pay for Dane Court. Then you put us up for holiday. And now this?"

"My pleasure." He paused. "All day I've been trying to find the right moment to tell you this news—I've been given the job at Cambridge. Seems after I turned them down twice they offered it to someone else; therefore there were days when I thought it was over. But she didn't take the job, and now it's mine. I start in the new year."

I threw my arms around him, startling both of us. "That's wonderful," I said and stepped away.

"Yes, I believe it is."

I smiled at him and jostled his arm. "A new job, by golly."

"Yes," he said. "Even this old man can start over."

"I do believe you can." I braved another touch to his arm.

Jack took two steps toward me, but no more.

Should I tell him what I'd seen on his desk? Ask him if he was in love with Ruth Pitter? The questions quivered below my throat, wanting escape.

He spoke first, almost as if he could read my mind. "I read another one of your poems last night, 'One Last Spring.' Did I tell you that? I meant to if I didn't."

"No, you didn't." A warm blush filled my face.

"'Out of my heart the bloodroot.'" He clasped his hands behind his back and quoted my words. "It's no wonder I quit poetry, I have neither ear nor hand for it as you do."

"Thank you." I leaned against the windowsill and soaked in the beauty of his voice reciting my poetry. "You can't know how much that means to me, to have my words praised—especially since Macmillan turned down my *Queen Cinderella* proposal. I'll have to write the entire thing to sell it."

"Then you will."

"Do you ever think of writing one more Narnian chronicle? Just one more? Because you know it will sell?"

"I think it's best to put an end to it when the readers are clamoring for more rather than when they're weary of the whole everlasting thing. There will be seven of them published in seven years. Sometimes you must know when it's enough."

Discernment fell down on me with great weight: *You must know when it's enough.* I would *not* ask him about Ruth Pitter or his feelings for her or for anyone else. I must know when it is *enough*. And I must trust God—again and again I was learning and relearning to trust the Truth who had entered my sons' nursery. The rusty and decrepit habit of trusting in only myself, only abiding in my own ability to make things happen, died hard and slow.

I glanced up to see outside the opposite window, where groups ambled toward the deer park and riotous flowers blossomed in the gardens.

"Tourists," I said, pointing out the window at a family with four children running behind. "I was one, and now here I am in your Magdalen rooms. It seems quite miraculous, Jack."

"They will knock on the door, you'll see." He came to my side, and together we looked down at the park. "They expect King Caspian or a man in long black robes with the keys to God's kingdom, and all they ever find is an old balding man with glasses." He laughed, and the family below looked up. He waved, and they wandered away.

I rested my head on his shoulder, only for a moment. "Thank you, Jack. Thank you so much."

He'd leave in the morning, and the boys and I would have the run of the house and gardens, and I of his college rooms.

This was dangerous territory in the land of love—he wasn't yet gone, and I already missed him.

CHAPTER 41

You are all the gold of all the rocks
Precious in my fingers; brighter things
"SONNET XLII," JOY DAVIDMAN

October 1954

I opened the front door of Avoco House to see my mother and father standing there in the brisk October day. Mother was prim and proper in her hat and pearls, her buttoned coat and lacquered hair. Father stood in a three-piece suit with his moustache greased to stand out as if at attention. Both looked as if they'd come from a party instead of a long journey across the ocean.

"Mother. Father," I said and hugged them both. "Welcome to London."

Their suitcases were propped on the sidewalk where the cab driver in his bowler hat and suit waited to be dismissed. I motioned to bring in their bags. "I'm glad you're here." I ushered my parents into my home.

"Oh, darling, this is such a lovely neighborhood." Mother's voice grated against my ears for a moment until I realized that I had become so accustomed to the melodic English accents that even my very own accent sounded rough around the edges.

After paying the cab driver and shutting the front door, Father silently roamed around the house. "This is a nice place. Much nicer than I expected, with your financial condition."

"Yes, it's been tough, Father. You're right. But people here are generous—the landlord has given me a fantastic price." I motioned for them to follow me. "You have the boys' room, right here."

"How have you survived here?" Mother asked. "That horrid ex-husband of yours not sending money. And you being in another country. I've been worried."

"Worried?" I almost laughed, but held back. If she'd been oh-so-very worried, maybe I would have heard from her more than in a random letter here or there. The only reason they were here was to see London on their way to a tour of Europe and Israel. And of course they wanted to meet my famous friend, C. S. Lewis.

I cleared my throat. "Are we going to talk about money and misery before you've even had tea and put up your feet?" I tried to smile. "Why don't you wash up and meet me in the sitting room for a cuppa?"

As they shut the door to my boys' room, I boiled water on the little gas circle and set biscuits on a flowered plate. I heard their murmured voices, but not the words. I wondered what they were saying, how they were judging this change in my life. Letters had been exchanged, but rarely had I confided my true feelings to them. What was the point? Could they have possibly understood? I hadn't told them of my health problems. I hadn't told them how I missed my boys but felt boarding school was best. I hadn't told them that even though the job in the dank printing press basement was misery, I was bereft that it had closed down, leaving me in even a greater pinch for income. Or how I'd entered a writing contest and lost—another way I thought I'd make money and hadn't.

It had only been two months since I'd left the summer enclave of Jack's rooms, the pureness of those sacred hours alone working while my boys ran through the woods and took a kayak Jack had bought them out on the pond and ran through Whipsnade Zoo. We'd cooked together and gathered plums, apples, and beans. When we'd departed, they'd voiced what I felt: *Why can't we just stay here?* But I was back in London now, and they were back at Dane Court.

"Darling?" Mother's voice called out.

"In here," I answered.

She smiled as she entered the room and went straight to the window to look out over my tiny garden. "Not quite the acres of vegetables you had on the farm, but you've made this your own." She turned to me, and for one moment I thought there might be tears in her eyes. "Your garden outside and bright fabrics and paintings inside. You've made yourself a home."

I laughed. "Did you think I was living in a bloody hole?"

"I didn't know, darling. I just didn't know." She squinted at me. "And aren't you quite the anglophile now, with your little words like *cuppa* and *bloody*. Next thing I know you'll have an accent."

"Maybe I'm just trying to fit in," I said, "but yes, one does pick up these things quickly. I'm the only American around far as I can tell."

Father's cough caused us both to turn to him. "You very well could have been living in a hole, for all the support you've received from that no-good ex-husband of yours."

"Oh, he's not so bad, Father. He does what he can; it's just that he can't do very much. I took his sons across an entire ocean, and he misses them. He lost his house also, and he can't seem to hold down a job. It's not like he's living it up and stiffing me."

They both stared at me with such surprise that it made me laugh. My mother's large brown eyes, so like mine, didn't blink.

"Surprising, isn't it? To hear me defend him? I think I just rightly shocked myself," I said. "But you're right. Money managing has been a dismal failure of mine. I'd expected more from my writing, and more from Bill's."

"We can help you, Joy. I don't know why you don't ask us for assistance." Father set his hat on the kitchen table and straightened his moustache, which did not need straightening.

"Well, Jack pays me for typing, and Bill is getting caught up with payments. I'm writing as fast and furiously as I can. I have some pieces out, and I'm hoping for more from my novels soon. If I accepted anything from you it would be for the boys."

"What do they need?" Mother fiddled with her pearls. "We have money set aside, you know."

"No, I didn't know, but can we talk about this later?" I asked. "I want you to enjoy your first day without worry."

Always with my parents there were two conversations: the one on top and the one beneath. Here's what rested below. I would not tell them that I had crawled to the bank just two days before, and in that bank, while trying to sort through the disaster of an empty account, I'd wept before a man in a three-piece suit and bow tie who had taken pity on me and given me some grace with time to fill the account.

They sat at the table and I poured them tea, which they cradled in their hands as their critical gazes flitted from the window with its checkered red cloth curtain to the walls where I'd hung drawings the boys had made, and then again to the window.

"What would you like to do today?" I asked. "It's your first day, and I know how tired you must be. Maybe just a walk in Trafalgar Square? A visit to Westminster Abbey and then a quiet dinner?"

"That sounds nice," Mother said.

We sat for a long while around my table while they gave me news from home. "Howie is fine," was all they told me about my brother.

"My grandsons," Father asked. "How are they?"

"Oh, Father, just wonderful. We had three weeks here in London after a month in Oxford. They've made friends. You'll see them when we visit their school in a few days."

"They feel as if this is home now?" Mother asked.

"This is their home. They know their way around, and they are free here. Although Douglas scared the living daylights out of me last week before he left for school. We went to the park, and he saw kites—he is obsessed with kites after flying them on Shotover Hill—and he followed them to find a group of avid flyers. He spent so long talking to them that Davy and I believed we'd lost him. I was wrecked. We came home and I called the bobbies. Hours later he just ambled to the front door all sheepish and apologetic, claiming he lost track of time. Meanwhile I thought him kidnapped or worse. So, yes, this is home."

"And it's good that you've made friends with famous people." Father sat straighter with the proclamation.

I ignored him and stood. "Let's get some fresh air and I'll show you around the neighborhood." I smiled at them both, hopeful. "Autumn here is gold, all gold."

"Dear," Mother said and stood, "I do love your haircut. You look sweet and put together. And you're wearing makeup. Are you in love?" She giggled like a child, and I cringed.

I patted my hair. "A woman can take care of herself for her own sake."

"Well, it's just that you never have."

I stared at her impassive face for only a moment. "Let's go, Mother. Let me show you my new city."

"When do I meet Mr. Lewis?" She dabbed her lips with her pinky finger.

"Tomorrow," I said. "You'll meet him tomorrow."

———

The next day the Piccadilly Restaurant glistened with crystal chandeliers and polished tabletops, cut-glass goblets and silverware polished to its ends. Mother stood next to me in the lobby. Pearls hung from her ears and surrounded her wrist in a bracelet. She wore a black suit with rhinestones. Rhinestones! A lacy pink shirt peeked from beneath her suit jacket.

"Did you see that man just look at me?" she whispered to Father and me. "Even in England the men aren't polite enough not to stare at a beautiful woman." She straightened her pink hat and blinked demurely.

Father, on her other side in a suit pressed to cardboard, took her arm. "Don't let it bother you," he said. "They like to admire. There's no harm."

I was uncharacteristically speechless. Mother still, all these years later, ambled around in her delusionary haze of beauty where all men wanted her, and Father was there to protect her from the sexualizing of her innocent glamour.

"I just hope Mr. Lewis likes me," she said.

"Have you read any of his books, Mother?" I asked, glancing around the room for any sign of him.

"No, but I've read the articles written *about* him."

I wanted to laugh at the absurdity of this entire afternoon—my parents meeting C. S. Lewis—but instead someone seemed to have kicked apart a bees' nest in my gut. "Okay, just remember that we can't monopolize his time, Mother. He's in town for a debate with Dorothy Sayers. He can only have tea."

"We understand, dear," she said.

"There," I said and felt a settling of my buzzing nerves. I pointed to Jack as he walked into the dining room, his eyes searching for me, finding me, and then his smile breaking wide as it had that day at the Oxford Hooker speech, all those years ago.

He approached us with long, wide strides and immediately held out his hand to my father and introduced himself, and then to my mother.

"Thank you for inviting me," he said, and together we all sat.

For inviting him? Urp. I'd almost begged him. *Please come satisfy my parents' curiosity, they won't leave this alone. You never have to see them again.*

He was here for one reason only: because he cared enough about our friendship to satisfy my request. The talk and tea were smooth, if also a wee bit awkward, until Father talked of Prohibition and how ardently he'd believed in its mandates all those years ago. "There is right and wrong," he always said, and said again. "No gray. No in-between, right, Mr. Lewis?" He directed his question across the little table full of teacups and biscuits on flowered plates.

"Father." I bristled at his harsh self-righteousness. "You believed in Prohibition for everyone but yourself. Don't you remember when I poured your apricot brandy down the drain because I thought I was being helpful? Not wanting you to go against your very own beliefs?"

Father attempted to laugh and yet looked to Jack. "Impetuous, this one. She would as soon throw out her father's brandy and get smacked than just leave it be."

"See?" I said. "That's the very thing. I thought I was right when all along I was wrong. And smacked to boot."

The joke, if it was a joke at all, fell flat. The table sat silent.

"I shall just stop trying to be funny," I said. "I always think I can pull it off and then I don't."

"Dear, you're very funny when you're not being rude," Mother said.

Jack leaned close to me, whispered so near my ear I felt his breath. "I'm doing my best here."

Under the table I nudged him with my foot and suppressed a laugh.

"Mr. Lewis." Father lowered his voice as if about to lecture. "Our daughter has told us that you are moving your career to Cambridge, leaving Oxford."

"I am. I shall start there in the new year." Jack glanced at me. "It is Douglas who is quite upset that I'm giving up the nobility of an Oxford man. It seems I'd done my job convincing him that it was of the highest order. I have outdone myself to my own debit."

"But isn't that the case?" Father looked down his long nose to Jack.

"Father!" I spat his name. "This new job is an honor. They have created a position for Jack's expertise."

"As you say." Father picked up his teacup and leaned back in his chair as if posing.

We allowed Father to talk all he wanted after that, not bothering to add or intervene. I longed to reach under the table and hold Jack's hand, allow him to be the balance in this wobbly world.

When we'd finished, Jack stood first. "I can't be late for my debate. Ms. Sayers and I will debate Kathleen Nott, and I must prepare. She can rattle. It was a pleasure to meet you both. Would you like to join me for lunch at Magdalen one day next week?"

"Jack, no, you don't—" I started, but Mother interrupted.

"We would be honored. Yes, that sounds lovely. Better than all the sightseeing my daughter has been trying to plan. I'd rather shop and see Oxford than traipse into a cathedral or museum."

As I bid Jack good-bye, I whispered, "By golly, are you aiming for a halo?" He only smiled in return.

As he walked away, I looked to my parents with slightly altered eyes. All of a sudden their approval didn't mean quite as much. I didn't need them to understand my life or why I chose it. I didn't need them to soothe or placate me—something they had never been able to do anyway.

"I'm tired," I said. "I might go back to the house and rest while you two go shopping on Regent Square. Tomorrow we'll visit the boys at Dane Court."

"Go on, Joy," Mother stated with closed lips. "Your father and I will get along fine and see you soon."

I stood, and Father did also to face me. "That Mr. Lewis is quite the friend to you, isn't he?"

At last we could agree on something. "Yes," I said. "He is."

The remainder of my parents' visit was as hurried as it was frenetic. Mother needed to go to Woolworths every other day and somehow needed at least six trips to the laundry. There were outings to the neighborhood shops, and even at night we needed to walk the streets to see how the shops appeared in the dark. Oh my, there were the promenades up and down Regent Street. Mother absolutely needed to see the hairdresser and the doctor (imagined illnesses). There was the cleaner and the chemist and the green grocers. I tried as desperately as I could to get them to sightsee, but alas, not much.

When we visited Dane Court, my prig of a father eyed the entire thing with an eagle eye bent toward insult. I at once thought of the many insulting editorial letters he used to send to the local paper, and how he raged when they didn't publish them, because you see—he knew how to fix everything. If everyone in the world would only listen to him, all would be well and good and true. I thought of how Mother often reminded me that my birth was so difficult that she had to leave and recover at a dude ranch for months. Maybe that was where we went wrong—it all started with difficulty.

There were also dinners and gifts and the time they told me that Renee and Bill's marriage had caused a great rift in the family at home—everyone had taken a side. I told them that my side was here in London and no one had to choose another.

When they departed, they offered me enough money to get through a few months without worry. I was gifted a warm winter coat, and the boys new clothes along with bikes. I hugged them with tears in my eyes. I wasn't sure if the tears were happy or shameful.

"I never wanted to have to take your money or gifts," I told them. "But I'm very grateful." I hugged the heavy coat close and buried my fingers in the thick wool.

Mother hugged me tightly, more so than she had since I was a little girl. "You are going to be okay, Joy. We will stop and see you on the way back to the States."

Father, who did not hug, offered a swift good-bye.

As soon as they were gone, I collapsed on my bed. But instead of sleep coming as I'd planned on that autumn afternoon, I stared at the cracked plaster ceiling. What a whirlwind it had been. All that energy in my quiet house, all those embers of memories of childhood ignited by a comment or a look.

I couldn't have gotten through those weeks with as much peace as I had without Jack. Twice Mother and Father had visited with him. When my father uttered an idiocy that bothered Jack, I saw his pain for me in a twitch or eye movement so subtle no other man or woman would have known. When my parents were gone for an hour or more, I would call him on the rickety phone just to hear his voice across the lines. But mostly we wrote—back and forth about what we did during the day, and how and why and what it made us think about.

The Underwood sat on my desk, a clean sheet of paper rolled into its belly. I set my fingers to the keys, wanting to write a sonnet about these past days, about my gratitude for him, but nothing came. I was full of gladness but empty of the need to write another pain-filled line of poetry. Something unalterable had shifted within me during my parents' visit. We'd been a team, Jack and I, and this luxury was more than I had ever thought possible all those years ago when I sent that six-page letter to Oxford, England.

I sat back in the chair and twisted my neck to look out the window at the trees like charcoal drawings against a blue sky, and as clear as that firmament I understood that I would not wrench one more love-starved sonnet from my soul.

They were complete.

CHAPTER 42

The shadow of pain is lifted from my eyes
And I see how gold you are

"SONNET XLII," JOY DAVIDMAN

New Year's Eve, 1954

The parties had begun all around Cambridge that New Year's Eve. Men and women walked the streets in their finery, the holiday lights strung twinkling on the lampposts.

The year had ended with Britain's removal of military force from the Suez Canal, Winston Churchill's eightieth birthday, and an air disaster of a Boeing 377 crashing at Prestwick airport. Neither Jack nor I had ever boarded an airplane, and now together we vowed we never would. "What a terrible way to die," we'd said in unison. In America, Ellis Island's immigration port had closed, and the Red Scare and the Cold War continued. But we were there, in Jack's new Cambridge rooms, surrounded by warmth and safety as the crazy world spun.

"Cambridge is so quaint," I said as we stood surrounded by boxes.

"It is." He stared absently at the mess I was there to help him unpack and organize. He didn't like chaos, or any disarray other than that of his own making. "It's a perfect tiny college, so unlike the cynical Magdalen." He glanced at me. "But that does *not* make it feel anything like home."

"It will."

"Oh, Joy, what have I done? I had a job I loved, and perfectly nice rooms, and now I've gone and upended it all." He frowned when he spoke, attempting levity, but I heard the distress creeping below like the ivy on the stone walls outside.

"Oh, Jack, I do believe you've ruined your life. Why would you do this to yourself? Three times the pay for half the work. And you can return to Oxford every Friday to Tuesday." I shook my head. "Terrible. Just hideously awful."

His laughter filled the room, echoing off the walls. He sat on a box labeled *Books*. "What an exhausting and exciting way to end 1954," he said. "Starting here as the new year begins."

I sat on a box across from him. "Let's get some of these unpacked so we can find out what we need to buy for your rooms."

He shook his head. "Do you realize they give only one glass of port at dinner? One!"

"What did they give at Oxford?"

"Three," he said.

"Oh, the misery!"

He loosened his tie before a quick glance my way. "Wait, have I said thank you for coming to my inaugural address, Joy? Or have I been a delinquent and unworthy friend by not saying it out loud?"

"Even though I wasn't invited?"

He blushed, his cheeks dark red.

"Oh, I'm joking, Jack. Don't look piqued. It was stupendous. You should have heard everyone talking about it as they came out of the room. I guarantee they'll be forever quoting the line about medievalists—'Use your specimens while you can. There are not going to be many more dinosaurs.' The room was packed with so many robes and hats I could barely see you there, but I did listen."

"I knew you were there, and it was calming. I was quite nervous. My first lecture, and there was all that recording equipment. I felt like I was inside a glass bell trying to make an impression that would last for all my tenure."

"It's a lecture they will talk about for years. But I must disagree with you on one point."

His eyebrows rose. "Do tell me."

"You made the case that the break between cultures came with the fall of Rome or the Renaissance, but I believe it was with the rise of science as logic."

His mouth broke into a great smile. "Oh, you do?"

"I do. Are you sure you didn't sacrifice accuracy in the name of entertainment?"

"No, I'm not sure at all. Now must I rethink my entire inaugural lecture?" He smacked his hand on his knee.

"You didn't agree with everything I wrote in *Smoke*," I said to soften the blow—if it was a blow at all.

"We mustn't always agree," he said. "Sometimes that is the intrigue." He stood and ripped open a box and took out a pile of books.

I did the same, both of us in a jolly mood. The empty dark wooden bookshelves began to fill as we unpacked. From a dusty pile, I held up a copy of Dante's *Divine Comedy*.

"'Abandon all hope, ye who enter here,'" I said with great dramatic flair.

He bellowed that laugh and then furrowed his brow above his glasses. "'The devil is not as black as he is painted.'"

We were off and running: as we unpacked, we chose a book and then quoted a line from memory. If we doubted the truth of the line, we'd check inside. When I pulled Charles Williams's *The Greater Trumps* from the box, the very book my husband had written a foreword for, I flubbed the line "Nothing was certain, but everything was safe—that was part of the mystery of love." Instead I stated, "'Everything is safe, that's the mystery of love.'"

"Aha!" Jack bellowed. "You aren't perfect."

"Perfect? Far, far from it, Jack. As you well know."

Yet he didn't flub one line. Not one. Soon we were competing to quote the most absurd or dirty line, one that might make the other blush. In any other small room with any other man, this might be considered flirting, but not with Jack—it was only great fun. Wasn't it?

I plucked a book from a box and dusted off the cover. It was *Phantastes*. I smiled and held it up to Jack without a word—we knew what it meant to both of us.

"'Past tears are present strength,'" Jack quoted and reached for the book.

"Oh yes! That's so true." I pressed the volume to my chest.

He reached over and eased it from my hands, held it up. "This book isn't so much a book as a thunderclap." He ran his hand over the cover. "Do you think anyone else could play this little game with us? Anyone who has the same photographic memory?"

"If there is such a someone, I don't know them."

He shook his head. "And neither do I."

This game, which he won, though I gave him a great run for his money, went on well into the night.

At last I stood and ran my hands along the spines of newly shelved books. "Jack, it's almost midnight. Let's be done with this for the night."

"Almost midnight?"

"Old lang syne," I said and brushed off my shirt, which was covered in dirt and book dust. I was bone tired and yet unwilling to forfeit five minutes with him if he still wanted me near.

New Year's Eve—would this be the moment when he would close that space between us with a kiss? Would he see and feel what flickered in his new rooms? As the tower outside tolled midnight, the bells echoing and clanging, he collapsed onto his desk chair, then swiveled toward me. "A new year. I can't think of a better way to begin it than with you."

"Yes," I replied. "A very brand-new year."

———

Back in London, January's gift was deep snows with fat snowflakes and bitter cold, which brought me the flu. Set in bed for a week, I had much to think about with my new Cinderella book. Warnie had sent valuable books and research. Although I couldn't get my brain to work well enough to write, I could make it read.

A deep and broken part of me wanted to give up on the writing. *Smoke's* low sales in America seemed the last disappointment I could tolerate. Good reviews and all that, but otherwise a loss. Soon it would release in England and I waited, hoping that Jack's preface and large name on the cover would help. Money was an ever-present worry.

Jack settled easily into Cambridge, and we both wondered aloud how he ever could have thought of turning it down in the first place, much less twice. We spent as much time together as we could—whether I was editing his book or helping him choose a hearthrug for his room. I hand-delivered pages with the excuse that he needed them straight-away, but really just to be near him. And he too stopped in London for no other reason but to linger at my side. He met more of my friends and even accompanied me to the Globe Tavern to meet the sci-fi boys, where he was both revered and stared at with curiosity.

Although I had a busy social life and was beginning to find my place in the London crowd, I missed Jack when he was gone; I was at peace when he was near. What category of his four loves could possibly contain this definition?

The evening was cold when he and I stood in my backyard, bundled in our coats and scarves as he smoked a cigarette and talked about a meeting he'd had at Cambridge. Twilight fell across his face, lighting it aflame.

I turned my palms up and let the light puddle there on my gloves as if it were resting before disappearing. "Look at that," I said.

"Patches of Godlight." Jack touched my gloved hand as if he too could hold the twilight.

We paused, both of us seeming to hold our breath. He wrapped his fingers through mine and drew me closer as he dropped his cigarette to the ground. We were face-to-face, only inches between us. Neither of us spoke.

I was afraid to move, to speak, to break the twilight spell that held us both in its Godlight. With his other hand he touched my cheek, the fuzziness of his glove tickling my skin. I leaned into his palm just as Sultan had once done with me, and he allowed that tender moment before dropping both his hands and taking a step back.

My breath held, and the tremor of desire flamed below my stomach. "Why do you stop yourself, Jack?" I asked, my voice deep and quiet.

"Stop myself?"

"I need to understand why you stop yourself from kissing me, just when I believe you will."

"Oh, Joy." He hesitated. "I don't want to cross over to eros and destroy the love we do have. I can't lose you or this deep, abiding friendship. And the church forbids our union. In their eyes, you're technically still married. And I'm an old man—too old to start again or change."

I took his hand again, pressed it to my heart. "I've watched what's happening to poor Princess Margaret. I see how the Church of England views divorce; I've watched from afar the abdication crisis of King Edward, how his love for Wallis made him choose between the crown and love. He chose love. Sometimes that's what happens; love is preferred, but usually not. Usually the crown or the god or the family or the duty is chosen. I understand this, of course. Lives are altered. Completely settled, lovely lives can be altered by love. And who wants change? Hardly anyone at all." Frustration crept into my voice. "But I don't understand why you keep the most vulnerable pieces of your heart from me. Why do you draw near and then fall back? Because I can *feel* your love."

"Joy." He exhaled my name and took a step not closer but farther away, as if I had pushed him, and maybe I had. I dropped his hand.

"I've spent all of my life in an attempt to *find* Truth and moral good, and then to *live* it. I can't discard my moral habits for feelings, which are just that—feelings."

"The virtues," I said. He'd written about them at length, and I discerned that they were as ingrained in him as the wrinkles now radiating from the corner of his mouth and drooping eyes.

"They are my footholds for moral goodness. Morality is about choice."

"You think God is judging you for wanting us, or because I'm divorced?"

"God doesn't judge by internal disease but by moral choices. We must protect our hearts."

Anger, my old and familiar companion, surged. "You're spouting theology and empty words. I read what you wrote about sex—that it's either in marriage or else total abstinence. But sometimes love changes things. Or love *should* change things."

He reached for his pipe and then his hand dropped as if even that was too much energy to muster. "We can't just surrender to our every desire—man must have his principles and live by them regardless. Our nature must be controlled or it can ruin our lives."

"But how?" I sounded like Davy when he asked ten million questions as a child, never satisfied with the first or second answer.

"If I attempt virtue, it brings light to my life. If I indulge desires, I invite fog and confusion."

"Oh, Jack, that logic takes no account for the heart. How can you tell a heart what to do? I'm incapable of such things." I turned away from him, desire's fire alchemizing to anger.

"I'm trying," he said. "Because I must."

"I think it's time for you to leave." I took a step toward the back door, not wanting him to see the pain quivering on my face and the frustration shaking my body. His logic would not quell or explain.

"Joy." His voice was soft, but I didn't turn back to him.

"Your logic," I said as I opened the door to enter the house. "It offers no rest for the heart."

He was instantly next to me, his hands on my shoulders to spin me around to face him. "Don't turn from me," he said. "I can*not* bear that. If we can't indulge in eros, surely we have all the beauty that remains in philia." He pulled me close to wrap his arms around me. Twilight turned to night and my head rested on his shoulder and the palm of his hand was on my neck, stroking my skin with gentleness as if consoling a small child after a frightful storm.

But this wasn't fright he was trying to subdue; this was desire. His mind might twist firm around logic, but his body divulged the truth.

It was he who let me go, and gently touched my cheek before leaving me quaking without another word.

CHAPTER 43

Blessed are the bitter things of God
Not as I desire but as I need

"BLESSED ARE THE BITTER THINGS OF GOD," JOY DAVIDMAN

Spring, 1955

Three months passed until I was able to return to the Kilns for the rising of spring. Touch between Jack and me came easier now, a hand on the knee or wrist, a hug in greeting or farewell. But still Jack was chaste in the way he knew how, keeping that last inch open.

"You know," I said, handing Jack a pile of letters I'd answered for him that morning, "when your first letter arrived I was afraid to open it, believing that Warnie might have written instead of you." I tapped the pile now in his hands. "Now I feel sorry for the poor bloke who receives my reply instead of yours."

Jack shook his head. "For some of these questions posed, your answers are better than mine. The recipient should feel privileged to have your hand in it." His voice was subdued, quieter than usual, and I took this to be a cue for peaceful work. I too sat, settling into my chair across from him. Pages of *Queen Cinderella* in my hand, I began to edit my work but found my mind wandering.

It was spring holiday at the Kilns. March of 1955 had arrived not quite like the lion it was rumored to be, but more like a heralding of all goodness and light. My sons ran through the Kilns and through Oxford as if they'd lived there all their life. *The Screwtape Letters* was out in paperback, and I was editing Jack's biography and indexing Warnie's history book. Our days together were languid, long and comfortable.

What a flip,

I'd written to Belle just the night before.

I once shared a bed with Bill, was part of his writing and his life, and yet I felt such contempt. And here I share love, esteem, and need, and yet *not* the bed. It's taking some adjustment, but I won't give it up. Not as long as he wants me here.

When I glanced from my pages, Jack was staring at me. His face, that endearing face, his sleepy eyes hooded.

"What is it?" I asked, knowing the curtain that fell over his dark eyes when something bothered him. No more could he hide from me than I from him.

"Now that I'm settled into Cambridge and have more free time, I'm dry as a bone. I have no more ideas, Joy. What if I'm done?" He leaned back in his chair and crossed one leg over the other. "Really bloody done?"

"What are you talking about?"

Jack rose and strolled across the room, his hand out as if seeming to miss his walking stick. He stood in front of the window, pulling aside the blackout curtain and pressing his palm against the window. "Maybe it's over for me. My writing, that is."

I stood to walk to him. "Even if that were true, which I doubt it is, your body of work is so profound already."

"That isn't the point and you know it. If I have nothing left, what is there of me for God to work through? There must always be more until there isn't."

"Let's brainstorm. Let's throw out the ideas you love the most. I know you're not dry." I settled back into my own chair. "Is there anything you've started and put away?"

"Of course there is, but I put it away because it didn't work."

"Sometimes things need time to grow in the soil of the imagination, to percolate in the unconscious, to unfold without our dirty hands all over them."

He smiled at me. "Yes." Then he walked to the side table where he kept the liquor on the bottom shelf. He chose a decanter of whiskey and poured two glasses and motioned for me to sit opposite him at the game table.

Did he notice my new haircut or new pearl earrings or the way I did my very best to make him see me as a woman? No. Instead he stared at me with an intensity that told me he wanted only to solve his dry spell, and I was the possible source of water.

I sat across from him. "Is there anything you've abandoned that you might want to pick up again?"

"One of my very first short stories rests unfinished. 'Light,' I had called it."

"Well then, what of that?"

"I don't believe I have the heart for it as of yet."

"Then let's go here—what fascinated you the most as a child?" I asked, already knowing the answer and wanting to guide him to deep water.

March winds howled outside. A storm was on its way, but neither of us mentioned it.

"Myth," he answered. "I could write another allegory like *Screwtape* or *Pilgrim*. Or another children's book, but those seem to have run their course."

"And what myth do you think of the most when you think of myth at all?" I asked.

"Cupid and Psyche," he said without hesitation.

"Well then . . ."

"I've already tried that." He sat in a posture of defeat, lit a cigarette as if the conversation were over.

"You give up that easily, my lad?"

He didn't laugh, but a smile eased slowly from the corner of his lips. "I wrote a play about this myth, also tried prose, a ballade, couplets. I've approached it from every angle, but still I think of it often." He poured another whiskey in his glass, sipped it. "I've even dreamt of the sisters."

Cupid and Psyche: it was a myth about the most beautiful of three sisters, Psyche, who was sacrificed to the gods, her older sisters complicit, only to be rescued by the winds and then discovered by Cupid—a love story at its finest. But when Psyche disobeyed Cupid and looked directly at him in the night, she was cast out to the forest, and then sent by Venus to fulfill impossible tasks. When Psyche finished the tasks with the help of the river god and magic ants, she was reunited with her true love. I knew the myth well—it was one of my childhood favorites, complicated and chock-full of envious gods, jealousy, true love, and mystical rivers.

"I first read of the sisters in *Metamorphoses*," I said. "I was as jealous of the beautiful Psyche as if I were the older sister in the story. I felt as if I'd sent Psyche into the woods to be sacrificed. But I couldn't have; I never would have stolen her happiness on purpose as her sisters did."

"Not even to save her?" he asked. "Maybe her sisters took away her happiness because they believed they were saving her."

"There, Jack. You've got it." I popped my hand onto the tabletop. "Write about *that*."

He closed his eyes and exhaled a long plume of smoke. "The sisters weren't taking away her happiness but trying to confirm reality."

"Yes, *saving* her, not destroying her. That's it. Your story is hidden in there."

"In this version . . ." He stared past me to whatever Muse spoke to him. "In my version, Psyche is motherless, so her older sister is raising her."

"The beautiful older sister who isn't quite as beautiful but—"

"No," he bellowed in a friendly way and stood with his whiskey to look down to me. "This time she's ugly. She's the opposite of Psyche.

And she loves Psyche with such obsession that—" He slammed his hand on the table with glee. "Yes."

"More . . ."

"*That* love," he said and bent down to look me in the eye, "will be what destroys. When love becomes a god it becomes a devil. And the ugly older sister will turn her love for Psyche into a god."

"Jack, go write. And don't stop."

"Thank you, Joy." He blurted these words, and in a great burst of happiness, kissed me on top of my head. He hurried away to begin writing that very night.

I touched the top of my warm hair, his kiss lingering there as his words echoed across my consciousness: *when love becomes a god it becomes a devil.*

By the middle of the next day Jack brought me chapter one, written in his tight scroll of liquid ink.

I sat at the desk in my bedroom where I'd organized the multiple projects I was immersed in. He hadn't entered that room while I stayed there, always offering me privacy. But that day he burst in as I was muddling through Warnie's history book, indexing it with a growing headache.

"Joy!"

I startled and stood. His mere presence in my room brought a warm flush to my thighs and belly.

"What?" I laughed and was conscious of how I appeared: I wore an A-line dress I'd bought in London, sleeveless and dainty. I hadn't yet brushed my hair, and it fell over my shoulders. I was barefoot.

But he noticed none of this. He held out his hand with a sheaf of handwritten pages. "Will you type these? And then tell me—am I on to something at all?"

He sat on the edge of my bed, unaware of anything but our creative collaboration. I returned my attention to the pages. "Do you want me to type now?"

"First . . . read."

I sat and began to do just that. Orual, the name he had given Psyche's ugly older sister, was speaking from her old age, from the knowledge of her imminent demise. *I am old now and have not much to fear from the anger of the gods.*

From there the prose and the story unfolded, confounding and enchanting as an original myth, as if he'd spent months on the pages.

Orual was the eldest daughter of the King of Glome. She told of their castle where she and her sister Psyche; their nurse; and the Fox, their beloved tutor, resided. But mostly Orual told the reader of Psyche and her beauty and Orual's great love for her—blinding love. Orual's ugliness was described in detail, and the reader discovered that in her old age she wore a veil to cover her face. When I reached the end of the chapter I looked to Jack, who had not looked away.

"I'm envious that you can write this in a night and half a day, and it can hold an entire story in its hints and foreshadowing."

"I'm not here for praise, Joy. Tell me where it lacks."

"Let me type it and write notes, not off the cuff."

"A little off the cuff?" He smiled; he already knew, as I did, that I would never turn away from that smile.

"Okay, on first blush. I need to understand *why* the Fox loves poetry so much, and I want a hint of who he will become to Orual. He seems integral and interesting. He needs to hint at what is to come."

"Yes." Jack took the papers from me and a pencil from my desk, making a mark in scribbled handwriting.

I looked at him. "Jack, I want to tell you something."

"That it's a terrible idea to head down this road, to write this book?"

"No. Not that at all. I want to tell you about the day I received your first letter. A winter afternoon in January of 1950. Five years ago now."

He nodded at me and set the papers to the side, crossed his legs, and leaned on his elbow. "Yes?"

"You'd asked for my history, and I didn't know where to begin. I spent hours thinking about it and realized that my life had been made of masks, many of them. And I decided that afternoon that I wouldn't wear any of them with you. I decided that I would show you *me*. That I would be barefaced. And here—in your story—you have Orual covering her face with a veil."

He stared at me for so long that I almost wished for Orual's veil. Then he spoke. "Never hide your face from me. It is precious and dear."

I smiled. "Sometimes I wish I could, but I cannot."

"*Bareface*," he said. "That should be the title." He stood and held the pages. "I haven't been this excited about my work in a very long time. How can I thank you?"

"Get out of here and finish it."

Or take me in your arms and set me down on that bed and make love to me.

The forbidden thought flew by unspoken. Jack rushed out of the room to return to his true love: the page.

Over weeks, we braided our themes and stories together into this novel—the new myth set in Glome, a fictional Greek town: two sisters, princesses—one beautiful, one ugly. Orual loved her younger sister with a destructive possession and narrated her case to the gods—how she'd only meant to protect and love her sister even as she caused her to lose true love by forcing her to face "reality." Meanwhile, even as Orual eventually became Queen of Glome, she loved a man she could never have: her loyal advisor Bardia. Although Orual eventually came to self-knowledge, self-love, love for the gods, and reunion with Psyche, much destruction had been wrought along the way.

I saw both Jack and myself in the pages we forged together, but in Orual's obsessive and possessive love for Psyche I caught more than a glimpse of myself. *God*, I asked, *how much of Jack's creation was of me?*

Finally one night, after the second whiskey, I asked. "Jack, do you think I'm ugly?"

He jolted as if I'd prodded him with electricity. "Whyever would you ask that?"

"You put my words into Orual's mouth many times. And I'm not a blonde," I said, a meager attempt at a joke.

"I do *not* think you're ugly. You are beautiful. It's not your countenance in Orual, Joy. And many times I feel I am Orual also."

"And are you the Fox? Orual loves him, and he's devoted to her but doesn't love her the same. Are you . . ."

Jack's kind expression didn't change as he spoke. "How can I know what parts of us are threaded through this story? But one thing I do know—this story would not be what it is without you. Its depth and intimacy would not exist without who we are together."

Much of our friendship and our lives found its way into that novel: my Fairyland and his North, his Island. Our views on longing and need and joy. Our accusations and questions for the gods. Our shared history of mythology and its ability to offer meaning. And for me, the problem of obsessive love. There was a tangled twine ball of us in that myth, unraveling day by day with our discussions and our readings, our bantering and our debate. There were moments in the writing of that novel that we merged into one without ever touching.

We were consumed and distracted by Orual and Psyche—we talked about them even as we picked apples or walked to Oxford or sat in the garden. Over dinner or beers it was Orual, the Fox, and Psyche who joined us.

"All I've ever read or done has led to this novel," he told me as we walked through Oxford, untangling how Psyche would be removed from the tree in the forest where she'd been bound and sacrificed.

"I feel the same, Jack. Although I'm not writing it, I feel the same." I paused and touched his arm. "As it's always been—we use stories to make sense of the world."

He'd stopped right there in front of the bookshop and faced me with his lopsided fisherman's hat and his red cheeks, with his great admiration. The cobblestone streets were wet with rain, small puddles rippling in the dip of the road. A priest on a bicycle rode by, ringing the small bell on his handlebars and waving to us both. Jack paid him no mind but spoke right to me.

"You *are* writing it, Joy. I'm putting the words on paper and so are you with every word you speak, every question you ask, every thought you offer, every page you edit. *We* are writing it."

"What will *we* call it?" I asked. "Still *Bareface?*"

"Yes." He was resolute in this title and smiled when he said it. "Because eventually for love to be true, we must show our *real* faces."

"What is it in the end, what is it that must happen at the end of the story? The shattering of Orual's self-centeredness?"

Jack nodded. "The journey from possessive love to wholesome love." Jack looked off as if not speaking to me at all, as if Orual herself stood behind us and slowly lifted her veil. "From the profane to the divine: union with the divine through love."

"Yes," I said in agreement that went far beyond the words he spoke.

The book eventually came to be titled *Till We Have Faces*. It braided our spiritual journeys together like two stories from the same Father, parallel and mystical, infused with nature's divine ability to change us.

Through the process of its writing we had become as bound together as any man and woman.

Only one step remained, and it was not my step to take.

CHAPTER 44

Love me or love me not, the leaves will fall
And we shall walk them down. I have my joys

"SONNET XLI," JOY DAVIDMAN

June 1955

Jack took only three months to finish that novel, his greatest in my not very humble opinion.

Alone in my bedroom on Avoco Road, I typed the final pages on a June afternoon. With birdsong outside the summer window, and my boys calling out in a game they played with neighborhood children, I read the end of Jack's novel, *our* quarrel with the gods and love and obsession. My fingers were set on the keys when my breath caught under my ribs, and my heart paused as I read the last line of the novel.

I know now, Lord, why you utter no answer. You are yourself the answer. Before your face questions die away.

Questions that die away.

Answers I sought.

Questions that haunt.

All my life I'd been searching *outside* myself for the answer to this one inquiry: do you love *me*?

Seeking, always seeking. Always scrambling. Always losing. *This,* I'd thought more times than I could count, *this* is the answer and *this* is the mask and *this* is the way. I had done the same to Jack—I had made him the answer.

I'd wanted him to answer a question that only God himself could.

I'd heard Jack say more than once, in a pub or at lunch or in front of the fireplace with Warnie, the way out of the petty self almost always "requires the seeing of deception." What Jack called deception was what I called illusion.

It was as clear as if someone had walked into the room and ripped the veil off my soul, forcing me to stare into its darker depths. Much of what I'd done—mistakes, poems, manipulations, success and books and sex—had been done merely to get love. To *get* it. To answer *my* question: *do you love me?* Even as I gave love, was I trying just to gain it? Had it really taken the fictional Orual to show me the truth?

In my bedroom, I fell to my knees on the hard floor and rested my head on the edge of the mattress, pressing my face into the softness.

The face I already possessed before I was born was who I was in God all along, before anything went right or went wrong, before I *did* anything right or wrong, that was the face of my true self. My "bareface."

From that moment on, the love affair I would develop would be with my soul. He was already part of me; that much was clear. And now this would be where I would go for love—to the God in me. No more begging or pursuing or needing. It was my false self that was connected to the painful and demanding heart grasping at the world, leading me to despair. Same as Orual. Same as Psyche. Same as all of humanity.

Possibly it was only a myth, Jack's myth, that could have obliterated the false belief that I must pursue love in the outside world—in success, in acclaim, in performance, in a man.

The Truth: I was beloved of God.

Finally I could stop trying to force someone or something else to fill that role.

The pain of shattered illusion swept through me like glass blown through a room after a bomb.

All had been turned around. No longer was the question *Why doesn't Jack love me the way I want him to?* But now *Why must I demand that he love me the way I want him to?*

I was already loved. That was the answer to any question I held out to the world.

"Mommy?" Davy's voice called out from the hallway. "Where are you?"

I wiped at my face, realizing it was wet with tears. Love overwhelmed me—a sweeping wind of complete acceptance. I stumbled to my feet and threw open the door to pull my son into a big hug.

"I love you, Douglas Gresham," I said.

He laughed and pushed me away. "Have you gone loony?" He squinted. "Are you crying?"

"Sometimes we cry when we're happy," I said and tousled his hair as love pulsed around me. A sense of calm so pervasive I didn't recognize the stillness inside. It might pass—the need and fear might rise again as old and familiar comforts. But deep down, I knew the Truth now.

"I do *not* cry when I'm happy," he said with that big Douglas smile. "I just wanted to know what's for lunch."

"A picnic," I said. "Let's take a picnic to the park. Go get your brother, and let's get outside and enjoy the sunshine."

He ran off calling his brother's name, and I stood in the hallway of my rented rooms and smiled. I had it all, everything I craved, and I hadn't even known.

It had not taken a man's body to finally open me to true love, but a man's myth and God's unwavering tenderness.

CHAPTER 45

Love universal is love spread too thin
To keep a mortal warm

"SONNET XVIII," JOY DAVIDMAN

In that summer of 1955, barely did I register what went on in America anymore: there was Elvis and the civil rights uprisings. There was talk of the US sending troops to Vietnam, and Senator McCarthy finally ending his hunt for Communists. Meanwhile in England, Winston Churchill had resigned in April; Tollers's *The Lord of the Rings* had been released and was making the huge splash it was meant to make. Yet I was immersed in the Middle-earth of the Kilns, as if nothing else were happening. The soil felt as I did—ready for more and more of what had already been born.

My writing was also fertile. I'd sold a proposed new work about the seven deadly sins called *The Seven Deadlies* to Stoddard and Houghton— telling them that the virtues become deadly when they become self-righteous. I had the idea to write of a protagonist who was a modern Pharisee, an intellectual prig who presented himself at heaven's gate for admission.

None of it felt like work: the correspondence I helped Jack with every morning, the editing and indexing for Warnie, and typing for them both. I'd also finally sold pages of *Queen Cinderella* under the title *The King's Governess*. And the English version of *Smoke on the Mountain* was actually selling copies (probably due to Jack's name on the cover). Jack had adjusted to Cambridge, and the free time, more than he'd had at Oxford, allowed his writing to flow.

We gloried in the summer weather. We swam in the Thames at Godstow, slightly snockered and accompanied by a swan. Even the half-mile walk to and from the grocery could not tamp down my happiness. Jack paid the food bills, and I cooked for all of us; it felt surreal and dreamy.

We'd come to be dear friends with Jack's pal Austin Farrer, whom he introduced to me as "one of my co-debaters in the Socratic Club, and the Warden at Keble College." But of course, as with anyone, Austin was more than his introduction; he was a dear friend to Jack, and his wife, Kay, was a mystery writer. We hit it off over our very first whiskey, and now she paid me to type the handwritten pages for her novels. We lingered long hours over finished dinners and empty glasses with Austin and Kay.

One black and loathsome cloud rested over all this beauty, one I'd kept from Jack: the British Office was niggling around on renewing my paperwork. If they didn't agree to renew, I would have to return to America. The only way to stay was if I married a citizen. I needed to find a lawyer, write a letter, something, anything. I could *not* return to the States. I wouldn't. I would do whatever needed to be done.

For me, bad news always seemed to arrive in the middle of the most tranquil moments.

"Mummy," Douglas had asked in his thoroughly English accent only an hour before, "what is that?" He poked with his muddy shoe at my satchel on the floor where the certified letter poked up, its official document obvious among the typed pages and scribbled notes.

I shoved it deeper into the bag. "Nothing to worry about," I lied. Just the British government informing me that my work visa was over, and unless I was married to a citizen it was back to Dante's Inferno with me.

I was deep into typing the final edited pages of *Bareface* in Jack's Kilns study one August afternoon, still not having told him. Outside my sons were laughing, and the merriness swooped to the open window like a bird. They were helping Paxford clear the garden for more summer planting, setting netting over the tomato plants.

In a repeat of last year, Warnie was again too sick with the drink to journey to Ireland with Jack. I'd encouraged Warnie to go to AA. It had been one of our very few disagreements, a lengthy and heated discussion by the pond. In the end, he agreed to go to a hygienic bastille in Dumfries, Scotland, but *no* AA.

Again it was the four of us at the Kilns for summer break—Jack, Davy, Douglas, and I.

I took that contemptible letter from my bag just as the ringing phone in Jack's house startled me with its coarse sound. I answered. "Mr. Lewis's residence."

"I'm calling for a Miss Davidman," the voice replied in a crisp English accent.

"Speaking." I stood to look out the window and watched Davy run off to the pond.

"This is Dutton Publishing. Please hold for the production manager for *Surprised by Joy*. Mr. Lewis has told us to direct all questions about production to you."

"Yes," I said. "I'll hold."

Jack's voice rose to the window. "Get cleaned up, Davy. It's the most dreaded time of the day."

Latin tutoring.

Davy's polite voice responded with words I didn't understand, and Douglas called that he was off to fish.

"Miss Davidman?"

"Yes?" I returned my attention to the phone.

"We have a question about page 32, where Mr. Lewis discusses his boarding school."

I spent a half hour or more on the phone answering production questions before I rose to fetch the laundry from the line in the backyard. Jack and Davy toiled over Latin in Jack's office, and I ambled outside. Sunshine had dried the clothes, and I took them down, burying my face in one of Douglas's shirts, inhaling the sweet smell of summer and my son.

"Mommy?" Douglas bounded from around the bend, a fish flopped over and dead in his hand. "Will you give this perch to Mrs. Miller? Please? I'm going to Oxford with the boys."

"I'm folding laundry, son. Take that fish to the kitchen."

And off he went, running all hilter and such with a group of boys following.

"Have fun," I said into the empty wind he'd left behind.

So different, my boys were—Davy tense and studious and Douglas gulping life by the mouthful. Still they sparred; after taking boxing classes at school they practiced with each other, ignoring my dissuading arguments that boxing was a disgusting sport. Davy was also studying magic, while Douglas studied the pond's rich life.

Slowly I folded the clothes, setting them into the basket with great care. It had become these small things that nourished me. If I could have allowed this life to be enough in New York, could I have saved my marriage? Why had these tasks, the ones I now did with a happy heart, once been such drudgery, Sisyphean tasks that took me away from my writing?

I folded Jack's shirt, a white button-down that needed mending, and I set it aside to remind myself to take a needle to the collar that evening.

No, it wasn't *entirely* within my will.

What I had with Jack—the intimacy and understanding, the collaboration and laughter—transformed everything in its path: every chore, every moment suffused with great love.

I mused over how much had changed between Jack and me. Chad and Eva Walsh had come to visit us a few months before. Eva and I had taken a long walk alone, and she'd whispered to me, "Are you two in love?"

I told her the truth. "I believe I'm alone in that budding emotion."

"I don't believe that," she said.

"Honestly, Eva." We reached the end of the path and stood before the pond. "He has no interest in anything more than this deep friendship, what he calls philia."

Eva had turned to me and shaded her eyes against the evening sun. "I see the way he looks at you. It's like no one else exists and you have a secret language. He looks to you first when he says something, as if he's checking with you."

My chest filled with this hope that Eva's words offered, but I knew the truth. "It is love, but a different kind to him. The man has been a philosopher since he was eight years old and he picked up Dante—it's his medieval world view." I shook my head with a smile. "His complete dedication to the virtues keeps him from falling into the kind of love that captures a heart. He knows how, after all these years, to guard his heart behind the moral goodness he's practiced. He belongs to God and the church almost more than most priests I know."

"But he's not a priest, and you're a woman, and a vibrant one to boot." Eva drew closer to me and took my hands, one in each of her own. "Be patient, Joy. The heart has its own rhythm and timing."

"I don't think it's a sense of timing, Eva. I must accept the golden friendship that we do have." I paused. "And there's more. His friends are suspicious of me—especially Tollers, who calls me 'that woman,' and he cares what Tollers thinks, cares a lot. I'm divorced. I have children. I'm a New Yorker. I have Jewish ancestry. There are reasons." I glanced at the sky, thunderheads forming. "And the last time he loved wholly—his mother—he lost her in the most catastrophic way. He's cautious. Temperate."

"Joy, give him time."

I shrugged and looked back to her dear smile. "These are only guesses, Eva. How could I know? I've come to know him better than anyone except Warnie, but still how could I *truly* know? He tells me he is too old to begin another love affair and that philia is our destiny."

I hugged her as Chad approached from the far end of the pathway, calling his wife's name.

As I folded the last of the pants, I reminded myself to tell Jack of the phone call from Dutton, scooped the basket under my arm, and ambled to the back door of the house. When I entered the common room, the sight of a woman in Jack's chair startled me. It was too dim to make her out exactly, but she was definitely a woman, reading a book and curled comfortably with her shoes tossed to one side of the chair.

"Who the hell are *you*?" I asked, rage flaring in a dark burst of the old angry-Joy.

She startled and dropped the book, stood and stumbled before pressing her fingers to her temples. "I'm Moira Sayer. We've met before."

"I don't think so." I held close the laundry basket and took two steps toward her.

She held to the edge of Jack's chair. "I have every right to be here, same as you. I'm George Sayer's wife. Jack said I could come here to read while George worked at Magdalen."

George.

Sayer.

This was the first friend of Jack's I'd met at the Eastgate. Moira, his wife, with whom I'd had tea only last year.

"I'm so sorry." I clutched the basket tighter. "I'm *very* sorry." I fled the room with the heat of shame burning through my skin. Would I ever learn? Or change?

I carried the basket upstairs and left a pile of Jack's clothes outside his room and took the remainder to the boys' room. I then entered my downstairs bedroom and closed the door to sit and drop my head on the desk.

How did I slip backward into horrid old habits so easily? Into jealousy and rage, as if they were as welcoming as a warm river swim?

It only took a few moments until the knock arrived.

"Yes?"

"Joy?"

I opened the door to Jack.

"I'm sorry," I said. "I was an ass to your friend. She startled me; I didn't know she was here. I think I must have deeply embarrassed you." I shook my head. "My anger—sometimes I still find myself at cross purposes with the world."

He laughed. "Oh, it's not so bad. I explained to her that I hadn't told you she was here, and you having such terrible eyesight didn't know she wasn't an intruder meant to steal my manuscripts for her own." He laughed, with that merry twinkle in his eye.

"My terrible eyesight?" I tried to laugh, but nothing came out.

"Yes, what with your glass eye in one and your cataracts in the other."

"Jack. You forgive too easily and warmly. I'm not accustomed." I smiled and exited the room to join him in the hallway.

"Let's get out into the sunlight," he said.

"Yes, let's gather some beans and tomatoes for dinner."

"Very good," he agreed. "And then we'll walk into Oxford?"

Together we scooted down the thin hall, where I grabbed a basket for the vegetables and an apron to cover my dress. Then we were outside to the summer sunshine again. Moira had gone, and neither of us acknowledged her absence.

I glanced around the grounds. "Where's Davy?"

"He's decided that he must lay down bricks for us to walk on from the house to the pond; he's out gathering them from the old kilns and setting them into the deep mud." Jack motioned toward the pond. "He's down there."

"Well, isn't he turning industrious?" I laughed and squinted into the sun. "Building walkways. I wouldn't have guessed it."

"Joy." Jack bent over and popped two green beans from their stalk and dropped them into the basket. "What made you buggered with Moira?"

"I assume jealousy."

"Jealousy?" He made a *tsk tsk* noise, teasing.

"Yes," I said quietly. "I know it's wrong," I leaned down and chose a ripe tomato from the vine, placed it in the basket. "Like with Ruth Pitter."

"You're jealous of Ruth Pitter?" He almost laughed, but my seriousness checked him.

"I've read her poetry. She's a more gifted poet than I am, Jack." I held up my hand. "There's no use arguing that, but that's not the point—she's in love with you." I bent to pick another tomato, but my finger pressed too deeply into the delicate flesh. Red juice trickled down my arm. I dropped the fruit to the ground and wiped my palm on the apron.

"That's not the case, Joy. We are longtime friends. We've been writing to each other for years now. We discuss writing and cooking and gardening and poetry."

I faced him, my hand shielding my eyes from the late-afternoon sun. I wanted him to hear what he had just said. In that sentence he could have been describing *us* as surely as he was describing her.

"What is it?" he asked when I didn't respond.

"She's not any different from me, is she—to you?"

"Ruth any different from you?"

"Yes."

Jack pressed his hands together as if in prayer and shook his head. "You're right. This is jealousy speaking. You are here standing in my garden, after answering my correspondence and editing my work. You are right here with me and we are heading to town for a beer. Tonight we will read and play Scrabble and Davy will beat me at chess. Douglas will fall asleep talking a mile a minute." He paused.

I took in a long breath. "I see when my ego takes charge. I've come to realize how my past affects me now—criticism and cruelty mingled with attachment have proffered a neurosis I'll spend the rest of my life overcoming." I paused. "I can't get this Christian thing right. How does one get it *right* at all?" I slapped my hands together in frustration.

"Get it right?" he asked quietly. "What exactly is getting it right?"

"Sometimes I forget to turn to him, and then the woman I have been for all of my life rises up and is no less damaging than she was before."

"God is no magician, Joy."

"Oh, how I could use some magic—it might take all of my life, what remains of it, to surrender fully."

"All of this life, Joy, and maybe most of the next." He winked but then drew closer. "As with our art, we must surrender and get ourselves out of the way if any good is to come."

"Must I surrender again and again?" I paused for effect. "And again?"

"I believe all of us must."

Our basket was full by then, the vegetables enough for dinner, when I told him, "The truth is I was already on edge—you see, I might not be here for long."

His eyes widened. "What do you mean? Whyever not?"

"The British Home Office won't renew my paperwork again. I'll have to take the boys back to the States."

"Joy, I'll not let you be sent back home. We'll find a way to make sure you stay."

"There is only one way to stay, Jack. And that's marriage. So unless I take myself over to the Globe Tavern and pick myself a good Englishman to seduce, it looks as if I will be packing for America."

"You can't leave," he said. "I will not let you return to that terrible place." He took my face in his hands. I dropped the basket, tomatoes and green beans scattering to the earth.

I placed my hands on top of his. "You don't want me to go?"

Our faces were close now, his lips near mine, his eyes shadowed by sadness.

"No. I would miss you too terribly. I have come to depend on you, Joy." He dropped his hands and placed them on my shoulders, drawing back a step.

My body trembled with the need for him, and I could feel the same from him—a thrumming below the words and the touch. He pulled me close and held to me, and I rested my head on his shoulder.

"You musn't leave."

CHAPTER 46

Now, having said the words that can be said,
Having set down for any man to see

"Sonnet XLIV," Joy Davidman

"I have something I want to show you." Jack stopped on the Oxford sidewalk next to one of the ubiquitous red phone booths. August heat pressed upon us, and a woman pushing a pram strolled past, smiling at Jack in recognition.

"You do?" I asked, redirecting his attention to me.

It was only the day before that I'd told him about the British Home Office. He hadn't said another word and I was nervous, reticent to bring it up again. Davy browsed through Blackwell's, and Douglas ran off to find some friends to punt with at the Cherwell.

"I do." He waved his hand. "Follow me."

We moved a few blocks down the road, and he stopped in front of a split brick house, 10 Old High Street.

"This is for sale," he said and pointed.

"That's nice." I continued to walk forward. Noticing the goings-on in town during our daily walks was as much a part of our routine as his morning correspondence.

He placed his hand on my shoulder, stayed me. "I can help you buy it if you'd move to Oxford," he said.

Then the strangest thing happened—I had nothing to say, no fanciful retort, no witty comment. I stared at the little house, the dark red color of the geraniums planted in window boxes all around the city.

The house was split with exact mirror images of two thin front doors set next to each other—a duplex. There were two upstairs windows, two down. A brick wall ran across the front of the house and pruned shrubbery hid the bottom half of the lower windows.

"Move here?" Even as I asked, I already saw us—Davy, Douglas, and me—with boxes and furniture, books and toys, Sambo the cat, our lives in tow and moving into this house within walking distance to the Kilns, to town, to a better life.

Jack moved to stand before me and took both my hands.

"I've thought of little else since you told me that you might have to leave. I knew in the sleepless night that I would do whatever it takes to keep you here. We can marry, a civil marriage of course, and you can move here." He pointed to the house, the FOR SALE sign pasted in the window.

"Marry me?" I tried to swallow the laugh but could not. "This might not be the most romantic proposal."

"It's not meant to be romantic. It's meant to be sincere. I want you to stay here. I want you near to me."

From the threat of returning to America to the thrill of having my own place in Oxford. He wanted me there. He wanted me near. And yet, a marriage of convenience? I smiled the truest way I could, and together we turned to stare at the house. "A real house," I said. "I haven't had one since I left New York. A real *home*."

Jack's cheeks rose with his smile. "Yes," he said. He spun his walking stick in a circle and tilted his fisherman's hat to me. "Home."

Back at the Kilns later that evening, Jack had fallen asleep in his chair when I jostled him awake. "Oh, buggers. I nodded off." He stretched and smiled at me. "I hope I wasn't snoring."

"Snoring? Of course you were. But that's not why I woke you." I looked at the folder I'd set on the table. "I have something for you. Something I thought I would never give to you, but now I am. It's time."

"You are oh-so-serious, Joy. What is it?" He shook the bleariness from his voice and eyes.

I held out the folder, my hand trembling same as my heart. "I've been writing these for years, Jack. They're sonnets."

When he proposed a civil marriage, I decided, standing there on an Oxford sidewalk with the sun beating down on his offer of both a house and marriage, that I would give these to him.

He plucked from me the beige folder with the word *Courage* written on the front, his hand brushing mine.

"Courage?" he asked.

"Yes, I needed it to hand these to you."

"Sonnets?" He beamed. "You've been hiding your poetry from me? And now I have a great treasure to read?"

"I think you will have to decide for yourself if they are treasure or trash."

What I didn't tell him, what he would find for himself, was that the sonnets dated as far back as 1936. I'd spent hours putting the verses together into a coherent storyline, a progression of sorts shadowing the loves I'd felt before and my growing love for him. I'd woven the past and the present together in a collection that might illustrate the clearest vision of my heart. It was bold. It was an action that might very well embarrass me and break my heart.

The sonnets swung wildly from passion to despair, from desire to embarrassment. But I wanted him to take that wild journey so that he might finally understand the larger arc of my abiding love for him. I also included fifteen poems that weren't part of the forty-five love sonnets, poems painting pictures of our days together—from "Ballade of Blistered Feet" (our first hike on Shotover), to my "Sonnet of Misunderstandings" after leaving him that Christmas morning, to the last one titled "Let No Man."

He flipped open the folder, carbon copies of every troubled-heart sonnet exposed to his eyes, to his knowing. But I couldn't hide anymore. As Orual lifted her veil, so I handed him the folder.

"I've stopped writing them," I said. "The last one was after my parents' visit."

His eyes grazed the cover page, on which I'd typed a silly rhyme and note to him—*Dear Jack, here are some sonnets you may care to read . . .*

"You've stopped writing poetry? Whatever for?"

"No," I said with a smile. "Not all poetry. Just *that* kind of poetry. You'll understand when you read."

I stood as he sat in his chair, evening falling through the windows like honey.

"It's the only gift I've got." I quoted the opening letter in his hand. "You have given me so much, and now you offer me a home here in Oxford. This is a gift in return."

His eyes radiated tenderness, and then he began to read. I walked away and left him with the love sonnets—with the poetry and with my heart.

It was the next afternoon, late in the day, as I stood in the kitchen sifting through the mail and humming a tune from an old song I hadn't thought of in years—Bing Crosby, "Swinging on a Star"—when Jack came to me. I'd spent the day in the garden, and I was dirty with the sweet earth under my fingernails and swiped across the kitchen apron over my flowered dress. Tired and satisfied.

"'Between two rivers, in the wistful weather; Sky changing, tree undressing, summer failing.'"

Sonnet VI. From the days of our first meeting.

"You've read them." I dropped the mail to the table.

"Not all of them. Not yet. I want to savor them as slowly as a fine glass of wine. They are stunning and, as I've described your work before—flaming. The imagery and heartache and aching loss are palpable. I'm honored that you offered them to me."

"You understand those sonnets are for you?" I wiped my hands on the apron, mud smudged across it.

"But some were written before you met me. Some of these are for other men. Other men you've loved." He spoke quietly, and I could hear in his tone that he didn't abide well the thought of me loving another man. Was it jealousy or fact he stated?

"Yes, but they were always meant for you. Can't you see that? Still they are *for* you. The collection, and how I ordered them . . . they are the trouble of my heart."

"The trouble of your heart." Jack stepped forward. "There is no trouble of your heart. It is exquisite."

I paused in the beauty of his praise, wanting to dive deep into the timelessness of his words. Decades of love poetry were now in his hands.

"You are magnificent, Joy."

"Jack." I said his name, tasted his name with the same love I always did.

He exhaled and drew one step closer. "This is an extraordinary journey for an old man. I never expected someone like you to come into my life, and I've been set in my ways and worked to live the virtues. We've talked of this before, but maybe it is best explained by something my mate Owen Barfield once said about me in a great debate over beers—that I cannot help trying to live what I *think*."

"Well, my dear." I smiled at him. "I want you to live what you *feel*."

"It's not as easy for the rest of us as it is for you."

I tapped his chest, the place of his heart. "Why do you close that door in your heart that lets me in, the room that is all ours?"

"You *are* in there." He leaned forward. "I feel your love, and it changes me every day. But I can't force my long-set patterns to change. I don't know *how*. When I met you, you were married, and then divorced. Our union would be adultery." He paused.

It was then that I quoted a sonnet. "Love. 'You can be very sure it will not kill you, But neither will it let you sleep at night.'"

He laughed. "Sonnet III." Then he grew serious. "And you are very correct."

I shook my head. "You are bloody infuriating."

He ignored my comment, drawing closer. "Joy, I'm late for Evensong at St. Mary's. Then on to a pint at the Six Bells. You'll accompany me?"

"Oh, tonight I think I'll stay in and enjoy the quiet."

He frowned but nodded. "I'll be back soon."

As he walked off he glanced back over his shoulder at me as if the two of us carried a great secret of sonnets together, and indeed we did.

CHAPTER 47

What a fool I was to play the mouse
And squeak for mercy!

"SONNET XLIII," JOY DAVIDMAN

April 1956

My wedding day, if one could call it such, yet who would have thought there'd be another?

At my new home on 10 High Street in Oxford, I stood in front of the mirror buttoning the front of the cream dress I would wear that day to my second wedding, although it was clear it wouldn't be a "real" wedding at all. Just in the nick of time to save me from another visit and plea to the courts for an extended visa.

Jack knocked lightly on the door.

"Come in." I spun around to face him.

He entered with that smile I loved. "You look beautiful, Joy." He straightened his tie and smirked a little bit. "'The angels disapprove the way I look at you.'" And he came closer, brushed my hair from my shoulder.

He'd just quoted from "Sonnet XXXVIII."

He'd been doing this for months now, privately inserting sonnet lines into our daily lives: whether in my backyard while I planted tulips and daffodils or tossed a net over my garden to keep the birds from destroying it, or while we hailed a taxi to attend a party. For the past eight months, since I'd handed my heart over in those sonnets, he'd become softer and more affectionate.

I straightened his tie. "You look mighty handsome for your first wedding day."

He placed his hand on top of mine and held it there until the anguished cry of Douglas echoed from across the house.

"Mummy."

"What is it?" I patted Jack's tie and stepped out of my room.

Douglas tore down the hallway and stopped in front of me, his hands held out in supplication. There in his palms were the remains of what I assumed was his precious budgie bird, Chirpers.

"Sambo ate Chirpers," he wailed. "The horrible cat ate my bird."

"Are you sure it was Sambo? Maybe it was Snowball?" We had adopted a new kitten, a white fluff of shivering fur.

"It was Sambo!"

"On my wedding day?" I tried not to laugh, but what else was there to do? It was a mean and nasty bird anyway, although I would never say that to Douglas.

"It's not a *real* wedding day. And Chirpers is dead. Dead."

I took the bird from my son and covered it with my other hand.

Jack appeared behind me. "We will give Chirpers the proper Christian burial he is due. He is now flying among the other cat-destroyed birds in heaven," he said.

"I hate cats." Douglas wiped at his tears and stomped away. The front door slammed hard enough to shake the floor.

Davy was somewhere close by, probably delving into his newfound passion—Shakespeare.

I took Chirpers to my bedroom where I found an old shoe box and placed him with care while Jack headed out to console Douglas.

What an odd little family we were.

———

We'd been on Old High Street for seven months by then. On a blazing hot August afternoon, after Jack had left on a delayed journey to

Ireland with Warnie, the boys and I departed from London. We'd settled into the three-bedroom half-brick house with a sitting room, a kitchen, and even a tiny dining room. On moving day, while boxes and tattered furniture were being dragged through the front door, we three had stood in the backyard and stared at the spacious lawn we shared with the attached identical house. Both plum and apple trees stood in our yard, echoes of the past.

"Beauty for ashes," I said to my boys. "God redeems what's been lost."

Of course they only stared at me with confusion and then tossed off their shoes to feel the soft grass beneath their feet.

"Oxford is much better than London." It was the first time in a long time I'd seen such a wide smile on Davy's serious face.

"Yes, my beautiful boy, it is," I agreed.

Months fly by in many ways, and those months had been the best of ways, even with my continuing and confusing declining health—oh, it's just middle age and stress, the doctors continued to say. Walking had become difficult—rheumatism, I was told—and I only forty-one years old. When had *that* become middle age? Davy tried to teach me to use his bicycle to get around easier, but I couldn't even put the weight on my hip to get on the seat.

Oxford became home quick as a flash, and I began to entertain again. Friends and neighbors visited. I cooked, made plum jam from the fruit of the backyard, gardened, and of course wrote and edited as I'd always done. The White Hart Pub was a block away, and its gardens were as lush as a tropical jungle, so I often ordered a pint and sat at a wobbly table to write.

Jack spent long hours with the boys—he'd bought them a horse to pasture in the back acreage of the Kilns, and he allowed Davy to buy books to his heart's content in Blackwell's. There was a football for Douglas and clothes for them both. Jack had come to love them and they him; it was obvious and endearing.

Surprised by Joy had been released the previous month to great acclaim. How many times I was asked if the title referenced me.

"Oh, that would be lovely," was my pat reply, "but no. It's the essence of Jack's lifelong search for something he found as a child in a miniature garden—joy."

I worked on *The Seven Deadlies*, for which I'd been paid an advance, but it seemed a dead end. Forgetting what I'd concluded when I wrote *Smoke*—writing theology was not my forte—I was being stretched to the limits. I took breaks from my own work to type like mad on Kay Farrer's mystery pages, which not only brought in money but also proffered a favor for an admired friend. I niggled away on short stories and still hoped to make something of my Queen Cinderella novel. I typed for payment, but did not and would not give up on my own work.

And oh! For my own ego's benefit—I'd been asked to speak at the Pusey House about Charles Williams, and at a London church on the problem of being a Christian Jew. In many ways it felt that my love for God, my soul, my family, and my friends had become a magnet, drawing all the broken and scattered pieces of my life together.

Bill and I continued a rigorous correspondence—sometimes I begged for money, sometimes I thanked him. I offered news and always kept him updated on our sons' lives—Douglas playing on the under elevens football team. Davy corresponding with Tollers about *The Hobbit*, learning runes and the Erse alphabet. I told him of Davy's favorite pastime— roaming through Blackwell's Bookshop for as long and often as he pleased, as Jack gave him a large book allowance. And of all surprises— Douglas had begun writing poetry!

"A golden peacock flies," one poem began. I hoped I painted a picture of our happiness for Bill, for it *was* a happy life.

Jack was alongside me every day he came to Oxford from Cambridge, and many whispered that he'd moved in. What vivid imaginations they had.

There had been a night I thought we were on a "date"—when he took me to see *Bacchae*, the great Greek tragedy. In the dark of the theater he had taken my hand. With our fingers wound together and the great tragic ending of the play approaching, I believed in more for us. But alas, after leaving that darkened theater our natural rhythms returned—philia, banter, beer, and laughter.

Every Sunday we went to church together at Holy Trinity, where he and Warnie had gone for years, attending the service without the organ and sitting behind the pillar so the priest could not see when Jack disagreed with his sermon. Always, the three of us slipped out directly after Communion and walked to town for a beer. There were sections of the liturgy that fed my soul and others that made me bristle with argument.

One splendid evening in the beginning of the year, I dug out a fancy dark-blue ball gown from my days in New York. Surprised to find that it still fit, I wore it to attend a dinner that Jack threw in my honor at Magdalen. Here I met his friends I'd heard about but never encountered. I behaved. I smiled demurely. It was a smashing evening that ended with a cab ride full of laughter as he imitated each one of his friends. We were a team, the two of us understanding each other in a way that no one else could or ever had.

Twice I'd been to meet Jack before or after an Inklings meeting, which is where I learned that Tollers's talking tree, Treebeard, was modeled after Jack.

Just when I believed I'd learned all I might, there was more to discover about this man. I was confident in this: it was only the beginning. I felt we were on a threshold, a precipice. We had a lifetime to grow closer and come to truly know each other.

A lifetime.

And who knows what that lifetime is made of? How many days, or hours?

———

"Jack." I faced him as I plucked my purse from the hook on the wall to leave for the registry office. "Is this meant to be a secret? This marriage?"

"It isn't so much a secret as it is between us. Because it's not in the eyes of the church and we aren't living together, it is ours to hold close. Of course Dr. Humphrey and Austin Farrer will be there today, so they will know."

"I want the world to know," I told him.

He smiled sadly and buttoned his jacket before looking directly at me. "We shall know, Joy. We shall, and that is what matters."

I smoothed my cream suit to leave for the office on St. Giles, down the street from our beloved Bird and Baby, where we would sign the papers binding us legally as husband and wife on April 26, 1956.

CHAPTER 48

Open your door, lest the belated heart
Die in the bitter night; open your door
"SONNET XLIV," JOY DAVIDMAN

"There might not have ever been a more sublime October," Jack said quietly. The lit end of his cigarette glowed, its own full red moon, and then fell in sparks to the ground. "The mornings cool, the days warm, and the nights like this. I can't remember another as beautiful."

The October moon was full, hovering over us in the back garden of my Old High Street house. We'd grown silent after hours of talking as we sat on the same bench, our knees touching.

I nodded, and although he wasn't looking at me I knew he felt the agreement. Kay and Austin Farrar and others had just left a little dinner party I'd given. Kay had whispered to me in the kitchen, "Austin and I agree that Jack seems more genteel in the past months. He's quieter and more relaxed. It's as if his sensitive nature has at last come through. And we all know it's because of you."

For dinner that night I'd cooked mutton the best I knew how, served mashed potatoes American style, and green beans I'd canned from last summer at the Kilns. I made the apple pie from my backyard apples and could almost taste summers in Vermont with the Walshes. The wine and conversation had flowed as smooth as could be.

It was eleven p.m. by then, and Jack was the last to leave. He was always the last to leave. Every day he walked to my house from the Kilns, and we worked or wandered into town.

"Today I bought fireworks for Guy Fawkes Day," I said. "So don't hoard any more or the boys will have enough to destroy your whole back forest."

"I'll tell Warnie," he said. "He's the one who stockpiles them. Oh! Has he told you? He's reading your husband's book, *Monster Midway*."

I laughed and rested my head on his shoulder. "I believe you're my husband."

"Indeed I am." Jack patted my knee.

I paused before delving into the subject I had held tight until all the guests had gone. "Jack, these days and nights have been some of the most treasured of my life. The dinner parties and friends. The conversation. I almost feel like I've made a life here."

He turned to me, his cigarette almost to the filter. He dropped it to the ground and crushed it beneath his shoe. "But?"

"There's talk about me. About us."

"What kind of talk?"

"Can't you imagine, Jack? The Oxford don who comes to the divorced woman's house until late at night, every night. People gossip." I paused. "Kay told me that Tollers is afraid of what Cambridge will think when they get wind of it. We appear inappropriate."

He attempted a laugh but it didn't work, so instead he quoted another sonnet. "'Would smile contempt, and in the brazen noon.'" He paused after the line when I didn't laugh or reply. "Since when have you started to care about what others think is inappropriate?"

"I care, Jack."

"Would you like me to not come round as much? Because I couldn't bear that."

I'd worn my hair down for the night, and it fell over my shoulders. The wind fluttered through and whipped it into my eyes as I spoke. "No, but I'd like to stop being your little secret. We're married. I know not in the eyes of God. I know not in the eyes of eros, you'd say." I stood then and looked down to him. "But we *are* married. And no one knows." Tears rose in my eyes, ones I'd held back for so long. "I feel as if you're ashamed of me. That you like to keep our friendship in this little cardboard box where only we and a few others have access."

"Joy, I have brought you into my life fully. I have introduced you to Oxford and Cambridge. I'm with you every day." His face fell with sorrow. "There isn't an area I have hidden from you."

"Do I embarrass you?"

Jack stood to face me. "You don't believe that, do you?"

"I no longer know what to believe about us."

"If you don't want me to stop coming round, what is it? Would you like me to tell everyone that we had a civil marriage so you could stay in the country? I told my very dearest friend Arthur in Ireland."

I held my hand to stop his defenses. "I just ruined the night," I said. "I'm sorry. I'm tired, and probably not making much sense. My old insecurities are rising. But keeping our marriage a secret feels clandestine and dirty. And dismissive."

"Joy." He took two steps closer to me, the aroma of the common room at the Kilns, cigarette smoke, and autumn air of crushed leaves engulfing me. He took my hands and pressed them to his chest as if it were something he'd done a million times before, not this, the first time.

"Would you and the boys like to move into the Kilns then?"

"Pardon?"

Had I heard him right? Had he just asked us to move in? Not a vacation, not a holiday or a feast, but to *move*. Were the wine and moonlight playing tricks? Were we another Janie and Maureen?

"I've been puzzling it out, and you've made me see that it's time to stop merely thinking about it. It's time to do it. We *will* make a life there, Joy. There won't be any more gossip, and I'll tell everyone that we've married."

"But not in the eyes of the church, and not in flesh?"

"The church will never allow it."

"King Edward abdicated the throne to marry Wallis Simpson, the love of his life. But that doesn't happen much—a love grand enough to defy the strict rules that make little sense." I paused. "Here I am, a terrible divorcée just as she was."

"No." The pain in his voice made me look up, and I watched his face crumple. He swiftly brought my hands to his lips.

I closed my eyes and let the sensation wash over me, the simple bliss of his lips on my skin, my heart racing for more, the autumn air ruffling his hair in the moment that he asked me to move in with him. He released my hands, and I opened my eyes.

His hand rose, and at first I couldn't imagine why, an exotic choreography in the dance of our relationship. Then his hand was behind my head, fingers wound into my thick hair, and with a slight tug he pulled me forward.

He kissed me.

Gently.

Finally.

My lips found his as easily as the sea finds the shore, as sun reaches earth. Our mouths soft, yet eager within the gentleness. My hands were behind his neck on the soft space beneath his hairline where I had often gazed as he walked ahead of me. I touched his skin. Against me, I felt the outline of a body I'd already memorized. All inside me loosened and untied, a surrender to anything he would want of me.

We lingered there for a few moments under that Selena-full moon.

Some things are more intense in the imagination, and some more powerful in reality. His touch and his lips—I could not have imagined the ecstasy of both. Nothing had ever been as worth waiting for as this.

He withdrew and rested his forehead on mine before kissing the soft spot below my ear. I shivered with the want of more. When he stood apart from me, holding both my hands, he smiled, but it wasn't a smile I'd seen before. This one, curled at the corners with his eyes on mine, was just ours. *Only* ours.

"Good night, my dear Joy." And with that, he was gone.

I felt almost as I had the night when God entered the cracked places of my ego in my sons' nursery—as if my boundaries had been dissolved, as if all that I was would become one with all that was another. Just as that night, it didn't fix anything, but it was the beginning of something that could change me, change *us*.

Pure love, it seemed, was not limited to a singular experience.

For two weeks I thought of little else but his kiss and his touch, yet I attempted to work. My mind spun back to that moment his lips found mine, and I'd discover myself standing stock-still wherever I was, my hand over my heart and my eyes closed. This was a state of longing and expectancy where time opened.

The days were blissful except for the aches in my legs and hips, but even this was colored by growing desire. When Jack broke free of Cambridge for short times, there had been more kisses: soft ones of promise without spoken words. He held my hand on the long walks through Shotover Hill. He slowly drew nearer, closer, as if he needed to court me when already I loved him.

When he was in Oxford, he stayed late with me as he always had, but now rested comfortably against me when we were alone. I hadn't pushed—waiting so patiently to experience who we would become when we lived together.

Would I move into his room? Did he still want us to hold fast to abstinence? My body would not allow me to think of much other than Jack and his touch.

CHAPTER 49

My friend, if it was sin in you and me
That we went fishing for each other in
The troubled waters of life

"SONNET XXXII," JOY DAVIDMAN

October 18, 1956

Only God knows when life will burst open, shattering all self-made plans and expectations as illusory as dreams. For me, it was a Thursday, a regular Thursday by all accounts.

My sons were back at school. Jack's final Narnian chronicle, *The Last Battle*, had just been released. Harcourt had published *Till We Have Faces* with its haunting black cover. We were both as thrilled as if we'd had our first child together, waiting for the reviews and readings.

Life had begun anew for both of us.

Autumn air rustled the birch tree, and songbirds called out to one another outside the open window of the small room where I typed pages for Kay Farrar's new mystery novel. The imminent move to the Kilns preoccupied me.

Sambo rubbed against my leg, his fur sticking to my flannel pants. I leaned down and tickled him behind the ear. "You happy too, old boy? You've adjusted to Oxford, haven't you?" He purred and walked toward the front door, looking over his shoulder. He wanted out.

I stood. That is all I did—stood and took one step.

And everything changed.

A white-hot, searing pain burst from my left hip. Fire shot down my leg and stripped breath from my lungs as I fell to the ground with a shriek of agony. For the fraction of a second I believed I'd been shot. I expected to see a hole in the wall or window, a thin river of blood trickling across the hardwood floor and seeping into the edges of my knotted rug.

The phone rang from the far side of the house in complete disregard of my agony, as if mocking me. Whoever was on that phone should have been able to hear me scream. I crumpled in on myself, folding into a fetal position with my leg bent at the wrong angle. The pain obliterated all senses but its own, selfish in its flooding anguish to be all I knew. I saw nothing, smelled nothing; the world existed only in the fire that was screaming through my body.

Slowly thoughts emerged, one by one. What happened? Was it bad? How had I fallen? Where was I? Had I tripped over Sambo?

No, I hadn't. I'd stood, and my leg had given out below me.

With meticulous and tiny movements, I crawled across the wooden floor.

You can do this.

Slowly.

You have to get help.

Don't panic.

Flames licked the inside of my thigh. I took long, deep breaths, but they caught in my throat and escaped as sobs against my will. I battled the mental fog of pain, struggling to think whom to call. I needed someone near, someone to come get me.

Kay. She was close by, only a block away. I finally reached the edge of the table. I couldn't stand for the phone, so I grabbed its dark, hairy cord and yanked it to the floor. It banged and clattered, scaring Sambo to lurch across the room with a loud *meow*. In what seemed like slow motion, I dialed Kay's number and waited through four long desperate rings for her to answer.

"Help me," was all I said.

CHAPTER 50

What will come of me
After the fern has feathered from my brain
"YET ONE MORE SPRING," JOY DAVIDMAN

My eyelids felt as heavy as granite, and I lifted them as if pushing a rock up Shotover Hill. In blurred vision I saw white curtains and glimmering steel, and I squinted against the glare. Where was I? The bed was hard and small, the pillow flat beneath my head as I lay supine. Somewhere far off, or was it close by? There was metal clanging against metal and the whispered voices of the serious. Cotton gauze covered my thoughts, and my brain wouldn't fire. Had I drunk too much? Was this a hangover?

Polished tile floors.

Fluorescent lights too bright.

I attempted to move, only slightly, when the pain arrowed from my hip in both directions—down my leg and across to my groin. An involuntary cry erupted, and I remembered everything in one flash: Kay and Austin squealing onto High Street to carry me to bed. Kay whispering that it was she who had been calling when I fell—a premonition that something was amiss. I'd had a fitful and harrowing night swallowing the leftover codeine from my dental work and never dulling the pain. At sunrise the ambulance was called and roared in to transport me to Wingfield Orthopaedic Hospital. The X-rays and needles, the crying out, and the blessed and blissful absence of pain when the medicine soared through my veins.

With my cry a nurse appeared, her white cap a swan in flight at Jack's pond.

"Mrs. Gresham," the nurse said quietly. "I see you're awake."

"Where is the doctor? I need to know what's wrong." My logical mind burst like a flash through the fog: Diagnose. Solve. Fix.

"You have a broken leg," she said in the weirdly placid voice of one trying to keep a hysterical person calm.

"I know that part." My voice was shattered, fragile as the remainder of me. Someone had plaited my hair into two braids, and they fell over my shoulders with white ribbons at the ends. I had never worn my hair this way, and the omen seemed morbid—I was no longer myself. The blanket over my left leg was tented, a metal cage below to keep the fabric from resting on the broken bones.

"Did I have surgery?" I asked.

"No, but the doctor will be in soon to speak with you."

She inserted a syringe filled with golden fluid into my upper arm, and I did nothing but watch her push in the needle, a distracted observer waiting only for the relief. What did Jack say about pain? *God's megaphone to the world.*

Well, God, I'm listening.

Then their names roared through my mind like twin lions: *Davy. Douglas.*

They were thirteen and eleven by then. Had anyone called them? Did they know I'd broken my leg? Where was Jack? Didn't Kay call him at Cambridge?

I turned my head to the window that ran the full length of the wall. Outside shimmered the glorious idyllic autumn of England. The views weren't any less beautiful than those from Jack's rooms, as the hospital was on Oxford's campus. The expansive green lawn, flowers crowding one another for attention, and roses so pink they seemed painted. But inside the room—metal and plastic, poles and sterile chairs of steel with the lingering stench of alcohol and vomit.

A great rustling came from the doorway, and my muddled thoughts wondered if they were bringing me a roommate. I turned my head slowly to see Jack rush through the door. He wore a wrinkled black suit; his tie was askew; his face was slack with fear.

"Jack!" My voice broke. I'd known it all along, but seeing him run through that door, his hair windblown, his eyes on me, I loved him as deeply as any man I'd known.

"Joy." He came to my bedside and knelt, not taking avail of the chair. "You're awake."

"You've been here?" I asked.

"Yes," he said and reached beneath his spectacles to wipe at the tears that had risen in his own eyes. "I've been here."

"You didn't have to leave school . . ." My voice trailed off.

Jack rose and brought the chair to sit and face me. "Is there pain now?"

"The medicine the nurse just shot into my arm says no." I tried to smile but could not. "What happened, Jack? I know I fell and then spent the night at home, but since they've brought me here . . ."

"You don't remember?"

"On and off, like broken puzzle pieces. I know there was an X-ray machine, and medicines and hushed voices. So much fuss for a broken leg, Jack. Too much fuss. Let me get the plaster and go home."

Outside came a great whoop of laughter from a group of students walking through the grass. Life was outside these walls and that window. I looked to Jack with a desperate plea. "I want to go home."

"There's news, Joy. The doctors have asked me if I'd like to keep it from you, but I cannot. Lies must not be told, not to you, not to anyone."

Fear engulfed me in a toxic fog, closing my throat and filling my chest with that familiar wing-flapping anxiety. I reached for Jack's hand and took it in mine, held to it as if to a life raft. "What is it?"

"They will come talk to you."

"I want you to tell me, Jack. What do you know?"

"It's either leukemia or another cancer." The two diagnoses scattered about the room like dark dust, like evil.

"Not the real kind," I said with some depth of understanding that there was no such thing as an "unreal" kind. "It's rheumatism. That's what they kept telling me. It's fibrositis, they said."

"They were wrong. Whatever it is, Joy, it's in your leg." Pain twisted Jack's face. He held so fast to my hand that I did not want to tell him that it hurt. "The doctors say the X-rays show that your femur looks as though it has been eaten by moths."

"Well then, maybe it has," I said, but a sob broke free. "Maybe Old High Street has a moth epidemic and we don't know and . . ."

Jack leaned close to me, wiped at my tears, and kissed me as gently as one can in a hospital bed. If I could have fallen out of that bed into his arms, I would have. If I could have dropped to my knees, I would have been on them already. Instead I clung to Jack, his hands tangled with mine. "No. It can't be something so bad as that. Not *now*."

He kissed me again and then, resting his hand gently on my cheek, said, "I can't lose you, Joy. I love you so much. I've been such a fool, such a bloody fool. I should have been loving you and saying it every day for as long as I've known."

"Jack . . ." My voice was quiet, as if I might scare away his confession. "You *love* me?"

"With all I am," he said.

"Because I'm dying? Is this a consolation gift?" I wiped at his tears and then at mine.

"Joy, you are not dying. And even if you are, this love has been here all along. Sometimes it takes a great shake from God to awake me from my insolence, to make me admit feelings that exist."

"Pain," I said and closed my eyes. "God's megaphone."

Tears were in the corners of his soft and full lips, and he kissed me again. I tasted his grief as he spoke, his breath then whispering in my ear. "Who knows when friendship crosses that borderland into love, but it has. Long ago it had, but it's just now that I can give words to the truth."

He lifted his head, and I touched his cheek. "I've loved you for so long, Jack. And here I am at my worst and you proclaim *your* love?

God does work in mysterious ways." I kissed him again and tasted the tobacco, the warmth.

"At your worst?" He shook his head and his spectacles fell from his face, landed on the worn cream blanket covering my diseased body. "You are beautiful to me, Joy. You are *all* that is beautiful." He tucked a stray hair back from my face. "All of my life I have thought of love in a literary sense, part of a story or fairy tale. But love is really true; I know that now. Eros—I haven't loved completely until now. I know that." His voice held the truth of every word spoken, a man broken by death's threat.

"Oh, Jack," I said, tears clogging my voice. "I haven't stopped loving you for one minute. Even when you told me not to, when you told me to accept philia, when you told me you loved blondes." I laughed and he did too, an absurd humor in a room smoked with fear.

Jack rested his cheek against mine. "I've kept you close, needing you as air and water, as garden and forest even while I told you no. When you aren't with me, I think of you. When you are gone, I miss you. I've been a tosser, keeping you near and yet pushing you away. You've become the other part of me. You're the very first person I want to share a thought or a moment with. Oh, the fool I've been."

He dropped his head onto my chest, and I placed my hand in his thinning hair, ran my fingers across his neck and then his shoulders under his shirt, felt the skin of the man I loved. "How can a woman be happy and fearful in one same moment?" I asked. "I have dreamed of us in this way for all these years. Here I am at my most ugly and there you are, loving me."

He lifted his face and smiled at me. That grin that had caught me at the Eastgate, the one he gave when I told a great joke or edited a mangled line or quoted a poem from memory or beat him at Scrabble with a Greek word he'd forgotten.

"Is it the pain meds?" I asked with a laugh.

He kissed me again. "Everything I've written since the day you walked into Eastgate has been tangled with you. How could I have not seen it at all?"

"It doesn't matter. It's now," I said. "You see *now*."

Then his face changed; the seriousness was etched in every line. "Let me get the doctor for you, Joy. We have so many decisions."

"For just a few moments, before we hear the death knell they might bring. Will you just hold me?" I paused. "Do you remember the poem I wrote, the poem I wrote when I was young and healthy? 'What will come of me; After the fern has feathered from my brain...'" I trailed off. "It was about my death, which seemed impossible, merely a concept."

"'Yet One More Spring.' I remember." He pressed both his warm palms onto the top of my head as the door swished open and two doctors entered with clipboards and stern expressions. "You will have many more springs ... many ..."

Jack lifted his hands, and I asked him without yet looking to the doctors, "My sons. Have they been told?"

"Not yet. I've sent for them. They'll arrive on the train tomorrow, and I'll collect them from the station and bring them here."

"Warnie?"

"Yes, and he's devastated. He loves you too. He could not even accompany me here; he returned to the Kilns."

The doctors shifted their weight, but I kept my eyes fixed on Jack. "When can I go home?"

"There's no going home to Old High Street, Joy. You'll be here for a long while, and then you are coming home with me. I'll never be apart from you again."

The first doctor stepped up then, and the long litany of my ills began.

It could be leukemia, but they believed it was another cancer, and that it had spread. My left leg bones were dust, and there was a lump in my left breast. There would be surgeries, and if cancer, then radiation.

"It's a dire diagnosis," the second doctor said. "If it's breast cancer, as I believe, then it has gone undetected for far too long."

"I've been to the doctor," I said. "I've been telling them how tired I am, how unremittingly *tired* I am. I've told them about the lump in my breast. About my heart doing funny jumps. About the pains in my bones. About my nausea. They said it was middle age and stress." Anger prodded my body to attempt to sit, but a great pain exploded, down my leg, up my side. "I told them," I wailed.

"How long has it been there? The lump. How long?" Doctor One looked at Doctor Two.

"At least seven years. I told my doctors in America about it, and then again Dr. Harvey here."

I looked to Jack, desperate to turn back time, to have someone tell me to take out the ticking time bomb in my breast. "Remember when I told Humphrey about it? At dinner that night? And he too said it was nothing to worry about. And then the eight doctors who prodded me in London and told me again that it was my thyroid. It can't be cancer. They would have known then."

"We can't change that," Doctor One said. "But we can do everything to treat it now."

"How?"

The list was egregious—leg surgery, removal of the ovaries, breast surgery, radiation. Rehabilitation. Months and months of it all, unless of course I died in the middle of the torture meant to save me.

When the room was empty, the doctors departed, and Jack gone to check on Warnie and bring me some things from home, I turned my thoughts to Jack and his pain, as mine was numbed by medicine. He had lost his mother in this same way, the greatest grief of his life buried fathoms deep in his psyche. All his life he'd avoided looking directly at that great anguish, and here I lay, making him relive it. Was it the reason he'd hesitated to love from the very beginning—the ghost of loss looming behind us, a menace of death?

"God," I said out loud to the empty room, "how could you be so cruel to those you love? You demand too much of us." I closed my eyes, and my weeping was silent as I allowed the knowledge to wash over me.

Jack loved me.

And I was dying.

CHAPTER 51

Love was the water,
Loneliness the thirst

"SONNET VIII," JOY DAVIDMAN

"Mummy?"

I jolted awake, a mother's reflex, pain shattering my consciousness. Douglas stood next to my hospital bed, and I held out my arms. "My poogles," I said and looked to Davy also, Jack at his side. "Come here."

They hesitated, still in their school uniforms and looking as scared as the day we'd landed port in England. My sons, who usually ran into me full throttle, who tossed themselves into my arms, hesitated.

"It's okay. I'm still me. Just don't hit the old lady's broken leg."

Douglas came to me first and then Davy. I held them close. "It's going to be all right."

Douglas touched the tented blanket above my leg. "Does it hurt?"

"Yes," I told him. "But they give me medicine. They're going to do some surgeries and then I'm coming home to you. God has enough grace for all of us."

"Jack says we can move into the Kilns now," Davy said. "Today." His voice shook with uncertainty, and I wanted to spring from bed, assure him of what I could not—that soon I would be well.

"Then you shall," I replied. "And I'll join you soon. We'll be a family." I stared at Davy with great intent, noticing right then how much he looked like Bill—that pointed chin and high forehead, his glasses on the perch of his nose. I almost saw a moustache that would some day appear. Would they grow up without me? Oh God. No! I'd moved to England to save them, not abandon them.

Jack came to join us, wrapping an arm around a shoulder of each of my sons and pulling them near.

"Tell me everything about school," I said. "I want to hear."

"Not now." The nurse had arrived without my knowing, her white hat pointing east and west, her red lipstick bleeding into the lines around her mouth. "You must rest. Surgery is tomorrow, and the doctors need to see you." She held a syringe in her hand, and the boys withdrew in horror.

"Go be good little poogles," I said. "I'll see you tomorrow. And soon we'll plant pole beans in the garden with Paxford and fish for perch in the pond. We'll fly a kite or go punting in the Cherwell."

Jack's face tightened against these statements, grief-stricken, and it hurt more than the shattered bones in my leg. It was his countenance that told me those things might never happen.

"I'm going to pray for you, Mummy," Douglas said with his shoulders back and a serious, grown-up look on his face. "I'm going to pray for God to heal you."

"Please do, my love."

Douglas ran from the room in a movement so swift that the curtains fluttered as if the window had been opened. Davy followed, fear coiled tight in his body and his fists at his sides.

I stared at the empty space where my boys had just stood, but now all I saw was the bedside table with a vomit bucket and a glass of tepid water. I spoke without looking at Jack. "You told them everything, right?"

"I did."

"Jack, no matter what happens, you must promise me you will never let my boys move back to America. You must make sure Bill never gets custody. Before I even go into surgery, I must make sure of this. I want papers drawn, a will that gives you full rights."

"Joy." Jack came to me and kissed me, as if this were the way we'd always been—a kiss before a comment or conversation. I closed my eyes to the sheer pleasure of it. "We have plenty of time to deal with that."

"We don't know that, Jack. You have to promise me they will never return to America, to his abuse and rage, to my cousin who betrayed me. This is home to them now."

"I promise, Joy."

"Will you go to them?" I took his hand in mine. "They need you, and they love you, Jack. You know that, don't you?"

"As I love them." He kissed me and left as a father to my sons.

I settled back into the pillow, into the floating anesthetic. I'd been exhausted for so long, and now I knew why—I was dying.

All my searching and doctors and wondering, and then the labeling of fibrositis and rheumatism and hypothyroidism . . . hadn't God known all along? Hadn't he seen the cancer growing, eating away at my insides? Could he not have intervened in human form? Sent a doctor to diagnosis it long before it ate me alive?

How could my body have gone on destroying me while I mustered my courage and resolve to rebuild a new life? My body worked against me as I tried hard, so bloody hard, to start over? Couldn't one doctor of the dozens I'd seen notice that cancer ravaged my body? That it coursed through my flesh?

I wanted to cry, "Thy will be done." It would be the best thing if I could, but instead, alone in that hospital room, I wept long, hot tears of despair and begged God for a miracle.

CHAPTER 52

I would create myself
In a little fume of words and leave my words
After my death to kiss you forever and ever

"Yet One More Spring," Joy Davidman

March 1957

Maybe I deserved all of it—the five months of surgeries and pain and vomiting, the weeks of fear and hospital transfers and inexhaustible disease. Maybe this had all been accumulating with each terrible thing I'd said or done in my life to beset me at forty-one years old. But did God work that way?

No.

He was not meant to be bargained with as he doled out punishment.

My leg was set and plastered and my ovaries clipped out; evidence remained in the form of crooked black stitches that ran along my stomach like tiny spiders. My breast lump had been excised—the cursed lump I'd known about all along but that had been dismissed. Radiation to the hip under groaning machines, and I'd swallowed medicines I'd never heard about before. The cursed-awful list of cancer's sites: in the left femur, the left breast, the right shoulder, and the right leg.

During these months I went from experiencing the mystical peace of God to black doubt and the abysmal dread of annihilation. But in the end, did I really believe all I claimed to believe? Did I believe God could exist at all? Or was he just like my Fairyland—a tactic to navigate life, imagining there was something more, something better, something out there that I'd longed for but that only existed in dreams? Maybe, just dammit maybe, there was nothing but being human and being in pain and in suffering until there was *nothing*.

In a ledger I could list the reasons I deserved this fate. I could list and I could flagellate myself, but the vile cancer was doing a just fine job of it all by itself.

Dear God, love finally arrived, and you will take me? Are you that selfish? That jealous? Is this my payment for loving Jack with such fierce intensity? For finally finding a life of peace? Or did I conceive you of my own making for consolation?

As Orual cried out to the Grey Mountain in defense of her love for Psyche, so I cried out to the God I'd felt and believed in and surrendered to in my boys' bedroom all those many years ago.

You will give me great love and then sweep me to the heavens—if they exist at all?

But did I believe God punished? The old wrathful God who smote his enemies and burned their cities? I was no better than Job or Jonah, railing against my lot in life. Just when it seemed everything might work out, that I might have the life I'd dreamed of for very, very long, I would die?

All my life I'd pushed too hard, tried too much, attempted to convince the head what only the heart can decide. But dying now? When I understood the grace of surrender? When love had arrived? What cruel injustice.

It took weeks, but I slowly emerged from that parched desert of doubt stronger in my faith than ever. Through reading and prayer, holding tight to Jack as he absorbed my doubt and pain, talking until we couldn't find another word, Jack and I found if not peace, then acceptance. *Grace,* I wrote to Eva, *arrived as I prayed.* Whatever my fate, I would be able to bear it with Jack at my side and my Creator's love surrounding me even as the doubt appeared and disappeared like smoke from the past, whispers of the woman who shadowed me and mocked my belief.

November was a kaleidoscope of pain and surgeries. By December I'd made it clear that only the two most basic of my desires remained: to live out whatever days I had left as Jack's wife in the eyes of the church and our community, and to keep the boys in England.

While frigid rain lashed the hospital windows, Jack came to me in the worst of the December nausea.

"I've gone to the bishop and presented our case for marriage."

"What did you tell him?" I asked. The nausea—I'd swallowed a pint of anesthesia when they removed my ovaries—was all consuming. I needed something, anything to assuage the suffering. Becoming Mrs. Lewis in God's eyes was a hope that burned as brightly as any light. I didn't want to be sick in front of Jack one more time. I wanted to be strong, to be the woman Warnie and he believed I was: courageous in the face of despair. But it was getting harder and harder.

"I told the bishop that your marriage to Bill never bloody counted because Bill had been married before you. But because they deem me a public figure, they are afraid they will be flooded with other requests, other exceptions. His answer was no."

"That's what you get for being a public figure." I tried to smile.

Jack didn't laugh.

In many ways, in such a short amount of time, our roles often reversed. Instead of it being Jack who held me, it was I who must quote from his favorite mystic—Julian of Norwich. All will be well, and all manner of things will be well.

I held his hand. "My love, the pain is cleansing me. Soon I'll be walking with a caliper splint and living with you."

Together we pretended it to be true, but it was only as real as Perelandra or Narnia.

Weeks passed; the boys returned to school. Eventually I felt well enough that Warnie brought me my typewriter. I began to preoccupy myself while waiting for test results, healing, and treatments by catching up on correspondence and informing everyone of my plight: My parents. Chad and Eva. Belle, Marian, and Michal. And finally, my brother—we reconciled as best as two siblings can when across an ocean with one of them at death's door. I knit and crocheted everything from scarves to mittens to tablecloths for the Kilns, as if I could move myself there with my hands alone.

It was the January doctor's announcement that almost destroyed us. "Months to live," he told us. "Months at best."

Together we took the news inside, let it churn our hearts to pulp. "If I could have made you love me all those years ago," I said, "we'd have had more time."

"Free will," he said and kissed me. "It's the only thing that might make love worth having."

I nodded in fear. "We cannot look at what horror has happened to us, but at how we will turn to God in it. If I only identify with the three-dimensional world I once believed in, I will despair. But we know better, Jack. We know there is more."

Jack's face, the ruddiness now white and sallow as if I'd drained him of his life as well, drew close to mine. "I want more of life here with you." His voice carried a tremor, and for one split second I thought I knew what he must have sounded like when he was a small boy and his mother was dying in the back bedroom of Little Lea. "I want more of you," he said.

"As do I want more of you."

During those months in the hospital Jack was at my bedside as much as possible. For three-day weekends he never left me but to sleep at the Kilns. During the times I believed I'd heal we relished our moments together; he sometimes sneaked sherry into the hospital. We recited poetry and read together. We talked of the future, whether it was a day or a month or more. We kissed and we held each other and felt great expectation of what might be. During the worst moments we prayed, feverishly we prayed.

"It's hopeless," I told him on a February afternoon when they removed the cast and found that the bones were *not* healing. "We must stop living in denial."

Crochet needles wrapped in gray yarn sat on my lap, abandoned mittens for Davy.

"It is not hopeless," he said with surety. "It is uncertain, and this is the cross God always gives us in life, uncertainty. But it is *not* hopeless."

"Jack, all I've ever wanted was to bring you happiness. And here I am bringing you pain. It would have been best if you'd never met me at all."

"Not met you at all?" He stood and paced the hospital room and then turned to me with fire on his face. "My life would have been but dry dust compared to having you in my world. With whom could I have ever been this close? *Till We Have Faces* would not exist. My biography would be but half what it is. My heart would still be hibernating, too troubled to feel." He came to my side and kissed my face, first one cheek, then the other, and then my lips. "Whatever we face together is better than never knowing you at all."

"There is so much to live for now. So much," I said and closed my eyes, shook off the dread.

"It does seem fate designs a great need and then frustrates it."

I smiled at him. "Now tell me how the boys are doing. Give me news from outside this cellblock of a room."

"I've restored the old falling-down guesthouse for them," he said with a grand smile. "Now they have a place all their own to play and hide. And guess what they found in there."

"Dead animals?" I asked.

"Your ham! On a top shelf. There it was. I used the guesthouse for storage during the rations."

I laughed so heartily that Jack wiped tears from my eyes. "I remember sending that to you."

"They ate it," Jack said with his own laughter. "They took it right back to the house, and Mrs. Miller opened that tin and it was still good." Then he grew serious. "I cleaned that little house because I think they need to get away as best they can."

"Or you need to be away from them." I kissed his hand, which held mine. "It must be a burden, Jack. I am so sorry."

"It's not a burden, Joy. I love them. But they do bloody well fight." He paused. "I don't believe Warnie and I ever brawled like that. Douglas often takes off into the woods leaving a roaring Davy behind; I found him one midnight skating on the pond under a full moon."

"They have been knitted together so differently."

"Yes. And that clashes. But also they worry. They worry about you. And they don't know what to do with those emotions."

"It breaks my heart in more places than my moth-eaten leg. If only we could promise them answered prayers." Immense weariness settled on me again, as it often did without warning. "Read to me, please. It takes away the pain." I closed my eyes. "Anything at all, Jack."

It was Shakespeare he chose that day, and I dozed, slipping in and out of the cadence of his words. It was only when I opened my eyes to see why he'd stopped that I realized he hadn't been reading at all, but quoting from memory.

Whenever I believed I could not love him more, I did.

CHAPTER 53

Could you listen to your devoted lover?
Listen just a while, it will soon be over

"ACROSTIC IN HENDECASYLLABICS," JOY DAVIDMAN

It was a Thursday, March 21, the spring equinox, the time I'd told Jack at our first meeting was a signal of new beginnings. He'd believed new beginnings were heralded by autumn. But it looked like I was right, for this was our wedding day. A *real* one.

My hospital room, now so familiar I could see it with my eyes closed, was cluttered with books and papers, with my typewriter and notepads. Newspapers and even a Scrabble game were scattered on the rolling table across from my bed, yet it would become a sacred cathedral in the next moments.

Plaster held my leg in place and my foot was propped high in traction, metal poles overhead, pulleys and gears, as I lay supine in the bed. Pillows were stuffed behind my back and shoulders to prop me. A clean white blanket was tented over my raised leg. My hair, brushed and clean with the help of the orderly, fell over my shoulders. From the wife of a patient down the hall, I'd borrowed a tube of red lipstick and swiped it across my lips.

Warnie came to my bedside first. "Joy, I have loved you like a sister, and now you will be my sister." His sober eyes were clear and yet filled with tears. "I have never loved you more."

"Warnie, look at us, loving each other and loving the same man."

He placed his hand in mine. "I pray for you every day."

Warnie moved away as Jack leaned close so only I could hear him, his lips soft against my ear, his voice filling me. "You have allowed me to become my true self with you. I hide nothing. Now let us become as one."

I took Jack's face in mine and kissed him, not as ardently as I'd have liked, for next to me stood the priest, Peter Bide, a former student of Jack's, his white collar a comma against his throat and his black robes swishing like smoke with every move.

"Are you ready, Joy?" Peter asked in such a serious tone that I wondered if he'd practiced.

"I believe I've been ready for this moment all my life," I said.

Jack squeezed my hand. "How is it that my heart is breaking and yet I've never been so happy?"

A ward sister in a prim habit stood with Warnie, who wore a suit pressed so straight he looked frightened to move. He smiled at me and held his hands clasped behind his back as if hiding something. Sober, his cheeks red with health, he stated to all present, "I love Joy as a sister, and now we will make it official."

Jack entwined his fingers in mine. He was handsome in his black suit and knotted blue tie, his hair slicked back. Without a cigarette or pipe, his mouth held only a shy grin. A great wash of love and admiration, and the realization of miracles, filled me with a swelling ecstasy that surged inside me like a sacred sea.

"Can I ask you something before we start, Father Bide?" I asked.

"Of course."

"How did you finally decide that this was sanctioned? That the Church of England would give permission? We've asked everyone we know, even the bishop."

"I asked the only source that mattered." Father Bide paused and closed his hands around the black prayer book in his hand. "The only court of appeal I thought had the final argument—and that was God himself. What would he do in this case? And the answer was clear."

"Then let's get married," I said and turned my face to Jack.

He squeezed my hand. "Yes, then let's be married."

So it came that on March 21, 1957, while I lay in bed in a nightgown with my left leg lifted high on ropes and pulleys, I finally married the love of my life.

Father Bide began to speak the words of the ceremony, and I listened to the melody of the Church of England's holy matrimony litany.

In the presence of God, Father, Son, and Holy Spirit

We have come together

To witness the marriage of Helen Joy Davidman and Clive Staples Lewis

To pray for God's blessing on them

To share their joy

And to celebrate their love . . .

Peter continued in the most serious voice, as if we were standing at the altar of Westminster Abbey and the queen herself was in the congregation—the hospital room no deterrence to solemnity.

"Jack," he finally said, "will you take Joy to be your wife? Will you love her, comfort her, honor and protect her, forsaking all others, and be faithful to her as long as you both shall live?"

"I will," he said, and then again for emphasis, "I will."

"Joy," Peter asked, "will you take Jack to be your husband? Will you love him, comfort him, honor and protect him, forsaking all others, and be faithful to him as long as you both shall live?"

"I will." Tears rolled from my eyes and down my face where Jack kissed them away, the wetness of them on his lips.

Warnie and the ward sister, whose name I never learned, also cried silently. Maybe it was the line "as long as you both shall live," or the boundless love that filled that room, I didn't know. Peter finished the ceremony—vows, rings, and declaration.

It wasn't the wedding a small girl dreams of—the white lace dress and a flowing veil. There were no bridesmaids or a symphony orchestra or long trails of white roses. But what does a small girl know of *real* love? I hadn't ever known how to dream. I hadn't known that love would arrive in the most unlikely of places—a hospital room where fear and despair usually reigned. I hadn't known that love could not be earned or bought or manipulated; it was just this—complete peace in the other's presence.

All the years wasted believing that love meant owning or possessing, and now the greatest love had arrived in my greatest weakness. In my supreme defeat came my grandest victory. God's paradoxes had no end.

Peter ended the ceremony with the final prayer. We closed our eyes, Jack's hands in mine.

"The Holy Trinity make you strong in faith and love, defend you on every side, and guide you in truth and peace; and the blessing of God Almighty, the Father, the Son, and the Holy Spirit be among you and remain with you always."

It was Warnie who let out a great whooping sound. "Congratulations, Mr. and Mrs. Lewis."

"My *wife*," Jack said, and laughed that resonating merry sound that had buoyed me all these months.

"My husband."

We set to laughter, and the ward sister shook her head. "I've never seen such celebration in a hospital room."

"Well, you've never seen anyone quite like the three of us," I said.

"No, I haven't."

I knew what she believed: that this was a deathbed marriage, one to satisfy the sad woman in the cast with cancer. But it was no such thing. It was holy matrimony between a man and a woman who had grown to love in ways that no words or explanations could contain.

It was then that Peter turned around and brought a tray to us both, offering us our first Holy Communion as husband and wife.

"Peter," Jack said when we had finished the Eucharist. "If I may impose with one more request."

"What is it?" Peter placed the tray on the bedside table.

Jack cast his eyes to Warnie and then to Peter. "I know you don't like to make much of it, but I do know that when you prayed over that young boy dying of meningitis, he recovered. I don't believe it is in you that healing is given, but if you would pray over Joy right now as my wife . . ." Jack's voice broke. "Please."

My wife.

Peter didn't answer with words, but instead placed both his hands on my head, the warmth of them comforting me. He closed his eyes. "Almighty God, to whom all hearts are open and all desires known . . ."

I closed my eyes to his prayer, his voice mingling with the cleansing power of a holy marriage and Holy Communion. The space around us shimmered, as sacred as if we knelt at a candle-festooned altar on red velvet cushions in the grandest cathedral on earth. If there was a time heaven might hear our pleas, this consecrated moment swelled around us, this boundless mystical silence beneath Peter's voice as he uttered the prayers of the Church of England and then those of his own, pleading for healing and restoration, but in the end, for God's will to be done.

After Peter finished, the silence extended, enveloping us all. The hospital and the world paused with us; time was suspended. It lasted for only seconds but felt an eternity in my soul. Outside, a songbird sang a single note. A tray banged across the hallway. A child called out below my window. A doctor called for a nurse, and the world began again.

It all began again.

CHAPTER 54

Under the quiet passion of the spring;
I would leave you the trouble of my heart

"YET ONE MORE SPRING," JOY DAVIDMAN

They sent me to the Kilns to die in April of 1957.

Helpless to assist, I closed my eyes and allowed the crew of many medical personnel to pack me: my medicines and wheelchair (for the possible day when I *might* use it); the bedpan and trays. Two nurses had been hired—day and night. This business of dying wasn't as simple as surrender to the great light. It was real and dirty and untidy. As Jack said, "A walk through the Garden of Gethsemane."

My emotions clashed brutally—everything one can feel I felt and usually all at once.

When I'd prayed to one day live at the Kilns as Mrs. Lewis, maybe I should have been more specific. Because that prayer was answered as they rolled in a hospital bed and settled me into the common room with the familiar egg yolk–yellow walls and blackout curtains, the well-worn chairs and leaning bookcases. The fireplace with the perpetual aroma of slag, and the faded carpet embedded with cigarette ash. It was my house now as Mrs. Lewis, and yet I might as well have been strapped to the floor to observe a life I'd never live, a happiness tasted and snatched away.

The bed had already been set up when the ambulance crew wheeled me in on a stretcher to gently lift me onto the sheets. But with a sudden shift of their arms a swift pain sliced through my leg, and I cried out.

"Joy!"

"Joy!"

Jack's and Warnie's voices comingled as they came running to the side of the bed from the far wall, where they'd been observing and allowing the attendants to do their work.

"I'm fine," I said through gritted teeth and tears. I settled back onto the hard mattress and tears ran down my cheeks, unbidden. I wanted to be courageous for them, for me, for the memory of me. But the pain and the lost happiness and the fear held sway.

It took some time for the hospital staff to unload and settle me and then to finally leave me alone with Jack, who sat next to my bed and rested his head on the pillow next to me in an awkward bent fashion.

"I want to take your pain away, Joy. I want to heal you."

I turned my face and kissed him. "And I want you to take me upstairs to your room and make love to me. For as long as you can. We can finally be together, and it's only my cancer that keeps us apart." A sob broke loose. There was no more courage remaining at that moment, only despair. And if God couldn't bear my despair, then he couldn't bear me.

"My love, the minute you are able, I will take you in my arms and to my bed." His voice was heavy beneath the burden, and he bowed his head.

———

Jack's and Warnie's voices were murmurs much like background music in a pub or a radio playing in another room. The cadence and accents, the elongated Rs and brief but lovely laughter carried me like waves. I was awake, but not in any real way that they would know I was. It was more like a dreamy consciousness of my surroundings while my eyes stayed closed and I floated in and out of knowing. Much like a dream where one was in one situation and then another without the synapse connection carrying them forward—nothing was in between.

Lying supine—my leg in plaster and a contraption much like a circus performer's trapeze hanging above my thin bed—nausea suddenly overwhelmed me like a rocking boat lurching me forward. My eyes flew open and I reached up to grab the triangular handle bar and pull myself to sitting. I wasn't given warning; my body was slow with warning bells for anything at all, and I vomited all over the clean bedsheets and warm brown blanket the day nurse had tucked in around me. I groaned with not only misery but also with embarrassment.

Jack was at my side, so quickly that maybe he'd been standing there all along. "Joy, I'm here." Then Warnie too.

"I'm sorry." I fell back on the pillows in shame.

Warnie, lit with the evening sun filtering into the room, held a silver kidney basin—the ubiquitous throw-up basin we'd brought home from the hospital. How I'd hoped that leaving the hospital after five months would mean leaving these accoutrements behind. No such luck.

Jack hastily yanked the blanket from its moorings and then grabbed the bowl from Warnie to lickety-split spill the liquid into it. Warnie placed a wet washcloth on my forehead as I moaned, humiliated and emptied. This was not how I wanted to be seen or remembered.

Jack placed the basin and the blanket on the floor as the nurse bustled in to research the commotion. Jack's precious face obliterated my view of all else in the room as he bowed over me. In an instant his lips were on mine with a kiss full and kind and overwhelmingly imbued with compassion. He heeded no mind to the sickness that remained on me, to the propriety of asepsis; he only loved me.

I'd felt certain of his eros in the months before this unsterile kiss, but perhaps some small and niggling part of me had believed it pity or forbearance, that his medieval virtues compelled him to love me in my dying. But non! It was this wink of time when I whorled toward understanding, into and resting in the arms of the love we shared—an uncommon and vulnerable combination of the four loves we'd traveled with and toward: agape, storge, philia, and now, unquestionably, eros. Our journey—riddled with both pain and joy—culminated in a kiss I would never have anticipated as the revelation it became, as the comfort and mastery of love.

Jack rested his head on my pillow, and when I thought he might stroke my head or cheek, instead he began to pray, an earnest prayer that God would give him my suffering, allow him to bear my burdens. Then he rested for a while facing me with his eyes closed and his lips ever so gently on mine.

He'd aged during these last months: I could see this. His hair was thinner, as was his face, but to me he was even more beautiful. His full and beautiful mouth. His deep eyes.

"You want to take my suffering but you can't, Jack. It's mine to carry. You're the one who told me there is no bargaining with God."

"No." He lifted his head from my pillow. "Your pain is not yours alone anymore. It's ours. I want to carry it for you. I'm asking God."

"This is mine, but *with* you I can bear it. It's you who's guided me here—to faith: I know I'm beloved."

"You are beloved by more than God, Joy. By me. By Warnie. By your sons and all the friends who have embraced you; I've never seen anyone make friends as easily and quickly as you." His voice cracked, and he rested his head on my pillow. "I love you with all my being."

"I love you too," I said in a faded voice. "But just because we love God and are committed to him doesn't mean we are exempt from the pain and loss in this world. We can't ask to be the exceptions."

We rested there for quite a while, the sounds of spring outside: wind, birdsong, and Paxford's voice calling out. The creak of the floors told us Warnie was upstairs. The kitchen pots and pans clanged together as Mrs. Miller made lunch. I fell asleep quickly and deeply, as I often did now, a sudden sleep completely different from the slow falling of an unmedicated rest.

I awoke when Jack's head lifted from my pillow.

"Poetry," I said. "Let's read."

He scooted back his chair and fetched Wordsworth from the side table. "Before we read, I have something to tell you."

"Is it bad news? Because I'm not sure I can take anymore."

"It's Bill."

I girded my heart with what armor remained and clenched my hands into fists at my sides. My foot, raised in traction, began to throb again—the birth pangs of a greater pain. I reached for the bottle of pain pills and swallowed one. "Tell me."

"He's written to us."

"Let me see."

"I don't think you should read it, Joy. You just need to know that he's demanding that if . . . if something happens to you, he wants the boys back with him. He laid some terrible accusations at your feet. But don't trouble yourself; I've written back to him in the sternest way possible. He will not and cannot have the boys return to America."

"Let me read it," I said. "Now."

He didn't argue, but rose and left the room. His footsteps echoed up the stairs to his office and then back down again. When he returned he handed the letter to me.

Dear Jack,

it began . . .

There were condolences about my prognosis and a reference to the fact that Bill's only spirituality was in Alcoholics Anonymous, and then the dagger:

Let me tell you my side of the story.

I read on with an invisible hand around my throat.

He told Jack that when I'd left five years ago, I'd been "disturbed." He claimed my mind had been a mess and my heart set on Jack. He wrote that I'd never made very much of my writing career and that he'd supported me in the *Presbyterian Life* articles so that I could feel good about myself. He claimed I left my boys too long (he was right), and that when I'd returned I'd been both angry and hostile. And there was more. His bitterness was so palpable it thrummed off the page and into my body, an electric current.

Bill ended with this.

There is nothing more my sons need than their dad.

I closed my eyes and then dropped the pages to the floor, and Jack allowed them to scatter like trash. "No."

"We won't let him, Joy. We will not allow it."

Grief began to heave within me, then made way for anger. My eyes flew open and I attempted to sit, for a moment forgetting that I was bedbound. The traction pulleys clanged against each other in pro-test, and a knife-pain sliced down my left thigh. But anger won and I slammed my fist into the mattress.

"His accusations, Jack. What a woman that must *be* for all of those things to be true. A horrible woman. One I wouldn't want to even know, much less be."

"It's Bill's way of telling a story he needs to believe." Jack's voice low and quiet, a balm.

"And nothing of his affair with my cousin? His anger or his rages or his alcoholism and breakdowns? His suicide threats that kept us captive? He doesn't say why I might have been angry when I returned home? Only that I was bitter and what else . . . violent? What a farce."

Jack rested his hand on my arm. "Joy."

I took in a long breath.

"Please get me a pad of paper and a pen. I must write back."

"I already wrote to him."

"Then I'll add to it, Jack. I can't let him leave this as a legacy, these pages of lies." Tears flooded my eyes, and I wiped furiously at them. "I'm tired of crying. Of hurting. I want only love now. Only love. It should be all that remains."

"That is what we have." He kissed me again and reached for the poetry book. I closed my eyes, let the hostile fury ride its wave, and listened to Jack quote Wordsworth. "'I wandered lonely as a cloud . . .'"

Inside my mind I heard Bill, but when I opened my eyes to Jack, I knew that whatever Bill believed or whatever he'd written did not and could not affect the love that breathed between Jack and me.

I understood for the first time the apostle Paul's words, "Death, where is your sting?"

CHAPTER 55

Beyond the foaming world; here is the chart
Of the last journey, past the last desire

(LAST SONNET, LAST LINE)
"SONNET XLIV," JOY DAVIDMAN

June 1957

"Your cancer has been arrested."

These words fell so casually from the mouth of the doctor in the white coat and tortoiseshell spectacles that I thought I might have misheard him.

I sat in my wheelchair with Jack standing at my side and stared at the drops of dried blood on the doctor's sleeve, his stethoscope hanging from his neck like a dead snake, as the words sank into my consciousness with soft mercy.

"Arrested?" Jack and I asked simultaneously.

The man nodded, his brows knit together in confusion. "Not *healed*. But the disease has been arrested. Your bones are solid as a rock, at least for now." He paused and fiddled with his stethoscope. "We don't understand. If you'd like to call it a miracle you could. But it is *not* what we expected. You, Mrs. Lewis, are growing new bone. Your body is depositing calcium into your bone, strengthening it. Honestly, when we sent you home we didn't have any other plan but to keep you comfortable. Death was imminent."

"But it isn't now." My voice didn't rise with a question. "It isn't imminent now."

"No, not from this cancer, it is not."

Jack and I had come to the orthopedic hospital for my monthly
checkup, girded as always for the worst news. Jack, Warnie, and I
had reached a grieving acceptance, but on that day we were granted
a reprieve. We hoisted our hearts onto that life raft and held tight to
each other. Jack bent over my wheelchair, his lips on mine, and a burst
of laughter after the kiss. "Bloody good news."

———

It was early evening in the common room when the truth flooded
me—it was a miracle. "You took my pain," I said to Jack in stunned
realization, the truth taking my breath. "Your doc, Old Lord Florey,
told you that you have a quite obscure case of osteoporosis, while now
we discover that I'm healing."

Not only had Peter Bide prayed over me, but also Jack, asking to be
my substitute. Was there a greater love?

"What?" Jack was red-faced and groaning, strapping a body brace
around his waist to support his back. I perched in my wheelchair with a
bright metal caliper that held my leg fast in its straight position.

It had been six months since my diagnosis, three months since
they'd sent me home to die. We had been told to prepare and pray. But
one by one the accoutrements of illness had fallen away: first the pain
pills were banished, and then the trapeze above my head gone, then
the night nurse fired (she was dreadful as it was). After that, when Jack
was at Cambridge, I began sitting to crochet and knit, to write letters
and welcome visitors, perched on my bed with our poodle, Suzie, and
old cat, Tom. Then came the day when I was able to sit in a wheelchair
while Jack wheeled me outside. I'd wept with relief in the pure June air,
the fragrance of the pine and spruce, the wet ground and fecund earth.

Then eventually I had walked there, with a limp of course—my left leg now three inches shorter than my right.

In what seemed an additional miracle, or maybe just a relief that felt miraculous, Bill had ceased in his threats to take the boys to America. While I'd recovered, while I'd slept, Jack had written Bill the most scathing letter of his life, explaining to him that he would not return the boys, who were both frightened of him. *Whose happiness would you foster by forcing them back to you now?* Jack asked. Douglas also wrote to Bill, telling him of his need to stay in what was now his home. We didn't prod Douglas or write the letter for him—this was of his own accord, my precious son whom Jack called "an absolute charmer full of just the right amount of mischief." Whether it was Jack's letter or Douglas's appeal or my own dying pleas, I would never know.

Life again held promise. I touched Jack's hand. "They gave me my death sentence and now I've grown bone. And you've lost bone. You're in pain and in need of a brace, and I'm relieved of so much pain." I stood shakily from the wheelchair, using a cane to bear my weight. "You shouldn't have done that . . . you shouldn't . . ." I gasped on the words. "I'm just now coming to understand what the doctor told us today. I'm getting stronger and you're getting weaker. Or at least your bones are. Why did you do this?"

"I didn't do anything, Joy. God granted my request, if that is what happened at all." He smiled through the pain and then stood straight. "And look at that, I finally figured out the bloody straps." He patted his waist where the brace held fast. "Now look at the youthful figure this gives me."

Our laughter entwined and filled the room, and also seemed to fill the world.

We grabbed our individual canes. I wanted to be outside, to touch the greenest leaves of summer, to taste a tomato off the vine, to feel the sun run down my face like honey. I wanted every sensual experience in the world. I wanted to run my hands across Jack's body, to dip my fingers into the cold pond, to inhale the summer air, to roll in the grass. Some were possible and some soon would be: I was alive! And in remission.

"Jack." We took a few hobbling steps together down the hallway and through the front door to emerge into the sunshine.

"Yes, love?"

"Can't you see? Honestly, can't you see? It's a miracle."

"Miracles, my love, never break nature's laws."

"Jack! I'm growing bone. You are losing. You are my . . . substitution."

"Let's not get into the land of fancy." He stopped in midstep. "But I thank God every minute I remember."

"Thank him for your pain?"

"Yes, and for your relief." He stopped and kissed me deeply. "The love I have for you has built a bridge to my true self, Joy. The self I only momentarily touched before you. If this pain is part of the bargain, so be it."

"Why did it take us so long to *see* this? To *know?*"

His answer was merely a kiss. *Sometimes that is the best answer*, I thought, and I kissed him in return.

We walked slowly, every step a triumph, as I'd once been told I would never walk again and that my grave would be my resting place by now. I stopped before the garden and released Jack's hand to touch his face. "The very fact that I'm standing here and the cancer has been arrested feels like a miracle that you orchestrated."

"Love always chooses for another's highest good, but I don't know if I chose this. I only know that I would have, and maybe God has done the same."

"I will choose you every time, Jack. Even with this cancer. Even with this suffering. Even with *all* that came before, I would choose you and this one evening in a garden, our bodies leaning against each other."

Jack drew me as close as he could with calipers and braces, with canes in the way and pain deep within our bones.

Silence, the sublime sort, hovered for a long while until I asked, "Did you write this morning on the new book?"

"I did, but I was also counting the minutes until you awoke. I couldn't focus knowing you were waiting. It's difficult to focus on the Psalms when love like this is sleeping downstairs."

He kissed me with the passion I'd dreamt of for many years. I tasted his pipe tobacco and his humanness and soft mouth. I wanted every inch of the man I loved so dearly.

I didn't know if others understood his deep love for me. I'd wondered and then let it go—it didn't matter anymore what Tollers or the Inklings or the Sayers believed. Maybe Jack had admitted his love or maybe he hadn't, but all that mattered was that I grasped the truth. He loved me when I was brash. He loved me in my weakest state. He loved me after I stopped trying so hard to *make* him love me. He loved me when I was outwardly unworthy. I thought of Aslan and his words in *Prince Caspian*, "You doubt your value. Don't run from who you are."

I looked over the Kilns property washed in twilight, the golden light of another day's end, another day Jack and I had together. "It's time to fix this place up a bit."

"Oh, Mrs. Lewis, I wondered how long it was going to be before you said so."

"I mean, honestly, could you possibly still want your blackout curtains and crumbling walls and yellow paint?"

"I could."

I laughed.

"Remember all those years ago in the pub the night before you left for Edinburgh?" he asked. "It was on your first visit when we talked of what it meant to show our real faces, when you told me of your decision to always show me your face without veil. That was love, Joy; it's what we're doing now." His brown eyes seemed fathomless, their depths holding the answers. "Although it was your mind I loved first, it is not what I've loved best. The heart of you is the heart of me now, and I want to know it fully."

"You just want me to stay around so I can help you with your work," I joked, but knew he was being true.

He pressed his cheek to mine and we were there, skin on skin, touch on touch. "It isn't the work you do or the pleasure you give, it is *you*, my beloved, that I want. You."

I kissed him with the same urgency and fervor I would have had when I was well and had rung the bell all those years ago and Mrs. Miller had opened the door. I wound my hand behind his neck and pulled him closer until his free hand, too, was in my tangled hair.

His voice was thick with desire; I had come to know the tone, feel the fullness of it. "Since the day we met and walked over Magdalen bridge and spoke of trees and rivers, I've preloved you in the same way my poems prewrote my prose, in the same way your poems and essays preloved God."

We were quiet, each lost in the desire that had come suddenly for him and exquisitely long ago, flourishing in time, for me. Just the week before I had heard him tell Dorothy Sayers, "Sometimes love blooms when a third adversary enters the scene, and what is a more worthy adversary than death?"

"Look at us," he said, drawing back to take me in. "Two crumbling old people acting as if we're in our twenties and desperately in love." He took my hand. "Come with me, Joy."

I followed him inside and slowly up the stairs, my caliper making a noise like a hammer on wood with each step. His bed, now ours, waited for our bodies to rest and to make love. Coming together was slow and luxurious and only ours, never to be shared or talked about in the world. On our soft pillows, my body long against his, skin on skin, I rested my head on his shoulder and a righteous grace overwhelmed us both.

We had traveled our individual and secret roads to this destination, both with our childhood mystical hints of nature that followed us—in a small box of moss brought to him by his brother or an ice-laden forest in a Bronx park for me. The signposts and messages along the way had been palpable and evident in hindsight—the lions I'd been drawn to all my life and his Aslan; my Fairyland and his North; George MacDonald and mythology; our lives intercepted and interrupted by the Hound of

Heaven; our poetry, our writing, and our reading—all pointing to this one moment in time: *Kairos*.

But how could I have known how to read those hints and messages? They'd been scattered across many years. Only now did I know. Only now.

"I love you, Clive Staples Lewis."

"I love you, Helen Joy Lewis," he said. "For as long as we have. For as well as I can."

Epilogue

At the sound of his roar, sorrows will be no more.
When he bares his teeth winter meets its death. And
when he shakes his mane we shall have Spring again.

The Lion, the Witch and the Wardrobe, C. S. Lewis

Grace does not tell us how long we have in our life, or what comes next—that's why grace is given only in the moment. Unmerited mercy is never earned.

After that June evening in our Kilns garden, against all doctors' prognoses, I was gifted three more years with Jack, three more years with my sons and my friends and the very earth that drew me to God. Three more years until I clung to the great Lion, buried my face in his mane, and dropped to my knees in surrender.

Much has been written and told of those three years when Jack and I were husband and wife. I didn't deserve it: the ecstasy in the pain, the redemption of the past, love that surpassed all understanding. But God and Love don't dole out their gifts on merit.

Our bodies slowly healed and came together in the love and passion I'd dreamt of for all those years, but more so. There are experiences that even imagination can give no due. No sonnet or words of lovelorn pity can draw one to love as our bodies were finally able. As Jack once wrote, *Eros has naked bodies. Friendship naked personalities.*

We celebrated our honeymoon in Ireland a year and a half after I'd been sent to the Kilns to die. Boarding the plane, we laughed that we had once vowed never to step foot in one of those dangerous monstrosities—oh, how love changes things. His childhood best friend, Arthur, picked us up at the airport with congratulations and a hearty laugh. It was obvious he was thrilled to see his true friend in love and married. Jack and I cozied up at the Old Inn in Crawfordshire. It was there that I met his storytelling and gregarious extended family, feeling left out at times but surrounded by love. My eyes soaked in the exquisite landscape of the Emerald Isle Jack loved. I was able to walk more than a mile by then, and we relished each day in what I called Gift Time and "unconvenanted mercy."

When we returned, Jack performed a series of radio addresses that so shocked the conservative American station that they banned his teachings on the four loves and sex! Oh, my man telling the world that "the roughness, even fierceness of some erotic play is harmless and wholesome." Laughter, he said, "is the right response of all sensible lovers." It wasn't quite what they expected to hear from him.

In those years I planted the garden with Paxford and cooked with Mrs. Miller. I redecorated, updated, and renovated the Kilns while rejoicing in nourishing friendships. Jack, Warnie, and I laughed and read and wrote, seeking the most out of every day as well as we could, as often as we could. Thanks to Jack's resolute love, Bill was unable to take our sons back to America, and our little family flourished at the Kilns. Belle and the Walshes came to visit, as did my parents and others, encouraging my heart as well as my body. I had reconciled with my brother, but I never saw him again.

As much as we could, Jack and I sneaked away for private weekends in cozy inns, understanding the Damocles sword that swung above our heads, ever making the time more valuable, palpable with grace and thrumming with desire.

Toward the end we flew to Greece, the land of our beloved myths, where we climbed the Acropolis and drank the finest wines with friends. It was our last journey together.

But that summer evening in our garden, how were we to know what would happen after our deaths?

I left Jack on July 13 of 1960, more than ten years after I opened his first letter. He grieved with such ferocity that he described death as an amputation. He wrote of this enveloping grief, and it became one of his most beloved books—*A Grief Observed*. Again pain and loss were redeemed in the service of our lives. This is how he describes us in that book: "I know that the thing I want is exactly the thing I can never get. The old life, the jokes, the drinks, the arguments, the lovemaking, the tiny, heartbreaking commonplace."

The tiny heartbreaking commonplace, yes indeed.

He became the most extraordinary stepfather to my sons. He wrote two more books, and he would say to all who listened, as he'd always said to me, "These books and these works would not exist without Joy's love and life, without my love for her."

Three years after my departure Jack developed a heart condition and died at home in Warnie's arms, and he too discovered that even his prolific imagination couldn't do justice to the great unknown.

It was not Fairyland or the Island, nor the Great North, but all of it and none of it all at once.

He was buried in the graveyard of his beloved Trinity Church. Warnie chose the epitaph, words from Shakespeare's *King Lear* that had been a quote on the family calendar the day their mother died. *Men must endure their going hence.*

Books would be written about both of us, mostly Jack, of course. Schools and classes were dedicated to his theories and his works. An Inkling Society was founded and movies made of our life. There would be scholars and theologians who dissected our writing, our stories, our mistakes, our poetry, my sonnets, and our foibles. No one would ever get all of it fully right—who could? Strangers would wander our garden while taking a tour of the Kilns, and also Oxford and Magdalen.

My sons, my heartbroken sons, would delve into their own faith—Davy in the Jewish traditions and Douglas in Christ. Both would grow up and find their own loves and lives, and Douglas would write of these days and produce the Narnian movies. There would even be a sign on my 10 Old High Street address that states *The former home of writer Joy Davidman, wife of C. S. Lewis.* There would be memorials and statues and reading rooms in America at Wheaton College with our papers filed in boxes alongside six more of the most important British authors of our time.

All of these things and many more would happen, but on that evening, the one in the garden, Jack and I knew nothing of what would come to pass. We merely leaned into each other, our bodies and our weight supporting and propping us, two trees entwined, unable to stand alone.

"To me," Jack said, "you are star, water, air, fields, and forest. Everything."

These most beautiful proclamations of love would be some of the very lines to be etched on my memorial stone after I finally closed my eyes, Jack beside me. When I would discover that all there is, and all there ever will be is this: Love, waiting for our surrender, from where we came and where we go.

With the great roar of Aslan, I ended my life with these words, whispered in truth to Jack: "I am at peace with God."

Remember Helen Joy Davidman

D. July 1960

Loved wife of

C. S. Lewis

Here the whole world (stars, water, air

And field, and forest, as they were

Reflected in a single mind)

Like cast off clothes was left behind

In ashes yet with hope that she

Re-born from holy poverty,

In lenten lands, hereafter may

Resume them on her Easter Day.

A Note from the Author

Becoming Mrs. Lewis is a work of historical fiction inspired by the life of Joy Davidman and her improbable love story with C. S. Lewis. The world's fascination with Lewis (Jack to his friends) and his only wife, Helen Joy Davidman Gresham (Joy), has never abated. Their eros-story led to some of C. S. Lewis's greatest works on love, grief, and faith, yet Joy is rarely offered credit as the muse, editor, best friend, and beloved wife she was to this revered author.

When I read *A Grief Observed* and felt Lewis's palpable pain in losing the great love of his life, I wanted to know more about the woman he loved so fiercely.

You see, I fell into my own kind of love with Lewis when I was twelve years old and read *The Screwtape Letters*, years before I knew what the words *satire* or *allegory* meant. I read Lewis's other works later in life with as much abandon and fascination. When I learned about Joy Davidman, I felt an odd kinship with her Lewis-adoration. Who was this woman? Who was this poet and novelist who had lived a world away from Lewis both culturally and literally and yet fallen in love with him?

A brilliant writer herself, Joy was a multi-award-winning poet, a novelist, a critic, a protégé of the MacDowell Colony, and much more. She graduated college at fifteen years old and received her master's degree in fiction from Columbia. Her résumé is nearly as long as Lewis's.

Everything about Joy seemed ill-matched for an Oxford don and author of Narnia living in England. She was a married woman who lived in upstate New York with her two young sons, and she was a converted Jew, former atheist, ex-Communist. On paper there was not a more impossible pairing. Everything blocked the way to love, but in the end it was not impossible at all.

With intense curiosity I began to read Joy's work. Her poetry, essays, books, and letters flamed with talent, pain, and insight. She was a force of beautiful prose that many tried to squelch and inhibit. Then there were the conflicting narratives about her life—some complimentary and others outright unkind. Who was she *really*? A brash New Yorker who inserted herself into Lewis's life or a brave and forthright woman of such brilliance that Jack loved and trusted her, while she also threatened the men and women who wanted to shove her into what they believed was her rightful place? This was a woman diverse, courageous, and complicated, and a woman whom C. S. Lewis loved with all of his being.

Joy often seemed not to care what others thought of her—but I did.

This work of fiction was meant not only to explore her life, work, and love affair, but also to delve into the challenges she faced as a woman in her time—or by any woman even now trying to live an authentic life while also caring for her family and pursuing her creative life, art, or passion. We are often woefully negligent of the women next to the men we admire, and Joy Davidman is one of those women.

There has been a shroud of mystery about what might or might not have occurred between Joy and Jack during the years of 1950–1956 (as all the letters between them have been destroyed). But some of that unknowing recently changed. In 2013, in a neglected corner of a closet belonging to Joy Davidman's friend Jean Wakeman in Oxford, Joy's son Douglas Gresham discovered a box of unpublished stories, essays, novellas, unfinished novels, and poems written by his mother. Inside this box was a sheaf of papers labeled *Courage*, which included forty-five love sonnets written by Joy Davidman and dedicated to C. S. Lewis. These poems and love sonnets were just released in 2015 (*A Naked Tree: Love Sonnets to C. S. Lewis*, edited by Don W. King).

I had already read most of Lewis's work by the time I was introduced to Joy, but during the writing of this novel, I reread many of my favorites with a new eye—seeing Joy's influence on the prose and in the women who were Lewis's characters. How had I not seen it all along? I wondered. Why do we not give credit to the women who inspired some of our favorite writers? I want the world, or at least you, the reader holding this book, to know of her influence on his works.

It was Joy's friendship, intellect, writing, encouragement, and love that influenced most notably *Till We Have Faces*, *Surprised by Joy*, *Reflections on the Psalms*, and *A Grief Observed*. Many times she was both inspiration and co-author.

For me, C. S. Lewis was an Oxford don, a scholar and a poet, a Christian apologist and an imaginative genius, a master at prose and theme. He has been a man with theories and quotes that both inspire and infuriate me, and I was surprised to find that it was Joy's life that brought Jack alive for me in a new way.

In this historical fiction, the letters and dialogue between Joy and Jack, as well as their family and friends, were created by my imagination. Although this is a work of fiction, my desire was to stay as close to the bone of the existing and factual skeleton as possible—thus the inspiration, occasional snippets, phrases, and quotes in the letters, in dialogue, and in Joy's internal musings have come from actual events, letters, poems, essays, biographies, and articles written by and about them both, as well as speeches they gave.

As with any life, there are discrepancies within the many stories that have been written about both Jack and Joy; there are myths and assumptions that have been told and retold. I did my best to gather all of the information, compare it, and unravel it to tell a story that relates an emotional truth. This novel was written with the backbone of research and the work of those who have come before me, yet in fiction, imagination and inspiration must fill the gaps. I have attempted to capture Joy's courage and fierce determination, as well as tap into the landscape of her heart.

I often felt like a detective digging through conflicting testimony and coming to my own conclusions as best I knew how on this side of their love story.

In the beginning of this journey, it was Joy's early biographies I turned to, most notably *And God Came In* by Lyle Dorsett, *Through the Shadowlands* by Brian Sibley, *Jack's Life* by Douglas Gresham, *Lenten Lands* by Douglas Gresham, and the biography *Joy* by Abigail Santamaria. The extensive critical work, articles, and edited collections by Don W. King, professor at Montreat College, brought me even closer to her life and work. Yet it was Joy's own writings, poems, and letters that drew me nearer to her heart.

During the writing of this novel, I traveled to Wheaton College's Wade Center in Wheaton, Illinois, where most of Joy's and Lewis's papers are housed and carefully curated, along with a research collection of materials by and about six more renowned British authors. Joy's (as of now) unpublished letters, poems, and personal papers were immaculately filed in numerous boxes—a treasure trove for a novelist. Alone in the Wade Center reading room, surrounded by Joy's handwriting, her letters, her poems, her divorce decree and passport, Joy came alive for me.

This novel is written in a key of empathy for this extraordinary woman. I can only hope that I've captured some of her lionhearted courage, conflicted and sometimes disparaged choices, as well as her abiding love for the man we know as C. S. Lewis, but whom she knew as mentor, best friend, and in the end her lover and husband. The man she knew as Jack.

I could not have come to know her as I have (and it is only an imagining of the heart, not a scholarly attempt to dissect her work or her actions) without the insightful, dedicated work of so many others. In addition to the works mentioned above, I found the following texts to be useful in my own research and strongly recommend them for further study and insight.

SUGGESTED FURTHER READING

Armstrong, Chris R. *Medieval Wisdom for Modern Christians: Finding Authentic Faith in a Forgotten Age with C. S. Lewis*. Grand Rapids, MI: Brazos, 2016.

Bramlett, Perry C. *Touring C. S. Lewis' Ireland and England*. Macon, GA: Smyth and Helwys, 1998.

Davidman, Joy. "The Longest Way Round." In *These Found the Way: Thirteen Converts to Protestant Christianity*, edited by David Wesley Soper. Philadelphia: Westminster, 1951.

Davidman, Joy. *A Naked Tree: Love Sonnets to C. S. Lewis and Other Poems*. Edited by Don W. King. Grand Rapids, MI: William B. Eerdmans, 2015.

Davidman, Joy. *Smoke on the Mountain: An Interpretation of the Ten Commandments*. Foreword by C. S. Lewis. Philadephia: Westminster Press, 1954.

Davidman, Joy. *Weeping Bay*. New York: MacMillan, 1950.

Dorsett, Lyle W. *And God Came In: The Extraordinary Story of Joy Davidman*. Peabody, MA: Hendrickson Publishers, 2009.

Gresham, Douglas H. *Jack's Life: The Life Story of C. S. Lewis*. Nashville: Broadman and Holman, 2005.

Gresham, Douglas H. *Lenten Lands: My Childhood with Joy Davidman and C. S. Lewis*. New York: Macmillan, 1988.

Gilbert, Douglas, and Clyde S. Kilby. *C. S. Lewis: Images of His World*. Grand Rapids, MI: William B. Eerdmans, 2005.

Hooper, Walter, ed. *The Collected Letters of C. S. Lewis*. Vol. 3, *Narnia, Cambridge, and Joy 1950–1963*. New York: HarperCollins, 2007.

Hooper, Walter, ed. *C. S. Lewis on Stories and Other Essays on Literature*. Orlando, FL: Harcourt, 1982.

Hooper, Walter. *Through Joy and Beyond: A Pictorial Biography of C. S. Lewis*. New York: Macmillan, 1982.

King, Don W. "Fire and Ice: C. S. Lewis and the Love Poetry of Joy Davidman and Ruth Pitter." *VII: An Anglican-American Literary Review* 22 (2005): 66–88.

King, Don W. "A Naked Tree: The Love Sonnets of Joy Davidman to C. S. Lewis," *VII: An Anglican-American Literary Review* 29 (2012): 79–102.

King, Don W., ed. *Out of My Bone: The Letters of Joy Davidman*. Grand Rapids, MI: William B. Eerdmans, 2009.

King, Don W. *Yet One More Spring: A Critical Study of Joy Davidman*. Grand Rapids, MI: William B. Eerdmans, 2015.

(Anything by C. S. Lewis, but most importantly for this novel)

Lewis, C. S. *The Four Loves*. New York: Harcourt Brace, 1960. First published 1960 by Geoffrey Bles.

Lewis, C. S. *A Grief Observed*. New York: HarperOne, 2015. First published 1961 by Faber and Faber.

Lewis, C. S. *The Great Divorce*. New York: HarperOne, 2015. First published 1946 by Geoffrey Bles.

Lewis, C. S. *The Horse and His Boy*. The Chronicles of Narnia. London: Geoffrey Bles, 1954.

Lewis, C. S. *The Last Battle*. The Chronicles of Narnia. London: Geoffrey Bles, 1956.

Lewis, C. S. *The Lion, the Witch, and the Wardrobe*. The Chronicles of Narnia. London: Geoffrey Bles, 1950.

Lewis, C. S. *The Magician's Nephew*. The Chronicles of Narnia. London: The Bodley Head, 1955.

Lewis, C. S. *Mere Christianity*. New York: HarperOne, 2015. First published 1952 by Geoffrey Bles.

Lewis, C. S. *The Pilgrim's Regress*. Grand Rapids, MI: William B. Eerdmans, 2014. First published 1933 by J. M. Dent and Sons.

Lewis, C. S. *Prince Caspain: The Return to Narnia*. The Chronicles of Narnia. London: Geoffrey Bles, 1951.

Lewis, C. S. *The Silver Chair*. The Chronicles of Narnia. London: Geoffrey Bles, 1953.

Lewis, C. S. *The Screwtape Letters*. New York: HarperOne, 2015. First published 1942 by Geoffrey Bles.

Lewis, C. S. *Surprised by Joy: The Shape of My Early Life*. New York: HarperOne, 2017. First published 1955 by Geoffrey Bles.

Lewis, C. S. *Till We Have Faces*. New York: Harcourt, 1984. First published 1956 by Geoffrey Bles.

Lewis, C. S. *The Voyage of the Dawn Treader*. The Chronicles of Narnia. London: Geoggrey Bles, 1952.

Sibley, Brian. *Through the Shadowlands: The Love Story of C. S. Lewis and Joy Davidman*. Grand Rapids, MI: Revell, 2005.

Santamaria, Abigail. *Joy: Poet, Seeker, and the Woman Who Captivated C. S. Lewis*. New York: Houghton Mifflin Harcourt, 2015.

Tolkien, J. R. R. "On Fairy-Stories." In *Essays Presented to Charles Williams*. London: Oxford University Press, 1947.

Zaleski, Philip and Carol Zaleski. *The Fellowship: The Literary Lives of the Inklings*. New York: Farrar, Straus and Giroux, 2015.

Acknowledgments

This novel captured my heart and my imagination as quick and bright as lightening. I owe its fiery force not only to the fascinating and courageous life of Joy Davidman, but also to so many others who contributed to the understanding of her life. I asked, I prodded, I read, I researched, and I could not have written this alone.

From the day I said it out loud, "I want to write a novel that tells the story of Joy Davidman beyond *Shadowlands*," there were friends and family who supported the idea with such enthusiasm that they propelled me forward. I am astoundingly grateful for this tribe of writers who knew about it from the from the start and offered an ear, advice, and all-out love: Ariel Lawhon, Lisa Patton, Lanier Isom, Kerry Madden Lundsford, Paula McLain, Mary Alice Monroe, Joshilyn Jackson, J. T. Ellison, Laura Lane McNeal, Karen Spears Zacharias, Dot Frank, Kathy Trocheck, Kathie Bennett, Tinker Lindsey, Lisa Wingate, Jenny Carroll, and Mary Beth Whalen—you buoyed me when I wavered and kept my confidence. Blake Leyers, with her first read, asked me the questions I didn't even know I needed to answer, and I am grateful beyond measure. To Signe Pike—how do I thank you? This editor (and author) extraordinaire read it from beginning to end and together we took it apart, found its troubles and its triumphs.

Lyle Dorsett (author of Joy's first biography, *And God Came In*, an Anglican priest and professor at Samford University Divinity School) is a prince among men. He spent hours with me talking about Joy and her life, her possible motivations and her triumphs and despairs. His prayers and his prodding to "write a story about her life" meant more to me than he will ever know. Also professor at Montreat College and author of numerous works about Joy Davidman, Don King's work was invaluable as I sent him emails and questions and read everything he wrote about Joy and her writing and poetry.

I would not have finished this novel, at least not in the form it is in, without my sacred time at Rivendell Writer's Colony under the ministrations of Carmen Touissant. It was there that I often found the heart of the story when I felt it was missing. My love and gratitude are in equal measure.

To the authors who have written about both Joy and Jack before me, whose work introduced me to several facets of them both, I am indebted and grateful (listed in the Author's Note for suggested further reading).

The Wade Center at Wheaton College and most notably Elaine Hooker were invaluable. As I sat in the reading room with Joy's papers, passport, divorce decree, poetry, and letters, she came alive for me in a way I hadn't expected. The Wade Center's support and careful curating of her papers (and C. S. Lewis's) allowed me to discover Joy in a deeper way. Elaine answered unending questions and guided me to the papers I needed the most. All authors should have someone like her in a place like this.

To my agent, Marly Rusoff, who believed in this story from the very beginning and championed it to its very end. My gratitude is as endless as my emails.

To the extraordinary team at HarperCollins/Thomas Nelson— you are a gift and a pleasure and I am grateful for every single one of you. To Amanda Bostic who understood not only the story but also why I wanted to tell it from the get-go. Working with you has been one of the greatest pleasures of my publishing history.

To Paul Fisher, Allison Carter, Kristen Golden, Jodi Hughes, Kayleigh Hinds, Becky Monds, and Laura Wheeler—you are the dream team. To TJ Rathbun and Ben Greenhoe, who filmed and produced our videos—you somehow saw the same vision as I did when it came to telling Joy's story. I am immeasurably grateful, and working with you was one of the best days of this publishing journey. And to L. B. Norton, the copy editor extraordinaire—your eye, your spirit, your generosity and humor made this editing experience more than I could have ever hoped for.

To my team who loves Joy with the same passion—I am grateful to each and every one of you. To Jim Chaffee of Chaffee Managament, who appeared in the most synchronistic and powerful way at just the right time. How happy I am to have you on our team: your insight and energy are boundless. To Meg Walker at Tandem Literary—your calm spirit and innovative creativity are stunning. To Meg Reggie, as always, from my very first novel, you are a gem and a creative genius. To Carol Fitzgerald and her team at Bookreporter, who helped me build a website I adore (and I am sure Joy would love also).

To my friends, who allowed me to talk about this subject endlessly and still hang out with me. I love you—Tara Mahoney for her humor and belief, Kate Phillips for her unwavering confidence, Barbara Cooney for sitting with me through the tough parts, Sandee O for bringing me back to center always when I need it most, and Cleo O'Neal for walking and talking when I needed to ground myself again.

To Douglas Gresham (Joy's son)—I am profoundly indebted to you and grateful. Your insight and kindness to a complete stranger who wrote about your brilliant mother was stunning. I am honored to now call you friend. Thank you, Douglas. Thank you. Your legacy holds true to the integrity and kindness of both Jack and your mother.

And my family. When I first told my parents of this idea, they were as supportive of me as always, and yet a sparkle came to their eyes. They knew what Lewis had meant to all of us. I found my first C. S. Lewis book—*The Screwtape Letters*—in my dad's office at home. I hope I've done them proud here. To my sisters, Jeannie Cunnion and Barbi Burris, and their extraordinary families who support me no matter my eccentricities. To my sisters-in-law, Serena Henry and Anna Henry, who heard so much about Joy and still listened and still asked and anchored me to family when I needed it. To Pat Henry, for tolerating my distant stares and forgotten dinners and early-morning huddles in my office—thank you and I love you. To my children, my love for you is beyond measure and as I wrote every word of this novel I thought of you and your wild and beautiful lives unfolding in their new ways, as always, Meagan and Evan Rock, Thomas and Rusk.

DISCUSSION QUESTIONS

1. Did you know much about Joy Davidman before you read this novel? Did you come with preconceived notions of who she was? How did those change during the novel? What was the most surprising part of this story for you?

2. Joy wrote to Jack in search of answers on her spiritual journey. Was she looking for a friend? Advice? Both? What kept them writing to each other for so many years without meeting face-to-face?

3. Not many people supported Joy's choices to first travel to England and then move there. There also didn't seem to be much support from Jack's friends as their friendship and then love story bloomed. How did Joy find the strength to overcome the resistance? How did they survive this disapproval to come together? What were the strengths that allowed them to resist the naysayers?

4. How did the time and place—1950s England when women weren't even admitted to Magdalen College where Jack taught—affect their love story? Would it be different today? *How* would this story be different today?

5. Joy often thought about her past—both her love affairs and her family life. How did the past influence her personality and decisions? How did it affect her self-esteem and self-love? How did she come out on the other side?

6. Joy and Jack enjoyed an almost three-year pen-friendship before ever meeting. Can friendships begin with words and notes?

Can one become friends through letters alone? Can we be more vulnerable on paper than in face-to-face contact?

7. Joy wept when she left Davy and Douglas to board the SS *United States* the first time. Have you ever had to make a tough choice to "save your own life" or do what you thought might be the right thing for yourself but caused pain for yourself and others?

8. Many of Jack's last books, most notably *Till We Have Faces*, were shaped by his friendship and love with Joy. Can you see her life and influence in his works written after 1950? If so, which ones and how? How did their co-writing, editing, and long talks affect his work?

9. Jack's descriptions of Joy included this sentence: "My pupil and my teacher. My subject and my sovereign. My trusty comrade, friend, ship mate, fellow soldier. My mistress. But at the same time all that any man friend has ever been to me." How did Joy not only change Jack's life but also his heart?

ABOUT THE AUTHOR

Patti Callahan (who also writes as Patti Callahan Henry) is a *New York Times* bestselling author. Patti was a finalist in the Townsend Prize for Fiction, has been an Indie Next Pick, twice an OKRA pick, and a multiple nominee for the Southern Independent Booksellers Alliance (SIBA) Novel of the Year. Her work has also been included in short story collections, anthologies, magazines, and blogs. Patti attended Auburn University for her undergraduate work and Georgia State University for her graduate degree. Once a Pediatric Clinical Nurse Specialist, she now writes full time. The mother of three children, she lives in both Mountain Brook, Alabama, and Bluffton, South Carolina, with her husband.

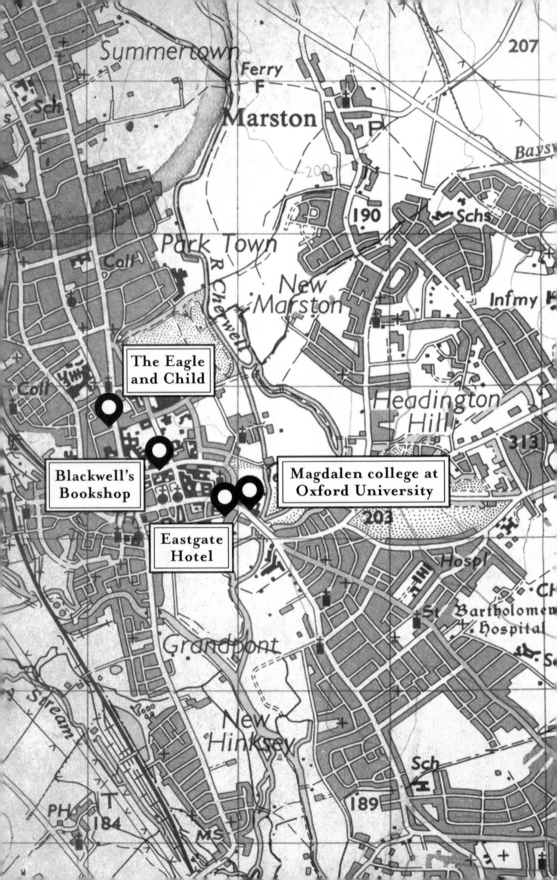